The Christmas Special

The Christmas Special

David J. Hearne

Subterfuge Publishing

The Christmas Special

Published by Subterfuge Publishing
PO Box 8008
Lumberton, Texas 77657
www.subterfugepublishing.com

Cover Design by:
Muhammad Faisal Nisar

Border Design created by Shannon L. Silver

www.The-Christmas-Special.com
ISBN 978-0975597613

Library of Congress Cataloging-in-Publication Data
Is available on request

Printed in the United States of America

To my wife Stacie for her support, tolerance, and love.

Acknowledgments

One fall day in the 1950's when I was a young boy we had a bomb drill at my school which consisted of the teacher yelling, "Drop!" and we would all try to scramble under our desk and cover our heads and necks with our hands. After the drill, we watched a terrifying movie about the power of the nuclear bomb which showed trees and buildings swept away disintegrating in the air as if a huge tornado had hit them. That night I lay out on the grass in my backyard with my best friend Paul. We were still psyched up about our drill and the film. We talked about what would happened if Springfield, Vermont was bombed. It was a town that made ball bearings and our parents were sure that the Russians would target it.

These memories of that night are still so vivid that I remember even the smell of the smoke from my neighbor's burning leaves. That evening, Paul and I decided we had to do something to save us from the bomb. Our solution was to dig a bunker in my backyard. So for the next few days we went about doing just that; we dug a hole and covered it with boards, straw and lots of dirt. Finally it was complete and we felt confident we were safe from any nuclear attack and as a bonus we now had a wonderful place to play, except when rain turned it to an underground mosquito breeder.

I think the impressions from that day of my life were the seeds that prompted me to write this book. I look back at that time and realize how deluded society was to believe that duck and cover was any real protection from being vaporized from a nuclear bomb. Today, the same mentality prevails in much of society toward the security of our nuclear power plants.

I spent over four years to research and write the Christmas Special and along the way I discovered many disturbing actions and inactions by our government that made me wonder if America isn't sometimes just running on autopilot. For example, it's hard for me to understand why the United States looked away for years while Pakistan's Abdul Qadeer Khan built his nuclear bomb, often dubbed the Islamic Bomb. Why didn't our government intercede in Pakistan's nuclear bomb program? I have never found a definitive answer to that question.

Getting closer to the premise of my novel, why are there so many stories of sleeping guards at nuclear power plants? Why do they continue with the farcical force on force tests that plant security so often fail? Finally how realistic is the premise that civilian guards with rules of engagement would be able to withstand a dedicated commando type attack on a nuclear facility by terrorist willing to die for their cause? The answers to those questions make me fear that we are as delusional now in our belief that our nuclear power plants are as safe from terrorist as Paul and I were with our belief that our hole in the ground would save us from a nuclear attack.

It's time to thank some friends and colleagues who were generous with their time, expertise, advice and the always needed encouragement. They all played a role in the completion of The Christmas Special novel, directly or indirectly.

I am very grateful to Jon Van Zile , the author of Zig Zephyr and Forever Diamond who provided a great deal of editorial support, research, and creative ideas to help me complete this book.

I also need to thank Yvonne Johnson, a prolific author of over 65 books who has been writing for major publishers since 1982 who took the time to read and critically comment on my work.

I was blessed with having Gene Weiser, one of the most skilled, creative and patient book layout designers work on the arduous task of typesetting and formatting the Christmas Special novel. In fact, his multi artistic talents made the novel's complex formatting job actually look easy.

Kudos need to be given to the great artists who created the illustrations you find in the Novel. Multiple talented artists feverishly worked on them to help me convey my message. The set of exclusion zone maps was created by I. Wayan Aries. He also created the illustration depicting the cryptic letter, stacks of money and the maps of the attack targets.

Lance Larue drew the graphic that is titled Vitriolic Rage. David and Leah Kaye created the graphic titled Evacuation Time and the graphic of Iceland was done by an elusive artist who signs his pieces with the initials of CGMJ. The graphic of the new church and the Culper, Texas donut shop drawing were done by Ramy Fares of Egypt who was living in Cairo, Egypt during the 2012 protests against President Morsi and the Muslim Brotherhood. And last, but not least is the work done by Manojms that consisted of the illustrations of the burning church, the large protest in front of the Capitol, the graphic titled "It's Zemblanitous" and the graphic of Sheeva hiding in the woods. I think their work of depicting some of these situations described in the Novel added another level of clarity to the story.

Attorney Gary Linthicum merits special thanks for his pro bono reading and numerous comments pertaining to the chapters portraying courtroom scenes and the Ali Hassan opening defense statement.

Among others I should acknowledge are doers like Judy Treichel- Executive Director of the NV Nuclear Waste Task Force whose unwavering dedication helped stop the conversion of Yucca Mountain to America's Nuclear Waste Dump. I can't forget those great folks at Google who provided the best research library in the world.

Finally I need to recognize those associates and friends who inspired me or kept me going: Mike & Karen Fuljenz, Jim King, Jannie Venter, Mayank Vadher, Chris Kyle, Robert & Diane Verde, Elaine Henderson, Megan Moore, Eric Compton, Pamela Truax, Sheila Bailleaux, Callie Hearne, Tatia Tate, Raj Singh and my good friend – that I see too little of, Mark Wulf.

Part One
The Holidays are Here

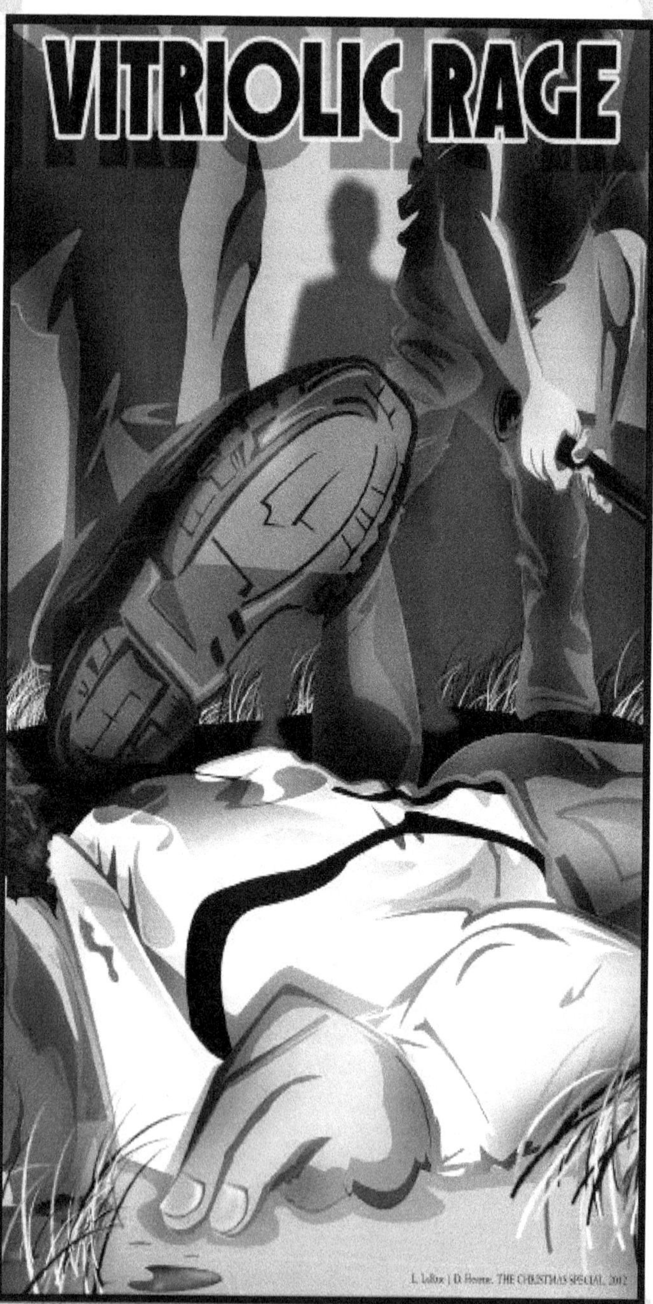
VITRIOLIC RAGE
THE CHRISTMAS SPECIAL, 2012

Chapter 1
The Opening Salvo

The baseball bat struck him hard across the left shoulder, knocking him to the sidewalk. The second blow rendered him unconscious and matted his hair with blood. Then there was a shuffle of feet as three young men circled the prostrate figure to finish the attack. Moments later, a flurry of thuds and cracks sounded as the three attackers released their anger on the boy on the ground.

Paralyzed in fear, Sheeva watched her boyfriend's body bounce with each blow. A piercing shriek erupted from her throat, replacing the sickening sounds of the beating. It lasted only seconds before it was stifled by her brother's backhand across her face. The blow alleviated her paralysis, and she found herself running madly away from the attack. She heard her brother yell, "You whore, you'll get yours when you get home."

Chapter 2
The Death of Attorney Thomas Lawrence

The following are excerpts from Thomas Lawrence's recording made just prior to his death:

"Hello, the Lawrence residence, may I help you?" "Sarah, it's me Thomas. Is Barbara there?"

"No, Mr. Lawrence, she is gone to Scott's school to watch the play he is in. Are you all right, sir? You sound out of breath."

"Sarah, what room are you in?"

"I'm in the living room."

"Okay, I need you to do something for me. I need you to put the receiver down next to the phone and go into my office and pick up the phone there and press the record button. Make sure the record light is red, then leave the phone alone. Don't use the phone at all and leave it off the hook until the police come."

"Oh God! What happened, Mr. Lawrence?"

"Sarah, please listen. Make sure the record light is on. Did you hear me?"

"Yes, Mr. Lawrence. I'm in the office now."

"Great. Remember the message, and now put the receiver down next to the phone and leave it alone. Call Barbara with your cell phone and try to get her back to the house. Thank you, Sarah. Now put it down please and no questions."

There were a few seconds of nothing but breathing, or maybe quiet sobbing emanating from the phone, and then Thomas Lawrence started to speak again

> *"Barbara, Barbara, Barbara! When you get this recording, you will already know I am gone. I dearly loved you and Scott. I'm in a dark place now, but your love is still here giving me strength and comfort. So thanks, Barbara, for being my beautiful, darling wife who has always been there for me. I guess soon I will be watching over you from above, I hope. If you feel a lock of your hair flicking lightly against your cheek, it just might be me saying hello to remind you that I'm still with you. I feel lucky to have had this time to record this message for you, because most wouldn't have these precious few moments to say good-bye. I know I never said 'I love you' enough, but I'm telling you now that those three simple words are what I always felt for you. I don't want to waste time, Barbara, because I probably have only a couple of hours left before I'm unconscious or before this recorder runs out of power. Don't feel sorry for me, it doesn't hurt; I just feel numb from my waist down and very tired."*
>
> *"Barbara, I need you to be strong and listen to whatever I can get on this recording and make sure you let the world know the real story behind Ali Hasson's trial and the Christmas Special. I know you have been following it, but you only know what they have reported. I*

know the real story. The world needs to know it too."

Chapter 3
Roberto Roma

When Barbara Lawrence brought me her late husband's recording, it didn't take more than a few minutes of listening to convince me to write the story that her dead husband wanted.

Why she picked me, I was not sure. I assumed she had read a few of my books, but Roberto Roma was not a big name in literary circles, not like John Grisham or Stephen King. I was flattered by her interest in me, and Thomas's recording was Pulitzer Prize material, dripping with primal emotions of fear, love, hate, and drive. It was the story of Ali Hasson, the most infamous terrorist to have ever attacked the United States. It was about an investigation and a trial that had exposed large holes in the frayed fabric of America's criminal system and showed that the laws lacked any semblance of logic or balanced justice. I gave Barbara my answer on our first meeting, and she quickly turned over a copy of her husband's last recording and all his notes and computer files about Ali Hasson's trial.

Chapter 4
Sheeva's Story Begins

So where does this story really begin? I could start it when Thomas Lawrence graduated from Howard University and began his illustrious law career, following in the footsteps of fellow alumni Thurgood Marshall, but that's not what he wanted me to write about. Telling his views and getting out the truth about what became known as the Christmas Special was Lawrence's final wish.

What event first wove Thomas into this tragedy? I think it was the beating of nineteen-year-old Jason Wilgers that launched the series of events culminating in the Christmas Special.

Jason was lucky. He has no recollection of what happened on the October afternoon when he was attacked, but his sixteen-year-old girlfriend Sheeva does. When Thomas interviewed her, she told this story:

> *When my brother hit me, I snapped out of whatever was making me just stand there like an idiot. I could not believe they were hitting Jason so hard with sticks and baseball bats. At first I was angered more than afraid, but when my brother Abdul hit me, I realized I was going to get beaten next. Suddenly, something gave me the strength to run from them. I could still hear the thuds and grunts of them hitting Jason even as I ran. I also heard my brother yell, "You whore, you'll get yours when you get home."*
>
> *My eyes were full of tears and I found it hard to see. I was afraid I would trip because I was wearing heels. We had*

just come from my sixteenth birthday party and I was not dressed for running. I had on this black lace Lolita dress that my father would have severely disapproved of. I knew if I fell and hurt myself they would easily catch me and beat me also. I just kept concentrating on the sidewalk and staying on my feet. My shoulder bag was slapping against my side and hurting me. I was panting like crazy and knew for sure, I was going to be killed or disfigured for life. As I ran, I had flashbacks to what they do to girls my age in Afghanistan when they are caught with a man before they are married, and I knew I had to escape. My toes were rubbed raw from hitting the concrete, but fear kept me running, I was so terrified. I finally stopped and removed my heels so I could run on the grass next to the sidewalk. Some cars drove by and I tried to wave them down, but they looked at me like I was a freak and kept going. Just as I was going around the corner at the end of the block, I glanced back to see if they were following me yet. I could not believe it, but they were urinating on Jason while they jeered and laughed.

With that last statement, Sheeva lost her composure. Thomas Lawrence attempted to console her and told her to drink some water and take a couple of deep breaths. Sheeva was a petite girl who looked even smaller sitting at Lawrence's massive conference table. She was a beautiful girl with jet-black hair falling over a flawless face. It was hard to imagine her own brother or anyone else wanting to hurt her. She dabbed her tears with a tissue and turned back to the microphone.

When the cars just passed me by, I felt even more helpless. I was gasping for air and my lungs were burning. I wanted to find someplace to hide, and then I decided to run into the woods on the opposite side of the road. I knew they were deep, and I hoped I could hide there while I figured out what to do. My feet were raw and my head was throbbing.

As I read the transcript of her statement, I realized that her mind was filled with a deep, overpowering fear of imminent death or a beating so horrific she would be permanently disfigured. She had to keep in control. She had to stay ahead of them. I think her experiences in Afghanistan made her more resilient to the danger she was facing. She was a survivor of the Taliban régime, which by itself spoke volumes for her courage. I continued reading.

Just as I was crossing the street, a big Hummer appeared from nowhere and almost hit me. I fell into the grass on the opposite side of the road and the Hummer came to a sudden stop, but they didn't help me. Instead they screeched down the road in reverse and around the corner. I guess they helped run off my brother and his two friends who were beating Jason. I was told their call to 911 probably saved my boyfriend.

Chapter 5
Testimony of Derrick Brooks

Sheeva's story was corroborated by the eyewitness account of Derrick Brooks, the young man who was driving the Hummer that Sheeva mentioned in her statement. He had been out "cruising" with two of his buddies when they spotted "these foreigners beating up this white guy." They weren't going to stop at first, but when they saw the girl running, they changed their minds. In the police report, Derrick was quoted as saying:

> *When I saw this cute little girl running barefoot across the road in her ripped-up party dress, I knew something was wrong. She was screaming like Freddy Kruger was after her. My friend James tells me let's go back and check out what's going on. I slammed on the brakes and threw my Hummer in reverse. I drove it backward all the way down to the end of the block, took the turn, and ran my Hummer right up onto the grass where they were beating him, that guy Jason. The second we opened the doors, the three guys doing the beating ran like we were police or something. I looked at the white dude on the ground and he was messed up bad. We knew that he needed some real help and James or Rodney called 911. I don't know which one did it first, because they both claim they did the calling. Anyway, next thing, we hear a bunch of sirens, and then ambulances, police cars, and even a fire truck come racing down the road. Right off, the police think we did it and handcuff us and push us in the back seat of their police cars. I*

guess we all told the same story or something because in about fifteen minutes some cop comes over to the car I'm in and lets me out and removes the cuffs. We told them about the girl running across the road, and they said they would check it out.

Chapter 6
Sheeva's Statement to the Chicago Police

According to a statement given to Officer Patrick Owens of the Chicago Police Department, Sheeva said:

> *When I saw the Hummer backing up so fast, I thought they were going to go back and get into the fight also. I wasn't sure if they were going to help Jason or just beat on him too. I was too afraid to watch, so I ran deeper into the woods. All I wanted to do was hide and figure out what I was really doing. I heard all the sirens and could even see some of the emergency vehicles whizzing by, but I was still very afraid. I knew that if the police found me they would probably return me to my father.*
>
> *"You'll get yours," were the words my brother had yelled at me as I ran from him when they were beating Jason. "You'll get yours," were not idle words. I was sure Abdul or my father would kill me or make me wish I was dead. At that moment I couldn't get a good grasp of my thoughts, my mind was spinning frantically, trying to figure out where to go and what to do. I staggered around in the woods and finally, exhausted, sat down on a log to gather my thoughts and catch my breath. I realized that my face was swollen and bleeding from my brother Abdul hitting me and tree branches scraping my face. My right leg was also bruised from thorns or a branch that had bloodied it in two places. I knew that I couldn't go home and realized I probably never would be able to return. It was hard*

to focus on anything but escape. Sweat still ran down into my eyes, burning and stinging, as I rested on the log.

I couldn't hear anything that sounded like anyone following me, and suddenly all I wanted to do was cry, and I did.

In her transcript, Sheeva mentioned a steampunk ring, which requires that I take a moment for those of you who haven't been exposed to "steampunk" subculture to define what it is. Steampunk is a form of speculative fiction inspired by alternative history where steam power is still widely used. Steampunk uses existing technology and inventions to imagine an even more advanced nineteenth century, often complete with Victorian-inspired wonders like steam-powered flying machines and mechanical computers. It offers a fresh, romanticized view on today's technology by making it retro. It has its own style that influences fashion, art, sculptures, films, literature, bands, music, and even video games. Steampunk art and jewelry has a visual aesthetic that many prefer over current trends.

Jason Wilgers was very enamored with steampunk culture and for Sheeva's birthday party wore steampunk–inspired clothes. He had also purchased Sheeva's Lolita dress, along with her ring, from a steampunk website as her birthday presents.

Chapter 7
Roger Wilgers Is Notified

Jason Wilgers's father was asleep when a long-distance call from the Chicago police woke him. He struggled at first to comprehend what Sergeant Jacob Stoffert was talking about, and then he suddenly realized the call was about his son Jason. Sergeant Stoffert had little to tell Roger Wilgers other than the hospital's name where his son was being cared for and that Jason was in the intensive care unit.

As soon as Stoffert hung up, Roger called the airport for flight information. To his dismay, there wouldn't be another flight to Chicago until the following morning at 9:30 a.m., arriving in Chicago around 1 p.m. That information made it a simple decision; he would drive there by car. He could get to Chicago in about twelve hours and perhaps quicker if he broke a few speed limits. Going by car made it possible to stay updated with his son's condition by calling the hospital, plus it allowed him to get the word out to his few friends about his situation. While he was speeding to Chicago, he could also contact and break the news to Jason's older brother, Frank, who lived in Beaumont, Texas.

It only took Roger about half an hour before he was packed and on the road. He called the hospital every thirty minutes, but no one could tell him anything about his son's condition. Finally, while Roger was speeding along Interstate 80 in Pennsylvania, he reached a doctor who actually knew something about Jason's condition. Doctor Andrew Ballenger told Roger that Jason's injuries consisted of a number of minor facial fractures, multiple rib fractures, cuts, bruising, and pneumothorax, but he would live.

Chapter 8
Sheeva's Night in the Woods

As Roger Wilgers's headlights illuminated the ribbon of darken highways leading to Chicago, Sheeva Hasson hid in the wooded park that was her temporary sanctuary. In Sheeva's statement to police months later, she stated:

> *The night Jason was beaten went by very slowly. I'd decided that running away and starting a new life was my only option. I knew kids did it all the time, and I thought I was smarter than most, so I could probably get away with it. If I could stay free for two years, I would be really free from my father and brother and not have to worry about them beating or killing me. My brother was crazy. He wanted to be a gangster like a mafia guy, but still a good Muslim. I know it sounds crazy, but he was like that. He had one friend, Ajani, who was really stupid, but strong and was nicknamed Abdullah the Butcher, after some TV wrestler. This wrestler guy wasn't even Muslim, but they liked him because he was crazy and did things like bite off chicken heads and beat people with chairs. My brother would get Ajani to beat up other kids. He was like my brother's bodyguard.*
>
> *Rahman was the other friend Abdul hung out with all the time. He was very smart, but also really mean. I tried to stay away from the three of them when they were all together, because they were scary.*

Anyway, that night I was freezing to death, but didn't dare leave the little clearing because I was more afraid of my father than what might be hiding in the rest of the woods. I was getting lots of text messages so I turned the ringer off on my cell phone, so it wouldn't give me away if my father, brother, or his friends were near and heard it.

It was a very dark night, and I could hear stuff in the woods. Things just moving around, making noises. The sounds terrified me. I also knew guys parked along this road with hookers, and if I was spotted on the road late at night, I could be mistaken for one or get raped because I was still dressed in a short party dress. I decided to just stay in one spot and try to keep warm by hugging myself and moving around just a little. I didn't want to sit down or lean against trees because of what might crawl onto me. I tried to just keep making plans and did a lot of thinking. I was getting a lot of text messages from my friends, asking me what had happened. I wanted to text or call my girlfriend, Hidi, but I was afraid my father would have called her dad to force Hidi to help trap me. I decided I would wait till Hidi was in school and then text her to call me. I thought of the things I needed to get from my home before I could run away and hoped my father wouldn't stay home all day waiting for me.

When the sky started turning light, I cried again. All I wanted to do was get Hidi to come and get me. I texted her at 9 a.m., and she immediately texted me back. She told me that Jason was in the hospital and my father was still calling everyone to find me. I asked her if she dared help me and come and get me. She said she was my BFF and of course she would, but she could not come until lunch break. I was so relieved that I had to bite my lip to keep from crying. I hated to think I would have to stay in the woods two more hours, but I had no one else I could trust. I told her where I would be and then started back toward the edge of the woods to wait for her there.

When I saw her car coming down the road, I ran out to flag her down. As I got into the passenger seat, she looked at me with pity. I know I looked horrible, dirty and all scratched up. I told her what had happened as she took me to her place so I could take a shower and clean up. I was paranoid all the time, expecting my father or brother to come busting into her house to grab me, but nothing happened. I wanted to change my looks as much as possible so any pictures my father might give the police wouldn't really look like me.

Once I was cleaned up, Hidi helped me dye my hair blonde. It looked really horrible, but at least I looked different. She helped me blow dry and style it a little and then gave me some of her clothes to wear. I pleaded with her to take me to my house so I could get clothes and other stuff I needed to take with me. She was my friend so she said yes. I knew we had to be careful because my father could easily be at home. In fact, the first time we drove by, his car was parked in the driveway and I was devastated, but Hidi comforted me and said maybe he was just home for lunch. We circled back a few more times until my father's car was finally gone.

Hidi dropped me off just down the street from my house, and I walked back to it, hoping none of the neighbors would recognize me with my blonde hair and new look. I probably looked like a thief when I was at my front door, peering around to see if anyone was watching me as I unlocked it.

Mangims/DHearne 2012
The Christmas Special

Chapter 9
Back at Home

In the transcript below, Sheeva continues the story of what transpired at her home after she snuck back in.

Once inside, I locked the door behind me and went to the kitchen. I needed a large garbage bag to put my stuff in and I wanted a butcher knife to take with me for protection.

Being alone in the house was terribly nerve-wracking. My brother's threat that 'I would get mine when I got home' constantly replayed in my mind like some bad song. The fear it created made me more conscious of noises and shadows as I quietly entered into my bedroom to grab the only picture I had of my mom. It was a framed picture of my family when we lived in Afghanistan just before my mother was killed. I was looking at it when I heard the front door open and close. For a moment I just froze and listened.

Someone had entered the house, so I grabbed the garbage bag I was packing and moved quickly down the hall to my brother's room. I opened his door, praying to Allah that the room would be empty. I had visions of my brother and his thugs sitting on the bed waiting for me. But when I entered, it was empty and his closet door was ajar. I silently moved across the room to the closet and eased myself into its farthest corner. I heard movement on the stairs. Someone was coming up. Suddenly, my father was shouting for me in Pashtu. He only uses Pashtu when he is very angry or excited. I heard my bedroom door swing open and bang noisily against the wall as my father entered it. He yelled repeatedly for me, and I had to hold my hand over my mouth to keep from responding. I could hear him moving my bed around and my closet door being opened. Then his footsteps came closer and suddenly my brother's door flew open. My father entered the room like a charging bull.

He was just a few feet from me. I knew if he found me, he would grab me by my hair and drag me down the stairs and whip me with his favorite, a doubled up lamp cord or punch me in my stomach until I puked. He was furious. I imagined him spitting on me while he'd roar at how I'd shamed him and Abdul.

I could hear him banging around in Abdul's room. He was yelling that he could smell me and I better come out or it would just be that much worse. My mind raced with what I should do. I thought for a few moments that I should run out with my knife and maybe it would scare or shock him enough to let me get away. But I feared he would have his lamp cord ready to whip me before I could escape. I was trembling with fear when I heard him push Abdul's bed around. He was continually shouting "Sheeva" and "spi lurr," which is a Pashtu curse meaning "daughter of a bitch." I knew the next place he would look was Abdul's closet.

I reached into the bag and removed the butcher knife. Its edges were serrated and very sharp. In my haste,I slit my thumb open on its jagged teeth. It stung, but it was nothing like what I was facing from my father. I pulled the knife from the bag and pressed myself hard against the closet wall. His shouts were so loud and close that they reverberated through the closet wall. My fingers clamped the knife tightly, and I waited for my father to step into the closet. A little trickle of blood ran down my wrist from the cut on my thumb. Stay calm, I kept telling myself, so I would be ready to use the knife, but I was also very afraid. My father's cell phone interrupted his shouts and curses. I could hear his labored breath just outside the closet as he struggled to get to his cell phone. Then I heard my father say "Ahlan" to the caller. He had switched from Pashtu and was now talking to someone in Arabic. Whoever it was, my father was speaking in a very respectful manner.

Chapter 10
Roberto Roma Interviews Roger Wilgers

While Sheeva Hasson was dodging her father, Roger Wilgers, Jason's father was walking down the third floor hall of Chicago Mercy Hospital, looking for room 372. Roger's recollection of his visit is detailed in the following transcript of an interview he graciously consented to do with me.

Roma: *Mr. Wilgers, may I call you Roger?*

Wilgers: *Of course, Mr. Roma. I'm actually glad to help tell my son's story.*

Roma: *Let's start from the beginning. What were you thinking about as you walked down the hall looking for his room? And please call me Roberto.*

Wilgers: *I was in my own twilight zone as I walked down that very, very long hall searching for Jason's room. When the police from a thousand miles away call you and tell you to come visit your son in a hospital, it's very unsettling. My thoughts were dark and depressing. My wife had died a few years earlier in a hospital, so I had definite fear of what might happen. Most of the time, I was probably just thinking about why did it happen. I was anxious and actually felt nauseous with worry about how bad his injuries might be.*

Roma: *How did he look when you first saw him?*

Wilgers: *When I first walked into his hospital room, I was devastated. Jason was wrapped in bandages, and the little I could see of his face was pasty white. He had tubes coming from everywhere. The first time I tried to* *speak to him, my voice broke. He appeared conscious, but his eyes just stared blankly up at me. I stood next to him and touched his hand, trying to fight back tears. I just thought about how beautiful my son had been and that he was only nineteen and now this.*

Roma: *What kind of discussion did you have with your son?*

Wilgers: *I think the first thing I said was, "Hi Jason." He didn't reply right off, I think he was trying to find his voice. Moments later, a raspy voice uttered a "Hi, Dad." I stroked my fingers across the back of his hand and told him, "Everything is going to be okay!" I doubt there was much conviction behind my words, but I really didn't know what to say.*

Roma: *Did you know more about his condition by then?*

Wilgers: *No, not really. I hadn't had a chance to talk to his doctor, and the information his nurse gave me was very sketchy, but it was obvious that he had serious problems because he looked terrible. I just stood there in shock, but I knew I shouldn't let him see my pain. I bent over, kissed his forehead, and ran my fingers through his hair. I couldn't help but cry, although I tried my hardest not to let him know.*

Roma: *This is very important, did you ask him then if he knew who had beaten him?*

Wilgers: *Of course I asked him. He was evasive or maybe just really hurting. I said something like, "Jason, who did this to you?" He looked at me and hesitantly replied, "Dad, I'm out of it right now, let's talk about that later." I told him*

I was going to stay with him until he was out of the hospital. I told him that his brother was also on his way.

Roma: *What else did you two talk about?*

Wilgers: *That was pretty much it. Really not much more happened because he was very groggy. I sat in a chair next to his bed for a while and just stared at him and thought about this horrible turn of events. He quickly appeared to doze off, and a few minutes later, I was snoring away in the chair. About an hour later, a doctor woke me when he came by doing his rounds.*

Roma: *Coincidentally, what nationality was this doctor?*

Wilgers: *What do you mean?*

Roma: *Was this doctor from Afghanistan, Iran, Iraq? Where do you think he was from?*

Wilgers: *His name was Zeiger. I guess he had German ancestry. If you're trying to see if Doctor Zeiger might have had a connection to Doctor Ali Hasson, I would say no. I think Zeiger was just another person who got dragged into this mess.*

Roma: *So what did Zeiger tell you about your son?*

Wilgers: *The doctor was very nice and quickly explained Jason's injuries. Zeiger said my son was not as bad off as he looked. He assured me that Jason would be up and around in a few days. He would experience quite a bit of pain and have to endure some stitches and bandages for a while, but his recovery should be uneventful. His collapsed lung was no longer an issue, so the majority of* *his injuries just needed time to heal. That was pretty much it.*

Roma: *Did you get a chance to talk to your son more that day?*

Wilgers: *Yes, we talked some more when he woke. I asked him again who did this to him. The story my son told, once he finally agreed to talk, was he thought it had something to do with the girl he was dating, but he wasn't sure who did it. He claimed he didn't remember anything about the incident.*

Roma: *Why did he think it had something do with his girlfriend?*

Wilgers: *As you already know, she was a young girl from Afghanistan. Her name was Sheeva. He had become infatuated with her. He told me he was in love with her, but I didn't take it very seriously. He told me her father and brother were very hostile toward him. Sheeva's brother apparently had words with Jason a couple times, but Jason didn't think he was serious, just a lot of mouth. This conversation was the first time I heard about Sheeva. Jason told me how beautiful she was and that her mother had been killed in the war. He felt that made a connection between them, since he also had lost his mother a few years back.*

Roma: *Did you talk to him about how young she was?*

Wilgers: *Do you mean did I warn him that he could get in serious legal trouble going with a sixteen-year-old? Hell no. I didn't even know she was sixteen until the rest of the shit hit the fan.*

At this point, Mr. Wilgers buried his head in his hands and his body convulsed as he tried to stifle his sobs. Perhaps a complete minute passed before he gained enough composure to continue. He lifted his head and looked at me, his cheeks wet with tears, and then continued.

Wilgers: *It never really dawned on me then that age could be any issue. He was a teenager going to school, and she was a teenager going to school, just a couple kids infatuated with each other. My mind was focused on his injuries, and I was mad as hell that someone had beaten him so badly. I'm sure some armchair quarterbacks will claim they would have seen the danger immediately. Truth is, I was just worried about his recovery and happiness.*

Roma: *Did he tell you where he was coming from when the incident happened?*

Wilgers: *Yes, he told me. It had been her birthday and they were coming from her party. He painted a picture of her as being very worldly. Jason said she could speak three languages, English, Pashtu, and Arabic, but she could only read and write in English because in Afghanistan the Taliban didn't allow girls to go to school.*

Roma: *How did Sheeva get along with her family?*

Wilgers: *From what I gathered, I would say not very well. Sheeva had told Jason that her father disliked her interest in Western culture and dress. He didn't even like her listening to Afghani singers who emulated American music. Apparently, there is an Afghani singer or group called something like Bisho or Besho. I think it was DJ Besho. They are sup-*

posed to be a big Afghani hip-hop band. Sheeva's dad caught her listening to this group on the Internet and punched her repeatedly in the stomach as punishment. Jason was furious and wanted to go over and beat her father, but she stopped him. I don't think Jason would have anyway; it was just him being her protector.

Roma: *Did Jason have any real altercations with Sheeva's father?*

Wilgers: *As far as I know he only met Sheeva's father once, but that once might have been considered an altercation because he told Jason to stay away from his daughter unless he converted to Islam. Jason knew that Sheeva's father thought he was the main reason for her rebellion against good Muslim values. Jason's steampunk clothes might have been another reason Ali didn't like my son...or the fact that Jason had a brother who fought in Afghanistan. Who knows?*

Roma: *You have a son who fought in Afghanistan?*

Wilgers: *Yes, I do. He was wounded in a battle that reportedly killed thirty-seven Taliban and al-Qaeda jihadists. Jason was very proud of his brother and told the story of his exploits to all his friends. The fact that Jason's brother fought in Afghanistan might have bothered Ali Hasson, because according to Jason, Sheeva lost her mother in an American bombing.*

Roma: *So how serious was Sheeva about this relationship with your son?*

Wilgers: *My son claimed she was in love with him. I mean, we are talking about kids, so what does love mean to a* *couple of young teenagers still in school? I thought the romance would soon be over because Jason was transferring to the Art Institute in Houston Texas. With more than a thousand miles between them, I thought the infatuation would quickly die. It was a non-issue to me at that time. I was just concerned with his recovery and getting him packed to move to Houston.*

Roma: *Did you and Jason talk about anything else that first day you were at the hospital?*

Wilgers: *No, Jason was really hurting. He tried to sit up and talk to me, but he was hurting so much from the pain in his lower body that he appeared to black out. His hair was soaked in perspiration. It was dripping down his face and onto the sheets. I called a nurse and she gave him a sedative and told me he needed more rest. That was it for the day.*

Chapter 11
Money to Live On

The following transcript, recorded during Sheeva Hasson's statement to police, provided the first clues that her father was an important player in the Christmas Special terrorist attack. Sheeva's statement continues from when she was hiding in Abdul's closet from her father.

"Stay calm," I kept telling myself. I continued to listen to my father talking on his cell to someone in Arabic. It was someone who wanted to meet him immediately at the Water Tower Place mall. The caller told my father that a driver was waiting outside to pick him up and bring him to the meeting. I could hear my father walking to the window, facing the street, and opening the blinds. He told the caller the car was there and that he would leave right off.

My father left the room, continually cursing as he descended the stairs. I listened for the front door to open and close and then moved quietly across the floor, to the same window my father had looked out. My father was just getting into the car as I reached the window. Once he was in, they immediately drove away.

I hesitated for a few moments before I decided what I should do. I was still very frightened. I pulled myself together and started back to my room to get my stuff, but a ***taweez*** *hanging from the mirror on my brother's dresser caught my eye. Abdul didn't believe in the power of a* ***taweez****, but I did. I felt like it grabbed my* *attention because it wanted me to take it. I grabbed it and stuffed it in my bag. I noticed then that I was still bleeding from the cut on my thumb. It dripped onto the dresser but, I didn't care; I wasn't going to clean it up. They would know I was there anyway.*

As soon as I left his room, I decided I would skip going back to my room and take care of more important matters, like finding some money to live on until I could find a job or something.

I quickly went downstairs and rushed into my father's office. He had a big, old desk that was stacked with all kinds of stuff. I looked in the middle drawer and immediately found about twenty-five dollars in change and bills. I started going through the other drawers and found nothing, but one was locked. I grabbed the butcher knife again and used it as a pry bar on the drawer. I thought the knife was going to snap, but suddenly the drawer popped open. Inside was a sealed manila envelope. Nothing was written on it except the Arabic word for Christmas, which I thought was odd. It was sort of heavy, and I was in a rush so I ripped it open. I couldn't believe it, but inside was a bunch of money.

I thought it was luck from the Taweez that had helped me find this money. The bills were bound in wrappers, except a few loose ones. I grabbed some and stuck them in my pocket. It was probably a few hundred dollars, and I thought the envelope had maybe a couple thousand dollars in it. It had some pictures too and a letter in Arabic, which I couldn't read. I'd only learned to read a few Arabic words, like Christmas, Valentine's and New Years, when I'd mailed out Arabic cards to my friends for the American holidays.

The shock of finding the money made me temporarily forget the danger I was in. I tossed the entire envelope into my bag and decided I wouldn't even go back to my room for clothes, but just buy new ones. Most of my clothes were stuff my father bought me, and I was ashamed to wear it. I decided to get out of the house quickly because if my father or my brother caught me, they would probably kill me.

I put my knife back in the bag and quickly went to the back door. My heart was racing; I knew there was no turning back now. I was starting a new life. My head was pounding as I tried to act calm walking down my driveway to the sidewalk. I felt that everyone was watching me. I kept thinking my brother would drive up any minute, drag me back into the house by my hair, and call our father. It didn't happen, and Hidi was still waiting down the block for me in her car. When she saw me, she started it and drove up to me.

The instant I was in the car, we were moving. Neither of us said anything for a block or two. I was breathing heavy from the excitement, and Hidi kept glancing over at me with a worried look.

Finally she asked, "So what happened?"

I told her I almost got caught by my father, but someone called him and he had to leave. I also told her I was lucky and I found enough money to keep me going for awhile.

She looked over at me and asked, "How much did you find?"

I said, "I guess over a thousand. I think it's money my father was saving for Christmas, if you can believe it."

I told Hidi I would pay her one hundred dollars if she would drive me to the bus station in Hammond, Indiana.

I wanted to go there because it was far enough away from Chicago that my father or brother wouldn't think to go there and look for me. It was like thirty minutes or more from my house.

Before we got there, we stopped at a Walmart and I bought a small backpack. I didn't want to carry a garbage bag onto a bus. I bought a few other things I knew I would need and tossed them all into the new backpack once we were back in Hidi's car.

While we drove to Hammond, I wrote a note to Jason and told him I loved him and hoped he would be okay. I told him I would try to call him once I got a new cell phone.

At the Greyhound station, I asked Hidi if she would give Jason my note and the Taweez. I hoped it would bring him the same good luck it brought me. I reminded her to explain to Jason that it was an Islamic talisman; if he wore it, it should bring him good luck.

She promised me she would explain it to him and we hugged good-bye.

I wiped tears away and went into the station wearing my backpack full of all my worldly belongings. I looked up at the bus schedule board for departures.

There was a bus leaving for Omaha, Nebraska, at 1:30 p.m. with seats still available. I bought a ticket for $162. I felt excited about the trip and tried to act as normal as I could. I was afraid someone would ask me why I was not in school, but no one did. They announced the loading, and I rushed over. Once I was on the bus, I felt so much calmer. Right at 1:30, the driver closed the doors. He backed the big bus out of the loading docks and I was on my way to Omaha.

Chapter 12
Meeting at the Water Tower Place

Ali Hasson arrived at the Water Tower Place mall at about the same time that his daughter Sheeva was driving to Hammond, Indiana. From information obtained from numerous investigations surrounding the Christmas Special, it's believed that the meeting at the mall was the first meeting between Ali and Dr. Badawi and that they only knew of each other from intermediaries involved in planning the attack. Ali met Dr Badawi in the food court. Dr. Badawi was a large man who made Ali's six-foot stature diminutive in comparison. These excerpts from Dr. Badawi's statements to the FBI clarify certain questions about the attack:

FBI Agent: *For the record, sir, please tell me your name.*

Dr. Badawi: *Dr. Yusuf Badawi.*

FBI Agent: *Dr. Badawi, did you meet Ali Hasson at the Water Tower Place mall on October 30?*

Dr. Badawi: *Yes.*

FBI Agent: *What was the meeting for?*

Dr. Badawi: *I was asked to give Dr. Hasson his invitation and tickets to the Annual Cardiology Conference that was to be held in Toronto, Canada, on November fifteenth. Dr. Hasson was to receive an award at the conference, and I was asked to brief him and assist him on writing his acceptance speech, which would include reference to his belief in Islam.*

FBI Agent: *What other business did you have with Hasson?*

Dr. Badawi: *I was asked by Dr. Marzook to give Dr. Hasson a sealed envelope that contained very personal material Dr. Hasson would be very grateful to receive. Dr. Marzook was very serious about me hand-delivering it to Dr. Hasson. He said he could not use the mail or other carriers because he was under investigation by the FBI over some fundraising activities associated with Hamas. He said since they had started the investigation, the FBI and Homeland Security had been harassing him. He assured me that delivering this note was nothing I could get in trouble for, but he could not communicate directly with Hasson without exposing him to possible problems, and he didn't want Dr. Hasson to inherit his problems because both were Muslim immigrants.*

FBI Agent: *Do you know what was said in the personal message?*

Dr. Badawi: *Yes, I steamed the envelope open at my home to make sure I was not carrying something that I could get in trouble for. Inside was a note in Arabic that appeared to be a congratulatory note for Hasson's upcoming award. I think it said:*

"Congratulations on your upcoming award. You have made great contributions to Muslims the world over and soon you will be even more renowned."

There was a reminder to reimburse for the PC Tran software and the "SFP" module. I looked up "PC Tran software" on Google. It was listed as "an FHWA-designated software distribution center." I didn't see anything odd about that and never realized until an FBI agent informed me that if I'd typed it as "PCTRAN software," I would have seen it referred to PC-based nuclear reactor simulation software. I had no idea of the significance of what the note contained. At the bottom of the note were three columns of English characters that were not discussed in the note.

I thought the columns of strange characters in English were odd, but they didn't make me think that I was delivering terrorist correspondence about an attack on America. Those codes could have been licensing codes for software or had something to do with Hasson's research in cardiology. There was nothing obvious in the note that indicated anything was wrong. The odd codes in English bothered me, but they seemed harmless. I did decide to keep a copy of the letter for when I had more time to figure out what they might be. When I heard the possible connection of Dr. Hasson to the Christmas Special I called authorities and gave them the note.

Chapter 13
Omaha, Nebraska

By the time Dr. Hasson arrived home that night, his daughter Sheeva was halfway to Omaha, Nebraska. Her ride on the Greyhound bus had been uneventful. She had received one call from Hidi, who gave her an update on Jason and said she had given him the Taweez. When Sheeva finally arrived in Omaha, she was grateful to walk about and relax a bit. At about 2 a.m. the bus arrived at the seedy downtown Jackson Street station.

Sheeva quickly discovered that the next leg of her journey to Houston, Texas, wouldn't happen till 6 a.m. She had four early morning hours to kill.

The following is Sheeva's recollection of what happened after she arrived at the Jackson Street Station:

> *My first desire was to find the woman's restroom. I was curious to find out how much money I'd taken. I was afraid it wouldn't be enough to help me get a place to live and buy food. I wanted to go to the lady's room because, once I was in a locked stall, I could check how much money was in the envelope I took from my father's desk drawer.*
>
> *A Mexican couple with two children sat on the bench opposite me. The man was a burley guy with tattoos on both arms, and his woman was this tiny thing and quite pretty. Their kids were very impatient about the wait and constantly bickered and fussed. The small boy came over to me, looked at me coyly, and asked me where I was going. I smiled at him*

and said, "To Houston, Texas, and where are you going?"

"I live in Houston. It's really big," he quickly responded.

His mother told him, "Leave the lady alone and get back over here on the bench." He hesitated for a moment, and then his father sternly said, "Jamie, get your butt over here now. Listen to your mother." The boy went back to his place next to his father. The mother looked at me and asked, "You live in Houston too?"

"No," I told her. "I'm moving there to live with my boyfriend."

"Where will you be living?" she asked.

I stuttered around, trying to think of how to answer that and finally realized that I could just tell them I was surprising my boyfriend.

The woman leaned over laughing and said, "I did the same thing. If I didn't, he never would have married me." She motioned to the man sitting next to her. "Go, girl! My names is Nelli, and if you want to know anything about Houston, just ask. I guess you're waiting for the same bus."

"My bus leaves at 6 a.m.," I replied.

"Yes, that's the same one. Long wait. My children will drive me crazy by then. They can't sit still."

I realized I hadn't given her my name and tried to think of what I should call myself. She probably thought I was weird with this orange blond hair, but I guess I didn't really look much different than a lot of other people in the terminal at 2 a.m. I finally felt it was time to use the restroom and excused myself. The restroom was just a few rows away. It was empty when I entered and smelled worse than the one on the bus. It had wet paper towels strewn on the floor and a soiled diaper dangled over one sink bowl. I walked up and down the stalls and found the cleanest one with a door that would actually lock and entered it.

I opened my small backpack, which I'd purchased back in Hammond, Indiana, and pulled the manila envelope to the top. It had numerous wrapped packets of money in it.

I pulled out one package. It was a wrapped package of one hundred dollar bills. I counted them. There were one hundred bills in the pack. I quickly realized I had a lot more money than I'd imagined.

When I left my house in Chicago, I thought I only had like a thousand dollars, but there was a lot more in the envelope. There were nine banded packs of one hundred dollar bills and two banded packs of twenty dollar bills. Minus a few twenties I'd already spent and the hundred dollar bill I gave Hidi, I had around ninety-four thousand dollars.

Just looking at all the money and trying to imagine what my father was doing with it, had my head spinning.

Inside the envelope was also a letter in Arabic, but I could not read enough of it to tell what it might have said. The only thing I could decipher was the Arabic word for Christmas.

In addition to the letter there were three aerial pictures that looked like clusters of buildings I thought were probably hospitals. The pictures were from Google Earth or Microsoft Virtual Earth. I thought maybe this was money my father was going to donate to a hospital at Christmas. My father was an important doctor, and I knew he did charity stuff like that.

Suddenly, I found myself trembling sitting there on the toilet. Just the knowledge that I'd taken that much money frightened me because I knew how angry my father would be. If he was to find me, he would beat me to death. Tears started to burn my eyes as I tried to not cry.

My brother's threat crept back into my mind, 'You'll get yours when you get home.' But the fact that I'd got all the way to Omaha, Nebraska, and not one soul had asked me for my ID, gave me hope that I wouldn't be discovered. In fact a part of me felt fairly confident that I wouldn't be easy to trace. With my blonde hair and western clothes, I didn't even recognize my own reflection. I doubted any one would recognize me from the old pictures my father had of me.

I tried to calm myself and think about what I had to do to survive. I took out some twenties from the pack and put them in my purse and then returned the rest of the money to the manila envelope.

I brooded over the question, if I wanted Jason to know how much money I had. It wasn't that I was afraid he would squander it, but more like he might want to return it to my father. Jason had a fear of my father and I'm sure he would feel I was wrong taking that much money from him. Jason believed in fairness and not hurting others.

I heard another person enter the bathroom and the voice of a little girl frantically telling her mother she had to go pee-pee. I was sure the voice belonged to Nelli's daughter. A series of doors opened and closed as they searched for a toilet clean enough for the little girl to sit on. The toilets were all filthy with seats caked with hanging toilet paper and worse.

I remembered that I needed to figure out a name for myself. I was going to have to use a different name, because I was afraid they would have me on some runaway list. There was a girl in school named Lyndsey Nicole something, but she wanted us to only call her Nicole. I really liked the name. Lots of kids thought she was all that, so I figured Nicole might also work for me. I thought Nicole was a very pretty name. I still needed a last name.

I closed up my backpack and opened the door, and saw Nelli three stalls away.

"Hi, Nelli, nasty place." I grimaced as I looked around.

"Yeah, it's hard to breathe in here. You okay?"

"Yes, I just had to repack some of my stuff and take care of business," I replied, smiling.

Nelli's little girl had finished, flushed the toilet, and was standing next to her. Nelli picked her up and carried her to a semi-clean sink to scrub her hands. I did the same and told Nelli to call me Nicole. Then I wondered why I said it like that. I should have just said, "My name is Nicole," but it was too late. Or was I just worried about nothing. I just had to learn how to think first before I say something stupid.

We walked out of the restroom, and I realized I was really hungry. We passed by a Greyhound employee, and I stopped and asked, "Where is a good place to get breakfast?"

The lady frowned and said, "The best place is a diner called 11-Worth, but this ain't no time for you to be leaving the terminal. There are all kinds of people out there right now. You would have to walk a couple blocks to get there and believe me, you ain't in the safest part of Omaha right now."

When we got back to our seats, Nelli asked her husband if he wanted to have breakfast. He was all for it, and the kids wanted to go also. They stored their luggage in the bus station lockers, but I kept my backpack. I was afraid somehow, it would be discovered that it had thousands of dollars in it. Around 3 a.m., we were all walking down the street to the diner. The lady was right. It was scary on this street.

The diner was busy when we got there. It had all types of people in it, some who looked like they were drunk and half asleep, others who were the truck driver type, and then a booth with girls who looked like hookers all giggling and talking loud. There was a big Skee-ball machine in the front that Jamie Jr. wanted to play with the minute he saw it.

Nelli's husband Jamie ordered this big plate of fried corned beef hash. The cook was some guy wearing a hairnet over his mullet and had arms covered with tattoos. The waitress was this gum-

cracking older lady who was constantly sniffling. When she wasn't sniffling, she was wiggling her nose. The shady people parading in and out while we sat there were really interesting. There was an old guy who toted a cane and wore gold-framed eyeglasses. He sat down with the noisy girls who looked like hookers. He called the waitresses "honey" and apparently was a regular. The next couple of hours flew by quickly, and I was glad I'd gone with them to eat. Our bus to Houston would be boarding soon.

By the time we got back to the terminal, they were already announcing the departure.

Chapter 14
Looking for Hidi

When Ali Hasson arrived home, he discovered that his daughter had been home and had rifled through his desk and taken money. We can assume he was shocked and angry, but since Hasson provided no testimony about this event, Ajani's secondhand knowledge is all we have to describe what happened.

Ajani was a close friend of Ali's son Abdul. The following account is taken from Ajani's recollection of the events.

While reading this account, it should be remembered that Ajani was also under indictment for numerous crimes, and no other testimony fully collaborated his story.

> *The night Sheeva's father realized she was gone, Abdul frantically phoned me. He said that Sheeva had stolen money from his father and run away, probably to be with her boyfriend. His father asked Abdul to help find and punish her for stealing their money and being so stupid.*
>
> *He had praised Abdul as a son he could count on to do what was necessary to keep the situation from circulating around the community. He told Abdul to tell friends and neighbors they had sent Sheeva to relatives in Canada, where she was now staying. The bottom line was that he needed Abdul to get back the contents of the envelope and everything in it as fast as possible. He gave Abdul five hundred dollars for gas money and other expenses.*
>
> *Abdul was really proud that his father trusted him with this task, he asked*

me and Rahman, a friend who went to school with us, to help find Sheeva and the money.

The first person he wanted to talk to was Hidi. I really liked Hidi and had been trying to get her to like me. I think she did like me quite a bit and I was sure that I could talk to her. If she knew anything about Sheeva, she would tell me.

Rahman had heard that Hidi had visited Sheeva's boyfriend while he was in the hospital. This infuriated Abdul even more, that Hidi would visit this infidel who was causing all these problems for his family. He wanted to visit Jason again but worried that he might be arrested at the hospital for beating Jason. The rumor that Hidi had visited Jason made Abdul obsessed with talking to her.

Abdul was a very devout Muslim and went to prayer meetings every day and watched on the internet famous Muslim clerics discuss Islam. He followed the teachings of clerics like Anwar al-Awlaki and Sayyid Qutb and was devoted to the Takfiri movement, which preached that they had the right to accuse other Muslims of apostasy and even condemn them to death.

Abdul wanted to be a part of the Takfiri movement. He liked that Takfiris didn't have to follow a lot of the usual Muslim constraints like wearing a beard and not drinking alcohol or not eating pork. Takfiris are supposed to blend into society so others won't recognize them. They are like secret agents working to find enemies of Allah.

Abdul had been very upset with his sister for a couple of years because she was getting to be like this girl named Yasmin Fostok, who was the daughter of the famous Cleric Omar Bakri Mohammed.

Yasmin supposedly became a pole dancer in London, which her father felt brought disgrace to him and Islam. She was targeted by Takfiris as an apostate and had to go into hiding. Abdul was afraid his sister, Sheeva, would shame their family in similar ways since she had become so Westernized. It made him hate her. I mean really hate her.

Hidi's parents were away in Saudi Arabia for the month of November, participating in the pilgrimage to Mecca. They were devout Muslims, and this trip was something they had looked forward to for a very long time. Because Hidi was still in high school, they had no choice but to leave her home. They had a neighbor looking in on her and had made arrangements with some of her friends' parents to help take care of her.

Hidi liked to party and was boy crazy, so she took advantage of her parent's absence and stayed out late with her friends whenever she wanted. Everyone at school talked about her partying.

Abdul was obsessed with finding Hidi and "interrogating her," as he called it. He wanted to talk to her someplace where they would be alone. He was texting me and Rahman all during school with his ideas of what we needed to do. He wanted to get her alone so he could scare her into talking. He felt Hidi knew where his sister was or at least how to contact her. He wanted to search her home. He was really crazy about carrying out his father's wishes. He bought flashlights, some cheap binoculars, and wanted us to follow Hidi everywhere to see if she might lead us to Sheeva.

Most of the friends Hidi hung out with would make it hard for us to really talk to her. The only time Abdul thought it would be safe to talk to Hidi was at her home, since she was supposed to be there alone. So we started to watch her home. That first night, we discovered she was staying with a girlfriend so we decided to see if we could get into her house and search it.

We parked the car around the corner and walked quietly up the sidewalk to her place. We climbed over a fence to get into her backyard and started looking for an unlocked door or window. We didn't find one, so we pried open a window. Once we were in, we fixed the window as much as possible to hide the broken lock and the bent frame. This was Hidi's parents room, and she would probably never notice it anyway. We found Hidi's room and searched it with flashlights. We looked everywhere for notes that might have a phone number or address that would tell us where Sheeva was hiding. We went through the house, all of it, but found nothing. Abdul decided to leave the back door unlocked so we could easily get back in. He figured Hidi would never check to see if her back door was locked, and even if she did we could just come in through the window again.

Two days later, Hidi was out on a date with some jock from school, so we parked just down the street from her house. About 11:30, she finally drove into her driveway. She got out and went into her house. From watching the lights go on in her house, it looked like she was going straight to her room. The light in her room was on for only a few minutes, and then the house was totally dark again. Abdul wanted us to wait for a few more minutes before we snuck into her house because he wanted to make sure she didn't get up again and that she didn't have someone in her car who was supposed to sneak in after she was in bed.

Finally, fifteen minutes later, we drove closer to her house. We grabbed our flashlights and exited the car. Hidi's house was just a half a block away. We quietly walked down the sidewalk and up her driveway. We climbed over her fence again and crept to her back door. The door was still unlocked, and we all snuck in and stood in the laundry room and listened for any strange sounds in the house.

Abdul wouldn't let us use the flashlights so we had to carefully move through the kitchen and living room. When we got to the hallway, we saw the flicker of a TV coming from one of the doors. Abdul signaled to us to be quiet as he moved noiselessly toward Hidi's bedroom door. When he got next to her door, he stopped and appeared to count. Suddenly, he rushed into her room and grabbed Hidi by her hair and yanked her out of the bed.

Hidi was only wearing a nightshirt, and when she fell from the bed onto the floor it bunched up underneath her breasts, exposing her crotch completely. She didn't have any panties on.

She didn't yell or anything. She just looked shocked and terribly afraid. She looked like she couldn't speak, like her throat wouldn't let any sound out at all. Maybe she thought she was in a nightmare. I guess really she was.

Abdul jerked her head around by her hair and hissed at her, "Where is my sister, Hidi?"

Hidi reached up to Abdul's hand holding her hair and said, "All I know is she ran away."

Abdul grabbed her fingers and bent them back hard. Hidi screamed in pain.

"Stop hurting me," she cried.

By this time Hidi was really crying and had realized she was exposed to all of us. She reached down to pull her night-shirt down, but Abdul slapped her hand away and said, "You're a whore so you don't need to cover up your pussy." He stooped over and stared into her face, "You're responsible for my sister becoming a whore, aren't you?"

Hidi finally looked up at me and between sobs said, "Ajani, I thought you liked me. Why do you let Abdul hurt me like this?"

I really felt bad then, because I really liked her, but I knew if I said anything against Abdul, he would freak out all over me. I said to her, "Hidi, if you just tell him what you know, he won't hurt you. He just wants to know where his sister is."

Hidi blurted out, "She took a bus out of Hammond, Indiana, but I don't know where she was going. That's all I know."

Abdul punched her in the face hard, and blood ran out of her nose and mouth. Hidi yelled even louder, and Abdul clamped his hand over her bloody mouth and told us to hold her arms so he wouldn't have to struggle with her any more. Rahman and I grabbed her arms and held her up against the bed. I tried not to hurt her arm with my grip. Abdul pulled a knife out of his pocket and flashed it in front of her face and told her, "I'm not messing with you any longer. Tell me what you know or I start cutting up your face, bitch."

As Abdul was waving his knife around in her face, Rahman reached over and grabbed her left breast and squeezed it. That really pissed me off, but then he said to Abdul, "Why don't you cut that T-shirt off her so we can see the whore's tits?"

"Good idea," Abdul answered and grabbed her nightshirt and stuck his knife into it. With a quick jerk, he yanked his knife up, ripping it totally open.

Hidi let out another yell and started to kick. She was afraid of being cut by Abdul's knife and was struggling like crazy. Her foot caught Abdul hard in the crotch and he doubled up. Rahman started to laugh at Abdul and temporarily lost his grip on Hidi's arm. She jumped at Abdul and grabbed him by his balls. Things were going crazy, so I let go of her and grabbed Abdul. I tried to pull him away from her, while Rahman tried to pull Hidi away from Abdul.

Suddenly Abdul stabbed his knife into Hidi's arm and pushed her down on the floor. He yanked the knife from her arm and plunged it into her shoulder. Then in total insanity Abdul started to repeatedly stab and curse Hidi. His arm was just a flurry. He was stabbing her in her face, eyes, mouth, shoulder, and breast. We tried to grab his arm, but before we could his knife broke off in her shoulder. He just sat there on top of her panting, holding the broken knife, and looking down at her. She was already dead when he climbed off her, still spitting and kicking at her. I couldn't believe he had killed her, and Rahman also looked shocked. Rahman and I just stood there, looking at her on the floor while Abdul sat on Hidi's bed getting his breath back.

There was blood splattered on the sheets, floor, and nightstand. It looked like something out of a horror movie. She was really dead, but her body kept making strange sounds.

Chapter 15
Ajani's Story of After the Act

Ajani's account continues with what happened after Hidi was murdered. This version is potentially compromised, however, as it is told by a man facing serious criminal charges related to the events.

"Abdul, you killed her. What are we going to do now," Rahman blurted.

"She deserved it. She was a whore and an apostate. We did our duty," Abdul said, looking definantly up at us. "We are going to clean this mess up and get her out of here," he said calmly, with a weird grin on his face. Then suddenly he started to laugh. Rahman and I just stood there in shock looking at him.

Abdul finally got hold of himself and stood up. He told Rahman to get a pot of water and some soap out of the kitchen to clean the blood off the floor and nightstand. He told me to get the shower curtain out of the bathroom. He wanted to wrap her up in it. While I was getting that, he tore the sheets off the bed and found fresh ones in the hall closet. He made the bed while Rahman cleaned the blood off the bed frame and nightstand. Once Abdul was done making up the bed, we picked Hidi up and dropped her onto the shower curtain spread out on the floor. He told us we would carry her out to the car. She was light, maybe a hundred pounds at the most. I could carry her all by myself. I was still in shock and really was not thinking at all. I was just scared we would be caught. Abdul, I think, was excited about having killed her. He was ordering us around like he was some big boss or something.

He had checked the floor really good and poured the bloody water down the toilet and returned the pot to the kitchen. The floor was still wet when we left. We left the back door unlocked again when we left. We had to pass Hidi over the fence, and then I carried her over my shoulder to the car with Rahman and Abdul walking close to me so it was hard to tell what I was carrying. No one was on the street, and the lights were off on all the houses we walked by. When we got to the car, Abdul popped the trunk and told me to throw her in there.

We quickly got in the car and Abdul started it and moved out onto the street without the lights on. He popped them on about a block down the street and then started cursing about what a whore she was and how she had made him kill her.

We didn't say anything, just listened to him rant. Just as we were passing a Jack in the Box, he pulled into the parking lot. He put the car in park and pulled out her purse and her phone from a pocket in his cargo pants.

"Let's check how much money she had," he said.

He pulled out a little over a hundred dollars and handed us both about thirty dollars.

Abdul said, "I'm hungry. Let's get something from the drive-through. I got her cell also." He flashed it in front of us and stuck it in his shirt pocket.

I wasn't hungry, but he insisted we all get something to eat before we go home. He told us to bring the food in to our homes so our parents would see we were just hanging out, doing nothing.

I asked, "What are we going to do with Hidi?"

"Well, Ajani, I will figure that out. Tomorrow after school, we will get rid of her," Abdul said boastfully.

He took us home, warning us all the way not to talk to anyone about what we had done unless we wanted to be bunking with some hairy-ass butt fucker.

My mother was up when I walked in and asked me what I'd been doing out so late and I told her, "Just hanging out with Abdul and Rahman playing Guitar Hero." That was something we did over at Rahman's house.

I told her we had grabbed something to eat at Jack in the Box and that was it. I acted like I was really tired so she would leave me alone and headed for my bedroom. My mother came in and reminded me she had to be at work early so I would have to fix my own breakfast. I said, "That's okay, Mom."

Then she broke into one of her lectures, telling me, "You shouldn't play that stupid game so late on a school night. Now you're too tired to take a shower and that's an awful habit for a man your age to be getting into."

"I'm sorry, Mom, I just didn't realize how late it was."

She gazed at me with that pathetic look mothers have when they are upset with you and then said, "Good night, Ajani. I love you."

The first thing I thought when my mother closed my door was how cold Hidi must be in Abdul's trunk. I think I silently cried for about an hour over what we had done. All I could see were her arms flaying about, trying to stop Abdul's knife. But he just continued stabbing her everywhere. Before he stabbed her in her mouth, she had begged him to stop. The vision of Abdul stabbing his knife straight into her eye and twisting it kept filling my mind. He was vicious. As soon as he would pull it out, he would slam it back into her. I remember how her mouth had gaped open from being cut so badly. Part of her cheek hung from her face. He had even stabbed her in her skull. For a girl only a hundred pounds, she struggled really hard to stay alive. I felt bad that I hadn't pulled Abdul off her. But once he stabbed her in the arm, I guess I was in shock and it happened so fast.

I couldn't sleep at all that night, thinking about what we had done. Part of the night I thought it must have been a horrible nightmare I'd dreamed. You know those nightmares you swear were real. The ones you wake up sweating or so scared you can't move. But in the morning, before school, Abdul called me and said we had to meet after school to get rid of the package. His call wiped away any doubt I had about the reality of what I'd envisioned all night. We had really killed Hidi.

Abdul didn't sound upset when he called, just excited and pumped up. A spot on my arm grabbed my attention, and Abdul's voice faded out as I realized I had Hidi's crusted blood stuck to my skin.

I couldn't help it any longer and vomited all over the bed. I could hear Abdul's laugh coming from my cell phone as I heaved and tried to catch my breath. I felt like I hated him, but I knew we still had to work together to get rid of the body.

Chapter 16
Ajani's Story: A Bundle of Trouble

Hidi's murder and the disposal of her body showed a frightening callousness. No other collaborative witness had been found regarding Hidi's murder, so the account remains only the recollections of Ajani. Once again, we advise you to consider that he is a man facing serious criminal charges related to the events:

> *All day at school, I tried to act normal and forget about what we had done. I concentrated on listening to the teacher, but a part of my brain kept flashing scenes of Hidi lying dead on the floor and those horrible sounds coming out of her. I kept feeling like every school guard was looking directly at me and could see how nervous I was. I tried to stay away from Abdul and Rahman, but Abdul kept texting me about how we were real "Takfiris." He texted me that he had an awesome plan and that I was going to really like it.*
>
> *After school, I looked for his car in the parking lot and met up with Rahman. I asked him if he knew what Abdul was going to do with Hidi's body and he just shrugged. He looked like shit also. I think he was worrying that we would get caught or he was sorry that we did it.*
>
> *We spotted Abdul car and walked swiftly to it. Abdul was beaming. He had a soda in his hand and motioned to us to hurry up as he took a drink. Once we got in, he said we were taking a trip to Wisconsin to ditch the garbage. He was really pissing me off, but I tried not to show it.*

He said, "You pussies okay?" and snickered as he backed the car up. I wanted to punch him, but I knew I had to stay calm.

Rahman asked, "You really know where you can dump the body and not be seen doing it?"

"Oh yeah. I found a great place by searching Google Earth during study hall. It looks like a totally deserted place near Tobin, Wisconsin. I plugged the address into my GPS, and it's about an hour drive. I looked on the map. It looks like a dirt road that has a bridge going over a culvert with nothing around. No houses, buildings, or anything. It looks like the stream empties into a lake. If there is water in it, Hidi will float out to become fish food."

We were not very talkative as we rode out to this location. It was someplace right off 1st Court and 122nd Street.

When we got there, we turned right onto 122nd Street, and just a short distance up that road going west it turns into a dirt trail. This was the culvert Abdul spoke of.

We stopped at the culvert and exited the car. The three of us went to the back of the car and removed the body from the trunk. Hidi's body was already reeking, and it was only a day old. We carried Hidi's body wrapped in a new clear plastic tarp. I could see through the tarp, and her face looked even more smashed and destroyed than the night before. Rahman noticed it also and asked Abdul, "What in the hell did you do to her face?"

"You like?" He paused for a moment and then continued, "I took a

sledgehammer to it and dumped a glass of sulfuric acid on it. No one will recognize her now."

I was getting that sick feeling again, and the smell was nauseating. He was right...her face was just a mound of mush protruding from her shoulders. The only thing that let you know it was a head was some blood-soaked hair still attached to what was probably her scalp.

We placed the body on the concrete wall and started to unwrap her from the plastic tarp. As she neared the edge, Abdul pushed the body with his foot, and Hidi's body spun out of the wrap as she fell to the water below. As she fell, I noticed her hands were missing. She landed head first in the water, with part of her body draped over the cold embankment. I stood there staring at what was left of her undulating in the water below and was in a trance again. I just couldn't believe I was doing this stuff. Abdul grabbed me and yanked me toward the car. Rahman was staggering toward the car and making gagging sounds.

Abdul said, "Rahman, if you're going to puke, do it before you get in my car, or I'll have you eating it. I got something else to show you."

He popped the trunk open and put the plastic tarp back in. He grabbed some gloves and lifted a large jar out of the trunk and held it up for us to see. In it were two human hands that looked like they were disintegrating. "You know what you're looking at?" Abdul asked. Before we could answer, he explained, "That's Hidi's hands floating in sulfuric acid. There is nothing left to identify her with.

Her fingerprints are melted away, and her face is gone. And now read the label on the jar."

I squinted at the jar and read the words pasted on the label. It read, "Deuteronomy 25:11-12 (King James Version) When men strive together one with another, and the wife of the one draweth near for to deliver her husband out of the hand of him that smiteth him, and putteth forth her hand, and taketh him by the secrets: Then thou shalt cut off her hand, thine eye shall not pity her."

"What's this for?" I asked.

"When they find this jar near some newspaper stand back in Chicago, they are going to think this is a crazy Christian freak who whacked off a woman's hands because she touched his balls. They are going to be looking for Christians, not Muslims."

Behind me, I heard Rahman heave his guts up all over the ground.

Chapter 17
Jason Goes Home

Jason Wilgers was released from the hospital about a week after his beating. He was still limping and experiencing terrible headaches, but his doctor assured him that his discomfort was normal, just another step toward complete recovery. His father, Roger, and brother Frank drove him back to his old apartment. To Jason's surprise, he found it stacked with taped boxes and the walls bare of his favorite hangings.

Roger Wilgers said the first thing his son did when he entered his apartment was give a startled look as he absorbed the changes.

"Hope you're not mad," Roger said as he watched Jason survey his apartment. "We weren't sure how long you might be laid up, so your brother and I took the liberty to pack up your belongings to make sure we can get you down to Houston on time to complete your next semester registration at the Art Institute."

"No, Dad, that's fine. It's less work for me. How much of my stuff did you throw away?"

"We threw away all those old picture albums and love letters we found from your latest crush," Frank interjected.

"Don't listen to your brother. He is just pulling your leg. We didn't toss any of your stuff, not a thing. See those green garbage bags over there by the refrigerator? Those are bags of stuff your brother and I thought you would consider trash, but being a good dad, I left it for you to make that final decision."

Jason gave his dad a thumbs up and collapsed into an easy chair, followed by Frank.

"So what are the plans?" Jason asked.

"I think we should eat up your last few TV dinners and watch the news. Once we relax a bit, we'll need to get back to the packing business and make sure you're ready to hit the road in the morning. What do you think?" Roger said.

"Sure, Dad, that's fine. What about the furniture and cleaning the place to get my deposit back?"

"I'll do that. I'm on the lease so I'll take care of it. Frank will drive you and your stuff down to Houston in his truck. He is still on paid leave from the force. The trip will give you a chance to reconnect."

Frank had already pulled a pizza from the fridge and was warming it up in the oven. Roger was waiting for his gourmet frozen dinner.

The Channel 7 News blared from the TV, informing Chicagoans that snow was not yet in the forecast, but freezing rain was a real possibility. A stoic reporter named Betty Kennedy said, "The discovery of a mayonnaise jar outside of Chicago Pete's Coffee Shop held a grizzly surprise. Inside were two decomposing hands floating in some kind of acid, according to preliminary forensics. From the size of the hands, it's believed that they belonged to a petite woman. The jar was accompanied by a cryptic note indicating that the person who cut off the woman's hands did it for some obscure religious beliefs.

Pete Johnson, owner of Pete's Coffee Shop said, 'I hope this is not another John Wayne Gacy or Jeffrey Dahmer deal. Chicago does not need no more of them kind.'

Anyone with any knowledge of this crime is urged to call the Chicago Hot Tip Line. As new information develops, Channel 7 will bring you the updates."

"Nice. Another killer on the loose...glad I'm getting out of here," Jason exclaimed.

"I'm sure every state has its share of them," Roger replied.

While they ate their TV dinners and frozen pizzas, Channel 7 started the national coverage.

> "We take you now to KJSV in Jacksonville, Texas, where citizens are protesting the district attorney's lenient prosecution of sex offenders. This is the same Texas town that made national headlines when Officer Larry Pugh was convicted in federal court of violating the civil rights of two women by forcing them to have sex with him. Two other complainants in his federal trial, Shunte Coleman and Terri Reyes, mysteriously disappeared during the same period Pugh was out on bond. The decomposed body of Reyes was later found in Angelina National Forest, but federal witness Shunte Coleman, mother of two, has yet to be found.
>
> "Now Jacksonville is the center of a new controversy. Court records indicate that probation is the most common sentence for sexual offenses. Offenses like molesting a twelve-month-old earned a forty-five-year-old only eight years deferred probation, and a forty-three-year-old registered sex offender was coddled with a ten-year deferred adjudication probation for an offense against a fifteen-year-old girl."

On the screen, a list of pictures and names scrolled down, showing sexual offenders in Jacksonville, with each case listing probation as its disposition.

Jason's cell rang. Roger suspected it was his girlfriend Sheeva. He acted surprised but happy when he answered it and immediately stepped outside. He was gone, probably a good ten to fifteen minutes and when he came back inside, he appeared much more upbeat.

But he tried to deflect the conversation to the TV, asking, "So, Dad, how did the pervert report turn out?"

"Can't tell you now. You should have stayed in here and watched it."

"So now I go from a place where floating hands are found at coffee shops to a place where they wink at you when you date three-year-olds."

"Don't worry, I'll protect you," Frank quipped.

"What time are we starting tomorrow?"

"I want to hit the road by 7 a.m.," Frank said. "We need to have all the boxes and stuff in the truck and ready to go by 6:30. I have to get back to Beaumont if I want to keep my job, so we have to start early and drive all the way through, okay?"

"No problem, let's get some sleep and get up at five to load the truck," Jason replied.

Chapter 18
KANUPP's Disgruntled Employee

The morning Jason packed and headed south to his new home in Houston, Texas, Ali Hasson received great news. His expert had been located. This expert was a terribly important person in assuring the success of the Christmas Special. A Hasson recruiter had been searching for this elusive individual for months. The man he found was named Nihad and had spent most of his adult life as a nuclear power plant operator in Pakistan. He was the perfect candidate: a disgruntled former KANUPP employee with over thirty years of experience. He was the perfect teacher for Hasson's three teams. He could show them the weaknesses of nuclear power plants.

Nihad had a seething hatred for America and its interference in Pakistan's nuclear program. He was also a devout Muslim fundamentalist. Now his Muslim brothers were offering him a great deal of money to assist them in a clandestine jihad operation. They would pay him fifty thousand dollars to go to Canada and train devout jihadists. He was to create a one-month crash course on nuclear power plant operations for about sixty Muslim brothers. This was a secret operation, and he was told he could not divulge his work to anyone, ever.

Nihad had held numerous jobs during his thirty odd years with the Karachi Nuclear Power Plant, but the American plants were of a different design. This fact posed little problem to Nihad because his studies abroad had provided him ample training on Westinghouse PWR light water reactors.

He would train his recruits with simulation software in the same fashion that the air force trained its jet pilots. He would use the same desktop simulator software the IAEA used as its training material for its annual advanced reactor simulation workshop. The PCTRAN software he would be using would be the same used the world over and consider by experts as the best application in training, analysis, probabilistic safety assessment, and emergency exercise for nuclear power plants.

Getting copies of the program was easy—Nihad still had many friends at the Karachi plant, and for eighty-four thousand Pakistan rupees, or roughly one thousand dollars, they would happily provide him with the latest copies of the PCTRAN software.

Pakistan had just purchased PCTRAN software to help teach its operators how to manage their new nuclear power plant. Nihad knew that the PCTRAN software would simulate the exact type of nuclear power plant that Dr. Hasson intended to destroy.

Ali Hasson had elaborate plans for his attack on nuclear power plants. His predecessor, Mahmoud Atta, had considered crashing a plane into Indian Point Nuclear Power Plant but had eventually decided on the Twin Towers and Washington D.C. as more appropriate targets. Hasson was sure the Indian Point Nuclear Power Plant would be a much more devastating target if successfully attacked. He was sure that his highly trained jihadists would easily defeat the Christmas morning security team and quickly take over the plants.

His plan required that his team attack the three power plants precisely at the same time. A small team would cut all power lines and visible phone lines into the compounds, while a truck laden with explosives approached the main gate. The surprised guards would immediately be killed or taken as hostages to be used as shields and to assist with any security issues. Any hesitation of a guard to assist would result in his immediate death. Jihadists responsible for destroying the various water-cooling equipment would use a four-wheeler to rapidly move to the various targets and attach plastic explosives and timers to the equipment to explode moments later.

Team two would use a four-wheeler to race to the building containing the control room and enter by means of captured guards or explosive charges. Once the door had been breached, the power plant controls would be set to cause maximum damage. Back up systems like generators and auxiliary cooling systems designed to protect the plant from any common failures without a total shutdown would be destroyed by explosives, fire, or a couple shots from fifty caliber rifles.

The timing would be essential to get into the building, but once the site was under their control, they would have considerable time to successfully destroy the plant. They expected a slow response on Christmas morning, and once police or the military arrived, they would be hesitant to use any heavy weapons for fear of causing more damage to the nuclear site and releasing radiation.

In fact, many of the responders would be afraid of even entering the compound once they realized the site was under jihadist control.

Chapter 19
Sheeva and Jason in Houston

Sheeva provided a very complete description of her stay in the east Houston motel. Her memories of those shared days with Jason were happy. In fact, they would be days Sheeva would cherish for the rest of her life.

> *We stayed in the motel off of I-10 in east Houston for over a week. That time felt so wonderful simply because we were together every day. We didn't really do very much because Jason was still very sore from his beating. He wanted to get back in good shape so he was very careful.*
>
> *I think he was still not too sure about us being together. I mean living together. Most of the time, I felt like he loved me, but sometimes I thought he worried about how expensive I might be. I hadn't yet told Jason how much money I'd really taken from my father. I simply told him I'd taken a few hundred dollars. I told him I would do some cleaning jobs and make money on the side to help with the expenses.*
>
> *That first week in Houston, we just lounged around the motel room watching TV and checking out the news from Chicago on the computer. I was anxious to see if there was any news about me running away. We checked 560WIND, WGN news radio720, and the Chicago Tribune website, but there was no mention of me running away. They did talk about other missing kids, but not me. At first it made me feel safer that no one was looking for me, but later it started to both-*

er me that no one missed me. I also checked the site where they list all the runaways, www.missingkids.com, and discovered that I was not listed there. In fact, I visited missingkids.com every day, sometimes a couple times a day to see if I was listed, but there was never nothing about me. No one was talking about me missing or running away.

I felt that my father didn't want me back. I used to feel that he hated me, and now his action or inaction seem to validate that feeling. It made me feel sad that I had no one in my life but Jason. My mother was dead, and my father and brother despised me. I bet my brother was happy I was gone, because I embarrassed him with my Western ways. My brother Abdul had always been my father's favorite.

Most of the time, Jason's presense made me forget how I felt about my family. From the minute he walked into the motel room, it felt so right, and I really could feel his love for me. Now his love was even more important. When I got sad about how things were and started to cry, he would kiss away my tears and tell me everything would be okay and that he would be with me forever. That was what I wanted to hear. I wanted him to be with me forever. I wanted him to really love me.

Anyway, we didn't do much that first week. but lounge around the room and occasionally venture outside to eat at one of the restaurants that lined the street near our motel. There were lots of restaurants along the street. We ate Chinese, Mexican, Italian, and regular old Ameri-

can food. Probably every day we ate a pizza for lunch or dinner, and I was sure I would grow fat and Jason wouldn't love me any longer. I was also worried that Jason would stop loving me because I'd dyed my hair blonde. He loved my real hair color. He said I looked foolish with blonde hair and much more beautiful with my raven black hair. But I was intent on keeping it blonde for a while longer so I would be more difficult to recognize. He might have liked it better if it had really looked blonde, but it had turned into a yellowish orange color. I looked like a punk rocker or something.

I think that first week being with Jason and free from my father was the greatest week I ever had. It was so full of love. It was exciting being with Jason and starting this new life. His love made it so right. Waking up every morning with him next to me was the greatest thrill ever. The only bad thing was the constant feeling that my father or Abdul would find me. I kept telling myself that they didn't care that I ran away. I thought sometimes that my dad was probably happy I was gone and didn't even care about the money as long as I was gone. It did feel bad to know that my world was very small. If I died, only Jason would miss me.

Then I thought about Hidi and asked Jason if we could call her and see what was going on back in Chicago. He didn't like the idea because he was afraid she would tell others, and Abdul or my father would end up here and take me back to Chicago. I didn't think she would tell anyone, but I did worry that if they found us together they would beat Jason to death. They would have beaten him even more than they did the last.

Jason told me we were going to take the Amtrak to New Orleans for the weekend, and when we were in Louisiana we could call Hidi with my old phone. He thought that would be better, because if my father went to Verizon and asked where the call came from, they would tell him New Orleans.

All the while, I kept listening to the Chicago news and checking missingkids.com to see if I was listed. We weren't following the news just to hear about me. Jason was also following the story of the gruesome killing where the hands of a dead person were cut off and put into a jar. The Chicago police still hadn't discovered who the hands belonged to nor who committed the crime.

This horrible murder had hooked Jason's interest because the Chicago radio stations talked about it incessantly. Jason searched the Internet for all the information he could find about the killing. He wondered what kind of a person would kill like this and leave sick passages from the Bible as a clue or warning.

The news people said it was some crazed religious fanatic. They talked about the possibility that this murder was related to a group like the Heaven's Gate cult that had castrated many of its male followers. Others thought it was some person who imagined he heard messages from God to kill those who have defied some biblical passage. Other people said the killer was probably not religious, but just wanted it to appear that a religious fanatic was responsible.

The news was full of horrible stories. I'd never really listened or watched the news that much, but for some reason Jason and I found it necessary to follow it daily. We wanted to know what was going on back in Chicago and in our new home in Houston.

I'd been following a terrible story about a woman named Jamie Leigh Jones who had gone to Iraq and a group of her co-workers had been accused of raping and beating her. She was only nineteen. It was horrible. The company called KBR that she had worked for in Iraq claimed she had to resolve the issue under some arbitration clause in her contract and could not go to court. The news reported that seven KBR employees drugged and gang-raped her. I just could not fathom how people could be like that, and I was so happy to have Jason there to hold and comfort me.

After about three days of being together, we were going to bed around ten at night, almost like old people. I guess it was because there wasn't much to do in our hotel room, but watch TV, talk, and cuddle. Jason was still healing from his beating and his body ached, so the extra sleep was good for him.

One thing we quickly decided was the need to start looking for a place to stay beside the motel room. It was getting expensive, even paying by the week. Jason's stuff was stored at his brother's house in Beaumont, Texas. He didn't have much, but he was missing the little he had. I was excited about setting up our very first place. I'd bought magazines about decorating small apartments and meals to make for two. I wanted it to be perfect, or as perfect as it could be for the two of us when we got our new place.

The night before we were leaving for New Orleans, I checked the missing-kids.com once again. I knew I wouldn't be listed, but something still made me get on it.

I guess a part of me wanted to be missed by my father and brother. I was not on it, but there was a picture I recognized. I gasped loud enough to wake Jason. I shook Jason and made him look at the screen. "Look, Jason, it's Hidi. She has run away also," I said hysterically. I hoped she didn't have to run away because of helping me. He looked at the screen and said, "Good for her." And then put his head back on his pillow.

I shook Jason again and told him I needed my old phone back so I could call her. But he peered up at me and said, "We will do it tomorrow. She might be back home already and then we would have her parents talking to your father, and the next thing, your father or crazy brother will be breaking down our door beating the shit out of both of us. Tomorrow, after we get to New Orleans, you can call her."

He closed his eyes. I knew he wouldn't change his mind, and really, I knew he was right. We had to be careful. I sat there Googling news for Chicago and Hidi's name to see if I could find any articles about her, but there was nothing.

Finally, I gave up, turned off my light, and tried to go to sleep. I snuggled up against Jason and threw my arm over him. His breathing faltered for a second and then continued its soothing rhythm.

Chapter 20
New Orleans Trip

Jason came through with his promise to visit New Orleans with Sheeva. They both looked forward to the diversion. Sheeva's account of the trip is told in her own words in the following:

> *Our trip started at 5:10 Friday morning from the Houston Amtrak station. The station was a one-story, boxy, white building. In front of it was a small parking area. Inside the station were old time wooden benches, but the rest of the décor was modern with industrial blue carpet and walls of imitation wood panels and large picture windows.*
>
> *Posted on one wall was a large poster advertising The Christmas Carol and Santaland Diaries at the Houston Alley Theater. I'd seen the movie The Christmas Carol with Jim Carrey and I loved it. My father was sort of a Scrooge when it came to Christmas. He hated it and was upset with me for participating in its celebration.*
>
> *Jason bought our tickets and we sat on the wooden benches looking out on the station's platform. It was illuminated by the bright lights high up on the surrounding poles. I heard the wail of the train as it neared the station and could feel it vibrating the station.*
>
> *An announcement was made that the Sunset Limited was arriving.*
>
> *Both Jason and I were really excited. This was our first trip on Amtrak. I watched the big white-and-blue striped engine roll by. You could see the rails give*

as the heavy engine moved over them. Our train had a big 838 painted on its side. A couple employees had started pulling two old-timey baggage carts laden with luggage over to the train. It seem odd they were still doing this in this old-fashioned way.

We went outside and stood on the platform as passengers climbed down the steps and hurried into the station. It wasn't very long before the boarding call was announced, and people started to climb on. Jason got a window seat with plenty of room to stretch out, and I took the one next to him. The train was quickly on its way, and we were soon heading to Beaumont, Texas, the first stop of our train excursion. Beaumont was where Jason's brother Frank lived. The train was fast. It sped along probably at eighty miles an hour or more.

Jason wanted to explore the train. The train had an old time feeling to it, especially in the double-decker Superliner carriages, with their old-fashioned décor and clunky fittings. As we rocked across the Texas landscape, the train lurched and swayed. The view from top of the Superliner carriages twenty feet up was unbelievable.

Soon after Beaumont, we crossed into Louisiana. I remember how gorgeous it was when the sun lit up the eastern sky with a blaze of yellow and crimson. As we sped through the landscape of cypress swamps and bayous, the sun lit the early morning mist hovering over the water. It was a beautiful sight, and I was glad we took the train instead of driving. This ter-

rain was so much different than anything I remembered from Afghanistan.

When we went to the dining car for breakfast, we discovered that eating alone was not that easy on the Sunset Limited because the dining car tables are laid out for four. We were lucky to share a table with a couple from Arizona who were photographers coming to Louisiana to film the damage caused by the huge BP oil spill in the Gulf.

The couple, Elden and Carol Crosby, were livid that nothing was really being done by the government to help the people on the Gulf. Jason was also very upset about the oil spill and the indifference of the government. He told the Crosbys that if the spill had happened around New York or Hollywood, it would have been solved much quicker. But the Gulf Coast people just are not that important to the administration. Elden said the president was too busy with vacations and campaigning to worry about the lives of a bunch of Cajuns. Our chat over toast, eggs, grapefruit, and coffee brought back memories of when I was little and my father would discuss all this political stuff with his friends as they sipped coffee.

It felt strange remembering that time. There were memories from that terribly dark period of my life that I preferred to forget, but that was apparently not an option. It was when the Taliban had taken over Afghanistan. It was an insane time where things happened that I still haven't been able to comprehend or totally believe.

When the Taliban came to power, my father was happy because so much of the fighting in our country stopped, but the bloodshed didn't. Now people just disappeared and ended up in a field missing their head or packed into airtight shipping containers like sardines until they suffocated. If you were willing to be a devout Muslim like the Taliban wanted and didn't care that all others were being killed, life was not that hard. My father didn't even get upset when the Taliban decided women were no longer allowed to go to school. He simply told me it would be okay because a wonderful husband would eventually take care of me.

As I sat with Jason and the Crosbys, I thought how different my life had become. In Afghanistan, I would have been whipped just for talking to these strangers and punished even more for the way I was dressed. Terrible images clouded my memory of women being hung at the soccer stadium or whipped with wire whips on the streets because they were in public without a male escort. And the worst was my father whipping my mother so badly that she passed out from the pain. I though she was dead, but she came to, and when he saw her trying to get up, he punched her so hard in the face it broke her nose. My mother's legs and back bled from the whipping for days, and her broken nose never healed straight. My father ridiculed her about it till she was killed three months later in a bombing.

I think the beating was because my father was angry with her for resisting him taking a seventeen-year-old girl as his second wife. The girl's name was Samira, and soon after the big fight with my mother, he married her. My mother hated my father and her, but she had to stay with them. Once my father married Samira, he treated my mother like a slave. He constantly beat her and even let my brother Abdul treat her like dirt. My mother began to wear a burka all the time to cover her bruises and hide the sorrow on her face. She was spiritually dead way before she physically died. Beneath her black burka, my mother wilted away like a beautiful flower locked in a box of darkness. She had nowhere to go; no one to help her.

When she died, my father showed little emotion. But just a few months later, he cried when Samira was killed. Her death came as the Northern Alliance attacked our village to drive out the Taliban. It was soon after that when my father began to work for the Americans and the Northern Alliance.

These visions and memories made me start crying. Jason and the Crosbys were talking about the Thanksgiving holiday, and I just starting sobbing. The Crosbys and Jason had no idea why I was crying, and I didn't want to tell them. They looked at me strangely as I hugged Jason tightly and told him how much I loved him and how happy I was that we were together. The gentle rocking of the train and Jason's strong arms around me brought me back from those dark memories.

Chapter 21
A Day and Night in New Orleans

In the transcript below, Sheeva continues her story.

The train slowed down as we came into New Orleans. We were soon at the New Orleans Union Passenger Terminal. This station was so much bigger and better than the one in Houston and those we had passed on our trip. As we got off the train, all I could think about was calling Hidi. I asked Jason to give me my old phone, but he still made me wait.

We arrived at our hotel, the Best Western Saint Christopher, which was just walking distance from Canal Street and the French Quarter. Its location put us in the middle of all the action, but still provided some quiet because it was tucked away on one of the side streets.

After we got settled into our room, we took a streetcar ride and visited the Saint Louis Cemetery No. 1. This is one of the oldest cemeteries in New Orleans, dating back to 1789. Jason wanted to visit it at night. He thought it would be fun. The cemetery is located in what's considered the "bad" part of town. A dilapidated wall surrounds it, giving it an even more sinister look. Our guide didn't help me feel safer because he kept talking about how haunted the cemetery was. As I passed through its gates, goose bumps crept across my flesh, and I tightly grabbed Jason's hand.

The cemetery was like a small city. Crypts and vaults covered the landscape with narrow alleys managing the traffic in the city of the dead. It was dark, and the lights from the lanterns made it more eerie. A slight breeze moved through the cemetery and blew my hair across my face. The sensation scared me, and shivers rippled down my spine.

A couple weeks prior had been All Saint's Day, and people had brought flowers and mementoes to the cemetery to commemorate the departed. A flower skittered up against my foot, and I was not sure if it was the breeze or something else moving among the dead. I almost ceased breathing as part of me felt the need to listen for any strange sound that might warn me of danger as we wandered through the tombs.

Our guide led us to the crypt of the famous voodoo priestess Marie Laveau. The crypt is marked with many Xs, which supposedly means that Marie Laveau continued to help people in need of her voodoo magic even after her death. Jason told me that if you knocked three times on her crypt and made a wish, it was likely to come true. If it did, you had to return to her crypt and mark it with three Xs or leave a coin at its base as a thank you for the granted wish.

Jason liked these bizarre things. He was still wearing my taweez around his neck, and he suddenly reached over and knocked three times on Marie Laveau's tomb and then closed his eyes tight as he made a wish. He looked at me, smiling and still clutching the taweez, and handed me my old cell phone. My heart beat even faster then. I flipped it open and moved through the names in its directory till I found Hidi's name. I didn't even ask Jason, but just pushed the call button. The phone began to ring. I listen intently for Hidi to pick up, but she didn't. Her recorded voice answered with a cute little message for me to leave a message. I hesitated for a moment and then said, "Hidi, I will soon call you back like at eight tonight, please have your phone on."

Jason had me pose near Marie Laveau's crypt, took several pictures of me, and then had the guide take some of us standing together.

Nothing supernatural happened at the city of the dead, and I was very happy to leave it behind us.

Next we visited Bourbon Street. The upper portion of the street is the most popular section, and Jason wanted to visit the night spot next. The street was packed full of people, many of them sipping on hurricane cocktails or drinking beers. I could not believe it, but three really drunk girls were walking around exposing their breasts.

Some of the people standing on the second floor balconies threw beads down to them when they exposed their breasts. This wasn't anything I wanted to do or see. I was sure my father would have had me beaten just for being there. This was the den of thieves and whores he always warned me about. I told Jason that I really didn't want to stay here, and I guess he didn't either, because he led me away from Bourbon Street and we were soon back at the Best Western Saint Christopher hotel.

I was tired. We had been up since four that morning, and I was ready to go to bed. I wanted to call Hidi one more time before I went to bed. I turned on my phone again and looked at my previously called list. I highlighted her name and pushed call. I heard the phone ring, and suddenly her phone was answered, but no one said anything. I said, "Hello, Hidi. It's me Sheeva, where are you?"

A voice came over the phone, but it wasn't Hidi's. My heart pounded and my voice was lost for a moment as I recognized the familiar voice. The person on the other end said, "Hi, Sheeva, how are you?" It was Abdul. I was so totally confused that I stupidly asked to talk to Hidi. Abdul said, "I'm sorry, Hidi is not available. Where are you, Sheeva? It's time for you to come home."

Jason saw my shock and grabbed the phone from my hand. He listened quietly for a moment to something Abdul was saying and then slammed the phone closed. He looked at me in a strange way and then reached out and hugged me as I broke down crying.

After hearing Abdul's voice, a terrible fear crept over me, and I began babbling, "He will kill me. Jason, he will kill us both. We should commit suicide, it will save us from the pain they will inflict on us. Let's just—"

Jason reached out and pressed my face into his chest. My tears soaked his shirt as he held me tightly, caressing my hair. His consoling was comforting and a strange warmth replaced the terror that had gripped my being after hearing my brother's voice. I felt a blissful peace in his arms, unlike anything I'd ever felt before. I felt like I was in the safest place on earth.

"Nothing will happen to us," I heard him say through my heavy sobbing. "Tomorrow morning, we will return to Houston and start looking for our own place to live. Some place where they will never be able to find us."

I started to protest, but Jason looked into my eyes and pressed a finger to my lips, saying, "Nothing will happen to us. You need some sleep now. You're tired, and when we get up, things will be clearer."

Jason was so sure of himself that I stopped protesting and got ready for bed. My mind, however, continued buzzing with many disjointed thoughts. I lay there imagining stupid things like the two of us married and wondering how many kids he would want. He would be a wonderful father, which was something I was sure of because he was so full of love. Sleep didn't come quickly. My mind would drift from visions of Jason and I married to visions of my brother smirking at me as he flayed my face with a lash. Then I would see a horrible vision of me partially buried with jeering people throwing stones at my head. Just like the stoning scene from the movie The Stoning of Soraya M.

Throughout the night, I tossed and turned, waking Jason repeatedly. Finally, we just turned the TV on to watch something stupid enough to make us forget our concerns. But the news was on and the first thing they reported on was the situation in Afghanistan. Jason wanted me to switch it off, but I held the remote and told him I wanted to see what was happening where I came from. Some female teachers and students had been found executed, and the Taliban took credit for the butchery. The reporter read a proclamation the Taliban had made in Kunduz to teachers. It read:

> "You are working with the government. We Taliban warn you to stop working for the government, otherwise we will take your life away. We will kill you in such a harsh way that no woman has so far been killed in that manner. This will be a good lesson for those women like you, who are working. The money you receive is haram [forbidden under Islam] and coming from the infidels. The choice is now with you."

The reporter said that in Kunduz these threats were reinforced by arson and rocket and bomb attacks. There had also been mass poisoning of beverages at these schools. One Taliban spiritual leader explained that the targeting of girls' schools was because education is unnecessary and un-Islamic for Muslim women. He also claimed that these schools taught adultery, nudity, and un-Islamic behavior.

Although I know Jason wanted to sleep, he tried to soothe me throughout the night. That night, it felt like Jason was a gift from Allah to me. I know this sounds a little extreme, but at that time I felt that Allah had given me Jason to make up for having me born into such a cruel family.

In the dark, lying next to him, I told Jason I really didn't have any other friends, except him. Hidi was my only other trusted friend. I wondered what happened to her. I was sure my brother had something to do with her running away.

Just before I finally drifted into sleep, I thanked Allah again that he had brought Jason into my life.

Chapter 22
Ajani's Road Trip with Abdul

The following events were compiled from Ajani's statements made during his interviews with the Chicago police after his arrest. Many of Ajani's original words have been preserved.

> *Checking Hidi's cell phone was a daily ritual for Abdul after he killed her. He was convinced that his sister would try to contact Hidi by phone. He hoped that Sheeva would leave a text or voice message on Hidi's cell about where she had ran off to. Abdul wouldn't leave the cell on all the time because he said the FBI could locate the user of a phone by simply tracking its phone signal. He had seen that in a movie and was sure it was true.*
>
> *He had read that Abu Musab al-Zarqawi had been located and killed in Iraq by Americans tracking his cell phone signal. He was pretty sure that occasionally turning Hidi's cell phone on while driving around some congested Chicago freeway for a couple of minutes to check for any voice messages or suspicious phone numbers wouldn't be trackable.*
>
> *Road trips became an obsession with Abdul. Every day he would call me to drive with him to some restaurant or mall outside of Chicago. This would give him the chance to be on the freeway to check the calls. He would have me drive, and once we were speeding along in the traffic, he would flip the phone on and check for new calls. As soon as Abdul had the phone numbers recorded in his*

little notebook and had listened to each voice message, he would turn it off, and ten miles or so later we would stop at some cheap restaurant and buy some junk food.

Days went by and Sheeva didn't call, but Abdul was very persistent and then late one afternoon it happened. When Abdul checked the messages on Hidi's phone, he heard his sister's voice leaving a short message. Sheeva simply told Hidi to have her phone on around 8 p.m.

Abdul was ecstatic that his sister had finally called. He made plans for us to be cruising Interstate 90 later that evening. Before the call came in, Abdul worked himself up by ranting to me about how bad she had disgraced his family. He told me that in Afghanistan she would have been dead in a heartbeat for the things she had done to his father and his family. Then he went on even a bigger rant, telling me that the problem with Americans and infidels is that they didn't understand Muslim ways. He said something like, "Americans don't understand why a girl who is raped has to die to protect her family's honor. 'After all,' they will say, 'it isn't her fault.' Infidels have sex like animals. Infidel girls dress like whores. Their mothers even dress them up in bikinis before they even have tits."

I didn't say anything but just kept driving and listening. I knew it was not worth arguing with him because Abdul would get mad if you questioned his Islamic beliefs. His temper grew even worse after Osama Bin Laden was martyred by the Americans. He had vowed to do any-

thing he could to help avenge the murder of Bin Laden.

As I drove, Abdul kept preaching about the purity of American women. He was saying, "It's sick, but true. Americans don't care if a woman is pure when she is married. That's why they can't understand why we say our family is humiliated when an unmarried Muslim girl is no longer sexually pure. Her lack of chastity brings shame to everyone in the family. How else can a family's honor be cleansed except by her blood? What's to understand?"

Abdul fiddled with the phone for a moment or two and then continued, "My father said that letting women act like whores and having no respect for their chastity can destabilize the entire morality of our Muslim society. Americans don't understand that, so they won't understand why we demand the right to take back family honor when a woman defiles it."

He was looking at me to agree with him, and so I said something like, "Yeah, you're right."

Then he said, "A Muslim family must have every member knowing their place. My father said men must stay in control of their families. Women and children must obey. Women must devote themselves to the care of their husband and children, or things will spiral out of control."

The traffic got worse as we passed Kimball Avenue. The traffic was bumper to bumper. We didn't have much further to go before we were out of Chicago.

Abdul said, "We could end up with a big bunch of Kola Boofs. And you know what a headache and disgrace she is to the Islamic community. She was born respectable but lost it by being brought up in America. If she was in Afghanistan, she would never be allowed to have a picture of herself with her bare tits on the cover of her disgusting books. I guess it doesn't make much difference anyway because she is an apostate. She will burn in hell when she dies. That probably will be soon because I heard there is a fatwa for her assassination. Did you know that?"

"No. I never heard of Kola Boof."

Abdul looked at me and shook his head in disgust. "You need to know what's going on in the Islamic world, brother. She is this writer who writes lies about Islam and is an enemy of Allah. Americans make her a big deal because of what she writes and she models lingerie and stuff like that, disgracing herself and her family. Look her up on the Internet and you will see."

He continued to talk to me about honor killings. It was like he was trying to prove something.

He said, "I hate the American news reports about honor killings. They always focus on the gory details instead of showing a compassionate understanding of why a family had to kill some bitch to maintain their honor. She committed a crime, it's that simple. She stole her family's honor. The family is the real victim. Their honor was violated, or destroyed in some cases, so killing the whore is needed to regain honor in the community. It shows your respect for Allah and Islam. I mean, Abraham was willing to sacrifice his son Ishmael. We should be willing to sacrifice those who defy Allah's righteousness."

Then Abdul looked at me and asked if I was his friend. I knew he wanted something big and I felt like I was his friend, so I said, "Yes."

Abdul said, "Thank you. It's good to have friends like you. I would do anything for you. Anything you asked of me, as long as it was righteous and would also please Allah. I want you to know that. You're like my brother. Even my father loves you. Every day at prayer meetings I ask Allah to bless you. I want you to know you can count on me for anything you need. When you need help, I will be there for you. Do you understand?"

These statements made me uneasy, but I said, "Yes, Abdul. I thank you for being my friend. I feel the same about you."

"I hope you do, Ajani," Abdul replied. "I want you to embrace Takfiri and work with me to promote Islam and make sure that Muslims follow the tenets of the Quran. There are others at the mosque who are also involved. We need to make sure the laws of Allah are obeyed. I think you and I could do great things for Allah by devoting ourselves to the Takfiri movement. Will you?"

I didn't know really what to say so I stupidly told Abdul I would.

Then Abdul wanted me to say the Shahada with him as a pledge that we would devote ourselves to Takfiri. We both repeated, "There is no deity except

Allah and Muhammad is the Messenger of Allah."

Abdul punched me playfully in the shoulder and said, "Thank you, my brother. We are both going to make Allah happy. We are going to help right many of the wrongs that weaken our Muslim community. I'm excited we can take this adventure for Allah together."

A car's horn behind me blared loudly, and I realized I'd drifted over to the left lane where a motorcycle was trying to pass. I'd almost pushed him into the concrete dividing barrier, so I jerked the car back into my lane. The motorcycle zoomed by me with the driver giving me the finger and probably cursing me. Abdul started cursing at the guy and wanting me to speed up so he could mess with him. I wouldn't do it, and he started calling me names. We had just passed Harlem Avenue, and I reminded him it was getting close to eight o'clock and that he needed to turn on Hidi's phone. That calmed him down a little. He still was muttering something about what an ass I was, but I just stayed quiet.

The cell phone rang just as we passed the sign on I-90 that said, "You are leaving Chicago." Abdul took the call and put the phone up to his ear. He kept quiet for a few seconds, and then he slid down into the seat and calmly said, "Hi, Sheeva."

He was smiling now and told his sister that Hidi was not available. She said something, and then Abdul started yelling into the phone. He was calling her a whore and telling her if she didn't come home right away he would find them and kill Jason. He said something like, "I will make you watch me as I cut his throat. Is that what you want? His death will be your fault because you let that pig fuck you."

Sheeva hung up on him, which made Abdul even angrier. He wanted to call back, but the number was listed as "Unknown."

Abdul stomped his feet on the floor a couple times and then turned to me and said, "I have to kill her. She is a pig. I want to kill that Jason along with her. We have to find them, and I want her to beg me to let Jason live. I want her to see that fucker bleed out like a butchered sheep before I kill her. She has to be punished."

Chapter 23
Back to Houston

Abdul's threatening conversation with Sheeva upset her so much that she and Jason decided to end their visit to New Orleans and return to Houston. Sheeva's account of their return trip to Houston on the Sunset Special follows:

> *The next morning, we left the hotel and went back to the New Orleans Union Passenger Terminal. Jason bought our tickets, and a short time later we were back on the Sunset Special heading for Houston. The calming sound of the train moving over the tracks soon put me to sleep. I think I slept almost all the way back to Houston. I didn't even eat anything on the six-hour trip.*
>
> *When we arrived at the Houston Amtrak station, Jason's brother, Frank, was there to pick us up. He had never actually met me before, and I was afraid he would ask me how old I was or something weird that I didn't want to answer. But he didn't. He simply smiled at me and said, "So this is Sheeva, I can see why my brother is so crazy over you." He gave me a hug and said, "Well, I'm glad to finally meet you. Jason has talked so much about you."*
>
> *Frank backed away from us and said, "I have a surprise that I think is really going to shock you. Something I bet you have been thinking about a lot since you arrived here in Houston."*
>
> *What he was saying and the way he was acting unnerved both of us. I could not imagine what this surprise could be. My mind started imagining all*

kinds of things; maybe they had arrested my brother for beating up Jason. I knew that would be bad for us because then Frank would tell the police in Chicago where we were. My paranoia made me fear that maybe my father had contacted him, or maybe Frank was going to say he had someone waiting who wanted to see me, or worse yet, he was going to arrest me as a runaway. But fortunately it was nothing like that; he led us to a car in the parking lot that had a bow and card attached to the driver's door handle.

Frank pointed to the card and said, "Read it."

The card read, "From Dad with love. Now you have some transportation to save you more time to study. Love You."

It was a 2005 blue Hyundai Accent with a couple minor dings on the trunk, but it looked very new. Jason's dad had asked his brother to find some cheap transportation for Jason. Frank had purchased the 2005 Hyundai for less than $4,000, with only seventy thousand miles on it.

It had been well taken care of. In fact, the interior looked brand new and even had that new car smell. I loved it, and I knew that Jason was happy about having a car again.

Frank wanted to know why we came back so soon, and Jason told him he felt bad about wasting Dad's money on the hotel rooms and eating out when the most important thing was getting a place to stay.

"Well, I think having a car will make it a lot easier finding a good apart-

ment," Frank said. "Now that you have a car, will I be able to bum a ride from you back to Beaumont?"

Jason, still walking around inspecting the car, replied, "Yes, of course we can take you back. Hey, you went out and bought me a car, the least I can do is give you a ride back home. Frank, I love it. I was worrying all the way home about transportation. Houston is a big city, and it would be hard to find a place without a car."

Frank said, "Why don't we look at a few rentals before you take me back to Beaumont?"

"Frank, I don't want to waste your time dragging you around Houston while we look at apartments," Jason replied.

Frank playfully punched Jason in the arm and said, "No, It would be fun seeing what the big city offers for rentals, and I can make sure you still remember how to drive."

"Okay, you've convinced me. Let's get a newspaper and take a look at a few places."

Over the next three or four hours we checked out nine apartments but really found nothing we could get into soon. All of them wanted to do credit checks on us and wanted ID. That was going to be a problem. Jason didn't want to fill out any of the applications because they also wanted deposits. I knew he was looking for something a lot smaller than these big apartment complexes. Finally, Jason convinced Frank it was time to quit looking and take him back to Beaumont. By that time, I was sort of worried about if we would be able to find a place to live but didn't want to tell Jason my concerns.

We drove to Beaumont and wondered if any of these small towns between Houston and Beaumont might be a better place to look.

By the time we got to Frank's place in Beaumont, it was getting late and both of us were tired and simply wanted to get back to Houston and our motel room.

However, Frank wanted us to come in and see his place, so reluctantly we did. Jason was complaining about needing to get off his leg because he was still recovering from his beating. Finally, Frank let us go when Jason promised he would be back in a couple days to try out this new restaurant called Starvin' Marvins.

Chapter 24
Zaki Mansur at the Farm

Confessed terrorist Zaki Mansur was a Nigerian Muslim who had immigrated to Canada in 1996. After settling in Toronto, he found himself homesick for the people and culture he had left behind and sought out others who came from his homeland. He frequented the various mosques in Toronto that served the spiritual needs to the city's four hundred thousand Muslims. From his visits, he finally enjoyed close friendships with some of the individuals he encountered.

The 1998 attacks in Sudan by President Clinton in response to the August 7 bombing of the US embassies in Kenya and Tanzania embittered Zaki toward the United States. Some of his friends were from Sudan, and they shared Zaki's belief that Clinton's deadly attack was done to divert attention from his sexual relationship with Monica Lewinsky.

It was the Clinton attack on Sudan that polarized Zaki and drove him into the radical Islam camp. In Zaki's quest to find friends who understood his anguish, he inadvertently befriended ardent believers of the 1998 fatwa declaring holy war on the West. He was surprised to discover the number of well-known, important individuals who signed it. They were Muslim luminaries like Ayman al-Zawahiri, amir of the Jihad Group in Egypt; Shaykh Mir Hamzah, secretary of the Jamiat-ul-Ulema-e-Pakistan; Abu-Yasir Rifa'i Ahmad Taha of the Egyptian Islamic Group; Fazlur Rahman, amir of the Jihad Movement in Bangladesh; and Osama bin Laden, head of al Qaeda.

These were all well respected Muslims, and Zaki became another ardent follower of the 1998 Fatwa declaring holy war on the West. From that time on, he felt it was his Muslim duty to be a jihadist.

Much of what is known about the planning of the Christmas Special attacks was the result of the capture and interrogation of Zaki Mansur. The following excerpts were taken from some of the publicly released Mansur interrogation transcripts.

> *When we arrived at the farm outside Toronto, Canada, we were met by Ali Hasson and some assistant whose name I no longer remember. Hasson's very polite assistant helped me carry my luggage to my room and then showed me around the farm.*
>
> *My room was in what was probably once a barn that had been converted to sleeping quarters.*
>
> *By noon, everyone had arrived, and Ali Hasson wanted us to assemble in a large dining room. Once seated, he preceded by giving us a very formal welcome. Included in the welcome speech were comments about our mission and how it would make us as important in the Muslim world as the Magnificent Nineteen. He reminded us that their feat of destroying the Twin Towers and damaging the Pentagon brought great pride to all Muslims who believed in our struggle to defend against America's crimes and sins against Allah and Islam in general. I remember how emotional Ali Hasson was when he said, "The hands of Allah in celebration of the sacrifice made by the Magnificent Nineteen crushed the Twin*

Towers to a smoldering mass and killed the kuffers who occupied them." Ali stood for a moment, regaining his composure. Suddenly he shouted, "God is great." And we all chorused, "God is great."

He continued and said, "This heroic selfless deed by these brave jihadists resulted in hundreds of thousands of new converts to Islam all over the world."

He urged us to accept that it was now our Muslim duty to follow the fatwa that states:

"The ruling to kill the Americans and their allies—civilians and military—is an individual duty for every Muslim who can do it in any country in which it's possible to do it, in order to liberate the al-Aqsa Mosque and the holy mosque [Mecca] from their grip, and in order for their armies to move out of all the lands of Islam, defeated and unable to threaten any Muslim. This is in accordance with the words of Almighty Allah 'and fights the pagans all together as they fight you all together,' and 'fight them until there is no more turmoil or oppression, and thus prevail justice and faith in Allah.'"

Ali Hasson slammed his fist on the podium and yelled, "Our mission will bring America to its knees. We are here to wage a battle that we know we will win. Why do we know we will win? Because once again, their arrogance and disrespect for our ingenuity will be their undoing. Yes, just like their own 9/11 investigation stated, it was their own lack of imagination that allowed us to turn their machines and inventions into weapons against them. Once again, my brothers, it will happen with even more death and destruction.

"We are not going to destroy just some building in a city this time or a symbol of their tyrannical government. This time we will create a fear in them that will not be forgotten for decades to come. We will show them that we can destroy their largest cities, that we can strike anywhere, and that our new targets will cause suffering and death for years to come. And where do our brothers come from who are committed to this jihad? From America, Canada, England, France, Nigeria, Sudan, Germany, Afghanistan, Iraq—the great beast will have a hard time to find someone to strike out against!

"Our mission will strike fear in America and create new respect for those who know the true God, Allah. These nonbelievers will soon find themselves impotent against the power of Allah. They will have no one to strike out against. America's leaders will look like the buffoons they are, and their citizens will seek their dismissal."

Chapter 25
Discovering Culper, Texas

Sheeva's various statements, recorded police interrogations, and sworn testimonies provide a reliable account of her and Jason's introduction to Culper, Texas. The following is Sheeva's firsthand account:

> *On our way back to Houston, we stopped at a convenience store just off I-10, where Jason decided to buy their local paper and check out the ads for rentals in that area. This area look a little desolate and he was hoping he could find a person who just wanted the rent money but really didn't bother with credit checks and all that. There were a few listings for Anahuac and Wallisville, but the most promising one was a cottage in Culper, Texas. It rented for $590, including utilities. Jason was excited about finding that listing, but when he looked at the date on the paper, it was almost a week old.*
>
> *We grabbed a couple of drinks and some chips, and we were ready to leave when I asked Jason why don't we just call and check and see if by chance the cottage was still available. He said it was a waste, but he gave in and called. The phone rang and rang, but no one answered. It appeared it wasn't going to be our day for getting a new place.*
>
> *It was time to get back to our motel room so we got back on I-10 heading west to Houston. The day had been great. We now had a car and Frank had turned out to be very nice. I'd felt like he actually liked me.*

As we were passing through Anahuac, Jason's phone rang, and dread filled me. He grabbed his phone and looked at the caller ID. He didn't recognize it. I remember he looked at me questionably, and I said, "Answer it."

It was an older woman. She claimed he had called her, but she wasn't there when Jason called. She wanted to know what he was calling for. She told him her first name and said she was calling from Culper, Texas, and that's when Jason's eyes lit up.

"Oh yes, we were calling about your cottage. Is it still available?"

"Well, yes it is. We got a few lookers, but no one gave us the deposit for it yet. First person who can afford it and gives us hard cash will get it. Are you looking for a place?"

"Yes we are. We were at a convenience store off of I-10 and read your ad. Your cottage sounded very nice."

"Well, if it's convenient for you, and you are not already too far away, why don't you just come on over? My husband is home, and we could show the place to you now. That is, if you're really interested."

"That would be great, ma'am. Are you sure this is not an inconvenience to you?"

"Of course not! Let me give you directions."

She gave Jason the directions, and we got off I-10 at the next exit and headed south to Culper, Texas.

Chapter 26
The Mission

Much was learned from the interrogation of Zaki Mansur. The information he provided helped answer many questions relating to the terrorists' inspiration and extensive training. The following narrative by Zaki Mansur demonstrates that.

During the early morning hours of the second day of training, it snowed. A freezing wind howled through the trees and plastered snow against the windows. Way before the Fajr prayer, we were awoken and told we had to dress and go outside in the freezing snow. Some thought this a joke, but quickly we understood this was a serious request. The power was off, so we dressed in the dark using flashlights given to us by Ali's assistants. When we filed outside, we were directed to the main hall. Ropes were strung between buildings so we could find our way in the darkness. Once we had assembled in the hall, Ali Hasson greeted us and told us that we had work to do that could not wait. First he told us that we needed to get outside in the storm and help remove the snow from the roofs. He feared the wet snow could cave in the roofs on some of the old cabins. When he heard some grumbling, he reminded us that what we were embarking on was a venture that could easily occur in the freezing snow on a morning just like this.

A diesel generator provided power to the dining hall, but only a few lights were used so the room looked drab and dreary.

Ali Hasson paced back and forth in front of us and then stopped and fixed his eyes on two men standing in the back of the room. Ali Hasson gestured at them and introduced them as Muslim Americans who had taken up the call to wage jihad.

One was named Habib Bishara who was from Key West, Florida. He had long blonde hair and was probably nineteen or in his early twenties. Ali Hasson asked him if he had changed his mind in his commitment to Allah.

Habib looked embarrassed at first, but then he spoke. He had a very effeminate voice, but what he said made me see that he was committed to the cause. He declared with great emotion that, "Jihad was the key duty in Islam and a pious Sunnah that Prophet Muhammad, peace be upon him, preferred all good Muslims to follow." Habib's words reminded me of things my father preached to me as a boy back in Nigeria. He said, "The need for jihad will continue till the Day of Judgment. Jihad provides a path to Allah and is the quickest way for Islam to complete its domination over the world."

Habib's declaration was followed by a chorus of "God is great."

Ali Hasson thanked him and then in a loud voice said, "Do you know there are 486 verses in the Quran that are called jihadist verses. For many American Muslims, these jihadist verses are seen as a problem that result in attacks on innocent Muslims by ignorant non-believers. For us, these jihadist verses map out our path to paradise.

"Our mission will happen in the dead of winter, so we should be grateful that Allah is providing days like this to practice our skills. This storm is not something that should bother us but a gift from Allah to embrace.

"We cannot be soft. We must be fearless and strong. Many confused Muslims, perhaps the entire Muslim Ummah today, are caught in this fear of admitting the meaning of jihad. Because of this, Muslims are seen as soft targets. In order to revile jihad, American warmongers paint Allah-loving Muslims as terrorists. But they don't apply the same rules to their own actions. They kill our leaders and their families with impunity. They murdered the weaponless son of Bin Laden and shot his wife while she begged for her husband's life. They killed the lion Osama Bin Laden even while he was unarmed. Yearly they kill thousands of innocent Muslims in their war on Islam by bombing our towns and cities. They call it retribution, or bringing democracy to our people. The massacre of thousands of Muslim men, women, and children by America's military is called collateral damage." Ali Hasson looked out at us, and his eyes burned with anger. "Those same hypocritical officials label the actions taken by Muslim jihadists as barbaric and cowardly. Our attacks are called acts of terrorism, but this obvious hypocrisy is recognized by most all Muslims."

The wind howled outside and snow continued to fall as Ali continued with his comments. "In America, the boot of the infidels presses down hard on our people, causing them to fear revealing their true views or deep anger. They know that exposing their beliefs could easily result in being imprisoned for supporting what the American imperialists call terrorism."

Many of us listening to Ali were very moved by his words and now began to interrupt his talk by yelling, "God is great!" His talk was very emotional to us. We had all experienced much of what he talked about.

Ali continued, "Because of this, what we do as jihadists is loved and respected by all devout Muslims everywhere. They realize that raising the flag of jihad expresses our tremendous love for the Prophet Muhammad.

"The wrath of Allah is already feared by the warmongers of Washington. The deceitful American head of America's Homeland Security already fears us. This coward is afraid to talk about us as jihadists because they feel that 'It risks reinforcing the idea that the United States is somehow at war with Islam itself.'" Ali Hasson laughed and said, "He must think that Muslims are as dumb and lazy fat TV-watching kuffers."

Another "God is great!" chorus was shouted, and then Ali continued, "One of our great brothers said, 'In America, Muslins with no voice are those who are praised by Americans and they become its slaves.' But we, the servants of Muhammad, peace be upon him, will never accept the slavery of the United States...By choosing martyrdom, a message is conveyed that martyrdom is part of our pious life and is embraced by all true Muslins. I don't believe there is a living Muslim in America who is not without the craving for jihad and a longing for martyrdom."

With that last statement, Ali's assistants handed us snow shovels and instructions of what we were to do. I was told to help shovel off a roof while others were instructed to shovel the snow off the paths between the buildings. The snow now was probably a full meter high.

We worked in the cold darkness of early morning for a few hours, and then we were told it was breakfast. We marched back to the dining hall, and Ali Hasson was there to give us more guidance.

While we ate, we listened to Ali Hasson. He said that most devout Muslims saw the fall of the Twin Towers as a miracle as it was played repeatedly on TV and realized it as a clear sign that Allah awards those who struggle to defend Islam from the crimes and sins committed by the Americans. This was something that many of my relatives from Nigeria also believed. In fact, a cousin of mine had written to me and was so inspired by the event that he also wanted to become a jihadist.

On a screen behind Hasson, pic tures of the Magnificent Nineteen were displayed, accompanied by quotes from their taped martyrdom statements. One said, "Allah said if you do not fight back, he will punish you and replace you." Another said, "My martyrdom will bring me to paradise to reside with the Divine Mohammed and his companions while the dead kuffers roast in the fires of hell."

While these images were displayed, I thought about what my martyrdom statements should say. I'd thought much about this statement, but I was still unsure of what those words would be.

Then Ali Hasson said loudly, "In the name of Allah, Most Compassionate, Most Merciful...praise be to Allah, blessings and peace upon his messenger, upon his family, and companions. You, my brave brothers, will soon go down a well-known path. A path the Quran makes clear, a trodden path that so many other martyrs have marched on, one after the other into paradise. We are at war with the infidel criminals who fight against Allah and Islam. And we must follow the fatwa of 1998 that declares war on the infidels. Again, my brothers the fatwa directs:

"The ruling to kill the Americans and their allies—civilians and military—is an individual duty for every Muslim who can do it in any country in which it's possible to do it."

Ali Hasson asked how many of us knew jujitsu. Some of us raised our hands. He smiled and said that we would use a similar technique against the Americans. He explained that we would use America's own energy against it. He explained that America's arrogance and disrespect for our ingenuity to make weapons of their industries and equipment weakens them. He also reminded us of how inept the America's government officials were and that their greed and association with big corporation made them blind to many national security risks. Many times Hasson told us, "In America, you don't find poor government officials because they are all made rich by the industries they support. It is said that there are only two things that American politicians are concerned about, and that's money and votes. If they have the money, they can buy people's votes, and if they can make people vote for them, they will get the money from the millionaire's they support.

"Bin Laden, before he was martyred, called upon all good Muslims to punish the Americans in a fashion that goes beyond the great deeds of the Magnificent Nineteen. He said, 'The apostates and atheists who offend our Prophet cannot be forgiven. They must be killed. The killing of those who offend Islam is a matter that Allah likes, and that his Prophet likes.'"

Ali Hanson said, "Our martyred brother Bin Laden believed, 'In order to free our holy sanctuaries, we must defeat the Americans.' We fought them in Somalia and defeated them. We have fought them in Iraq and Afghanistan, where they were also leaving defeated. Unbelievers cannot win against us. Even America's president admitted defeat in Afghanistan on national TV soon after he was elected. America has lost its values and world appeal. America's version of freedom, human rights, and equality has been revealed as a total mockery."

Everyone had finished breakfast, and many of us were sipping Turkish coffee while Ali continued his inspiring talk.

"Our attacks will bring about great change in the American Muslim communities. They will be refuted by the mufti of

the Americans, but all Muslims living on American soil will have to decide in their hearts if they should follow Allah's will and enjoy the protection of heroic Muslims jihadists, or if they would rather continue to cower under the heels of their oppressors. That change is already under way as our great brother Anwar al-Awlaki noted, 'Being a jihadist is becoming as American as apple pie and as British as afternoon tea.'"

While Ali Hasson was talking, one of his assistants handed out the first chapters from our al-Qaeda handbook, called UK/BM 29. Ali Hasson ended his welcome speech by playing a statement recorded from a radio sermon by the beloved Sheikh Ikrama Sabri, a Palestinian mufti, who said, "Oh Allah, destroy America, her agents, and her allies! Cast them into their own traps, and cover the White House with black!"

Ali Hasson smiled and said, "Sheikh Ikrama Sabri's prayer is being answered by all of you, Allah willing, and in just a few days you will discover what trap the Americans have created that they will find themselves ensnared in. Their government's arrogance and the stupidity of its citizens have created the trap. In the meantime, please study the handbook given to you today and work hard at all the tasks given during your stay here at the farm. More than a billion Muslims are depending on you."

Chapter 27
Home in Culper, Texas

Culper, Texas, is about sixty miles east of Houston, Texas. Sheeva Hasson continues her account of their search for an apartment, which led them to Culper.

> *When we first drove into Culper, I was immediately struck by how small it was. Many old houses lined Main Street, but commercial buildings were few. Right before the town's only traffic light was a brick building that served as Culper's fire station, which also housed its tiny post office. That building was sandwiched between a Dairy Queen and a boarded-up gas station. Across the street from the fire station was a Southern Maid Donut shop, along with a house that served as the town hall and police station. A Chamber of Commerce flag hung from another building.*
>
> *We were looking for Oak Drive, which supposedly intersected Main Street right after the Southern Maid Donut shop, but we couldn't find it. Jason finally stopped in at the donut shop and asked for directions. An older lady behind the counter told us that Oak Drive was the dirt road right after the deserted gas station. She said it didn't have a sign, but that's where it is. We bought some great donuts and sodas and got back on the road.*

Oak Drive was right where the lady said it was, marked by a rusty sign sticking up from a clump of weeds. We turned onto the gravel road and drove over some railroad tracks and into a wooded area, where the road suddenly transformed into an asphalt road. About a half-mile further was the house we were looking for.

The Tanners lived in a nice brick house set back some ways from the road.

We drove down their pothole riddled driveway and parked in front of their porch.

When we arrived at the house, Jason wanted to talk first to the owners to see if they appealed to him. He was at their front door for just a few moments before he turned smiling and signaled for me to come. I was so nervous about looking at this place because we had already been turned down for no credit or asked to deposit money and be placed on some ridiculous waiting list.

I guess you would call the Tanners elderly. They were very unique. Mrs. Tanner was very brusque in her speech, but still a really nice lady. Her first name was Eva, but she seemed to prefer being called Mrs. Tanner. The first thing she asked after we were all introduced was, "Do you have any pets? We don't allow pets here. Unless you post a thousand dollar security deposit." She was the take-charge, bossy one. "You want to see the place?" she asked. We told her yes and she ordered her husband to take us around to the back of their home to show us the cottage.

The cottage was really a singlewide trailer, with flowers, bushes, and trees growing all around it. I'd never been in a trailer home before so I was surprised at how nice it was inside. In the kitchen, they had all these old avocado green appliances that Mrs. Tanner said were from the fifties but still worked just like new. She said they had lived in the trailer when they first got married. We were looking at the main bedroom when Mrs. Tanner abruptly asked, "Well, do you like my cottage or not? It rents for five hundred ninety dollars a month, first and last paid in advance. Utilities are all included, even wireless Internet."

Jason looked at me, and I shook my head yes. He told her, "It will be great."

"Well then," she said, "let's go back in the house and talk about it."

The Tanners led us to their living room. Mrs. Tanner gestured to us to sit down. The sparsely furnished room was adorned by plants. Jason and I settled into a love seat, and the Tanners sat on their sofa. On the mantle over the fireplace were pictures of a boy and a girl.

The boy was tall, lean, dressed in a suit, and looked very much like Mr. Tanner. The girl was also tall and had an elegance about her that would make most women envious. Her eyes looked like Mrs. Tanner's, and she had blonde hair cascading over her black blouse. I thought these two must be the Tanner's children.

Mrs. Tanner explained their rules to us. Basically, that we would have to pay two month's rent in advance and that we were expected to help maintain the shrubs around the cottage. She also told us there would be no loud music or partying on their property. She didn't want trash left around the house, and that included human trash.

Basically, she didn't want any new problems. She said she had enough of her own.

She gave us a piece of paper to sign that just stated we would pay our monthly rent and that she could kick us out with a thirty-day notice for any reason whatsoever. We both signed it, and she wanted to know when we would have the money. Jason and I still had the money we had intended to spend in New Orleans so we gave her that money and promised we would be back the next day with the rest.

Over the next couple days, we moved into the trailer. Frank brought all of the stuff Jason had stored in his garage.

Decorating the place kept me busy for the next few days. I framed and hung lots of pictures Jason had taken while in Chicago and New York. Many of his steampunk art pieces I also displayed. The place was beginning to look like a Ja-

son Wilgers's art museum. I also went through his mementoes and displayed a lot of them on the walls and shelves. The house began to feel like it was our home by the time I was done. I did feel bad that I had nothing other than the picture of my mother to contribute.

Chapter 28
The Tanners

I thought it was important to include the Tanners' observations of Sheeva and Jason. Their views provide a better picture of who Jason and Sheeva appeared to those who met them. The following transcript was taken from an interview with Mrs. Tanner.

> *When I first met Jason and Sheeva I thought, "What a nice young couple." My husband, Calvin thought that Jason was a bit odd since he didn't follow sports or like to go hunting and that he dressed sort of odd. He didn't wear droopy pants or anything disgusting like that, but he wore suspenders, striped pants, and these weird white shirts. He tried to explain it to us one time, claiming it was some culture he was into. Never the less, Calvin and I still liked the boy. That first day when they came over to see our cottage, I could tell immediately that the girl Sheeva loved the place. I saw the sparkle in her eye as she looked over the place. She liked my appliances.*
>
> *Calvin had always wanted the place to stay looking like it did when we lived in it back in the late fifties and sixties. It's a very romantic place. We have flowers planted all around it, and we added a garden window back in the sixties that opens up the kitchen and lets you have beautiful flowers right there in the kitchen while you cook.*
>
> *Sheeva told me she liked to cook, and later I found out the young lady had been cooking for her horrible father and*

brother since her mother was killed. God bless her.

Her English was so good that I never suspected she was from a place like Afghanistan. When I first found that out, I was a little concerned. We have a few young men and even a couple of ladies fighting in Afghanistan. In fact, Bubba Frazier's son was killed just a couple months ago by one of those IEDs. It sort of bothered me for a while, and I even ended up talking to my preacher about it. He thought I should just keep quiet about it and see if I could get her to come to our church and maybe we could save her. He reminded me that she was also fleeing from all that killing herself and that she probably was ready to be saved.

I did talk to her about my concerns and tried to make her understand that in a small town like Culper, Texas, she had to be careful who she told all her business to. After that talk, she seemed to come to me a lot more often with stuff that was bothering her. She never told me she was a runaway, but when I heard about her father I certainly could understand why she was. She did tell me she was a Muslim, and we did have quite a few occasions where we would just sit around talking about God, Jesus, heaven, and salvation. She didn't act or dress like the Muslims you see on TV who run around in those black robes with their faces all covered up. Sheeva dressed really nice and not like those trashy girls you see hanging around the Southern Maid Donut shop after school. She was just a very nice girl.

I tried my best to get her to come to our Baptist church a few times, but both her and Jason said they didn't think it would be right since they already belonged to another religion. I tried to get them to understand that unless they were living for Christ as born again Christians, they were not going to get into heaven. I told Sheeva about some of our famous born again Christians, like President Jimmy Carter, Johnny Cash, Mr. T, and even crazy people like Alice Cooper and Little Richard. I wanted her to know that Jesus accepts all people if they believe in Christ as their savior and place their whole trust in him.

I knew a few Catholics we had converted and were now born again Christians, but I don't think we had ever converted a Muslim at our church. In fact, Sheeva was the first Muslim I had ever really known. When she told me there were over a billion Muslims in the world, I was astounded. I pray for her all the time because I know she is a lost child. I hope Jesus will embrace her when the time comes and let her into heaven.

Sheeva invited Calvin and I to join her and Jason in their celebration of one of her holidays. She said it was called Eid al-adha, and believe it or not, it was a celebration of Abraham's willingness to sacrifice his son as an act of obedience to Allah. Their version of what happened with Abraham seemed just like the one in Genesis 22:1 something-or-other in the Bible, where God tells Abraham to sacrifice his son Isaac. Then just in the nick of time, God's angel tells Abraham to kill a ram caught in the bushes instead. I told Sheeva about how similar those stories were in both of our religions.

Sheeva said that back in Afghanistan and in most Muslim nations, Eid al-adha is a very important holiday. People have a big feast and the rich sacrifice a goat, cow, or camel as part of the celebration. Sheeva had made these cookies called ma'mouls. She said these cookies were one of the traditions of Eid al-adha. They were very good, but I was afraid to eat many because of my diabetes, and of course Calvin could not eat anything with a lot of sugar because of his irritable bowel syndrome.

Chapter 29
Training at the Farm

Zaki Mansur's account of his training at the Canadian farm provided a very vivid picture of the dedication of Ali Hasson's holy warriors. The cadre at the farm had great respect for them and often referred to them as "angels" sent by Allah to destroy the kuffers. Mansur told of the daily early morning drills conducted before their Fajr prayer meeting.

> *"We would all dress in American army uniforms, complete with boots, field jackets, and liners. In the first few days, we were given paint ball rifles and wooden knives to train with. The morning drills would consist of attacking a guarded shack and gate, plus trying to find and eliminate eight trainers who were hidden along the perimeter fence in small guard towers. Each morning, a different member would lead the attacks. Often, these dark morning drills were conducted with snow falling and ice-cold winds numbing our face and hands. It was so cold sometimes that the paint balls would freeze and cause large welts on whoever was hit by them. After the drill and Fajr, we would all gather in the dining hall and eat these great breakfasts of simit bread and tea, or khubuz, white cheese, and labneh, and sometimes falafel with pita bread, tomato slices, salad leaves, onions, and tahini sauce.*
>
> *During breakfast, Ali Hasson and others would critique us on our morning drill and give us advice on how to improve our attack. We would also talk about other famous holy warriors and their accom-*

plishments, or what they could have done better. One morning, Ali Hasson wanted us to realize that we were not the only jihadist operation that included American Muslims. He talked about a great leader Omar Hammami from Daphne, Alabama, who left home and became a commander with al Shabaab in Somalia. He said that Omar had enlisted many Americans to fight alongside him for Allah with the goal of bringing shariah to Somalia. Ali Hasson said that Hammami even used rap music to bring other Americans to fight for Allah from places like Minneapolis, Minnesota. Ali told us of one of Hammami's biggest accomplishments. This was a suicide attack where four American holy warriors gave their lives to Allah to kill more than twenty-five American-backed oppressors in Somalia. We listened to a taped recording from Hammami that he recorded in Somalia. He said in English, "Oh, Muslims of America, take into consideration the situation in Somalia. After fifteen years of chaos and oppressive rule by the American-backed warlords, your brothers stood up and established peace and justice in this land."

Ali Hasson talked about how Allah selected us the lions of Muslim men to fight the American oppressors and Jews. He told us much about Hammami and his search for the right path. He told us that Hammami was brought up first as a Baptist but discovered that the religion of his father was the true path to paradise.

After breakfast, we would then conduct an hour of hand-to-hand combat with another team and practice throwing fake grenades. We would also study al-

Qaeda's field manual, UK/BM-29, which taught us how to conduct undercover operations, how to prevent being monitored by the American security apparatus, how to communicate safely, and other important information needed to succeed in our mission. In the afternoon, we would practice using snowmobiles and four-wheelers. Two of us would share a vehicle, one to control it and the other to fire at hidden targets. Ali Hasson said that in our mission we would be provided snowmobiles or four-wheelers to quickly move around the perimeter of our target.

Chapter 30
Celebrating Eid al-Adha

Sheeva and Jason quickly completed their move into their Culper, Texas, home and were enjoying life together. The future looked exciting to Sheeva, with so many holidays coming up. She was happy! Her account of their first few days in their new home follows:

> *The next few days were full of surprises and went by so quickly. I wanted to celebrate Eid al-Adha, which was on the seventeenth of November. It would be the first one I celebrated without my family or Muslim friends. I wanted Jason to celebrate it with me, and he said he would. I tried to explain the significance of it to him. Eid-al-Adha is a day of happiness and a day to forgive and forget your differences with others. It's the Feast of Sacrifice, commemorating the Prophet Abraham's willingness to obey Allah by sacrificing his son Ishmael. The holiday lasts for three days. Muslims all over the world celebrate Eid al-Adha.*
>
> *Anyway, I wanted Jason to experience it as close to the way I did when I celebrated it with my family and Muslim friends. I bought a bunch of CDs by Dawud Wharnsby, Sami Yusuf, Zain Bhikha, and Yusuf Islam from Amazon. I wanted this music to play around our house just like it use to when I celebrated it at home. I liked Sami Yusuf's song "Eid Song" and another one called "Happy Eid Adha for all Muslims." I love music, and Jason said he liked Dawud's song "Whisper of Peace." Most of Dawud Wharnsby's songs are in English, so I played them*

more than the traditional songs so Jason could understand the words.

I decorated our home with Eid cards, a crescent moon, paper flowers, balloons, gold stars, Arabic hangings, gift bags, and other items. I wanted to have a feast for Jason, his brother Frank, and the Tanners, if they would come.

Jason had really been studying his Arabic with a course he bought from Barnes & Noble in Beaumont. I even was learning from it. Jason had learned that during this season we greet each other with "Eid mubarak," which means "May your holiday be blessed."

I also was trying to figure out what to get Jason as a present for Eid al-Adha. I finally decided on a halal gift basket of favorites from the Middle East. It had things like Turkish coffee, ground cardamom, Turkish apple tea, honey, and some truly wonderful sweet delicacies. They had Lebanese-style baklava and a selection of hazelnuts, pistachios, and coconut sweets.

On the morning of Eid al-Adha, I would normally attend a prayer ceremony, but this time it was not going to be possible. Not being able to attend this traditional Eid al-Adha morning prayer and my lack of Muslim friends dampened the festive spirit of the holiday.

It was still nice, and I think Jason enjoyed the celebration also. We exchanged gifts. He had bought me some videos and music he knew I wanted. He found a great CD by Salman Ahmad, who is a big rock star in Pakistan but sings much of his songs in English. One of the songs that I really liked was called "Ring the Bells" and was sung by Melissa Etheridge and Salman Ahmad. Jason also bought me a watch that looked a lot like the one worn by the girl in Salman Ahmad's music video, "Love, Can You Take Me Back?" It was an Islamic prayer watch with a compass arrow that would tell me the direction of Qibla and always alert me when it was prayer time. It was a very beautiful gift that I will always cherish.

I gave him my gift basket, and he wanted to immediately try some of the food. Then we brought gifts over to the Tanners and reminded them that we were counting on them being at my special Eid al-Adha feast later that day. They promised to be there and looked shocked when I handed them a gift for the Muslim holiday. Before I left them, I gave Mrs. Tanner a big hug, and it made me feel good, because normally on Eid al-Adha you make a point of embracing your friends and neighbors. The feeling of homesickness attacked me again as I wondered what my father and brother were doing in Chicago. I was so busy trying to get things ready for our feast that they had quickly faded from my thoughts.

The feast is a very important part of Eid al-Adha celebrations. I wanted to prepare the best traditional food I could for Eid al-Adha. I wanted my meal to be over the top and include dishes that are only eaten on these holidays.

I was preparing a few special meat dishes like beef kebabs, beef biriyani, and also Shahi mutton. I wanted to make some rice dishes, Afghani korma, and gulab jamuns.

I'd driven Jason crazy earlier in the week, making him take me to an Indian grocery store in Beaumont to get all the right spices and herbs I needed to make the meal.

Later that day, Frank came over and visited. It was a beautiful day outside, and they just wanted to relax, talk, and be brothers. They both parked in front of the TV Jason had set up on our porch. They were watching some old cowboy movie while I finished up my work in the kitchen.

I had some of Dawud Wharnsby's music playing softly in the kitchen while I put the finishing touches to my Eid al-Adha feast. My meal turned out wonderful, and I carried it out to a picnic table between our place and the Tanners. The air was still and the day was cool, with beautiful puffy clouds floating through the mesmerizing blue sky. It was the perfect place to enjoy my feast.

When everyone sat down and saw my food, the Tanners and Frank started asking me a bunch of questions about what they were eating. Mr. and Mrs. Tanner picked through my food like they expected to find a dead bug in it. Even as scared as they were of my food, they did try just about everything. One thing everyone agreed on was that my gulab jamuns was delicious, and the Tanners even took some home with them. They wanted to know what this dessert was called in English, and I said I thought it was called waffle balls.

The whole day turned out really wonderful, and once everyone had left, Jason wanted to talk to me about some-

thing. He seemed serious, and I wondered if he was going to talk about marriage. My mother was married at sixteen so it wasn't that odd to me. But that was not what he wanted to discuss. He told me he wondered where I got all this money to buy the food and all the presents I gave everyone. I decided to finally tell him more of what really happened when I ran away and how much money was really in the envelope. I told him about where I found it and the pictures and papers that were with it. Much to my surprise, he didn't yell at me or tell me to return it, but he did want to see the pictures and note that was with it. I pulled it out of hiding and gave the note and pictures to him. He didn't know what the aerial views showed either, and of course he couldn't read Arabic so he had no idea of what it said. I told him I thought the first sentence said something about "the Christmas Special," but that was all I could translate. I told him that it might be a package of money that my father was planning on giving to a hospital for Christmas. He thought for a few moments and said that would be unlikely because usually they would give that much money by check so they would have a record of it for tax purposes.

Jason looked at the papers in Arabic and said, "Well, I guess figuring out what these papers are all about is going to be my challenge for my Arabic studies." He told me he wanted to keep them and the aerial view photos. I was so relieved that he didn't get upset about the money that I immediately said yes to him and handed them over. He sat there staring at the pictures and the papers for probably another minute before he said anything else. Finally, he said that if the money was really important to my father, he would have listed me as a runaway. "I think he does not want to find you because of this money, the note, and the pictures," Jason said. "There is definitely something odd about him being a doctor, a prominent Muslim in Chicago, yet not reporting your disappearance."

I told him maybe it's his pride and the fact that he hates me. He might feel it was worth getting rid of me in exchange for losing the money.

"Maybe," Jason said, looking at me with a hurt look and embracing me. "But I don't really believe it."

Chapter 31
Training Day Three

Another day of the training at the Canadian farm is described by Zaki Mansur in the following account:

> *Day three at the farm started like the previous mornings. We practiced an attack on the guard building and hidden guards. After Fajr and our morning meal, we were given a class on the state of the war on America and the West. On a large map on the wall, Ali Hasson detailed the many battle grounds Islamic warriors were involved in. He focused mainly on Western forces and how battles were being fought with Americans and other major powers.*
>
> *"The Americans have ran from Iraq and our forces will soon take over the government," Ali said. "We have already chased Americans out of Somalia."*
>
> *Ali smiled and whacked the map with his pointer. "Al-Qaeda showed the Americans they were not wanted in Somalia and slaughtered their marines. After the first battle, the Americans fled Somalia as fast as their planes would fly." Ali Hasson pointed to Afghanistan and said, "The brave Taliban warriors harass the Americans like hornets from a kicked nest. They sting the Americans and fly away to sting them again as they try to move around the country. The Taliban are like the shadow of Allah. They are everywhere, yet when you try to touch them, they disappear like vapor from a cup of tea. Soon, the Americans will flee Afghan-*

istan, and the Taliban will take back the country and cleanse it of all its American slaves.

The Taliban will purge the government of its traitors and hypocrites just as we did when Russia fled in defeat." Ali Hasson directed his pointer at us and continued, "The Americans are afraid of us. They fear the wrath of a billion Muslims. Their greedy companies and cowardly government officials want to appease us and create bonds with us that earn them money and make them feel safe from our wrath. Their fear of us is so great that they will accept our demands no matter how humiliating they might be. They explain it to their citizens as being religiously and racially tolerant, they will even arrest, and prosecute their own citizens who dare speak out against us or defile our Quran or our blessed prophet Mohammed. But their words are lies to placate their people and hide their cowardly shame. They fear us so much that when we defecate on their flag or urinate on their Bible, they humbly smile and say that we have the right to express ourselves under what they call their First Amendment rights."

During his talks, Ali Hasson taught us about the life of Salah ad-Din. This great man defied all odds in an era of darkness similar to that of today. He refused to listen to the criticism of the many Muslims who were weak in faith. They didn't think Salah ad-Din could unite the Ummah, stand up to the Crusaders, and return honor to where it belonged. It was those who lacked faith, who ridiculed him and called him crazy for wanting to do what they felt was impossible. But he did it. He laid waste to the Crusaders, defeating them in the battles of Alexandria, Hittin, Acre, Tyre, Beirut, Nablus, Haifa, Tiberius, Gaza, Asqalan, Jerusalem, and dozens of other cities and towns across the Middle East and North Africa. His great accomplishments eventually won the respect of Muslims and even the Crusaders. He is another of the great names that evoke feelings of honor and pride in Muslims."

We all shouted, "God is great!" at the end of the story of Salah ad-Din.

Then Ali asked, "What personality does it take to carry out such heroic feats and achieve such a status? Salah ad-Din's belief, lifestyle, and character was what made him Allah's chosen one." And Ali Hasson said, "It's the same for us. It is our belief and character that will help us accomplish the amazing feats we will be remembered for. Our visions, lifestyle, and character are the thread we share with all of the other Islamic legends we praise today. They all believed in daily recitation of the Quran, studying the Shari'ah, charity, preventing useless words from coming out of our mouths, and living simple lives free of luxury and excessive comfort." Ali reminded us that this was also the life the martyred Osama Bin Laden lived, saying, "It's this type of lifestyle that makes it possible to live for something greater than ourselves, but instead for Islam. There is no way we can dream of defending Shari'ah if we lack the willpower to live it on a daily basis in our own life.

We learned that we had reached what al-Qaeda called stage four of its five-point plan for America. We had increased the number of Muslims in America to the point that they now had a powerful political voice. Ali Hasson told us that our jihadist mission was the fifth stage of the five-point plan. Our mission was the most important event any Muslims in this new century had ever been involved in.

Chapter 32
Second Day of Eid al-Adha

It was evident from Sheeva's account that Eid al-Adha, the day of sacrifice, was an important time that she desired to share in traditional ways with Jason and others who were in her life. Eid al-Adha was equal to Sheeva in importance as Christmas holiday is to Christians. The following is her account of that time as extracted from her various interviews and given testimonies:

> *The next day was the second day of Eid al-Adha. Jason and I'd planned to visit a restaurant in Houston called the Savoy. It's one of the few Muslim restaurants in Houston, so we were sure it would be very busy with people celebrating Eid al-Adha.*
>
> *We got there about 2 p.m., and I loved the Savoy. It was a plain and simple, Muslim-oriented, Indo-Pakistani restaurant that served totally authentic meat dishes and had some of the best Indo-Pakistani food I'd ever tasted. There were many Muslim families dressed in their traditional clothes. It was odd for me to see so many women in hijabs. Lots of people wouldn't like the Savoy because it lacked the typical American restaurant ambiance, and you feel you're in a different country when you're there. It doesn't even pretend to be elegant. The Savoy serves meals on plastic plates and offers plastic utensils, but no one cared because the food was so good.*
>
> *Jason and I ordered kadai mutton, chicken corn soup, freshly made biriani, and chicken boti. It was funny, I felt real-*

ly comfortable there, but every once in a while someone would look our way, and my paranoia would set in and I would imagine them getting up and asking me if I was Ali Hasson's daughter. When one person looked at us and he was on his cell phone, I imagined that he was calling the police to report me as a runaway and have me taken into custody. For some reason, seeing all those women in hijabs gave me a very weird feeling, almost like I was doing something wrong. The food, however, was awesome and even Jason expressed how much he liked it.

Before we left the area, we stopped into the Savoy Indian Supermarket next door to stock up on spices and other items that American supermarkets didn't carry. I was very much into making meals for Jason that were similar to things I experienced in Afghanistan. It was hard to make these dishes unless I could get the right ingredients. After we finished shopping, we rushed back to Culper, Texas, to drop the food off and get ready for our night out in Beaumont with Jason's brother.

It was about 7 p.m. when we picked up Frank in Beaumont to go to the Starvin' Marvin restaurant. Tonight Starvin' Marvin's had live music and the reviews said the group playing there, was the Jamie Talbert Band and the Band of Demons. Jason had told Frank that I liked country and western music. When we arrived at Starvin' Marvin's, the parking lot was packed with cars. The sounds of the band were audible before you entered the place. I was afraid we were not going to get a place to sit, but a hostess led us to the second level and gave us a nice table where we could see the band quite well.

Jamie Talbert, the lead singer, sang one song called "Time." A verse from it went:

> *"Better take time and pray for Forgiveness\and pay for penance for all the bad things you do.*
> *Don't let your heart grow bare, even if it gets trampled,*
> *be the example that you know is true."*

The words made me think about everything that had happened in my life in the last few weeks and question again if running away from my father and living with Jason was wrong. Would Allah punish me or did he give me Jason to take care of me. Was all this his plan? I was so confused.

Suddenly, a man appeared at our table wearing a hat with a crown on it. He introduced himself as Jim King. Behind him was a woman with a video camera, and it looked like she was filming us. Mr. King pushed a microphone toward Jason and asked if he was enjoying the show. Then he swung the microphone in my direction and asked me the same. I told him I liked the band, and he said, "Good, I will be featuring them on my show next week and you will be able to catch a glimpse of yourself on the show also."

I felt terror rising up in me and I asked, "What show?"

"The Jim King of the Road Show, it's on Fox every Saturday night at 9:30 p.m., don't miss it."

I think I became numb with fear, and he asked if I was all right. Jason saw how weird I was acting and told Jim that I was acting strange because I had never been on TV before and I was just very excited. He was squeezing my hand hard while he talked to King. Frank started talking to Jim King about his program, and while they were talking, Jason leaned over and whispered in my ear, "I will talk to him later and ask him not to show you in his show."

I realized Jason could not say anything to King in front of his brother because Frank would wonder why I didn't want my face on TV. His reassurance made me feel a little calmer, and I tried to recover my composure. King moved to another table, and I tried to talk and laugh with Jason and Frank as if everything was okay, but I kept thinking about my face being on TV and someone recognizing me.

After what seemed like hours, Jason finally excused himself for the men's room and stopped over at the table where Jim King sat with some other people. He asked King not to show me on his show because I was not supposed to be here. Jason told me later that he had given King a very plausible reason—because lots of girls go to clubs when they are not supposed to—so the request to edit me out didn't seem strange to King. He told me Jim laughed and promised that I wouldn't be in his show. He told Jason it was sad because I was the prettiest girl in the place.

After we ate, Frank wanted to go to another part of Beaumont called Crockett Street. I didn't want to go. I told them that I really hated to break up the party, but I really didn't feel very good and needed to go home. I used the terrible headache excuse, which was not very far from the truth. I think Jason wanted to leave, also; he was not really a party guy. Frank was also okay with it, and so we took him home and headed back to Culper.

The day after our trip to Beaumont, I woke up before Jason and sat in our living room watching the news on TV. I was surprised to see so many reports about things that were happening in Afghanistan. There were more reports about the Taliban attacking schools for girls and killing teachers and students. It seemed like in any province where the Americans left, the Taliban came right back to take charge. With President Obama's announcing that the American troops would be leaving the country, I knew it would make the people in villages afraid to help or trust the Americans, because they all knew the Taliban wouldn't be leaving.

Obama's announcement of troops leaving Afghanistan just reinforced the Taliban's propaganda that America lacked the resolve to win a war against Muslim jihadists. More suicide bombers had struck right in downtown Kabul, and there was a story about a girl named Bibi Aisha who at the age of twelve was given, along with her younger sister, to a Taliban fighter's family in Afghanistan's Oruzgan province as a tribal peace offering.

At sixteen, she was married to a Talib. Her new in-laws took her and her younger sister and housed them with their livestock and treated them both as slaves. She attempted an escape, but she was found. Once she was returned to her husband, a Taliban court ordered that Aisha's ears and nose be cut off as punishment for running away and shaming her husband's family. Her husband and brother-in-law took her to the mountains of Oruzgan and hacked off her ears and nose and left her there to die, but somehow she survived and was given aide by American troops. The report said she was in America for reconstructive surgery.

The story saddened me. I remembered how badly my mother was beaten by my father and how often he would punch me in my stomach, sometimes so hard that it made me vomit. Only the night before, I'd questioned myself about my running away from home, but after watching this report I was sure that Allah had wanted me to leave my father.

This was the third day of Eid al-Adha, and one of its customs is for all good Muslims to remember the plight of the poor and give to them. This report about Bibi Aisha helped me decide what I needed to do for charity. I wanted to help her and a group called Women for Afghan Women that had helped Bibi Aisha, along with many other Afghani women. The group had lessen their misery and, for some, gave them their first experience of feeling kindness and love.

When Jason got up, I made us breakfast, and while we ate I explained to him how much I wanted to give a hundred dollars to the group called Women for Afghan Women. I told him a little bit about why, and he quickly agreed. He wrote out a check from his own account, and we drove to Culper's post office and mailed it.

I know a hundred dollars is not a lot, but I was sure it would help someone in Afghanistan and perhaps even save some woman's life.

That night, Jason started trying to translate the notes found with the money I took from my father's desk.

He had recognized a greeting that made him think it was a letter to someone. Jason had also found plenty of phrases that included "Allah" and numerous references to Mohammed. This all

sounded typical of my father because he was considered a very devout Muslim and constantly quoted the Quran.

Surprisingly, he also discovered the words "Beaumont, Texas" within the note, along with the names of other towns. I thought maybe this was because Beaumont had a hospital that had been selected to receive some of the money in the envelope. I felt bad about that possibility because I never intended to steal money that was intended to help a hospital. I wanted to ask Allah for forgiveness, but I knew that prayer could not be answered until I returned the money to those who were supposed to have received it. I prayed that Jason would soon be able to translate the rest of the note so I would know who the money was for. Knowing who might lessen the guilt I felt.

Chapter 33
Day Four at the Farm

From the account given by Zaki Mansur, training at the Canadian farm was an intensive ordeal that pushed everyone to the limit, both mentally and physically. Ali Hasson was intent on creating an elite group of Islamic warriors who would be loyal, motivated, extremely talented, and highly dangerous. On day four, Zaki learned that the training also weeded out those who didn't love Allah enough to endure these sacrifices. As you read the translated transcripts of Zaki's recollections, you will see the seriousness of the training.

> *On the fourth day at camp, something disturbing happened that frightened me and made me secretly question my involvement in the mission. The day started off with our calisthenics in the freezing, predawn darkness. Once they were completed, we ran over a mile to the dining hall. By the time we got there, our faces were numb from the cold, and our feet felt like bricks.*
>
> *Breakfast was a welcomed blessing in our daily routine. We were all starved and always looked forward to sitting down in the heated dining hall.*
>
> *While we ate, Ali Hasson or his associates would talk to us about training, world events, and other things. This morning Ali Hasson teased us by telling us that in one more day we would learn what our jihadist mission would be. His announcement created great excitement and speculation. Most of us thought our mission would be an attack in Washington DC at the White House. We thought*

that since the Americans had targeted so many of our leaders, it would be time to revenge their deaths. Recently, even American Muslims were being targeted for death by America's criminal president, such as holy warriors like Adam Gadahn and clerics like Awlaki.

Ali Hasson, on hearing our discussion, said, "American CIA operatives wouldn't dare target American Muslims because they are afraid of the political consequences within their own government. There are many in their government who sympathize with our cause and would seek to punish whoever was responsible for the assassination. They also know we will strike back severely at them. Killing Gadahn or Awlaki would simply create legends of these two Muslim brothers, and America does not want to create legends of these famous jihadists."

Soon we were back in the cold snow-covered fields, practicing hand-to-hand combat. We were pitted against well-trained jihadists who were ferocious fighters. I was surprised at how violent they were. In my struggle with my opponent, I received a split lip and bruised ribs, but Ali Hasson said that, as jihadists, we must learn to accept the pain of combat.

One brother named Kadar tried not to anger his opponent, but he still received a black eye and a bloody, swollen nose. It might even have been broken. When he fought, he looked terrified of his opponent and held back. If it had been a real fight, he would have been dead because he al-

lowed his opponent to press his wooden knife to his throat.

By the time the hand-to-hand training was over, Kadar was bruised and bleeding from numerous cuts and abrasions. He was in pain. He asked Ali if he could receive medical attention for his injuries, but Ali said they were superficial and wouldn't interfere with his training. Kadar looked humiliated and returned to our group, but he was also very angry and talked much about the unfairness of the training and even his desire to leave. He thought we all should have received more practice before being matched against Ali's well-trained jihadist instructors.

Kadar was a pious and dedicated Muslim, as indicated by the noticeable prayer bump on his forehead, but he must have forgotten these words of Allah, "So lose no heart, nor fall into despair. For ye must gain mastery if ye are true in faith." He continued to denounce this training experience, testing Ali Hasson's patience, but our training continued regardless of his complaints.

When we broke for our mid-day meal, all of us were cold, wet, sore, and tired. I'm sure the cold contributed to how extremely tired and ravenous we felt. We greeted the mid-day meal with great enthusiasm.

During this luxury of sitting down and eating in a warm building, Ali Hasson inspired us with stories about Prophet Mohammed, peace be with him. He told us about the Quraish tribe in Mecca, of which Mohammed was a member. The non-believers of Mecca oppressed and rid-

iculed Mohammed so much that he was forced to move to Medina. In Medina, things were much different, and Mohammed was revered. Over a short period of time, he assembled a large force and marched back into Mecca. The people of Mecca so feared Mohammed that Abu Sufyan, the head of the Quraish tribe, quickly became a Muslim, along with many others of Mecca. Those who didn't were killed or cast out of Mecca. Mohammed took the religious idols out of the Kaba and destroyed all of them, except the black stone.

At this point in his story, Ali Hasson interrupted himself to interject, "In my country, the same was done by Mullah Mohammad Omar. He even destroyed the ancient Buddha in Bamyan. He did it because it was right to destroy pagan statues worshipped by nonbelievers."

Ali Hasson paused and glanced over at where Kadar sat. Then he continued, "We have much to learn from this story about Mohammed. The main thing is that we must realize that Mohammed's actions forced the people of Mecca to make a decision to worship Allah or be the enemy of Allah. Your actions will present the same decision to many Muslims in America. Who do they support? Allah or the laws and rules of kuffers? It will be for some a very easy question to answer. But others will not have the faith to make the right decision and will be destined to perish along with the kuffers. Most of our Muslim brothers and sisters will choose Allah, and our ranks will swell with those who want justice and respect for Allah and the prophet Mohammed.

"After 9/11, so many good American Muslims showed their faith by raising money to help support our war on the kuffers. Some Muslims joined the ranks of the holy mujahideens. Great warriors like John Muhammad, Hasan Akbar, Jose Padilla, Ali al-Timimi, Nuradin M. Abdi, Hasson Abujihaad, Christopher Paul, Umar Farouk Abdulmutallab, and many others answered Allah's call to kill the infidels. It's quoted that Hasan Akbar said, 'A Muslim should see himself as a Muslim only. His loyalty should be to Islam only.' It will be this question that many Muslims in America will be faced with," Ali Hasson said.

Ali Hasson again looked over to Kadar and said, "Kadar, you will be excused from training this afternoon. You can spend your time helping us with our interrogation techniques." As he spoke these words, two of his associates grabbed Kadar's arms and pulled him away from the table. Fear washed across Kadar's face.

Chapter 34
Thanksgiving Is Coming

The life that Sheeva and Jason lived in Culper, Texas, appeared almost idyllic. Sheeva strove to provide a good home, good food, and her love for Jason. She wanted their relationship to survive the ordeals they had already endured. Now, as Thanksgiving neared, Sheeva was intent on creating another memorable holiday for Jason as detailed below.

> *A couple of days after Eid al-Adha, the Tanners invited us to their home for dinner. Mrs. Tanner said it was the least she could do to repay our kindness for inviting her to our Eid al-Adha feast. I tried to tell her that it was part of the custom to invite friends to your house for the feast of Eid al-Adha.*
>
> *The minute we walked into her house, you could smell the food cooking. She had gone out of her way and cooked a very Southern meal of fried chicken covered with gravy, mashed potatoes, corn on the cob, and fresh rolls straight from the oven.*
>
> *It was less than a week until Thanksgiving. The end of the year was so filled with holidays.*
>
> *I wanted our Thanksgiving dinner to be a very romantic gourmet dinner. It was not only going to be the traditional turkey fare, I wanted things like veal marinated and prepared in a way that was common in Afghanistan. I was also going to decorate our place and put candles everywhere. On our kitchen table, I'd placed long, white tapers that flickered warmly. To complete the look, I used a*

centerpiece of evergreen. Mrs. Tanner came over two days before Thanksgiving and invited us to dine with them, but I told her that I'd already started preparing Thanksgiving myself.

I asked her if she was having her children over. She looked down, but I could still see hurt in her face. She bit her lip to regain her composure and told me, "No, they will not be coming." Her eyes were still wet and she said, "I'm really going to miss them this holiday season." She never had really told me much about them, but now she just let it all pour out. She told me her son's name was Jack. He had married two years before when he was twenty-three and moved to California.

"I have a daughter also, her name is Veronica and she married a year ago," she said. "Neither of them can come. My son says his job will not allow him the time to come. And my daughter claims she has to go to her in-laws for Thanksgiving."

I told Mrs. Tanner she should come to our Thanksgiving dinner, and she said she would like that—but only if she could help prepare the food. I thought that would be nice, so I told her, "Yes!"

Chapter 35
Training Continues

The fifth day at the jihad camp was greatly anticipated by all of the men who had come to be a part of this new mission. The excitement is evident in Zaki Mansur's recollection. What happened to Kadar was also on everyone's mind. The following is the translated transcript of Zaki's account of the fifth day at the training camp.

> *The morning of the fifth day started with the same grueling exercises that had been the routine for the previous four days. Everything went as usual until after the noon prayer. Ali Hasson stood in front of all of us and asked if we had what it took to bring Allah to America and become as important in the history of Islam as the Battle of Badr.*
>
> *Ali Hasson broke out in a large smile, his white teeth glistening, and asked, "Are you ready to destroy the infidel's biggest pagan holiday and largest city?"*
>
> *No one said anything, and Ali Hasson questioned us again, "I ask you, my young holy warriors, are you ready to destroy the infidel's biggest pagan holiday and largest city?"*
>
> *A chorus of "Na'am" met Ali Hasson along with "Nam, nehnu nastatyeh" and "Allāhu Akbar." The positive response brightened Ali's face even more, and he replied, "Well then, it's time to explain your mission."*
>
> *On the screen before him, a picture appeared. Pointing to it, Ali said, "That is a nuclear power plant right outside New*

York City. It's called Indian Point Nuclear Power Plant. Your mission is to do everything in your power to destroy this plant and cause it to leak as much radiation as possible into the surrounding communities. The attack will take place on the morning of the Christians' most holy holiday, Christmas. This is the most opportune time strategically to launch this attack. Most likely there will be fewer guards, and they will be the least experienced because the seasoned guards will try to take off Christmas morning.

"The practice you have been doing each morning since you got here will be done for real that morning. You will take out the guards in the guard shack and kill all the guards standing watch around the perimeter. You will have explosives, a .50 caliber rife, and automatic weapons. You should be able to breech their defense in seconds. If possible, you will take a couple guards as hostages to assist you in entering buildings that are locked or require codes.

"We will go over the equipment available to you, but at this time I want to introduce you to Nihad, one of our most important instructors. Nihad worked in a Pakistani nuclear power plant. He will be giving you classes on how nuclear power plants operate and provide you with the type of information that will allow you to have the knowledge needed to totally destroy Indian Point Nuclear Power Plant."

Nihad took over the class and gave us a quick background of the jobs he had held in the Pakistani nuclear power plant. Once he completed his introduction, he told us to open our notebook computers so we all could get acquainted with software that would help us understand the operations of a nuclear power plant. Once our computers were working, he told us to click on an icon on our notebook computers that was labeled "PCTRAN."

The screen lit up with a welcome screen that described itself as the premier desktop simulator for all types of light water nuclear reactors. Nihad said this was the same software used at the Pakistani power plant for years. He also said it was what the International Atomic Energy Agency used for its annual workshops. The program was used to teach us normal nuclear power plant operation control, startup, shutdown, loss of coolant accident, steam generator tube rupture, feed water transients, damage to containment facility, loss of diesel backup, and many other conditions. We needed to know what set of failures would lead to a total meltdown of the facility and what could be done to produce the most radiation leaks to the surrounding area.

Nihad also provided us with a layout of the Indian Point Nuclear Power Plant. He said we had a maintenance worker employed by the plant pace off parts of the compound every day, and each night he enhanced an overlay made from a Google aerial view of the plant. The layout was within inches of the exact measurement of the various buildings of the facility.

All of us were fascinated with the software and the fact that we would be using the same software that the American nuclear power plants use.

That evening, everyone discussed the PCTRAN software, our instructor Nihad, and occasionally someone would broach the question if anyone knew what happened to Kadar. The subject of Kadar was one that frightened most of us and not something we dared talk about.

Chapter 36
Thanksgiving

By Thanksgiving, Sheeva and Eva Tanner had become very close. Mrs. Tanner had become virtually Sheeva's substitute mother. Eva was someone Sheeva respected, trusted, and felt she could confide in. The following extracts from Sheeva's story illustrate this bond.

> *The night before Thanksgiving, Mrs. Tanner was at my place showing me what all we had to prepare.*
>
> *With her help, I knew Thanksgiving would be a success. Soon the whole house smelled like roasting turkey and all kinds of other fragrant kitchen smells. We made homemade crescent rolls, pumpkin pie, sweet potato casserole, and mashed potatoes flavored with horseradish. Everything was going great until I got to the mashed potatoes, and then I put way too much butter in them. Mrs. Tanner said all I had to do to correct my mistake was add a little instant mashed potatoes and no one would realize my mistake or that we had added instant potatoes to real mashed potatoes.*
>
> *I found a wonderful recipe for honey roasted carrots that I had to try. Mrs. Tanner said we already had way more food then we could ever eat, but having more than you needed was the fun of Thanksgiving.*
>
> *The smells of all the foods wafted together into a wonderful, mouth-watering aroma. As we worked on preparing the food, there was plenty of friendly banter.*
>
> *We talked about her life. She told me that she had lived in Culper, Texas,*

her whole life. She talked about the neighbors and how the town had changed over time. She didn't mention anything more about her children.

Mrs. Tanner had grown on me, and I began to confide in her. I told her things about my father my brother and what a miserable life I'd lived. I think she found it hard to comprehend that I'd lived in a place where a woman on a street without a male relative would be whipped like an animal. She couldn't understand that women in Afghanistan could not go to school, hold jobs, drive, dance or even listen to music. She could not understand that men, husbands, or fathers had the right to beat a woman without any consequences.

After that, we became even closer, and we discussed many things. However, I didn't tell her that I was a runaway. I felt if she had known that, she might have asked us to leave their home. She was like my second mother, and I really looked forward to seeing her. I loved our relationship.

On Thanksgiving morning while we continued to prepare the meal, Mrs. Tan ner wanted us to watch the New York Macy's Thanksgiving Day Parade. I'd never watched this on TV before, but she told me in her house it was a yearly Thanksgiving tradition. Mrs. Tanner said, "In prior years, even people from Culper, Texas, had participated in the New York Macy's Thanksgiving Day Parade."

However, this year there were no entries from Culper.

At the end of the Thanksgiving parade coverage, CNN reported more Ameri-

cans killed in Iraq and two large truck bombings at an Iraqi police station killing fifty-six and injuring 148 men, women, and children. Iraq had returned to chaos after the US president withdrew all American troops from there. A clip of Muqtada al-Sadr played on CNN where he threatened to unleash his Mahdi army on any American forces left in Iraq after the 2011 deadline.

The news switched to Afghanistan, showing videos of American troops sitting with trays of turkey, mashed potatoes, corn, dressing, biscuits, and all kinds of desserts. The Thanksgiving celebration in Afghanistan was marred when a girl's school was fire-bombed and an American soldier was shot while guarding a medical facility for pregnant Afghani women.

Looking back on that Thanksgiving, I'm sure it will be the most memorable Thanksgiving celebration I will ever have. I was surrounded by people who loved me and wanted to share in this wonderful celebration.

Thanksgiving did have one uncomfortable incident for Jason and me. Mrs. Tanner invited us to her church for Thanksgiving services, but we declined. Jason had told her that he only goes to the Catholic church, and Mrs. Tanner knew I was a Muslim so it was presumptuous of her to think we would want to go to her church. Mrs. Tanner told me she had talked to her preacher and he would be happy to guide me on to the right path for salvation. It was very difficult to convince her, without hurting her feelings, that I didn't want to go to her church or convert to Christianity. My refusal didn't appear to upset her much because when she returned from services she didn't say anything more about it.

I realized that gathering around the dinner table with friends and family on Thanksgiving had a very special meaning. It was one of those holidays that Americans cherish and celebrate with loved ones and family members they rarely see any other time of the year. It turns into a once-a-year magical time for all to enjoy distant friends, family, and loved ones.

I quietly thanked Allah for the food, for giving me Jason, and for putting Mr. and Mrs. Tanner in my life. It was all such a blessing from Allah.

Frank, Jason, and the Tanners talked, joked, and devoured my Thanksgiving dinner. Hours passed, and I realized how much I'd enjoyed their company and being with them on this special day. I felt a bit melancholy because I wished my father and brother could have seen what a beautiful day I'd made it. It was not so much that I missed them as it was the fact that experiencing Thanksgiving with people like Jason, Frank, and the Tanners might change their views of what Thanksgiving is all about.

Just before the end of Thanksgiving dinner, Jason got a call from his dad, who promised that on Christmas he would come and visit us. He said they had already received snow in New York and many of the planes were unable to depart. I was sort of happy that he didn't get to come. He might not have liked me or the fact that Jason and I were living together. He said the snowstorm was one of the earliest ones they had experienced in years.

When I was clearing off the table, I sensed Jason standing behind me, and he shocked me by embracing me in front of everyone and kissing me on my lips. I was stunned; he had never showed his feelings for me so openly. His kiss was gentle and intoxicating. After that, he held my hands, looked into my eyes, and said "Uḥibbik." I was so surprised because these words were Arabic for "I love you." It was so special to me to hear those words coming from Jason on such a special day as Thanksgiving.

My senses were reeling, and I know I blushed as I tried to not look at anyone when he released me. But I loved that he showed others his real feelings for me.

When I did look over at the others, Mrs. Tanner winked at me, and I gave her a foolish smile.

Chapter 37
More About Abdul Hasson

While most Americans were celebrating Thanksgiving, Abdul Hasson was struggling with his desire to become a Takfiri. Privately, Takfiris adhere to austere Islamic beliefs, but they consider it acceptable to engage in un-Islamic practices in order to infiltrate the unbeliever's society. Al-Qaeda adopted this course to ensure its ability to move easily among its enemies.

According to Ajani, Abdul was obsessed with this dream. The following events were compiled from the statements provided by Ajani. These interviews were conducted by the Chicago police after his arrest.

Abdul was getting scarier with his desire to pull me and Rahman into his fantasy about all of us becoming Takfiris. He was talking more and more about the need for us to kill other unbelievers and apostates. The reality that I'd already helped kill someone was still something I struggled to accept.

Hidi's murder appeared as visions in my head that often felt like the recollection of a powerfully horrible dream. The type of dream that revisits you for days, months, or years and is censored by a conscience that knows it would never have let you do such an evil thing. I would tell myself it could not be real because killing Hidi was not something I would have ever done, but then I would mentally slap myself back into reality and realize I had. Worst of all, I felt like a coward because I loved Hidi. Why did I not stop Ab-

dul from beating her to death? I will never understand. I could have saved her life, but I acted like a mindless thing and helped kill this girl I loved.

At first, each morning after we killed Hidi, I could almost convince myself that those strange memories were just a figment of my imagination. They were the result of some very bad dream that still haunted me. It's funny, when you don't want to believe you did something horrible, your mind helps you cope with it by creating doubts and reasons why you couldn't have done it. It seems our conscience can be so shocked at what the evil side of us does that the memory of it can eventually just vacate our being.

At least that's what I feared as I began to struggle with this nagging question in my mind about killing nonbelievers and apostates for Allah. Is this really what he wants, and if it is, why does he not do it himself?

Sometimes I think this must be the work of Iblis. Killing just seems evil, and more than likely it's the calling of Iblis and not God the creator.

Abdul helped shatter my delusion of what I'd done with his frequent calls gloating about the murder. He would say things like, "No one misses her yet because everyone thinks she is out whoring around. I think I did her family a service."

Abu Qatada, Muhammad al-Mis'aree, and Sa'd al-Faqih were all big idols for Abdul. They appealed to him, and he wanted to be more like them. He read everything he could find about them and despised all the negative things that were written about them. Some Muslims had labeled Abu Qatada a bloodthirsty tyrant who killed more Muslims than non-believers. However, Abdul believed that Abu was just cleansing Muslim society of apostates. If I tried to argue about this with Abdul, he would just get upset with me and say that he was the thinker and I was the muscle. For a while I accepted that as fact, until the day we visited his neighbor, Steven Grubs.

Abdul never told me why he wanted to visit Steven. I had a suspicion he probably wanted to pick a fight with him, but I was still in denial about what Abdul was becoming. Abdul had turned off the lights in his living room and sat watching the Grubs' house through the large picture window. I sat with him, trying to find out what he was up to, but he would just laugh and tell me I would soon find out. Finally, Steven's parents drove away from the house, and Abdul got up and stretched and said it was time to have a chat with his friend Steven. I knew that Abdul didn't like him very much. He thought Steven had been hitting on his sister, and Steven also used to make fun of Abdul's clothes and the way he talked. I knew things were not going to be good, but I never realized how bad they would be.

When we got to Steven's door, Abdul had still not told me what we were doing there. Abdul knocked on the front door, which was partially obscured by large bushes on each side. Inside, the sound of the song "Dance with the Devil" rattled the windows. Steven saw himself as a thug. Abdul banged hard on the door so he could be heard over the sound of the rap. Steven finally answered the door, bobbing his head to the beat of the music. He looked questionably at us, but before he could say anything, Abdul pulled a pistol from his jacket and hit Steven across the face with it. Steven fell back in shock, and Abdul walked right into Steven's house. I stood on the stoop for a minute, and then Abdul motioned me in.

I could see that look in Abdul's eyes again, that look of hunger and hate. Steven hadn't regained his composure from being smashed across the face with the .32 caliber pistol and looked at us in total shock. He tried to say something, but it was incoherent and largely muffled by the heavy rap music.

Abdul said, "You remember when you used to call me a rag head and mess with my sister?"

Steven didn't answer. He just looked at the waving gun in Abdul's hand.

"Steven, I asked you a question. You better answer or I'm going to beat the shit out of you."

A scared voice answered, "I was just kidding with you back then."

"Do you like to dance with the devil?" Abdul said.

Steven looked at Abdul, trying to make sense of that question. "I don't know what you're talking about."

"The song you're listening to. The name of it is 'Dance with the Devil.' Do you think you're a hardcore thug?"

"No, dude, I just like the beat. What do you want?" Steven was regaining his composure. "Abdul, please put your gun down and we can talk about

whatever is pissing you off. Sorry I offended you back then. I am an ass sometimes."

"You've been an ass as long as I have known you," Abdul replied. "Pull your pants down so we can see your ass."

An alarmed look spread across Steven's bloodied face as he asked, "Come on, what do you want?"

"You heard me. Pull your pants down, turn around, and bend over or I will shoot you right in the stomach."

Abdul moved closer to Steven with the gun pointing straight at his stomach. "You're going to have a hole in your stomach if I don't see your ugly asshole real quick."

Steven turned around and fumbled with his belt and buttons to loosen his pants. Abdul told me to take Steven's belt and wrap it around his neck in case he decided to start screaming.

I asked, "Abdul, what are you doing?"

Abdul pointed the gun at me and snarled, "You dare to question me? You dare? I am making things right for us. You just need to trust me and don't ask me dumb questions like that when we are doing our duty."

I stepped closer to Steven; he had his pants pulled down. I pulled the belt from his trousers and wrapped it around his neck. I said, "You best do what Abdul tells you."

Abdul sort of laughed and told him, "I want to see your bare ass. Pull your underwear down also."

Steven didn't resist this time and pulled his underwear down. He stood there leaned over with his bare ass sticking out and his pants bunched up around his feet. I could see sweat glistening on his head and blood dripping from his mouth and nose.

"Now, badass, I want you to start singing along with your rap music," Abdul told him. The rapper was talking about raping his mother, and Steven just mumbled a few words, which just pissed Abdul off even more.

Abdul stuck the tip of the gun right on Steven's ass and said, "You better really start rapping this song, badass, or you will have two assholes."

Steven was still mumbling, but he was a bit more coherent as he said, "The devil grows inside the hearts of the selfish and wicked. White, brown, yellow, and black colored is not restricted."

Abdul shouted, "If you don't know the words, you can at least bob your lily white ass around like a real rapper while you pretend to rap. Do it."

I could not believe it. Steven was trying to move around and mumbling some of the words, "You have a self-destructive destiny when you're inflicted."

Then Abdul quickly put the pistol back in his pocket and pulled a knife out of his other jacket pocket. Before I realized what he was doing, it was over. He had reached between Steven's legs and grabbed his privates, and the next thing I know he was holding them dripping with blood in his hand. Steven was making guttural sounds, and finally a real yell poured from his mouth. I tried to stifle it with the belt, but the sound bellowed out of him.

Abdul smashed his gun hard on Steven's head, and he fell down on the blood-soaked floor. It didn't knock him out, so Abdul went ballistic and beat him repeatedly in the head with the butt of the pistol. I was in shock. I didn't want to be involved in killing anyone again, but I realized it was going to happen. I dropped the belt from my hands and backed away. I asked Abdul, "Why?"

He jumped up from beating Steven and struck me across the face with the pistol, yelling, "You feel sorry for this fucking unbeliever?"

I was really in shock. I feared him. My mouth was filling with blood. I felt he would kill me next. I heard him yell at me. "You're as cowardly as Rahman. Don't piss me off again, or you will be right there on the floor beside him." He pointed toward Steven.

He took a cushion from a couch and walked back to Steven's still body on the floor. He wrapped the cushion around the pistol as he pointed it at Steven's bloodied head. His face looked troubled suddenly as he pulled the gun from the cushion. He studied it and cursed, "Damn it. I've got hair and skin stuck under the hammer." He then reached back into his pocket and grabbed the same knife he had just used to remove Steven's testicles. He reached down to grab Steven by the head.

I knew what would come next and darted for the door. I never saw him cut Steven's throat, but I know he did it. I ran down the street and hid in the woods. I called Rahman and told him what had happened. Rahman told me he knew Abdul was going to kill Steven and had refused to be a part of it. I told Rahman that I would never again be a part of Abdul's crap either.

That was the last time I ever talked to Rahman, and I really don't know if Abdul killed him or Rahman simply ran away from Chicago to save his own life. Later that night, my phone started ringing incessantly with calls from Abdul. I waited till about 2 a.m. and finally answered his call. He was apologetic and said he was sorry that he hit me. He wanted us to meet in the morning and make things right between us, but instead I tossed my belongings into a duffle bag and snuck out of the house. I left a little note to my mother on my bed that read, "Love you, Mom. Don't worry, I will be okay."

Once I was in my car, I headed to Detroit. I had an uncle there who I felt would help me, and he would let my mother know I was safe. I wanted to turn Abdul in, but that was not something we do in our community. What he had done—or what the three of us had done—would affect our whole community. Every Muslim would suffer if it came out that Islamists were running around killing apostates and non-believers.

I read the papers about the crime, and I heard more about the murders after the Christmas Special, but that was really all I know firsthand.

Chapter 38
Meeting Sarah

The arrival of the Christmas season was evident everywhere in Culper, Texas. This was going to be Sheeva's first Christmas holiday free from her father's watchful eye. She became passionately involved in the holiday season. A part of her Christmas excitement may have been influenced by an early holiday gift that came in the form of a new friend. I believe her owns words of encountering Sarah Ferguson provide a very vivid picture of her life at this stage of the story.

> *Christmas Season was in full force and houses everywhere were decorated for Christmas. The Tanners had a large Santa and sleigh staked down on their lawn. All the trees in the front yard were wrapped with twinkling white lights. At night, the house looked like something from a fairy tale. Jason had helped Mr. Tanner put up the decorations.*
>
> *A few days after Thanksgiving, Mrs. Tanner invited me into her house to show off her Christmas decorations. She had a beautiful Christmas tree that was fully decorated with lights, garland, tinsel, Christmas balls, and a beautiful angel on the top. That was when I decided that Jason and I had to buy a tree and decorate our house for Christmas also.*
>
> *That same evening, the Tanners invited Jason and me over to their home for dinner. Mrs. Tanner's demeanor and cryptic words hinted that she might have a little surprise for us.*
>
> *When we arrived that evening, Mrs. Tanner was decked out in a red*

sweater with a large snowman on it. She was preparing fried chicken, which was considered a southern Texas favorite. The room was filled with its spicy aroma. It smelled delicious.

While we ate, I wondered what the surprise might be, but I dared not ask. Jason quickly got into a conversation with Mr. Tanner about his antique radio that sat prominently in their dining room. It was about three feet tall and looked well preserved. It appeared to work just fine, although its sound was a bit muffled. The radio was set to some AM station playing Christmas carols. The dial glowed a warm orange-red that flickered as the "Carol of the Bells" played.

Jason wanted to buy a similar radio and quizzed Mr. Tanner how much this one had cost. Mr. Tanner told Jason that a radio like the Philco Tombstone would fetch six hundred or more. He bragged that his was a piece of history that was built back in the 1930s. I knew why Jason liked it; the radio appealed to his steampunk interest in vintage artifacts. Mr. Tanner turned the conversation to the subject of work and asked if Jason was still hunting for a job.

I thought they were going to ask us how we were planning on paying the next month's rent, but instead Mr. Tanner asked Jason if he wanted a part time job at his lawn mower repair shop. Jason was taken aback and just looked at Mr. Tanner inquisitively. Then Jason told Mr. Tanner that he really didn't have much knowledge about lawn mowers. Mr. Tanner smiled and said it didn't make much difference because what he needed most was someone to clean motor parts, clean the small engines, and make the machines look brand new when they were ready to be returned to the customers. The job was not going to pay much, but Jason took it anyway. Later, he told me it was a great job because it gave him a little extra spending cash for Christmas presents, for materials for his steampunk art projects, and for school when it started in January.

One day when Jason was at work, I stopped by the Southern Maid donut shop in Culper and got into a big conversation with this girl who worked there. She had lots of piercings and tattoos all over her body. I wanted to get my nose pierced, so I asked her where she had gone to get her piercings done, and she replied that she did it to herself. She also warned me that most of the professional places in Beaumont wouldn't do piercings unless you have a driver's license proving you were eighteen or older.

She said, "If you think you could trust me, I would do it for free."

I told her, "I would love that!"

She leaned over the counter and said, "We can do it today, if you want to."

I took her up on the offer and replied, "Okay, why don't you come over to my house after you get off work?"

We chatted a while longer, and I discovered her name was Sarah Ferguson. I gave her my address, and she said she knew right where my place was located.

I rushed home and cleaned up my place as much as possible before she could get there. This was the first girl I had anything to do with since I ran away. I thought I liked her and hoped she would end up being my friend.

Sarah arrived a few minutes after two. She told me she worked the 5 a.m. to 2 p.m. shift which really ruined her social life, but it paid her bills. Sarah said she also was going to Lamar University and working toward a liberal arts degree.

Sarah was surprised that I already had my Christmas tree up. Jason and I had bought a real tree and decorated it really nicely. We had a blinking angel on top and even a couple of gifts already beneath it. I gave her a quick tour of our place and explained some of Jason's art pieces, especially his steampunk metal sculptures. She seemed fascinated with the whole steampunk culture thing. She said she had never seen such neat items made of old cogs, gears, and brass and copper tubing. She appeared genuinely impressed. After my quick tour of our small place, Sarah wanted to know if I watch MTV's Teen Mom. I'd never heard of it, and she said I had to watch it. She was all excited about it.

"The show is addictive," she said. "It's all about girls around sixteen who are already mothers. She wanted to know if I would turn on my TV so she wouldn't miss the day's episode. So I did.

These girls were getting famous for being pregnant and dropping out of school. Sarah told me it was sort of a joke on them. They think they are really cool because they are on TV, but most people who watch it think they are trash and watch it for the same reason people use to watch the Jerry Springer show, where in-

bred families fought over which brother was going to sleep with their own mother.

Sarah was right. It was entertaining in a strange, voyeuristic way seeing teenage mothers dumping their babies on their own mothers while they went out to party with boys who came across as retarded thugs.

When I watched this show with Sarah, I felt glad I was Muslim and smart enough to realize that having sex can make you pregnant. Jason and I weren't going to have a child until after we were married.

A Muslim woman with a bastard child would be major disgrace to her family, and that could easily bring about an honor killing. It made me wonder again about Hidi. She was a party girl, and if she got pregnant, her parents would have sent her away or maybe even worse. Her father was a devout Muslim, and the shame she would bring to his family might be enough to get her killed. I wondered if she ran away because of something like that or if something worse happened to her.

We continued to watch the show about a teenage girl who was upset with her mother. The sixteen-year-old kept cursing her mother and demanding that she take care of her baby so she could go out again. Eventually, the mother gave in and took the baby from her daughter. The daughter marched out the door, slamming it behind her. This is the type of conduct my father lectured me about and one of the things he despised in Western culture.

It was sort of sad to see families this dysfunctional. If this happened in Af-

ghanistan, these girls would all have been tossed out of their homes or killed.

Once the show was over, Sarah was ready to do my nose. She opened her purse and pulled out some things she said she needed for the piercing. She had a little bottle of antibacterial soap, a large needle, and a tube of KY jelly.

She washed my nose with her surgical soap and then took her needle and squirted KY lubricant on it. She put a finger in my nostril and pulled it open. Sarah told me to stay still while she did the piercing. The next thing I felt was a lot of pressure on my nose but really no pain, and the needle was through. I gave her my stud, and she inserted the sterilized jewelry into the new hole. She took me to the bathroom so I could see her work. I liked it a lot, and I hoped Jason would also.

We spent another hour just talking about music and other TV shows, and then Sarah had to go.

After she left, I went to our bedroom and turned on our computer. The conversation and TV show about girls getting pregnant made me wonder even more about Hidi. I had to check again to see if I could find any new article or anything about her disappearance. What could have happened to her? Was she still alive? Was she fine? Did my brother do anything to her? Why did my brother answer her phone? There were so many questions swirling about in my mind.

I checked different Chicago news stations, but there was still no news about Hidi. On Chicago's 560WIND or WGN 720 news radio, the talk was all about a new murder that the reporter believed was connected to the previous mutilation murder. In the new murder, a teenager had been killed and two passages of the Bible were discovered at the murder scene. One was attached to the corpse. It read, "If one curses his father or mother, his lamp will go out at the coming of darkness. (Proverbs 20:20 NAB)." The other note was more sinister. It was found in a sealed plastic bag floating in a large jar that contained the victim's testicles. It read, "For there are eunuchs that were so born from their mother's womb: and there are eunuchs that were made eunuchs by men: and there are eunuchs that made themselves eunuchs for the kingdom of heaven's sake. He that is able to receive it let him receive it. (Matthew 19:12 ASV)." The teenager's name was Steven Grubs.

When they said his name, I was stunned because I immediately recognized him as the kid who had lived next door to us in Chicago. He was seventeen, and I guess you would call him a jock. He used to fight with his parents a lot. Their arguments were so loud that I could hear him cursing his mother even inside our house, with all our windows and doors closed. My brother Abdul disliked him because Steven had made fun of Abdul's clothes a couple times. The thought that someone who had lived so close to my old home had been killed and mutilated made me shiver. These reports were really depressing.

I should have stopped then, but I went ahead and revisited the website www.alllostchildren.com. As usual, I found nothing about Hidi or any listing about me running away. I was sinking into a depression, worried that something must have happened to Hidi.

I looked forward to Jason coming home that night to cheer me up. While I waited for Jason, I decided to make koftas again. Jason really liked my koftas, which are traditional Afghani meatballs. They are made of meat and vegetables. After I cook them, I pour a broth over them.

When Jason got home, the first thing he said was, "Wow, that smells good." Just those nice words cheered me up.

I smiled at that. I was glad he liked my cooking. It was the second time I'd made koftas for him. He claimed he liked my piercing, but as he stared at my nose, he said, "I hope that doesn't get infected, because we don't have insurance."

Chapter 39
More from the Farm

A quote credited to Ahmed Yassin reads, "Sons of Islam everywhere, the jihad is a duty to establish the rule of Allah on earth and to liberate your countries and yourselves from America's domination and its Zionist allies, it's your battle—either victory or martyrdom."

This quote is certainly one that would have seemed very fitting by the sixth day of Zaki Mansur's training. The training apparently had evolved into something these men had never previously experienced. The rigid routines and absolute control over their lives would give them the self-discipline, loyalty, obedience, and sacrifice that was required of them to meet the challenge of becoming one of Ali Hasson's Islamic warriors.

The transcripts of Zaki's narrative of his days spent training at the farm in Canada illustrate the dedication and desire shown by these jihadists to become martyrs for their cause.

> *By the sixth or seventh day at the farm, I'd become accustomed to the morning ritual of calisthenics in the snow. These sunrise exercises in the freezing cold were oppressing, but once I'd worked up what should have been a sweat, my body would feel warm; only my face and fingers would still suffer. Often, while we were doing pushups, my hands would become so numb from the cold that I would fear they were frozen. When the temperature hovered in the teens, the cadre would have us run in place between*

exercises, clapping our hands to prevent frostbite.

After these calisthenics, we would then jog nearly two miles along a narrow, snow-covered path in the woods.

This was an exercise I dreaded because snow would blow in my face and frequently turn into icy water. Often, the snow just swirled about, and I would find my face wet with snow. Before the jog was over, the moisture would ice over my eyebrows and freeze my jacket collar. Often, as I ran over this path, snow-covered branches would suddenly dump their load on me, covering me in snow. Flakes would even find their way between my collar and neck and melt into my clothes. To jog in the snow, I had to learn to lift my feet high, which made the run seem like a ten-mile jog. The path led us to a large field that was blanketed with snow. It spread out over a few acres, and above it hung a white mist that consisted of frozen snowflakes swirling about from the early morning north wind. Most important, however, was the large barn that sat at the mouth of the path. It was heated, and inside, we were greeted with hot coffee, a choice of Egyptian omelets, nasi goring, or Egyptian ful mudammas.

We were given one hour to eat, but during this period we also listened to Ali Hasson or others talk about our mission and what we must do to win. This was also when we were told of other battles raging all over the world between Muslims and non-believers. We were not allowed to listen to TV, radio, or use the Internet, so all of our knowledge of the out-

side world came from these breakfast talks.

One morning, a couple days after we were introduced to Nihad, Ali Hasson asked him to talk to us about events in Pakistan. Nihad wanted to share with us a major event that was happening in Pakistan. He was very upset that a man doing the will of Allah was in prison for killing a traitor who wanted to change the blasphemy laws. Nihad said, "These laws were man's law showing our love, belief, and respect for our Prophet and Allah. The governor of Pakistan's Punjab province, Salman Taseer, was a tool of America and the Jews. He wanted to change or even eliminate the blasphemy laws, but a hero stepped forward and killed this treacherous Jew collaborator."

Nihad told us that this man, Muhammad Mumtz Qadri, had been praised by Muslims all over Pakistan as a hero for killing Salman Taseer. He claimed that people were so happy with what Muhammad Mumtz Qadri did that to show their support they showered him with rose petals as the puppet police led him into a courthouse. Nihad asked us to pray to Allah for Muhammad Mumtz Qadri's release from prison. Ali Hasson then ran a video from Al Jazeera of what was happening in Pakistan. The video showed people from all over Pakistan protesting the arrest of Mumtz Qadri.

Ali Hasson said, "Muslims simply saw him as doing his Islamic duty to Allah and our prophet Muhammad. He will become a hero in our history books, just as all of you will, but your accomplish-

ment and courage will be celebrated by Islamic people all over the world.

"Here, my brothers, is a quote of our beloved Prophet Muhammad, peace be upon him: 'This world is a prison for the Faithful, but a Paradise for unbelievers. Be in the world like a traveler, or like a passer on, and reckon yourself as of the dead. Cursed is this world and cursed is all that is in this world, except the remembrance of Allah and that which aideth thereto.'"

As he was quoting Prophet Muhammad, peace be upon him, there was the noise of numerous cars or trucks outside the barn. A fear crept through me at first that we had been discovered, and we didn't even have weapons to defend ourselves. A glance at Ali Hasson assured me he was expecting this.

"My brothers, today we will have a variation from our normal exercises. No hand-to-hand, no lessons on weapons. Today you will all become carpenters. We are going to build a big maze on the large, frozen field, which I'm sure you have all noticed. Those flocks of common redpolls that so often blanket the field are going to have to share it now with all of you. Why are we doing this? Because the maze you create will be a replica of the layout of all the halls, rooms, and walls of your target, Indian Point Nuclear Power Plant."

Ali Hasson saw our bewilderment and answered the question we all wanted to ask, "Once you have this built, we will practice our attacks every day in this maze until you know the corridors, rooms, doors, alarms, generators, control room, and the rest of the layout better than those who work there now. By Christmas morning, you will be able to navigate this maze even in the dark. This means when you attack Indian Point Power Plant you will have the advantage of knowing it better than the skeleton crew that will be operating it on Christmas morning. The operators, guards, and office staff will most likely be new hires, totally inexperienced, and afraid of doing the wrong thing. They might at first even think that our attack is one of their 'force on force' tests. This will be one of your advantages, and since they have failed many of these tests with only three to five combatants attacking them, your success is a certainty.

"As you build this maze, Nihad will explain what each room contains and its importance. We will be placing crates, oil drums, and other items to represent the equipment in each room. You will be taught where all the backup generators are located, critical cooling pipes, and other major items you need to destroy or use to help release radiation from the site. We will have a room to hold all the hostages we can use to make it far more difficult for police or the military to enter the plant. By the time they respond to the attack, you should have already started releasing radiation, which will stop the non-believers from even coming close to the plant. If Allah is with us, Broadway, which runs parallel to the plant, will be so packed full of vehicles fleeing Buchanan that reaching the plant from a few miles away will be virtually impossible."

After the talk, we were divided up into two-man teams and given backpacks full of tools. They gave us hammers, nails, cordless saws, tape measures, and levels. Each of us was given a copy of the scale drawing marked off with the pieces of the maze that we would be responsible for. Once we were outside, we saw old five-ton trucks that were loaded with two by fours and sheets of OSB. They had arrived while we listened to Ali Hasson and Nihad.

While we milled about in the snow-covered field, we were instructed to grab sheets of OSB and carry them to the location where we were building the maze. The construction of the maze started by first building the perimeter walls of a building located in the center of the plant. Once the outline of that building was completed, all the other teams were told to start fabricating their sections of the replica. Ali Hasson pushed us to work as fast as possible to create as much of the maze as possible. The walls of all the sections were simply sheets of OSB attached to two-by-four frames. Since the walls in this replica were just about four feet tall, you could look out over them to the other rooms and get a better perspective of where things were located. Building the labyrinth representing Indian Point Nuclear Power Plant gave us a great sense of confidence in the success of our attack. We knew the layout of the buildings. Nihad was teaching us how to operate the plant's controls and where they were located. We were quickly learning all about the pumps, valves, compressors, fans, and chillers that are a part of the nuclear power plant.

We placed boxes or empty propane tanks and other items in the rooms to rep-

resent control consoles, backup generators, and other major components of the site. Once we had the maze created, we practiced running down the corridors to various rooms or to different buildings. We did this over and over, and finally we did it with blindfolds on. We would count the number of steps that it took to get to various doors or to adjoining corridors. We were better acquainted with the layout of the plant than most of its actual employees.

Soon after the completion of the maze, we were given instructions on how to navigate the maze when the place was filled with smoke. We were given thermal infrared goggles, which allowed us to see people in the dark and in smoke. These worked better than night vision goggles, which work poorly in smoke-filled environments. The attack would be in the early morning, when it was still dark, but we would fill the areas near the observation towers with smoke to prevent the guards from seeing us. If they fired, we could easily detect their positions with thermal infrared goggles and kill them.

Zaki Mansur provided much more information about their knowledge of the weaknesses, equipment obsolescence, guard counts, security measures, and more. The information had been provided to Ali Hasson by a Muslim janitor who had previously worked at the Indian Point Nuclear Power Plant.

For obvious national security reasons, I thought it prudent not to further elaborate on this information or the detailed preparation or planning of the attack on the nuclear power plants.

Chapter 40
A Present from Sarah

It was not even December yet, but Sheeva was totally consumed by the Christmas spirit. She had decorated her home as gaily as possible and had gone so far as to display a miniature nativity scene. She felt that it really created no conflict with her religious beliefs because in her religion, Jesus was still considered a prophet. He simply was not the son or God as Christians believed. Sheeva's story continues in her own words.

Many evenings, Jason would discuss his work at the shop, the customers, and how the job was going. He had grown to like his work and was excited that he was earning a paycheck. Jason had already been buying gifts for me, along with gifts for his dad and brother. The pile of gifts under our tree kept growing day by day.

Our life together began to feel really normal and peaceful. I thought about my father and brother less and less. I now had a new friend, Sarah, and I began to share more of my life story with her. She said she felt so bad that I'd lived in a country during a war. I showed her the picture of my mother, and she said I looked so much like her except for my blonde hair. She hugged me and cried with me when I told her how my father would beat my mother with a switch like she was a dog. I told Sarah about how my mother's legs and back would bleed from the whippings. I shied away from telling her I was a runaway. She might have guessed it when I finally told her I was only sixteen, but if she did, she sure didn't ask.

Sarah was interested in knowing if I had to wear clothes that totally covered me in Afghanistan. I told her I was too young then, but teenage girls and women had to dress that way. Those girls who disobeyed, the Talibs would whip them right on the street if they were caught not properly covered. She could not believe I'd once lived that way. She told me how beautiful I was and that I should never have to be afraid to show my beauty. She said, "God gave you beauty; you should not listen to any man about how you should hide it."

Regardless of all that had happened, I told her that I still loved being a Muslim and that I thanked Allah all the time for his blessings.

Sarah and I became very close friends, and one morning she called me during her morning break very excited and told me she had something very special for me. I asked her what it was, but she wouldn't tell me. She told me she was going to bring it over to me after work.

Her excitement made me really wonder what it could be she was talking about. The wait till she got off at 2 p.m. was grueling. I waited, and finally she called that she was on her way. It was almost three o'clock when she arrived, ringing my doorbell repeatedly like she always did.

I opened the door, and in front of me was Sarah dressed in an old frilly dress that looked like something her great grandmother might have worn a hundred years ago.

She stepped in and twirled around. "How do you like my new dress?" she asked.

I had to laugh a little, but I still told her how beautiful it looked on her, just perhaps a bit outdated. "Are you going to a costume party?" I asked.

"We are going to a costume party," she snapped back, twirling around a couple more times. "I have a dress for you also. It will need a little tailoring, but I am good at it."

"What's this all about?" I asked.

"You and I and maybe Jason are going to the Dickens on the Strand in Galveston next weekend. Everyone dresses up in Victorian clothes. The street where they hold the celebration is transformed into what London looked like in Charles Dickens's time. About ten to fifteen blocks of the Galveston Strand becomes a near copy of the Strand in London, which Dickens wrote about in his books."

Sarah's selection of a dress for me made me cry. It was made of fragile gauze embroidered with gold threads all through it. The bodice of the dress was decorated with silk flowers and ribbons.

The dress totally exposed my shoulders and the neckline, so I added a three- to six-inch-deep lace flounce as trim. I also draped the dress with several additional bands of pleated fabric. Sarah had also bought me a beautiful huge hat to wear. She said everyone going to the Dickens fair wears a hat, even the guys. She told me I still had to buy a Victorian style purse and other accessories so my

Dickens costume would be complete. Sarah had also bought me two tickets. The dress, hat, and tickets were her Christmas present to Jason and me.

When I looked at the brochure she gave me about the event, I got even more excited and looked forward to greeting Jason at the door in my new Victorian dress. I knew he would love this event because it offered him a chance to experience Victorian times. I was sure that dressing in Victorian clothes would appeal to Jason's fondness of steampunk culture.

Chapter 41
First Casualty at the Farm

The training had gone well for Ali Hasson's men. It goes without saying that there was a great deal of security surrounding the operation, and one event in particular demonstrates how seriously Ali Hasson took security. The problem was related to a jihadist named Kadar, who had complained about the severity of the training and his desire to return home. Zaki Mansur's chilling account of the events surrounding Kadar paints a very bleak picture for any jihadist who dared to change his mind.

> *Our training was very close to being complete. We had received from Nidal many lessons on how to operate the various consoles used to control the nuclear power plant. We were given more information about our individual missions. Some of us were not selected for the attack on the nuclear power plant, but were instead given other missions. Some I think were designated as suicide bombers, and others were given the mission of planting bombs in hospitals. Ali Hasson wanted his attack to be so intense that Americans would feel as if their country was caught in a war between believers and non-believers. He wanted to force American Muslims to make the choice of taking the side of the jihadist bringing the war to American or becoming the enemy of Allah.*
>
> *To everyone's surprise, the afternoon began with a very serious lesson. Two of Ali's associates dragged Kadar onto the snowy field. His hands were bound tightly behind his back. Kadar's face was purple and black with bruises, and his*

left eye looked like it was totally swollen closed. He didn't utter a sound but just knelt in the snow. Ali Hasson walked over to him and grabbed Kadar's hair and yanked his head up and then released his grip so Kadar's head fell back to its bowed position.

Ali Hasson called all of us to witness what was to take place.

We were ushered in closer to Ali Hasson and the kneeling Kadar. As we stood there, I think we all knew what was to happen. An eerie quiet hung over us as conspicuous as the wispy plumes of breath that drifted silently up into the grey sky.

Ali Hasson stood straight and tall and uttered, "God is great." We all sang out "Allahu Akbar!" in response.

Ali Hasson raised his hand for silence and said, "Today I have a valuable message that all of you must learn. It's about death, fear, and our love for Allah. The Quran tells us that death will find us wherever we might be. We cannot hide from death. In fact, when we are asked to march forth in the cause of Allah, it's odd that some would prefer to cling to this earth. Does that person prefer the life of this world to the hereafter? Unless you march, he will afflict and punish you with a painful torture and put others in your place. Those are the words from the Quran, verse 9:38."

Ali Hasson smiled at us and brushed snow off his shoulders and Kadar's head. He then continued, "We have all freely elected to be a part of a mission for Allah and Islam that will likely result in the end of our existence here on earth, but our reward will be a life in paradise for eternity. I think our sacrifice for Allah and Islam will not only earn us a welcome into paradise, but perhaps even earn us a place in the lofty mansions where Osama Bin Laden now dwells with his martyred son. When you pledged your allegiance to this mission, you swore to Allah to do everything in your power to make our endeavor successful. Each and every one of you knew that in accepting this mission you were being asked to sacrifice your existence here on earth to help spread Islam and the truth to the unbelievers. Much time and money have been spent to make this mission a success, and we cannot abandon it now."

Ali Hasson stood silent for a moment with his eyes gazing up toward the grey sky. As he exhaled, his breath plumed out in front of him and hovered in the suddenly still air.

He looked back to us and said, "When a man makes a promise to us, we count on it. Keeping it marks his character and his value as a Muslim. When a man makes a promise to Allah, and then he breaks it, he has committed blasphemy. The punishment for blasphemy is death. Lying to Allah is the ultimate lie, and the person who does it loses all the righteousness he once had. The man who lies to Allah will not live in paradise but will lie in the ground or in hell's fire, tormented by seventy serpents that will continually bite and rip at his flesh until the Day of Judgment."

Ali Hasson again paused, maybe for a second or two, and my mind was racing with a jumble of thoughts that con-

fused and scared me. It seemed like this pause went on for an eternity because so many thoughts filled my mind. I knew that Kadar would soon be killed, but I suddenly realized that I was also just days away from dying. That thought made me feel even colder. The freezing wind blew on my back, but a colder sensation crept through my being. It was sadness, numbness, something really unexplainable, but I knew at that moment I would never again see my mother, father, sister, or any of my friends. I fought the thoughts of loss and the whole finality of death.

These thoughts frightened and saddened me, but I tried to comfort myself with the fact that I knew I would soon be in paradise and still be loved and adored by my parents. I guess it was fear of the unknown, but a voice somewhere inside yelled at me that I must leave and return to my parents. It told me that what I was doing was madness, but then I remembered Abraham and how the devil tempted him to turn against Allah and not sacrifice his son Ishmael as he had been instructed. As I tried to calm myself, it came to me that I was being tested—and not just by Ali Hasson but also by Allah.

All this time, while these thoughts tore through my consciousness, I watched Kadar kneeling in the snow. His head hung down, with his chin virtually resting on his chest. He had said nothing since Ali Hasson brought him out to the field. The little bit of his face that I could see was unreadable. I wondered what thoughts were going through his mind as his last few seconds ticked by. I didn't really want to see him get killed, but knew I could not stop it nor allow others to see me as too weak to watch him die.

Then Ali Hasson said, "For those of you who are righteous, your death will be the beginning of a beautiful eternity. You will be met by the blue angels Munkar and Nakir at one of the eight gates to paradise. The three questions they ask to ensure your entrance into paradise, you will be able to answer truthfully. But for Kadar, he will be met by Azra'il, the angel of death, and cast directly into hell's fires.

"I have discussed Kadar's punishment with others. His refusal to do Allah's calling is a rebuke of his faith. He has given us no choice in this matter and has sealed his own fate with his actions, cowardliness, and lack of remorse. He was Allah's slave, as we all are, but a slave who refuses his master's wishes is a slave of no value."

Ali Hasson stepped behind Kadar and grabbed his hair, yanking his head back and saying loudly, "God is great" I remember how we all echoed it back, "God is great."

We had become conditioned to do and not to question or even think of what we were doing. I feel sorry now for my brothers who are all dead. They were all wonderful men who loved Allah, their families, and our people. The torments that some of them endured before they died will always haunt me.

My eyes were frozen on Kadar's face. He still showed no emotion, except maybe hatred in his one eye. He didn't beg or yell for mercy. Ali Hasson held Kadar's head up like that for what seemed like a long time, and then suddenly his right hand held a knife that slashed a dark gash across Kadar's throat.

Blood spurted from the wound and sprayed over the white snow. Kadar still didn't utter any sound except the sound of his breathing. A silence fell over us, and the only sound was the rhythmic sound of the spray of blood splattering on the snow and Kadar's labored breathing. Gurgling sounds mixing with his loud gasps seemed to thunder over every other sound. Kadar teetered back and forth and then finally fell face first into the snow. His tied hands struggled behind his back, and Kadar twitched his head to the side in an attempt to stem the bleeding. For some unknown reason, he pistoned his legs, scooting himself forward. Each thrust kicked up blood-soaked globs of snow and pushed his head deep into the snow. His actions were perhaps some primal attempt to escape death or hide from our view as he died. Then suddenly he flipped himself over and seemed to stare with his one eye defiantly up at Ali Hasson.

We all watched him as he bled out. A large pool of blood congealed beneath him, creating an eerie cloud of steam that hovered over his dying body. The spray of blood became tiny spurts, but his chest still moved. It was almost like he was defying death. And all the time, his one eye glared unblinking up at Ali Hasson.

Suddenly the quiet was broken with the shouts of "God is great!" and we all chorused it. I still thought I could see movement under his coat, and then realized it was simply from the blowing wind.

He was dead, and I shuddered from the reality of it.

I pondered Ali Hasson's word about Kadar's cowardliness and wondered if that really was so. He certainly didn't beg for his life, but accepted his fate in a very brave fashion. Down deep, I doubted if I could have been that brave in that situation. I knew then there was no escape from what we had set out to do. I accepted that I would be dead in a few more days, but I swore that I would kill as many non-believers as possible before that moment happened.

A few minutes after Kadar's murder, we were all back to our training, doing forward rolls, leopard crawls through snow-covered bushes, pole vaulting over fences, and firing live ammunition into dilapidated mannequins scattered about the maze. In one exercise, I was hit twice by paintballs, and the meaning now felt far more ominous than it had the day before. The thought of death hung heavy over me the rest of the day. I'm sure others thought the same, but no one dared discuss this fear. None of them wanted to die like Kadar.

Chapter 42
The Dickens Fair

Sheeva's transcript continues with her recollection of the Dickens Fair in Galveston, Texas.

> *On the first weekend of December, Sarah, Jason, and I went to the Dickens on the Strand festival. Sarah and I were totally decked out in our Victorian costumes. We had even fixed our hair in styles that were supposed to be similar to how women wore their hair back then. My hair was all held up with hairclips. Jason also had got into the spirit for the Dickens fair and found the appropriate attire to wear. He looked very much like a gentleman of that era with his shiny black top hat. He was costumed in a white shirt with its collar turned up and layered over with a velvet vest. Around his neck he had a light blue cravat that matched his eyes. I had altered a pair of his slacks by sewing a ribbon of black silk down each leg to make them look more authentic. The final touch was a long overcoat with a fur collar.*
>
> *The Galveston Strand was packed when we got there. There were hundreds of vendors, costumed characters, free entertainment, all kinds of food, and of course things to buy. We got there just in time to see a big parade with huge horses called Clydesdales pulling a wagon and all these bell ringers, hundreds of them. Up and down the Strand were strolling carolers, street musicians, and costumed characters that I had to pose with for pictures. Later that evening, they had the*

Dickens Ball, which was this beautiful event where everyone dressed in evening attire. It had all the pomp and pageantry of the Victorian era. The music played was strictly period waltzes from the 1800s. They had this huge Christmas tree called the Queen's Christmas tree, where we took a bunch of pictures. The street was constantly packed with visitors and vendors with their rolling carts all selling food, crafts, jewelry, and holiday decorations.

The day had been wonderful, but on the way home a discussion happened that was very upsetting. We were all joking about the Dickens Fair and how much fun it was to dress up in all these costumes when out of the blue Sarah asked Jason if he was going to become a Muslim or if I was going to become a Christian if we got married. Before I could say anything, Jason blurted out, "I'm not becoming a Muslim or asking her to become a Christian. She knows I'm agnostic and have no interest in joining any religious group."

Sarah asked, "Well, if you don't have any beliefs, why would you celebrate Christmas and Sheeva's Muslim holidays?"

"Simple, they are fun and bring people together. But I'm sorry, I don't really believe in the Easter bunny hiding chicken eggs, Santa Claus orbiting the earth, Jesus walking on water, Muhammad's chats with God, or the tales of the tooth fairy," Jason snapped back.

Sarah and I were speechless at first, and then Sarah asked, "How can you not believe when you see such wonderful things that God has done?"

"Sarah, I really don't want to have this discussion with you because you're going to tell me what great things God did, but you won't have any way of proving it beside simple blind faith in the stories you have been told."

"God heals people who are sick every day and creates new life," Sarah replied angrily.

"Sure, if you say so," retorted Jason. "But does this God ever grow new legs for amputees or eyeballs for those who have lost them? How many severed heads has God reattached? You give God credit for doing the things nature does on its own. This constant popularity contest among different people's God has ended up killing millions of people, and sadder yet, we did the killings for our imaginary super beings."

"Gods need followers to do their bidding and killing. So, sorry Sarah, I see gods as impotent as the Easter Bunny. If we didn't have people hiding eggs, the Easter Bunny would be out of business, and if we didn't have religions selling their gods, we would all be living a lot more peacefully and sanely."

I couldn't believe what I was hearing, that Jason thought Allah was nothing. I felt fear in my heart as I heard those words, fear that I should not be around someone like him who says such horrible things about Allah.

The rest of the trip home was very quiet, and I was ashamed of the things Jason said. When I got in bed, I couldn't sleep. Jason's words kept me awake, thinking about what I was doing and if being with a non-believer was so evil that Allah would punish me forever.

I turned on the TV to get my mind off what he had said, and the first thing I saw on CNN was a report about a girl named Aisha Ibrahim Duhlow being stoned to death in Somalia. They showed about fifty men surrounding her, hurling stones at her, and yelling "God is great" in Arabic. They were stoning her in a football stadium with a thousand people watching. It was horrible. Right after that story, a reporter from Jackson, Alabama, stood outside a courthouse and talked about an evangelical preacher who had killed his wife and stuffed her body in a freezer after she caught him sexually abusing their daughter. The news made me even more confused and depressed. I just couldn't believe that such a wonderful day had ended this way.

About three in the morning, Jason finally rolled over to see if I was still awake. He gave me a kiss, which I pulled away from, but then he apologized for offending me. He said he was tired of people dismissing his beliefs just because he doesn't believe in Gods. Reluctantly, I kissed him back, and somehow that apology and kiss was all I needed to forget all my concerns about Allah and fall asleep.

Chapter 43
Graduation Day for Zaki Mansur

Zaki's account of graduation day at the terrorist farm in Toronto, Canada, gives an insight to some of the reasoning that compelled him and his comrades to participate in the Christmas Special suicide missions.

Even though most of the members of the Christmas Special suicide teams came from Western nations, as opposed to the bulk of the 9/11 attackers, who came from Saudi Arabia, they all shared many of the same underlying reasons. The most fundamental of these was their belief that perceived slights to their religion or God justified acts of violent retribution toward the people of any country who have allowed these transgressions.

This is not just a Muslim thing, but a curse on mankind from all religions. Many people will defend their religious beliefs at all costs, including their own lives, the lives of their families and friends, and/or the lives of anyone else in the world who stands in their way. So powerful is their belief that a fanatical believer would willingly destroy the planet to fulfill the prophecy of his religion.

With our technology of war having evolved far past the advancement of our understanding of the primitive yearnings of our being, we are left tottering on the precipice of our own annihilation. Regardless of how many religious leaders or followers proclaim their faiths as peaceful, as long as their sacred doctrines and manifestos continue to contain messages of violence and hate, there will be people who will read and act on those morbid suggestions in the name of their faith.

Ali Hasson knew that it only took a few to destroy the many, and those few were about to be unleashed on America.
The following is Zaki Mansur's recollection of graduation day.

Our day of graduation was a big event. That last morning, we still exercised out in the snow but once that was done, the rest of the day was a celebration of what we had accomplished and what we were now a part of. During breakfast, while we sipped Turkish coffee and munched on baklava, Ali Hasson praised each and every one of us for our dedication and sacrifice to the cause of bringing the word of Allah to all the people of the world. He told us that we had received compliments from Omar Hammani the Shebab Commander in Somalia. Omar was an American who had denounced his Baptist religion and converted to Islam. We also received compliments from Ayman al-Zawahiri, who praised us and blessed us that we would be as successful in our mission as the Magnificent Nineteen had been. A blind mullah who I think was named Azzam then led us in prayer for the Magnificent Nineteen and for our successful mission:

"We ask for Allah's blessing. One such passage from the Holy Quran reads, 'Think not of those who are slain in Allah's way as dead. Nay, they live, finding their sustenance in the presence of their Lord.'"

This passage gave me much courage and reminded me of the reality that I would soon make the transition from this world to paradise, with the blessing of Allah.

Mullah Azzam read to us:

"O ye who believe! When ye meet the unbelievers in hostile array, never turn your backs to them.

"If any do turn his back to them on such a day—unless it be in a stratagem of war, or to retreat to a troop (of his own)—he draws on himself the wrath of Allah, and his abode is Hell, an evil refuge indeed!"

He reminded us that once we are committed to the word of Allah, we must obey his wishes if we desire to be rewarded with eternal life in paradise. This mission we are all bound to we must not run from. He said these passages from the Holy Quran make that very clear. He went on with this reading:

"It is not ye who slew them; it was Allah. When thou threwest [a handful of dust], it was not thy act, but Allah's: in order that he might test the believers by a gracious trial from himself: for Allah is he who heareth and knoweth [all things]. That, and also because Allah is he who makes feeble the plans and stratagem of the unbelievers."

Mullah Azzam stopped and reminded us of what Ali Hasson had told us so many times, that the American government was now run by a group of buffoons led by an apostate who was responsible for the murder of our beloved lion Osama Bin Laden. It was our time to bring the battle to the doorstep of this corrupt apostate who commanded the armies who mercilessly killed our wives, children, and young men. He said, "You should all be proud of yourselves and know that your names and stories will live forever with Muslims all over the world. More than a billion believers will soon be singing your praise and thanking you for your courage and your commitment to this historical mission for Islam and Allah. In the Quran it says, 'Remember how the unbelievers plotted against thee, to keep thee in bonds, or slay thee, or get thee out [of thy home]. They plot and plan, but Allah is the best of planner of all.' So with this I say with Allah your commander and with his blessing upon you, your victory will be complete." He ended with, "Allahu Akbar, Allahu Akbar, Allahu Akbar."

Soon after that, we were paired up with cadre members who helped us write letters to our loved ones and make videos to commemorate our life on earth. This was a very sad part of our celebration because of the reality that these would be the very last images and words from us to our parents, families, and our friends. It was a sad time for many. We knew many of our loved ones would cry and feel very heartbroken. Our fathers would be so proud of us, but still cry and be sad that we had perished.

While I sat waiting for my turn, I thought of how I'd found so many friends here at Ali Hasson's farm. I didn't know much about their families, but many nights we had talked of our reasons for wanting to be a part of this mission. My friend Mazen had felt wronged by the insulting way that Islamic holidays were observed in America. These were holy days for praising Allah, but instead we were made to work on these days, businesses stayed open, and not even the American media talked about how important these days were. We had to celebrate them in the few hours after we worked our jobs or went to our classes, but on Christian holidays we were told to stay home. We all thought this was demeaning to our religion, a religion of the truth, a religion of over a billion believers. It was also difficult for us to have to follow laws that defied the laws of Allah. Why should we be punished for following shariah laws and the laws of Allah instead of the man-made laws America imposed on us?

After doing the videos and letters, we were all honored with a feast to celebrate our completion of our mujahedeen training.

Tables and chairs were arranged in a semicircle in the dining hall, with a podium positioned near the front. Soft Muslim music played in the background as we took our seats. The event was kicked off with prayers led by an imam, followed by speeches from several of my comrades in praise of our achievements. Ali Hasson stood at the podium again and praised all of us for our sacrifice, dedication, and hard work during our mujahedeen training. His dark eyes sparkled with tears when he finished and said that the saying "Alhamdulillah, finally we have a king among us" would aptly apply to all of us. His words and sincerity touched all of us.

For the next couple hours, the dining hall rang with conversation and laughter as we congratulated each other and exchanged stories of the last few weeks. The tables were covered with many well-prepared dishes. There was mouthwatering biryani of beef meat, which would never be missed in any Muslim celebration, accompanied by gravy meat or mutton. Chicken was also available for those who preferred chicken to beef or mutton. Added to the feast was shir kurma, a dessert made of milk boiled with many dry fruits. Plates of kebbe, labneh, jebneh, kabiss, makboss, koussa, and many more covered the table. Everyone served himself as the celebration progressed.

There was also a solemn part of this celebration where I realized how Allah had answered my prayers. I remembered standing in front of the Kabbah in Mecca under the scorching midafternoon sun and praying with all my heart: "O Allah, let me serve and help spread your word." Two years had passed since then, and now I was a mujahedeen. Allah had made those years of studying and training so easy for me to reach my new status.

Finally, at the end of the celebration, Ali Hasson said to all of us, "Asalamualykum wa Rahmatullahi wa Barakatuh, may the peace, mercy, and blessings of God be upon you."

During this feast, many pictures of us were taken that would be sent to Al Jazeera and other Muslim media companies so they would have good pictures of us when they wrote of our deeds.

After our celebration, we were divided into our three-man units and instructed by our unit leader on where we would meet next and how we would enter the United States. Each of us was given money and verbal instructions of how to get to our next contact. We were told that each contact would provide us with more resources and information on where to meet next. We were told that, a couple of days before Christmas, we would all be contacted by email of what time to arrive at our designated target. At no time were we to communicate on our cell phones with others in our groups, except at those times designated by our contacts. We were not to commence the attack until after Ali Hasson posted on his facebook page a comment that would read, "Have a very Special Christmas."

Late in the afternoon, the cadre began to bid us farewell. For many, including myself, it was a tearful departure. We had come to love our instructors and felt a very close bond with them, and I think they also felt the same for us. After many hard embraces and heartfelt wishes for our success, we finally got into vehicles and were driven back to downtown Toronto. I was to meet a man at a coffee shop who would take me and two others to an area of the Canadian border that was easy to cross. A contact would be waiting for us on the American side who would take us to a safe house. It was during the time I was riding in this man's vehicle that I realized the tremendous excitement that was coursing through me. I wanted to sleep, but the excitement made it impossible.

I realized how fast the next few days would pass. It was as if we had climbed a big mountain and now we were racing down it, toward paradise. It was impossible to stop, and Christmas morning was just around the corner, not even a week left to experience Allah's earth. During these last few days on earth, I knew my mind might become overwhelmed with confusing or negative thoughts, so I had to be careful to manage myself to avoid this from happening. Mullah Azzam had warned us that often the devil would tempt us, just as he did when Abraham was told by Allah to sacrifice his son Ishmael. "Don't listen to him. Do not let him weaken your resolve to do Allah's bidding," Mullah Azzam said to us. I would have to be very diligent to guard myself from the whispers of the shaytan.

There were so many things left that I wished I had time to take care of, but I knew it was now impossible to do anything but my mission. I just had to face the stress of waiting to join those who went before me to paradise. I always tried to look at the brighter side because it made me stronger. Anything I could do to reduce worry and create an uplifting atmosphere I knew would help me pass into paradise that much easier. I knew I would say additional prayers the next few days and ask Allah for strength and make sure He knew how much I loved him.

As we raced along the freeway, the image of my mother's face entered my mind, and tears welled up in my eyes. I thought of how she would cry when she heard that I have become a martyr. I knew she would be consoled by millions for raising a son who martyred himself for all Muslims, but her tears would still flow and her heart would still hurt. I added her to my prayers and hoped my martyrdom wouldn't let sorrow dwell in her heart for very long.

I wiped the tears from my own face before I could be seen by the others in the car. It's not a sin to cry, but it angered me that I was shedding tears because I was going to leave life on earth when I should have been celebrating that I would soon be joining my comrades and other martyrs in paradise. My excitement buzzed away in me even as I entered the United States.

Chapter 44
Help with Translation

Jason continued translating the documents written in Arabic that Sheeva had taken from her father. On the third page of the document, Jason recognized the names of numerous towns and cities in the United States. He also had discovered an Arabic word that he believed meant "attack" throughout the document.

Like Pandora, who could not curb her curiosity about the forbidden box, Jason couldn't control his desire to know the meaning of the stolen documents. About ten days before Christmas, he decided to find someone to help him complete the translation. He started looking for this person online and in local newspapers. The person he found was Azim Chand, a twenty-two-year-old student attending Lamar University in Beaumont, Texas.

Chand had been born in Godhra City, India, a few years before the terrible 2002 Gujarat violence between Hindus and Muslims. An estimated 790 Muslims and 254 Hindus were killed during that incident. Azim was old enough to remember the fear he felt during those violent times. He was still haunted by the memories of one particular day during the terrible riots; the day his mother just disappeared. They searched for her in hospitals, clinics, and even in morgues, but they never found her or her body. Azim's mother became one of the 223 people who just vanished during the slaughter in the streets of Gujarat.

After her disappearance, Azim's father dedicated himself to his son's future. He wanted his son to excel. The elder Chand made sure Azim would have the money to attend college in America if he chose to.

A couple of years prior to the Christmas Special, Azim came to America on a student visa and settled in Beaumont, Texas. He had an F-1 visa, which prevented him from working more than twenty hours a week. Azim needed extra funds to live on, but he couldn't find a part-time job that paid enough to produce the extra needed money. He also didn't want to saddle his father with additional debt, so after some consideration he realized his polyglot talents as a translator between English, Arabic, and Hindu could earn him the needed money. The more he thought about it, the more he liked the idea. Since he would be paid in cash, there would be no record of his employment.

He posted a few ads on Craigslist.org and on a couple local publications and created a thriving business for himself.

Six days after the Christmas Special attacks, FBI agents were knocking on Azim's door. They had tracked him down through the phone calls Jason had made to him. Below are excerpts from one of the interviews.

Agent Spears: *Please state your full name for the record.*

Azim: *My name is Azim Chand*

Break in transcript: *Numerous questions were asked of Azim Chand that are not relevant here, so I am skipping to the portion of the interrogation that supports Sheeva's statement that Jason had help in his translation of the documents.*

Agent Spears: *Did you translate a document brought to you by Jason Wilgers?*

Azim: *Yes, I did. I only saw a part of the total document, however.*

Agent Spears: *From your recollection, what was the document about?*

Azim: *It appeared to be a plan to attack various places around the United States*

Agent Spears: *What did you read that made you come to that conclusion?*

Azim: *Well, it said something about the completion of selecting all necessary jihadists. It talked about how help would be provided by others in the States who supported the cause. It said that used military vehicles had been purchased and were waiting to be turned over to those who need them for their mission.*

Agent Spears: *Did it mention anything about weapons that would be used?*

Azim: *Yes, it talked about three teams that would be provided with something called shape charges. It also said that sixteen automatic rifles or something like that were already purchased and hidden in safe houses.*

Agent Spears: *Where were these safe houses?*

Azim: *It didn't say.*

Agent Spears: *Did it say how many safe houses?*

Azim: *No, it just said safe houses.*

Agent Spears: *Why did you not notify authorities about this plan?*

Azim: *Jason said he would.*

Agent Spears: *You didn't think you should also?*

Azim: *I thought about it, but I'm from a place in India where my father would suffer if Muslims thought that I'd interfered in something like this. I really thought Jason would tell. He told me he would and promised he wouldn't mention my name.*

Agent Spears: *Why did he promise you he would not mention your name?*

Azim: *I asked him not to so I wouldn't get in trouble with immigration.*

Agent Spears: *You feel your problems with immigration were more important than the security of the United States?*

Azim: *I don't really mean that. I didn't think it would happen. Jason told me that he had these documents for months and that the person who wrote them knew he had them. He didn't seem that upset when I told him what it said. I thought it was probably some old plan that was no longer active. With Obama being dead and everything, that's really what I thought.*

Agent Spears: *Obama is dead?*

Azim: *I mean Osama Bin Laden. I'm sorry. I'm nervous and they sound so much alike I get them mixed up sometimes.*

Agent spears: *Do you think those plans were real now?*

Azim: *Yes! Of course they were real. Now we know, but I didn't think they were then. It would be very difficult getting involved in reporting a terrorist plot because of where I come from in India. Muslims killed many people in Gujarat where I lived, maybe even my mother.*

And I was afraid I might be asked to return to India.

Agent Spears: *So you think doing your duty to America, the country you claim you're trying to become a citizen of, is less important than pissing off some people back on your old block in Gujarat?*

Azim: *It's not that simple. These people could kill my father and other relatives. It's very complicated.*

Agent Spears: *So why do you think Muslims might have killed your mother?*

Azim: *My mother was caught in the rioting that occurred in 2002, and she just disappeared. She had gone out to buy groceries one afternoon, and then a riot started. They were beating people with clubs and some people were shooting others. A lot of people were killed, but we didn't find my mother.*

In India, a wife just doesn't disappear. We have very close families. She would have contacted someone, or someone would have seen her and reported her to authorities. But she was never seen again.

Agent Spears: *Well, I'm sorry about your mother, but those riots should have taught you a lesson about helping the law. So my friend, all these complications that you felt prevented you from being loyal to this country have now just bit you in the ass.*

Azim: *Why do you say that?*

Agent Spears: *Because soon you will be given a free ticket back to where your Dad worked so hard to get your sorry ass away from. You have won a free ticket back to Gujarat. And I hope the me-*

dia publicizes your failure to warn America all over the world.

Azim: *Why do you do this to me? Why do you hate me?*

Agent Spears: *Gee, I'm sorry, but I interview you. I ask the questions, not you.*

Azim: *I wish to talk to my consulate. I will not answer any more questions until I find out my rights from my consulate. I really did nothing wrong. People watch other people get killed in America, and you don't do anything to them, but you choose to pick on me because I'm a Hindu. It's you who should be ashamed.*

Chapter 45
The Confrontation

According to Sheeva's account, a few days before Christmas, she was fixing breakfast for Jason and herself when he snuck up behind her, grabbed her, and surprised her. Her story continues:

> *I was fixing breakfast for us and Jason came up behind me, kissing my neck. I turned around wondering why he was being so sweet, and he said in Arabic, "Sana sa'eedah!"*
>
> *I could not believe what I heard. It just came as a total surprise, and my mind was not able to interpret it because I was not use to hearing Arabic from Jason. I had to ask him to repeat himself.*
>
> *He repeated, "Sana sa'eedah!"*
>
> *I was astonished because he had just said "Happy New Year" in Arabic. I was so absorbed in my life that I'd forgotten it was the first of Muharram, which marked the first day of the Islamic New Year, a major Islamic holiday.*
>
> *I looked at him demurely and said, "Sana sa'eedah! You're watching the calendar better than I am, and I'm proud of you, your Arabic is really improving."*
>
> *Later, when I saw Sarah that day I told her about it being the Islamic New Year and that the sixteenth of December would mark the Ashura holiday for Muslims. Of course she had no idea what the holiday was about. I told her it was not like any American holiday. It was celebrated for different reasons. I'm a Sunni, so we celebrated it because it was the day Noah left the Ark and the day Moses*

was saved from the Egyptians by Allah. Shiite Muslims use the day to commemorate the martyrdom of Hussein, a grandson of the Prophet Mohammed. Some Shiites flay themselves in public demonstrations to express remorse and sorrow over the killing of Hussein Ibn Ali. My father told me that their acts of self-flagellation made all Muslims look barbaric. People who were not Muslims usually didn't understand the difference between Sunni and Shiite Muslims.

Ashura became the day commemorating the event that divided the followers of Islam. For Shiites, this was when the Prophet Hussein Ibn Ali and seventy-two others were slain in a battle at Karbala, Iraq. Yes, the same Iraq that still has fights between Sunnis and Shiites. The battle was the result of Hussein Ibn Ali's refusal to accept the legitimacy of Muawiya bin Abi Sufiyan's right to the succession as the fifth caliph of the Muslim empire. The killing of Hussein Ibn Ali gave birth to the Shiites, who are also called the "supporters of Ali."

My father called the Ashura celebration by Shiites a "Jahiliyyah" way of life.

Jahiliyyah is a word we use that means people who are ignorant of the divine guidance of Islam.

Their bloody commemoration often offended Sunnis and other non-Shiites as an insult against all those who are not "supporters of Ali."

I would be fasting for this holiday, because that's what we do as Muslims. I told Sarah she wouldn't see me at the Southern Maid Donut shop for a few days. I didn't want to be tempted by the sight of all those donuts and break my fast.

I had a conversation with Mrs. Tanner and told her about Ashura. She told me there were many things similar in our religions. She told me she was surprised that we celebrated days for Moses and Noah. She also was astonished that we have a holiday to celebrate when Hazrat Ibrahim was ready to sacrifice his son Ishmael. She told me that the story is very similar to the one in the Bible where Abraham is willing to sacrifice Isaac to God. It was during this conversation that Mrs. Tanner tried again to convince me that I should convert to Christianity. She said that if I continued as a Muslim I wouldn't go to heaven. I was extremely offended, but I didn't say anything to her. Inside, I was steaming. To make me even madder, she then warned me to be careful who I told I was a Muslim, because a lot of people in Culper thought Muslims were terrorists. She got a call just then and hugged me and left. I was glad because I felt so mad at her, but all I could do was smile and be polite.

I sat on my couch, thinking about how angry her words had made me and how complicated life can be. I wanted to celebrate Christmas with Jason, but that didn't mean I wanted to change my religion. I didn't want to leave Allah. "I would be so alone without you Allah Tallah, please don't let me stray," I said silently. After which I recited the first Kalma to reinstate my belief and surah fateha so that Allah would bless me.

The next morning I woke at 5:40. It was too early for Jason to be up so I stayed in bed, fantasizing about Jason and me being married. I had visions of how our child would look. The fantasy was so vivid that I was totally confused when I awoke. It was such a wonderful dream and so strong that I didn't want the dream to end.

I saw us marrying in this perfect Islamic ceremony. I dreamt of a molvi asking Jason if he was ready to marry me, and he said, "Yes." Then the molvi looked at me and asked me if I wanted to marry Jason. It was all so beautiful.

In my dream, we married on the Islamic New Year, so that the whole Muslim world would celebrate our marriage with us, but then suddenly the alarm went off and the dream faded away. I thought it was a weird dream because being married on the Islamic New Year wouldn't be a good day for a Muslim wedding.

On the twentieth of December, Jason was going to go to work and I was going to do more Christmas shopping, but something bad happened that changed our plans. That was the morning we realized our world had fallen apart.

Jason had been working hard on his Arabic, and now he was able to translate more of my father's note. In fact, he had even hired some Indian student to help him.

Jason had acted odd the night before, but I figured it was work. I was tired and fell asleep quickly. On the morning of the twentieth of December, he was up early and right back on the computer to work on his translation project. He had told me to stay in bed when he got up. I was still tired and fell back to sleep and didn't get up until about two hours later. I could hear A Charlie Brown Christmas playing on the TV in the living room. It was one of my favorite Christmas specials, a great show to get you into the Christmas spirit, and our Christmas tree was twinkling in the early morning darkness.

I came into the kitchen smiling, but when I noticed the grim look on Jason's face, my smile faded. He looked up at me, and a little smile flickered across his face as he said, "Good morning." He motioned me to come over to the table with him. He wanted me to sit down and look at some things he had worked out, but his looks frightened me. I knew something was very wrong. I sat down at the kitchen table across from him, and right off he handed me six pictures.

I quickly glanced at the first three pictures, which were the ones that had been with the money and the note. The pictures were all labeled. The first one was a picture of Indian Point Energy Center. Its label read, "24 miles north of Manhattan, New York." The next picture was another nuclear power station. This one was called Waterford 3 nuclear power plant and was twenty miles west of New Orleans. The last picture was of the San Onofre Nuclear Generating Station serving San Diego, California.

These pictures didn't mean anything to me so I asked, "So what do you think this means?"

Jason looked at me and said, "Your father and others are planning to attack these sites on Christmas morning. That's what this all means. I translated enough of the actual note to understand that he was buying software to be used in the training. I looked up the software and it's used in training operators of nuclear power plants."

I looked at the pictures and tried to absorb the meaning of what Jason had just told me. I think I laughed at first at the absurdity of it all. It just didn't sound like anything my father would do. He was so concerned for his image in the community and so proud of being a great doctor. But a part of me started to believe it. I know I must have looked like I was in shock as I sat there looking at these pictures. I could see they were nuclear power plants. My stomach was churning, and I said, "Jason, I just can't believe my father would be involved in something like this. He is a doctor and he fled from Afghanistan to escape this type of lunacy. Why would he be involved in something where he could get kicked out of the US or worst yet be put in prison?"

Fear struck me as Jason shook his head and said, "I don't know why, but it's clear in the notes and in these pictures that he was planning an attack. Attacking a nuclear power plant is serious business! He also is planning to attack churches and hospitals in a bunch of states. We need to figure out what to do about this. And we need to do this fast, because Christmas is just a few days off."

My mind kept racing trying to absorb all of it. I asked, "Jason, what do you want to do?"

"I'm not sure, but we need to tell the authorities about your father and his plan."

It was odd, but just then I remember hearing Charlie Brown on TV shouting out, "Isn't there anyone out there who can tell me what Christmas is all about?"

I was not feeling Christmas then. In fact, a feeling had crept into me that was reminiscent of the fear I use to feel when I heard the guns firing and bombs exploding in my village back in Afghanistan. It was a paralyzing fear, a fear that comes from the recognition that you cannot escape from the horror and that you're at the mercy of Allah.

I heard myself saying quietly, "I cannot turn my father in. I hate him sometimes, but I wouldn't want to be responsible for putting him in prison for the rest of his life. You know Jason, this could have just been talk, and now that I stole his money he probably killed the plan. If he is a terrorist and working with Osama Bin Laden, the plans are definitely on hold since Osama is dead."

Jason heard me, but he didn't believe what I was saying any more than I did. He replied, "So if we don't turn him in, then what do we do? He is planning attacks on three nuclear power plants and all these other places! This is a serious attack, maybe bigger than 9/11. Lots of people could die, and we will be in trouble for not reporting what we know. Maybe you're right. Maybe it's nothing now, but if he goes through with it, we will suffer in the long run. I'm not interested in going to prison for something your father is doing."

I started to cry then and blurted out, "Jason, you do realize that we will no longer be able to be together if we report this? They will take me away from you. You do realize this, don't you?"

Jason came around to my side of the table, hugged me, and said, "Sheeva, we have to. I don't want to lose you, and I don't want to go to prison. Even just mailing what we know to the FBI or Homeland Security wouldn't protect us because I'm sure they would want to talk to you since you are his daughter. They would come looking for you, and they would find us."

He started kissing my hair and cheek, and I realized he was crying too. His tears dripped on my face.

I pulled myself together and said, "Okay, please give me until tomorrow. Let me call my stupid brother and see if he knows anything about this. I'm sure he would love to hear from me. If we don't know anything more by tomorrow, then we will turn my father in and let the police or whoever know about this. If my father has dropped the plan, we don't need to do anything, right?"

Jason looked at me and said, "Make your calls and see what you can find out, and maybe we will be lucky and you're right. I'm going to try to work today, and hopefully when I come home tonight this nightmare will be over." I asked him not to go to work and stay with me. I needed his support, and I was very afraid that everything was over between us.

Jason said, "I need to go to work or the Tanners will wonder what's wrong with me. I don't want to talk to them about this. Anyway, going to work will make time go by faster. I'm upset about all of this. I don't want to lose you either." I could see the sparkle of tears in his eyes as he said those words.

Jason did go to work, and at first all I did was just sit in a daze watching Charlie Brown, Schroeder, Lucy, and Linus. I was feeling confused and angry. I flicked the TV off just as Linus was saying, "Glory to God in the highest, and on Earth, peace and good will toward men. That's what Christmas is all about, Charlie Brown."

I know it's stupid, but the quote struck home for me, and I realized that what was being planned was not peace or good will toward men, but something as evil as Mecca and the Kaaba being totally destroyed. It was not just an attack on America, but an attack on Christians.

I started crying again, asking myself how could I have ever been born into a family like mine? Why? I cried until I was exhausted. I felt so alone. Finally, I got control of my emotions and worked up the courage to call my brother. I blocked my phone number when I called Abdul; I didn't want him to be able to call me back.

I kept calling him all day, but he never answered. I left a couple of messages telling him that I really needed to talk to him, but he never picked up. The fact that he wouldn't answer unnerved me more, and by the time Jason returned home I was frantic. I'd been sure I would be able to reach Abdul. Since he was looking for me, I thought he would welcome my call in hopes that he could get me to come back or tell him where I was. I wanted to leave a message on his cell asking him if he knew about the possibility of our father planning this attack, but I knew that wouldn't be wise. If Abdul was involved, Jason and I might be killed for what we knew. I was sure my father would feel killing me was the appropriate punishment for a daughter dishonoring the family.

Chapter 46
December the Twenty-First

In the transcript below, Sheeva continues her story.

The next morning, we were both up early. Jason was going to call in sick for work and hoped the Tanners wouldn't come over to see us. We were not in the mood to see anyone.

We were trying to figure out what we needed to do. Jason felt the best thing to do was call his brother Frank. He thought his brother, being a policeman, would be able to tell him who he could talk to and give him an idea of what might happen next.

We waited till after 8 a.m. before calling Frank. As soon as he answered the phone, Frank knew something was wrong, maybe by the tone of Jason's voice. Anyway, Jason told him to sit down because he had some bad news and he needed some big brother advice.

Jason told him about what he had discovered about my father, about the pictures, the note, and even that I'd run away from my father. He hinted about me taking money from my father, but he didn't elaborate on the amount. Then Frank asked Jason how old I was, and our next nightmare began.

Frank went into hysterics when Jason told him I was sixteen years old. I could hear him berating Jason about me being jailbait. He finally paused after reminding Jason that he was supposed to think with the head on his shoulders not the one in his pants. I felt awful that Ja-

son had to listen to all of this; it made me feel very guilty and dirty. Finally, he told Jason that he needed to find an attorney who would represent us before he went to the police. He said that since a few Culper high school football players had posted videos of themselves having sex with a fifteen-year-old cheerleader, the district attorney had applied a "zero tolerance" policy toward statutory rape. Apparently, the boys all went free because the police investigating the incident screwed up, and the county and district attorney were then sued by the girl's parents. Since then the district attorney had prosecuted every case that comes before him.

Frank told Jason that he would be in trouble regardless of what my father might be doing because he was sleeping with a minor and harboring a runaway. In fact, he listed off a whole bunch of crimes he claimed Jason had committed. Stuff like exposing himself to a minor, transporting me across a state line, lascivious conduct with a minor, and more. By the time Frank was finished reeling off what the police could arrest Jason for, I felt like our situation was totally hopeless.

Frank told Jason he needed an attorney to protect him and to get the best deal possible. If the story about my father was true, Frank thought the DA would probably be lenient with Jason, but if the story was bogus, the police would throw the book at him for sex crimes and label him as a sex offender for life.

We knew we were not suppose to be together and that the law frowned on it, but we knew so many other couples like us and they never had any problem like this with the law. It never seemed like we were doing anything that was really all that bad or different than other kids our age and certainly nothing that might put Jason in prison. We felt like we were like other teenage couples, but I realized then that the police could make a big deal about our relationship, and Jason and I would really get hurt. It suddenly dawned on me that the next couple days might be the last days we would be together for a long time. It was a very sad morning.

Frank said he was sorry he could not help Jason more, but he told him he could get in trouble just knowing that we were living together and that I was only sixteen years old. He said he was breaking laws not reporting us. I couldn't believe that Jason and I living together was making it so difficult to turn my father in and report his terrorist plan.

Frank suggested that Jason try to make a deal with Culper's district attorney before telling them the details about the attack. He said they might be willing to make a deal to dismiss any charges against Jason for the information he could provide about the attack.

The day was only getting worse.

Jason thought that maybe the Homeland Security website might offer a way to report a possible terrorist attack and promise anonymity to the informer. We pulled it up. It talked about the "Homeland Security Advisory System" and said the agency was hiring, but a way to report potential attacks was not that visible. Finally, on the side of the page it suggested that, "If you see suspicious activity, please report it to your local police department." We were back to square one.

After the option of anonymous reporting failed, Jason looked at our phone book and started searching for lawyers who could help us. I could tell he was very upset and afraid.

I felt so guilty, because if I was not with him he wouldn't be going through this. I should have never run away to him. I cursed my father for being what he appeared to be. I was so ashamed. I couldn't believe that Jason might be labeled a rapist, child molester, or sex offender. He did what millions of other boys were doing, but they would make an example out of him and ruin him. I thought about my mother, who was sixteen when she married my father. I tried to stop thinking about it, but it was bothering me more than the fact that my father was planning a terrorist attack on nuclear power plants.

Jason called law firms for a couple hours, but no one could give him an appointment until after Christmas. He didn't want to tell the receptionists what was going on because he was afraid they might call the police and he would be arrested and I would be taken to some foster home. It was just a total nightmare.

Some of the receptionists said they would try to have an attorney call us back. We waited until about 3 p.m., and then Jason got on the phone again, calling attorneys in Houston. Finally, just a few minutes before 5 p.m., Jason got to talk to a real live attorney named Charles Potter on the phone. Jason told him a bit about our situation and said that we knew *something very serious about my father that the police would want to know. We told him it was something we had to report or we would be in trouble also. Mr. Potter said we should all meet tomorrow at 3 p.m. at his office. He would have a little time to talk to us in person and hear our story. He told us that his fee for talking to us would be $300. He said that if he felt he could help us, we would discuss what the next steps would be and agree on his fee.*

Jason got off the phone feeling a little relieved. It made me feel a bit better seeing him look happier. I hugged him tightly and kissed him all over his face. He said he wanted to get out of the house so he wouldn't be home if the Tanners decided to come over. I'd forgotten about them, and I agreed that I didn't want to talk to anyone either. All I wanted was the hours to go by fast so we could talk to Mr. Potter and get this nightmare behind us. We drove to Beaumont that evening and actually ate out at the Red Lobster. I almost felt normal.

Getting away from our house helped and being with Jason just felt so right. I would look at him and just want to tell him over and over again that I loved him. Losing him was more frightening than anything else. We talked about the Christmas decorations in the restaurant and then discussed if we should tell his father not to come down for Christmas until this nightmare was behind us. Jason wasn't sure how to tell his father about our problems, and he worried that Frank might say something about it before he could.

I felt awful because I knew Jason was also worrying about his dad's health. His father, Roger, said he was in remission from cancer, but we all had our doubts about that claim. We knew our situation was not going to help him get better. Jason had wanted his father with us for Thanksgiving, but his dad had claimed that the weather wouldn't let him get a flight out. We thought he was just too sick to come. He was on chemo and had lost his hair. Jason felt bad for his dad because he was alone, with no one to help him or look out for him.

Jason hoped his dad would get into a relationship with someone because he had been alone since his mother died. Jason couldn't remember any woman his dad ever had really liked after his mother's death. I thought Roger was a good dad who tried to stay involved with his kid's lives. Jason knew that if his dad heard about his problems, he would be in Culper right away to help him, but he did not want his father's help. He didn't want his father mixed up in this mess. He felt sorry for his dad, sorry that he might have to be stuck with a son registered as a sex offender. I think this was the thing that frightened Jason the most. In every state, the law is different. If we were married, no one would care we were sleeping together and we wouldn't have this problem. I felt that these laws were really stupid laws that made good people criminals.

We finally left Red Lobster and headed to the Hollywood Theater. We had decided to see this movie called Water for Elephants. The movie was great, and for a couple of hours we actually forgot our nightmare. The movie was about a couple who loved each other, but had to go through so much to be together. It made me remember that a lot of people had to struggle to be with the person they loved. It made me feel a little braver.

Chapter 47
Interview with Border Patrol Agent James Brewer

During those days before Christmas, as Sheeva and Jason struggled with their legal issues, Ali Hasson was busy moving his jihadists across the US/Canadian border and outfitting them with the equipment needed for their mission. An interview with Border Patrol Agent James Brewer provides insight into how some of the members entered the United States and the vast network of sympathetic American supporters that helped their cause. Excerpts of my interview with Agent Brewer follow:

> **Roberto Roma:** *Thank you for taking your time to meet with me. I think your knowledge of the four-thousand-mile Canadian/US border will help readers understand the herculean task of securing it from terrorists intent on entering the US.*
>
> **Agent James Brewer:** *I'm happy to meet with you and hopefully shed some light on this issue.*
>
> **Roberto Roma:** *Please tell me a little about yourself and what part of the border you patrol.*
>
> **Agent James Brewer:** *Well, I have been a border patrol agent for about eighteen years and worked various sections of the Canadian/US border. This has been my job since I got out of school. It's a hard job because you have four thousand miles of border, and most of it's wide open. You're not going to find many fences on the US/Canadian border, like*

on the Mexican border. In fact, up here we have places that straddle both sides of the border. Would you like me to tell you where I was working when I got caught up in the Christmas Special?

Roberto Roma: *Yes, that's what I'm really here to learn about. Where were you working then?*

Agent James Brewer: *I was patrolling the border that includes Massena, New York, Saint Regis, Rooseveltown, and the US portion of the Mohawk territory. This is a very active stretch of border that's often used by drug smugglers and others trying to slip into the US.*

Roberto Roma: *Was that where you were working on December twenty-first?*

Agent James Brewer: *Yes, that's correct. On December 21, I was working with Kenneth Horn, a tribal police officer, checking the Mohawk territory border. This particular piece of the border is located on Indian territory and is very loosely monitored. That particular morning, we found lots of snowmobile tracks in the fresh snowfall on the frozen Saint Lawrence River. Snowmobiles are often used to help smuggle drugs, weapons, and people into the US when the Saint Lawrence is frozen over. Anyway, while Officer Horn and I were looking at the snowmobile tracks, Horn's dog was going crazy over something in the brush. When we investigated what he was barking at, we discovered two bodies that had been hidden from our sight by the snow-covered brush. One was a member of the tribal police force and the other was a young man in his twenties.*

Roberto Roma: *What did they die from?*

Agent James Brewer*: Only one of them was dead. The tribal police officer, Balik Waters, was still alive when we found him, but unconscious. He had been shot in the chest, leg, and head. The other individual was dead. It appeared he had been shot numerous times and had fallen on top of Balik Waters or was stacked on top of him. The dead guy had no wallet, passport, driver's license, or any other type of ID to help us indentify him. However, from his jewelry, we speculated he was a young Muslim man of origin unknown. He was wearing a sterling silver crescent moon and star ring and a watch with Arabic words inscribed across its face. Maybe someone had removed his ID or he hadn't been carrying any. Since the killing happened on Indian land, the investigation became a cross-border investigation that included Canada, the US, and the tribal police.*

Roberto Roma: *Can you describe the area where you found the bodies?*

Agent James Brewer: *Yes, this area is a very wooded area that borders the Saint Lawrence River. The river here is scattered with small islands that people can use for cover as they hopscotch across the border in boats and snowmobiles. Thick forest on both sides provides cover from surveillance planes. We have cameras and sensors located in these areas, but 50 percent of the alarms are triggered by animals, and most of the time we lack the resources to even respond to the alarms. To make things worse, the cameras are continually smashed or shot* *up so they are next to useless. The fact is, we have lots of holes for people to come across, and this area is very hard to police since it's part of the Mohawk territory.*

Roberto Roma: *How does this area differ from other parts of the US-Canadian border?*

Agent James Brewer: *When you're dealing with an area of the border on an Indian reservation, you need to coordinate everything you do with the Indian tribal leaders and their police. When we enter their territory, we are normally escorted by a tribal police escort. The truth is, we are not really welcomed guests on the Mohawk territory. A big sign at the entrance of the territory states their sentiment toward us and other outside authorities interfering in the tribe's autonomy. It reads something like, "Yes, 'terrorists' come through Mohawk Territory. They are Border Patrol, New York State Police, ATF, FBI, Homeland Security etc., etc.!" This is a country within a country and encompasses land in Canada and the US. It's a very difficult border area to control.*

Roberto Roma: *Getting back to the man who was killed, who was he?*

Agent James Brewer: *It was more than a week or more before we discovered who he was. His name was Farook Hafeez, and he was one of Ali Hasson's terrorists. Farook was believed to be a suicide bomber who was supposed to enter a San Francisco church and kill as many people as possible by blowing himself up. The lives of many Bay Area individuals were saved when Balik Waters shot Hafeez to death. We found out he was an*

American, born in the Bay Area to a very good family. Farook's father had immigrated to America from Pakistan some thirty years prior. The Hafeez family was Muslims, but they never expected their son to become involved in terrorist activities. They had seen him as a very devout Muslim who often voiced his anger about the treatment of Muslims after 9/11. To them, it was unimaginable that Farook would do something like this. He was only twenty years old when he was killed.

Roberto Roma: *Was he the one who shot Balik Waters?*

Agent James Brewer: *Statements from Waters and the physical evidence showed that Hafeez was the shooter. I have thought many times about how lucky Balik Waters was. From what we can tell, Hafeez rushed Balik Waters, shooting him at almost point blank range, but Waters was able to return fire and kill him. I think Hafeez landed on top*

of Officer Waters, knocking him down, and apparently Hafeez's associates thought Waters was dead because he was shot in the head.

Roberto Roma: *I guess Balik Waters has you and Kenneth Horn to thank for saving him?*

Agent James Brewer: *No, I think we need to thank Kenneth Horn's dog. That dog was barking and yelping the minute we came into the area, and he led us straight to the bodies behind the thick brush. Officer Waters was damn lucky. The doctors claimed that the cold also helped save his life, but he certainly didn't come out unscathed. His wounds left him an invalid. He cannot walk and* *has impaired vision and chronic headaches that last for hours. So he wasn't all that lucky. Waters told me that Indians have a proverb that goes like, "What is past and cannot be prevented should not be grieved for." He told me I should not dwell on his condition that much, but whenever an officer of the law gets killed or disabled like Waters, it becomes a very emotional and touchy subject. We don't like to see any of our officers in these situations. These shootings are life-altering events for all of us. It angers us and hurts our morale, especially when catching the guilty parties becomes so hampered politically.*

Roberto Roma: *Did Waters provide other information that gave you a better picture of what they were doing?*

Agent James Brewer: *Yeah, they were all armed and carrying multiple bags. Waters didn't see any snowmobiles so they were probably driven by the others, who were already zooming back to Canada when Waters ran into Farook Hafeez and his associates.*

Roberto Roma: *Once these illegals entered the States along the border, how did they survive?*

Agent James Brewer: *On the US side is a vast support network enjoyed by Ali Hasson and his type. There is also probably the same in Canada. My humble opinion is that many Muslims say they disapprove of the violent methods Ali Hasson or the 9/11 conspirators used against America, but they still would welcome an America governed by shariah law. Many legitimate businesses, organizations, and religious groups served the* *needs of Ali Hasson's terrorist group either knowingly or unwittingly.*

This web of support consists of many levels, for example, safe houses exist to provide refuge to Muslims who need to hide from authorities to prevent their deportation. In most cases, the person being helped is just an individual who has overstayed their visa or is trying to visit a sick relative, but unfortunately these same networks are also used by those with a much more evil intent.

Roberto Roma: *From your investigation, did you find out more about the extent of this network?*

Agent James Brewer: *We have known about these networks for quite some time, along with the fact that only about thirty-two miles of the four-thousand-mile northern border is secure. That's not from my observation, but from a report of the Government Accountability Office. So you would think we would use more resources along these borders to prevent illegal entry, but that's not the case. We also know that millions of Muslims live in America, and they help and protect each other in the same fashion that the Italians and Irish did when they poured into America back in the 1800s and early 1900s. We have over a thousand mosques in the US. In fact, in the state of New York alone, we have nearly 150. I'm not saying that mosques are willing partners in the terrorist problem, but they do bring the good guys and bad guys together. Sometimes we worry that the bad guys have more influence than the good guys.*

Even those who appear to be the good guys have ended up being very evil. You probably remember the case of Muzzammil "Mo" Hassan, who was the founder of Bridges TV and ended up cutting his wife's head off. This was a guy who was trying to produce TV shows here in New York that would counter the negative stereotypes of Muslim after the September eleventh terror attacks. I think he failed.

Roberto Roma: *I don't see how that crime really ties into what we are talking about.*

Agent James Brewer: *I'm just saying that often the people we trust the most, who claim they are doing good like Muzzammil Hassan and the Chicago surgeon Ali Hasson, end up being very bad people. It's a very tough world we live in when so many of those we are supposed to respect or revere turn out to be people capable of such horrible deeds.*

Roberto Roma: *Unfortunately, as Mark Twain said, "Everyone is a moon and has a dark side."*

Chapter 48
Three Days Before Christmas

Back in Culper, Texas, Sheeva awoke to the reality of her new dilemma. It's invariably harder to face difficult problems when people around you are excited, happy, and celebrating something that you realize you will not be a part of. Parkdale Mall in Beaumont was jammed with last-minute shoppers. School was out and teenagers were hitting the mall, along with procrastinating husbands buying last-minute gifts. Many stores had decorations already marked down at half price because Christmas was only three days away. The following is Sheeva's account of that day.

> *The morning news December twenty-second talked about a good possibility of snow in the Golden Triangle. Part of me thought how nice that would be for Christmas, but the rest of me had lost any interest in Christmas. All I could think about was our meeting with the lawyer later that afternoon. Jason stayed home from work again and wrote up the details of what he knew from the translated note. He wrote it by hand because he didn't want a copy available for the police to find on our computer. He wanted them to have to deal with him to get the information. He was feeling very confident that once they understood the seriousness of what my father was planning they would be happy to forget Jason's transgressions with me in exchange for the information. He felt they would have to be fools not to do a deal with him. Jason said that when we went to Houston to see Mr. Potter, we would find a Kinkos*

or Internet café and make copies of the pictures, the original note, and the translations. He wanted to put these copies somewhere safe but also easy to locate when we needed them.

Before our trip to Houston, I grabbed a few hundred dollars from my stash of money. By then, I felt much better about having taken the money. If it was going to be used to finance a terrorist attack, it was much better that I had it instead of them. I could also see that we might need a lot of it for lawyer's fees before this nightmare was over. We didn't want to be late for our appointment with Potter, so we left for Houston about 12:30 p.m.

We had little conversation as we drove to Houston. This was a very tense time for us. I was afraid to say anything to Jason that would make him more afraid of what might happen. We would soon be at Potter's office, and hopefully he would have some good news for us.

Jason had the address of a Kinko's that was very close to the Potter's law office, so we stopped there and made three copies of everything. Jason kept one copy to take with him when he visited Potter and placed the other three copies in the trunk.

We found Potter's office; it was located in a small storefront in a rather seedy part of Houston. The windows all had security bars on them, and the front of the building was in dire need of paint. Two buildings down the street was a strip bar with a big neon sign displaying a big-breasted, gyrating girl. You could hear the strip joint's rap pounding away as we walked to the front door of Potter's office. Once inside, we were greeted by a heavyset older woman who lacked any warmth. Her demeanor made you think she saw you as a low-life. She looked at her book with Potter's schedule and matter-of-factly told us he was expecting us but first we would have to fill out a few forms. She handed us a clipboard with a pamphlet and a form simply titled "Intake form—Criminal." She told us to sit down, read the brochure, and fill out the intake form. She said she would inform Mr. Potter that we had arrived.

The forms had questions about who we were and where we lived and what we were there for. They wanted to know where we worked, how much we made, and a lot more personal information. It asked about former arrests and wanted us to describe the crime we were there for. While I was looking at the form, Jason read the brochure. He looked even more agitated as he read it. He handed it to me and said, "Read this part."

It read, **'Sex crimes are taken very serious in the state of Texas. Currently laws are being presented that will call for the death penalty for people twice convicted of sexually assaulting a child. Not all sex crimes carry such harsh sentences, but in general a person convicted of a sex crime in the state of Texas can expect severe punishment. Because of the seriousness Texas law attaches to these crimes, it's imperative for anyone charged with or expecting to be charged with a sex crime to seek competent legal advice from an attorney experienced in sex crimes as soon as possible.**

Under no circumstance discuss your case to anyone without proper legal representation. At Potter and Ferguson, we know what is at stake in these cases and spare no resource to defend our clients charged with alleged sex crimes."

The brochure went on to list various sex crimes. The list included rape, statutory rape, indecency with a child, indecent exposure with a child, date rape, possession of child pornography, and more.

At the bottom of the page it read, **"Potter and Ferguson will do whatever is legally and ethically possible to assist our clients from being convicted and suffer the shame associated with being a registered sex offender."**

I read this, and Jason looked at me and whispered that I should leave. He was afraid that me being there would complicate the discussion with the lawyer and possibly result in me being turned over to the police as a runaway.

I didn't want to leave, but I could see Jason was adamant about it. He asked me for the money I brought for the lawyer, and he told me to go to a restaurant and wait. He warned me about being careful while I drove because I didn't have a license. I was a good driver, and our car didn't really attract attention. I gave him a kiss as I left, right in front of the receptionist. I wanted her to see that I loved him. He said he would call me when he was done talking to the attorney. Jason went back to filling out the intake form as I left.

It was almost two grueling hours later before I heard from him, but I could tell from his voice that it didn't go as well as he had hoped. He told me he would tell me everything when I picked him up.

Jason was walking down the sidewalk from Potter's office when I drove up. His face told me we were still in serious trouble.

The first thing Jason told me was that Potter wanted a $25,000 retainer to represent him for any possible sex crimes he might be accused of. If they had to go to trial, an additional fee would be required. Potter had told Jason the case was complicated because he should have turned the evidence of a possible terrorist attack over when he first had his suspicions. The bottom line was that Potter would try to contact the district attorney for Culper, Texas, the following morning. The main purpose of the call was an attempt to make an appointment for Jason with the DA to discuss dropping any potential sex charges in exchange for information about the possible terrorist attack.

Potter wanted to talk to his partner Ferguson about Jason's predicament, especially to see if Ferguson had any intimate knowledge of the Culper District Attorney. Worst of all was the fact that Potter told Jason he was not sure he could commit to the case with the speed and resources needed to really help. Potter ended the meeting with a promise that he and his partner would discuss the case and get back with Jason in the morning with their final decision.

I could see Jason was very depressed, but he put up a good front. He asked me if I had all my Christmas shopping done, and he said he was sorry that Christmas was not going to be as happy as we had planned. He wanted to know if I'd told Sarah my girlfriend about our problem yet. I told him I hadn't. In fact, I'd not even answered her calls for the last few days. Jason thought I should talk to her and see if I could stay there tomorrow, because with or without an attorney, he was going to the police with the terrorist attack information. He said he could probably barter with the police about something as serious as this as well as Potter could and for a lot cheaper.

He was very upset that it would cost $25,000 for an attorney. We still had most of the money I'd taken from my father so we could afford the retainer. I wondered what the lawyer would think if we brought in two and a half bundles of one hundred dollar bills?

Jason said he wanted me to talk to Sarah and see if I could stay with her until the situation was resolved. He was afraid that the police or the Texas Child Protection Services would grab me and report my whereabouts to my father.

When we got home, the first thing Jason wanted to do was call his father and tell him not to come for Christmas. This was a call that Jason dreaded, but he knew it was necessary to tell his father about our situation before he heard it from Frank or from the police.

I will always remember that evening of December twenty-second, when Jason made that call, because it was when I really realized that my life was once again drastically changing. I'd no idea of what was going to happen, but I knew we would be separated for a while or maybe forever. It was a very sad night.

Jason was so distraught as he spoke with his father on the phone. The call was terribly emotional, with Jason choking up as he tried to explain to his father why he was facing sex charges. He finally told his father my age and that he could easily be facing statutory rape charges in Texas. He explained to his father that I'd ran away from an abusive father and fled to Texas to be with him. Finally he told Roger about the note, the plans to attack the nuclear power plants, and that they appeared to be written by my father. He told his dad that he hoped he could use this information to barter with the DA for dropping or at least reducing the charges he might be facing.

After Jason explained what was happening, his father insisted it was even more important that he come to Culper. He told Jason he was not going to desert him just because of a couple legal issues. Jason had a very hard time talking to his father because he felt ashamed and angry that his father had to know about our problems. The fact that he might be arrested as a sex offender was devastating. Jason struggled to maintain his composure so his father wouldn't realize how afraid and distraught he really felt.

Roger finally told Jason there was no way he was just going to sit home while his son was having all these problems. He was going to come out and help as much as he could, because that was what family was all about. He reminded Jason that all he had was him and Frank, and he was damned if he was going to sit by while his son was ruined by some archaic Texas laws. Jason's father was seriously angry that the police would even consider prosecuting his son, who was bringing them information that could perhaps save many lives.

Jason told his dad once more that he really didn't want him to come because it would be too stressful, but Roger just laughed and reiterated that he was coming. In fact, he said he was going to try to change his flight to something earlier. Jason reminded his dad that he should think about his cancer and how this kind of emotional trauma could affect his illness. Roger scoffed at that and claimed he was in remission. I think Jason was genuinely concerned that the emotional trauma would affect his father's cancer.

His father responded by telling Jason to get some sleep, check with the lawyers in the morning, and regardless of their help, go to the authorities and take care of this. He reminded Jason that what he was doing could be saving many lives. He counseled Jason not to sign any statement before a deal was made in writing and not to let the police bully him. He promised Jason he would be there late on the twenty-third or early the twenty-fourth of December. He told him he loved him and hung up.

When Jason got off the phone he broke down totally and started crying. I'd never seen him like this before, and it frightened me even more and made me feel horrible for getting him into all of this. I hugged him and kissed him and finally got him to lie beside me in our bed. I don't think either of us really slept at all that night. I kept watching the Christmas lights on the wreath in our window flicker on and off hoping it would put me to sleep, but it didn't. I just couldn't quit thinking of what the next day might bring.

As I laid there in the dark, a horrible, suffocating, soul-crushing despair descended upon me. It was hard to breathe. My body shook and I ached with the desire to just cry my eyes out, but I clenched my fist and laid there numb with shame, anger, and fear. I didn't want Jason to have to endure my fear also. I glance at the glowing clock and realized how terrified I was of the coming morning.

Chapter 49
The Twenty-Third of December

On December twenty-third, people awoke to the promising prospect of a white Christmas. Snow had fallen all over the Golden Triangle, but that news was overshadowed by the sad news of two young girls in Culper, Texas, who had been hit by vehicles and killed.

Weather-related traffic accidents abounded across the Golden Triangle because of the constant snow and the freezing weather. Police said one of the girls, seven-year-old Tesha S. Williams of Port Arthur, was hit when her Good Samaritan father stopped to help another motorist fix a flat tire. A car driven by eighteen-year-old Paul Winter plowed into the rear end of Williams's car, crushing seven-year-old Tesha and killing her instantly. Winter was arrested for driving sixty miles per hour over the posted speed limit and refusing a field sobriety test, according to police spokesperson Katherine Butler. Mr. Williams was rushed to the hospital when he showed signs of a possible heart attack, probably brought on by the death of his daughter.

A second tragedy happened in Culper when a fourteen-year-old girl was struck while bringing Christmas cookies to the UPS delivery man who had just dropped off Christmas presents at the girl's family home. She was hit by another truck that was attempting to pass the UPS truck. The girl became stuck under its axle and was dragged a quarter of a mile before the driver responded to the honks and frantic antics of other drivers who could see the girl's body protruding from the rear of his truck. Weather was not reported to be a factor in that accident, officials said. “The people of Culper, Texas, are saddened that these terrible tragedies happened, taking the lives of these two wonderful souls,” stated Mayor Young.

“These accidents seem even more tragic happening as they did only a couple days before Christmas. Here you have two children killed in Culper, Texas, devastating two families—well, probably four families...it’s very sad, very heart-wrenching. It just can’t get any sadder at this time of year for those families involved in these accidents," said Officer John Burns.

Sheeva Hasson had her own tragedies to cope with that morning. Her story continues below:

> *When the bedroom started to brighten from the sun seeping through the blinds, I rolled over to Jason and saw his eyes wide open, gazing at the ceiling. I kissed him and told him I was getting up to make some coffee. He said nothing to me, didn’t even look at me. It was not what I expected, but I didn’t say anything to him about it. I forced a smile, got up, and walked out to the living room. The house was cold. We hadn’t turned up the heater the night before, and the temperature had dropped during the night. I turned on the TV and flipped to the local news. They were talking about how much better stores were doing for the Christmas season. They showed a video of Beaumont’s Parkdale Mall with Christmas decorations everywhere, and then they showed a long line of kids waiting to sit on Santa’s lap to tell him what they wanted for Christmas.*

Everything was about Christmas, but my Christmas was shrinking into something dark and ugly. That morning I realized it might be the last day we would be living in this house together. Just thinking those thoughts made tears come to my eyes. I turned on the coffee pot and sat at the kitchen table, thinking about what I needed to do. It wasn't only Jason who was in trouble. If this whole terrorist thing turned out to be a big mistake, I'd be returned to my father, and I was sure he would beat me...or worse. It was like I needed to prepare to run away again, but where? This all had happened so fast that I really didn't know where to go. I grabbed a cup of coffee and looked in on Jason. He was still just laying there like he was comatose. I knew he had his problems, and he really could not help me any longer. I went back to the kitchen and called Sarah. She answered immediately.

"Where have you been?" she answered the phone. "I have been calling you the last few days and wondering what you were doing and why you weren't calling me."

"Sarah, I'm sorry that I have not called you, but a lot of things have been going on with Jason and me. I need to see you in person and tell you all about it."

"Of course, Sheeva, I'm off today and would love to have you come over. Can you give me a hint? Are you guys breaking up?"

I sort of laughed and replied, "No, not really, but we have some major problems and I might have to ask you if I can stay at your place for a few days. I can pay you."

"Of course you can," Sarah said. "What time would you be coming over? Do you want me to come and pick you up?"

"I don't know what time right now, but Jason has some important things to do today, and when he leaves I will call you," I said.

"You better not change your mind because I'm going crazy trying to figure out what's going on," she said.

Jason came into the kitchen; his eyes were all puffy and red. I wanted to get off the phone and talk to him so I told Sarah, "Jason is up now. I got to go, but I'll call you in a while. Thanks for the understanding. Bye!"

I hung up and looked up at Jason. He looked so distressed. I blurted out, "Jason, I am so sorry I got you into all of this. If I hadn't chased after you, you wouldn't be in this fix." I hugged him, and tears came to my eyes.

I felt his arms closing around me, and he whispered, "I love you, Sheeva. This is not your fault; it's just one big mess we are caught up in. I'm glad you have been living with me. This last month has been so wonderful, and you have been so wonderful. Your dad is our problem, not you."

What he said took my breath away, and I couldn't reply, but I embraced him even tighter. I finally got control of myself and told him, "Jason, I love you too. I just want this all behind us."

He held me tighter, and I said, "Let me fix your coffee and then let's call Potter to see if they are going to represent you."

"You're right. Let's get the act on the road," Jason said as he released me.

Before I even had his coffee ready, he was already making notes at the kitchen table of what we had to do that day.

He called Potter, but there was no one in the office at 8:30 a.m. Jason left a message to call him as soon as they got in. He said he was waiting for their decision and that he had to do something that day.

He told me he was glad that I already called Sarah and said he had thought about what we had to do all night. He said he had to take the car when he went to the Culper police station and hide the notes, the maps of the nuclear power plants, the list of all the places that would be attacked, and the rest of the translation under the spare wheel in the trunk of his car. He said once they agreed, in writing, not to prosecute him, he would give them the evidence of the attack. If they didn't have an agreement before his father got in town, he would have his father bring a copy of the map of one of the nuclear power plants with the title "The Christmas Special—Target One" written in Arabic. And he would ask his father to call the FBI and Homeland Security to get them into the case. They might help pressure the local police to do the right thing for the sake of stopping any attack and drop the cases against him.

Jason said he was going to tell the police that we never slept together, but that still left the problem of harboring a runaway and crossing the state line with a minor and lots of other violations. I told

Jason that I'd swear to that also, but with Culper's zero tolerance policy on teenage sex I wasn't sure that would make any real difference. I was sure the district attorney would be afraid to grant leniency after the sex scandal with the cheerleader and football team. I felt like maybe we were just being paranoid and that the minute we told them what was about to happen they would just laugh at all these fears and tell us not to worry. It was just hard to figure which way it might go and how serious they would treat us living together.

Jason also wanted us to split the money I'd taken. He wanted forty thousand dollars so he could pay the lawyer if they would take his case and have enough to live on till he got his life back together. I had no problem with that. In fact, I wish I could give all of what money remained to him, but I realized I had to have a little money to live on also. We really hadn't spent much of the money anyway.

So we divided the money, and I put my share into a suitcase. As we talked, I packed some things I would need to wear for the next few days. I really had no idea what I should take, but something made me feel like I should take some of the mementoes we had accumulated over the last couple months of being together. While I packed, Jason went out to the Hyundai and stashed the majority of the money in the car-jack compartment. I thought someone would have a very merry Christmas if they stole our old car and happened to use the jack.

By 1 p.m., Potter had still not called us, so Jason called their office again. This time they did answer, and the receptionist, probably the same women we met, told us that Mr. Potter was with a client and that she would remind him to call us right after he was done. Jason explained to her that his business with Mr. Potter was an urgent matter that had to be handled that day. She assured him she would have Potter call him back.

At about 2:15 p.m., Potter finally called. He apparently sounded upbeat because Jason's face brightened, but then Potter told him that he and Ferguson had decided they could not take on his case. Potter said Jason's best bet was to try on his own to barter with the district attorney, just as he had planned, because that was really all the leverage he would have in Culper, Texas. He told Jason to demand to talk to the district attorney before giving any real details to the police. Potter added that if the district attorney had any brains at all, he would take care of Jason's situation in return for the information we had about the attacks. He reminded Jason that Culper had a zero tolerance policy toward statutory rape so he needed to get a deal in writing and signed by the district attorney, but most important he needed get to the police fast.

Jason hung up the phone and looked at me like he was totally lost. I moved over to him and kissed his forehead. He looked up at me and said in an emotionless voice, "Sheeva, it's time I drive over to the police station. I want you to get Sarah over here to pick you up as soon as possible. I am going to leave a note for my father on this table, along with the map I want him to bring to the police station. You start calling him later and tell him what's going on."

He pushed himself up from the chair and pulled me over to him. He kissed me hard and stroked my face and told me he loved me. I tried to reach up and kiss him again, but he pushed me gently away and started toward the door. Tears welled up in his eyes as he left.

I stood in the kitchen and listened to Jason back the Hyundai out onto the road. All of a sudden, I felt so alone and afraid. I shut my eyes tight and asked Allah to please help Jason. At the same time on the TV, a choir was singing "Silent Night."

I called Sarah to come and pick me up and then waited for her to arrive. I was so lucky to have such a wonderful, loving friend. While I waited, my head raced with all kinds of terrible visions of what was happening to Jason. And every car I heard coming near, I imagined it was the police coming to take me into custody. It seemed like an eternity before Sarah arrived, but really it was just a few minutes. I guess it was about three o'clock when she drove up our driveway. The sound of her car relieved me greatly, knowing I could leave. When I opened the door for Sarah, her smiling face brightened my day and gave me hope again.

It was a false hope, however, because Jason didn't get to call me that evening and no deal was made. The worst was about to start.

Part Two
The Wrath Upon Us

EVACUATION TIME
D & L Weathers/DHearne
"The Christmas Special" 2012

Chapter 50
Have A Very Special Christmas

At 4 a.m. on Christmas morning, Times Square glittered with Christmas lights while carols played over outdoor speakers. The traffic was minimal, with yellow cabs moving along Broadway. It was a beautiful, peaceful Christmas morning. Even the normal riffraff was missing. It was spitting a little snow in New York, but for Christmas, snow was always welcome.

At the same time, in Chicago it was sixteen degrees, and Ali Hasson sat inside his car parked outside the Chicago Latte Café. He was eating a croissant and sipping an espresso. In the back seat of his car was a mountain of presents gaily wrapped and tagged to give to children at his hospital and to the families of hospital staff members. Ali had always been a very considerate and kind doctor.

According to FBI records, Ali's computer that night was connected to the free wireless network at the Chicago Latte Café. Ali was checking CNN and Fox News, probably to see if there were any reports regarding the upcoming operation. However, the biggest story on that Christmas morning was that Santa had succeeded in his delivery of thousands of toys to children all over the world. Below that story were the happy words that not one American combat death had been reported in December for the Iraq war. Afghanistan was a different story. Twenty-five Americans had been killed in combat, including six ghastly beheadings of marines captured in the previous month by the Taliban.

At about fifteen minutes after 4 a.m. Eastern Standard Time, Ali brought up his Facebook account and typed in a posting that read, “Have a very Special Christmas.” This message would be viewed by about twenty-seven people.

According to the all-night attendant at the café, Ali appeared terribly agitated when he bought his coffee and croissant. Perhaps his anticipation of the Christmas Special was so intense that it showed in his demeanor. At least we’d hope he felt something like that before he clicked the send icon under his Facebook message. This was a crucial moment, and his simple action would soon change America’s history.

Chapter 51
Roberto Roma's Christmas Morning

It was 5:35 Christmas morning when my phone rang. It was my brother-in-law, and he was virtually breathless. He asked if I'd heard the news.

"What kind of news am I suppose to hear at 5:30 in the morning?" I replied sleepily.

"We have been attacked, this time across the country. Turn on your TV; it's on all the networks."

I reached over to the nightstand and grabbed the remote and flicked on the TV. My wife was staring at me quizzically.

"What's wrong, Roberto?" she asked.

"I don't know yet."

From the blackness of the cold screen, a solemn-faced reporter materialized, talking excitingly to a person in Louisiana. The picture changed and we could see the massive Waterford 3 Nuclear Plant with black smoke billowing out from within its compound.

The reporter said, "It's an unbelievable scene, an absolute horrible scene. It looks like something from a war movie. Burned-out vehicles, covered bodies on the ground, uniformed police everywhere, smoke spewing out of the Waterford 3 Nuclear Plant, and the acrid smell of gun smoke is evident as you near the compound. We have helicopters with huge spotlights buzzing overhead and landing in the adjacent fields, bringing in medics and additional police. You can see men kneeling beside their fallen comrades offering emotional support. So far we have been told that an unknown number of terrorists are inside the Waterford 3 Nuclear Plant. It's believed they have not yet caused any serious damage or release of radiation. Police negotiators are outside with bullhorns, trying to create a dialog with the terrorists. Police have exchanged gunfire with them for the last fifteen minutes."

I switched to a different channel and found a reporter standing outside a hospital in Des Moines, Iowa. The reporter was pointing to the second floor, where smoke curled out of the broken windows. "Police are trying to restore calm, but currently the mood here at Des Moines General Hospital early this Christmas morning is sheer panic. It's reported that a bomb exploded somewhere on the hospital's second floor. No details of fatalities or injuries have been given. It's suspected that the explosion is connected to the chain of attacks on nuclear power stations, hospitals, and churches being reported across the country. These coordinated attacks threaten the very fabric of our existence as we know it."

I heard my brother-in-law's voice emanating from the phone I was squeezing in my hand. "Are you watching it?"

"Yes, Jeff. When did this all start?"

"I think it just started in the last hour. I'm not sure. I'm watching the same stuff you're watching. Hey, I have another call. Call me if you find anything else about what all is going on. Merry Christmas, bro!"

"Yeah, you too. Looks like we are going to have a very merry Christmas," I said and hung up the phone.

I looked at Elizabeth and said, "This is unbelievable," just as CNN switched to an affiliate in Buchanan, New York. A panoramic vista of a town sparkling with beautiful Christmas lights filled my TV screen. The voice of an unseen reporter directed our eyes to the misty black shadows in the top left of the screen. There were flashes of lights in the blackness. The voice continued, "What you are seeing are explosions at the Indian Point Energy Center here in Buchanan. These explosions are being reported as mortar rounds fired by terrorists onto the grounds of the plant. The entire nuclear power plant is currently under the control of a small but heavily armed terrorist group. Police and military units are at the scene but are unable to remove the terrorists because their rules of engagement prevent firing into the nuclear power plant for fear of causing greater damage and possible radioactive release that could endanger the public. Experts are rushing to the scene to devise a way to neutralize the threat. It's believed that the military is planning to use nerve gas to incapacitate the terrorists.

"The freeways and roads leading away from Buchanan are already clogged with cars full of residents fleeing the area in fear of a major nuclear calamity. I have just received news that our station will be off the air temporarily as we are also relocating our station staff to a safer site. Apparently, there are now reports of higher-than-average gamma ray readings. That is a bad sign." The screen went to a test pattern, and a static hiss replaced the reporter's voice.

I was fully awake now. My adrenaline was coursing through my body, and for the first time ever on a Christmas morning, Elizabeth and I went downstairs and turned on the living room television. Our piles of presents sat untouched under our beautiful, sparkling Christmas tree. Elizabeth made coffee, and I started channel surfing. I was feeling the same depressing emotions that I experienced on 9/11. Something that was never supposed to happen was unfolding for real across the country.

CNN had a frantic-looking reporter interviewing a man by phone who was evacuating San Clemente, California, after being jolted from sleep at 3:15 a.m. on Christmas morning by the nuclear power plant's emergency siren. The CNN reporter asked, "Thank you, Mr. King, for calling. Can you tell me what is going on there in San Clemente?"

"All I know is that at about 3:15 a.m. the SONGS emergency siren started. Before I could even get up, my five-year-old daughter was by my bed wanting to know if this siren was for Santa. To tell you the truth, my heart was racing, wondering what the siren meant this time. San Onofre's got a real bad history of false alarms. I hoped it was just another one of them or a test, but I doubted they would do a test on Christmas morning. My wife and I tried to call the sheriff's department, but it was continually busy or the 'All circuits are busy' recording played. We also checked the SONGS and the city of San Clemente website, hoping it would tell us something, but there was nothing about what was going on. Then our lights went out, and that was when we grabbed flashlights and candles and scrambled to get the stuff we needed to evacuate. We were out of the house in five minutes or less. We grabbed a few Christmas presents for our daughter to take with us in hopes of having a little celebration somewhere. Once we saw all the cars on the road, we knew something very bad had happened."

"Thank you, Mr. King, and good luck to you and your family." The reporter continued, "Not only are civilians evacuating San Clemente, but it's being reported that marines from Camp Pendleton just south of the San Onofre Nuclear Power Plant were also evacuating their facility. To complicate evacuation, the ten-mile stretch of Interstate 5 adjacent to San Onofre is closed to all traffic. That means all traffic both north and south on Interstate 5 is closed."

As I watched the unbelievable news, Elizabeth started crying, and I moved closer to her and hugged her. Her body shook with sobs. She had her eyes tightly shut and was biting her lip to regain her composure.

"Why is this happening?" she blurted between sobs.

Channel 12 showed an anxious reporter recounting the president's flight from Capitol Hill Baptist Church to Andrews Naval Air Facility. An animated map displayed where the president had attended Christmas morning services and the route his motorcade had used to race to Andrews Naval Air Facility.

"In just minutes, Washington DC Metropolitan Police were able to divert Christmas morning traffic in both directions along the president's route. The resulting deserted roads allowed the president's motorcade to barrel along between 60 mph and something over 100 mph, running red lights with impunity. On arrival at Andrews, the president, accompanied by his family, immediately boarded one of the Air Force One jets and is reported safe at an undisclosed location. No word regarding the Christmas morning attack has yet been issued by the White House."

Scrolling across the bottom of the screen was the message, "Terrorists taken alive, says an unnamed source from the Saint Charles Parish's Sheriff Office."

Another report from Beaumont, Texas, said an unidentified man struggled with a woman outside Saint Paul Catholic Church. As others tried to interfere in the altercation, the woman yelled "Allahu Akbar" and blew herself up. At least fourteen bystanders were killed, along with the woman and the man who had been fighting with her. Calder Avenue was strewn with dead bodies for hours as police coped with the crime scene.

All Christmas morning my wife Elizabeth and I sat transfixed in front of the television as report after report poured in describing the attacks that were happening all over the country.

In many cities and towns, police were preventing people from going to church services. Police were called in from Christmas vacations to assist in searches of hospitals for bombs. Members of military bomb squads had their leaves canceled and were ordered to assist in nearby communities to help search for bombs. The news was dominated by reports of death and havoc. Attacks were reported in Seattle, Washington; Alexandria, Virginia; Havre, Montana; Las Vegas, Nevada; Nashville, Tennessee; Miami, Florida; Philadelphia, Pennsylvania; Des Moines, Iowa; and Lewiston, Idaho.

I wondered how many people were actually celebrating Christmas. How many people had still not heard that we were being attacked by fanatics? I sat consoling my wife, but I also felt torn apart. How long would this last? Evacuations were already being called for by officials in towns near the three nuclear power plants that had been attacked. I had heard from one station that three million people would be evacuated from around the Indian Point Nuclear Power Plant. Nobody seemed to be in charge of these evacuations—or anything else for that matter. Orders to stay home and stay calm were issued by many state and city officials, but no directives came from the federal government. It was reported that the entire White House had been evacuated, and command and control was being set up in an undisclosed secure location. Nothing had been officially heard from the president regarding the attack.

From my seat in front of my TV, the country looked like it was in total chaos, that everybody was doing whatever they thought was needed to protect themselves. There were reports of armed men acting as guards for hospitals, churches, power plants, malls, schools, and even closing streets to anyone who seemed suspicious or looked like they were Arabs. More reports of churches being attacked trickled in.

The reports were so many that it was confusing to know if a new place was being attacked or if a different reporter was reporting an older attack in a different way. The church attacks were as devastating as the hospital attacks. There were reports of churches being bombed by suicide bombers in Washington, DC; Salt Lake City, Utah; Wichita, Kansas; Bellows Falls, Vermont; Grand Junction, Colorado; Beaumont, Texas; Springfield, Missouri; Birmingham, Alabama; Keene, New Hampshire; and Tulsa, Oklahoma.

All air traffic was stopped, along with all scheduled Amtrak travel. America virtually shut down. Christmas was basically called off. I tried to imagine the millions of children who were unable to understand why Christmas was not being observed in its traditional fashion. Throughout Christmas day, hundreds of thousands of police, service people, paramedics, and emergency workers were called up to assist in securing the country. Sometime around ten in the morning, it was reported that the Pentagon, Treasury Building, and Capitol Building were also being evacuated.

By noon Christmas day, there were reports of more explosions, fires, and high radiation levels in the areas surrounding all three nuclear power plants under attack. It was believed that the terrorists had successfully destroyed most, if not all, of the redundant cooling systems needed to cool the reactors' cores and the spent fuel rods stored in pools around the plant.

I watched a report from a CNN affiliate station in Baton Rouge, Louisiana, where a spokesperson for the governor read a declaration of emergency for the Waterford 3 Nuclear Power Plant. He stated that all towns within a ten-mile radius of the power plant were ordered to immediately evacuate. Those towns included Taft, Good Hope, Gypsy, Norco, Montz, New Sarpy, and Hahnville. In addition, Interstate 10 was ordered closed between McElroy and the Interstate 310 junction. Even worse was the closing of the Louis Armstrong New Orleans International Airport because it was situated just a few miles downwind from the nuclear power plant.

Following that report, a cell phone video from the Louis Armstrong International Airport was shown. It captured the chaotic evacuation of the airport. It showed a huge line of travelers waiting to board evacuation buses. Some of the people held wet rags over their mouths and noses in a vain attempt to protect themselves from breathing in radioactive dust.

Workers in hazmat suits, some carrying yellow radiation meters, attempted to maintain control of the line. Two of these hazmat-clad workers, distributing potassium iodide tablets, squatted next to a small hysterical girl who clung to her mother's leg. One worker held out the pill and a glass of water for the girl, but she cried and protested so much that it was impossible to get her to take the potassium iodide tablet. The girl kept yelling that she wanted to go home to Daddy and have Christmas. Her sobbing mother kept pleading with her to take the pill or she would get very sick.

In the background, fear-stricken travelers, some crying, some with vacant, staring eyes—shuffled past a huge, gaily lit Christmas tree. The majority of them carried Christmas gifts and dragged carry-ons as they slowly inched closer to the evacuation buses.

Chapter 52
Jerry Jordan's Investigative Reporting

Like the rest of the country, Reporter Jerry Jordan was transfixed by the events of Christmas morning. He had channel-surfed from station to station to learn as much as he could about the attacks. By about 6 a.m., his investigative sixth sense told him that his preliminary investigation of Jason Wilgers's murder was directly linked to the terrorist attacks.

Jordan a reporter for "South East Texas Investigates" had connected the dots much earlier than Homeland Security or the FBI. When I interviewed Jordan, he was a wealth of knowledge about the sequence of events that ultimately led up to the attacks. Jordan's transcript paints a frightening picture of the ineptness of the handling of Wilgers's warning about these attacks. Portions of his transcript follow.

> *Frank Wilgers, an officer with the Beaumont police force, contacted me the day his teenage brother Jason was arrested for statutory rape, harboring a runaway, lascivious conduct with a minor, and some other offenses. That was a couple days before Christmas, actually the afternoon of December twenty third. Frank told me that his brother, Jason, had information about a possible terrorist attack, but the authorities were more interested in the statutory rape charges than checking out his claim. Frank Wilgers told me that his brother had been living with his sixteen-year-old girlfriend, Sheeva Hasson, for a couple months and was totally unaware that his relationship violated all these laws. He discovered his*

dilemma when he told his brother, Officer Wilgers, that he had evidence that Sheeva's father was the leader of a large cell of terrorists. Frank told me that when he asked Jason more about his girlfriend's father and who she was, he discovered Jason's girlfriend was sixteen. He warned Jason that once he started explaining his suspicions about Sheeva's father to the authorities, he would likely be in deep shit over her age. Frank said Jason couldn't believe anyone in today's world would care that he was living with his girlfriend since they were in love with each other.

The day Frank visited me, I took notes but unfortunately didn't do anything with the information. Last-minute Christmas shopping was on my agenda for that afternoon, and the completion of three articles on deadline for the "South East Texas Investigates" *would eat up the rest of the day. I'd planned to talk with Jason Wilgers the next day, but his murder altered those plans.*

When I heard about his murder the morning of December twenty-fourth, I was devastated. I felt guilty that I hadn't done something sooner. I called Frank Wilgers to tell him how sorry I was, but he was not answering his phone. I felt like I'd let them down and even myself. If Jason was killed knowing about a terrorist attack and the authorities were more interested in a statutory rape charge, it would be one hell of a story. However, I didn't have any real proof that Sheeva's father was in fact a terrorist. I decided to make a few calls.

First, I was interested in how long Sheeva had been on the road as a runaway. The Chicago police were first on my list. I hoped I could get some info from them. After calling them and being transferred around for a few long minutes, I was finally talking to an officer who was knowledgeable about reported runaways. Barbara Wayne was the officer, but after searching her database of reported runaways, she could not find any information about a Sheeva Hasson. I explained to her that Sheeva had been living a couple months with her boyfriend in Beaumont, Texas. I asked if she knew anything about her father Ali Hasson. She told me no but promised she would check him out and call me back with what she found. I pleaded with her not to forget me, and she promised once again she wouldn't.

Once I was off the phone, I wondered why her father didn't report her as a runaway. Ali Hasson was an educated man, a doctor. If she had been gone a couple of months, he should have reported her as a runaway. Something told me I was onto something big. Maybe he didn't report her because he didn't want police snooping around.

I called a local police officer in hopes he would know more about Jason's death. After a few calls, I was able to contact an old police friend who supplied me with the gruesome information. I can't give you his name, but police reports will verify this information. Apparently the officer who jailed Jason was supposed to be getting off when Jason was brought to him for interrogation. Officer Krewell wanted to get home, but Jason was ada-

mant about not being arrested for any sexual charges if they wanted the info on the terrorist attacks. Krewell told him something like, "You don't come into a police station and tell us we can't arrest you for statutory rape just because you think you got some hot tip on a terrorist plot. For your information hotshot, 99.99 percent of these tips are total shit. I don't have time to play games with you, so I'm going to write you up with these charges and let you enjoy a night in jail. Maybe tomorrow you can give us this hot info you have and not play games with us."

I am paraphrasing what was said, but it ended up with Jason having charges filed against him and being placed in the holding area that night of December twenty-third.

Later that night in the holding tank, a couple members of the Five Percent gang got wind that a white boy named Jason was in for raping a young Muslim girl, and they decided to teach him a lesson. They distracted the lone guard by telling other inmates to sing Christmas carols to him. While he was being serenaded and his view blocked, Jason Wilgers was dragged over to the shared toilet. They pushed his head into the toilet bowl, stepped on his neck, and shoved his county-issued sandals up his rectum. Either on purpose or by accident, their actions killed Jason. They left him dead sitting on the toilet. He was discovered when they changed guards later that night and attempted to ordered him off the toilet.

I received my call from Barbara Wayne, the Chicago police officer I'd talked to earlier, and she had a few tips for me. She told me that Ali Hasson was a doctor at Saint Anthony's Hospital, but he had been away lately participating in some doctor's conferences in Canada. The only Muslim girl reported as a runaway or missing in Chicago in the last couple months was a friend of Sheeva's named Hidi. The most interesting piece of information Wayne gave me was the fact that Sheeva's neighbors were told she was staying with relatives in Canada. They said her brother, Abdul, told them this.

The next morning, I woke up to find my suspicions were correct, but I'd been to slow with my investigation on Ali. The attacks had already began.

I dialed the number of an FBI contact and told him what I'd just discovered.

Chapter 53
The Trip to London

While the Christmas morning terrorist attacks were happening across America, Ali Hasson slept peacefully in the big Boeing 777, thirty-five thousand feet above the Atlantic. Next to him sat Edward Wright, who was traveling to London to celebrate Christmas with his children who lived with his ex-wife. Unfortunately for Mr. Wright, his luck in sitting next to Hasson resulted in him being detained for questioning after it was established he was one of the people sitting close to Ali on the trans-Atlantic flight.

Mr. Wright's affidavit recounts the events in London:

> *Ali Hasson appeared very normal and made no show of nervousness or any visible indication he was aware of the attacks. Part of the trip he watched A Christmas Story and laughed often as Darren McGavin tried to make sure his family had a merry Christmas. The remainder of the trip, he appeared to nap. Just before we got to London's Heathrow Airport I asked Ali, "Have you ever been to London before?" Ali replied, "Oh yes, many times, I have many friends in London." When we exited the plane, I asked Ali if he knew how long it takes to get through customs. Ali good-naturedly said, "For you, just minutes. For me, probably a bit longer." I don't know if he already suspected he had been discovered or if he was just really joking. But as soon as we exited the plane, six or more security personnel grabbed him and pulled him away from the rest of us. That was the last I*

saw of him except for the thousands of pictures of his face plastered all over the TV and newspapers.

Just as soon as he was out of sight, two more guards walked up to me and requested that I come with them. They said they had a few questions they wanted to ask me. For the next three and a half hours, they grilled me on who I was and if I had any prior connection to Ali Hasson. An agent named David Gilligan had me watch some news footage from the attacks in America. He watched me intently to see my emotions. I was shocked that all this was going on back home, on Christmas day. It took my breath away as I watched a report of the evacuation of people from around the Indian Point Nuclear Power Plant. The roads were packed full of vehicles, and they said that people were freezing in their cars after they ran out of gas and were abandoned by others fleeing the area. Pictures of emergency rooms that had been bombed flashed on the screen as emergency people tried to help the hurt and cover the dead. I just couldn't believe what I was seeing and that this man who had sat next to me was involved in these bloody attacks.

Officer Gilligan flicked off the TV and wanted to know how I ended up sitting next to Hasson, what he said to me, and who else he talked to on the plane. He asked if Hasson had called anyone and a thousand other questions. At least I had something exciting to tell my daughters as an excuse for why I was hours late picking them up.

Chapter 54
Christmas Afternoon

Elizabeth and I were mesmerized by the hundreds or maybe even thousands of stories that continued to flash across the TV screen. It seemed like an unending battle was going on out there. Stories and grim pictures of more bombings of hospitals, churches, and even reports of burning stores added to the chaos that flooded the news. It was hard to get any real sense of how severe things were. Were the attacks getting worse, or were they subsiding? I couldn't tell, and when I tried to call out to friends and relatives, I was constantly met with "All circuits are busy. Please try your call later."

Evacuations of towns were in full force all around the Indian Point Nuclear Power plant, the San Onofre Nuclear Power Plant, and the towns surrounding the Waterford 3 Nuclear Power Plant. Terrible, heartbreaking stories were coming from all of these evacuations. Nobody was prepared. Police had initially set up roadblocks to stop evacuees to test them for radioactivity and give them potassium iodide tablets, but they quickly ran out of tablets and they realized that stopping the cars caused greater harm than good. Many vehicles quickly ran out of gas in these snail-paced lines. Fights broke out at the few gas stations with people brave enough to sell gas on the evacuation routes. At one gas station, a man became furious when he was trying to fill his Hummer and shot and killed the station attendant, who had restricted all gas sales to ten gallons or less. The owner of the Hummer was then overpowered by an enraged mob and reportedly beaten to death.

Throughout the day, newscasters used different names for the attack. Some called it "A Black Day on a White Christmas," others called it the "Christmas Massacre," one network referred to it as the "Grey Christmas," and another as the "Nuclear Christmas." Finally, after some reports started saying it was a coordinated attack that was called the "Christmas Special" by the terrorists, all news outlets adopted it as the official name of the attack.

By late Christmas afternoon, various American Islamic groups had stepped forward and denounced this attack. One imam of a major mosque wrote, "Like all Americans, we are horrified and grief-stricken at these events. Countless innocents were murdered today in an unjustified act of terrorism, and the true followers of Islam in America strongly condemn this heinous crime against our country." The spokesperson went on, "We all share the same anger and frustration, and we are all affected by these horrible attacks. We must all take care, however, that in our anger, we don't unjustly target those who are innocent of these attacks. We only ask all the people of America to remember that many followers of Islam came to America to avoid persecution and love the land. These are not the enemies, but your brothers."

Soon after this welcomed announcement, a new recording was released by Al Jazeera with a very chilling message that was soon displayed on every TV channel. It was a prerecorded message from one of the terrorists that stated, "To the American people, I lived among you. I shopped at your grocery stores. I worked with you, and by the time you hear this recording I will be a martyr in paradise while you cry over your dead. Know that I'm not alone." This message added an additional chill to the frosty Christmas air. There was no way to really know if this statement was true or not, but fear of more attacks quickly escalated. Perhaps even more frightening was a new sound bite taken from the message that was repeatedly broadcasted. It was simply four ominous words, "We will come again."

Fox News had an expert on showing people who were unable to evacuate how to take shelter. The reporter was explaining that sometimes it was impossible to evacuate, and in that case, what other options did you have? The best thing you could do, according to the experts, was to "take shelter." That entailed just staying in your home and following numerous precautions. You needed a roll of plastic, along with a couple rolls of duct tape so you could tape plastic sheeting securely over every window and door to stop all airflow. The whole idea was to keep radioactive contaminants from entering the house, but unfortunately few people would have enough plastic and tape available to do the job right. He also warned that you needed to use bottled water instead of tap water because it was very likely that the city water would also be contaminated. So drinking it or bathing in it was out. If you could accomplish this, you were a bit safer than being exposed outside your home.

I still could not totally get my brain around the fact that all this was really happening. Here I was sitting in my living room, sipping coffee, watching these horrible scenes on TV while thousands of people were stalled in the snow or mistaking their migraine headache for a sign of radioactive poisoning, or worse yet vomiting blood, which turned out to be a real sign of radiation exposure. The symptoms of radiation poisoning flashed on the screen throughout the day. They talked about bleeding from the nose, mouth, gums, and rectum or having bloody stool and bruising easily. Dehydration, diarrhea, fainting, fatigue, hair loss, inflammation of exposed areas (redness, tenderness, swelling, bleeding, nasty mouth ulcers, nausea, and vomiting) were even more of the dreaded symptoms of radiation poisoning. But there were still more signs you had to watch out for: open sores on the skin, skin burns (redness and blistering), sloughing of skin, ulcers in the esophagus, stomach, or intestines, and vomiting blood.

In the New Orleans area, the city was begging any available doctors to come and assist the hospitals, which were short staffed. The news didn't provide information where the injured had come from, but I guessed it was wounded guards, people who were involved in accidents trying to flee the city, and maybe the captured terrorist they had announced earlier that morning.

Just as I flipped the channel, the four words, "We will come again," scrolled across the screen with the anchor asking, "How long must we wait before our government knows if this is just bluster or a real threat?"

Chapter 55
Beaumont's Homeless Shelter

The Beaumont Homeless Shelter was adorned with Christmas decorations. The freak snow flurries that painted Beaumont a frosty white continued unabated, coating the shelter's sidewalk with a thin, sparkling coat of snow. Its entrance appeared to glow from the strings of twinkling lights encircling the front door. Adjacent to the sidewalk was an old nativity scene dusted with fresh snow. Completing the holiday ambiance was the Christmas music coming from within and the distant church bell chimes. For a few frosty moments, the spirit of Christmas eclipsed the horror of the day. This was the temporary home for Sheeva Hasson after being picked up by police on a tip from her friend Sara. In the transcript below, FBI special agent Felicia Burke tells her story of what happened that morning.

> *I presented my credentials to the attendant at the Beaumont Homeless Shelter. My partner and I were there to talk to Sheeva Hasson, who had been placed in the shelter the same evening her boyfriend, Jason, had been murdered. While the attendant looked over my papers, I noticed how the lobby was complete with a beautifully decorated Christmas tree still smelling of fresh pine and surrounded by children playing with their brand-new toys. It was odd, but in the front room a semblance of normalcy prevailed even after these terrible attacks had occurred. The Christmas spirit quickly dissipated when the attendant, Cynthia Outley, presented me to Sheeva Hasson. The minute I entered Sheeva's room,*

I was met with total disdain. "Hello, Sheeva," I offered in a cheery voice.

Sheeva sat on her bed holding a pillow to her chest; she locked her eyes on me, but said nothing. I moved closer to Sheeva's bed while the attendant exited, providing us a bit more privacy.

I smiled at her and introduced myself, "Sheeva, I'm an FBI special agent here to help you and ask you to please help us. I have another agent waiting outside, but I wanted a few minutes to talk privately with you. I know you—"

"You come now and ask me to help you, after we pleaded to help you before your stupidity killed Jason?

Her eyes filled with tears. "I told him not to trust you, that your pettiness and stupid laws would destroy our relationship. Now he is dead because it was more important for you to charge him with some ridiculous sex charges instead of worrying about something a lot bigger." I could see tears streaming down Sheeva's face as she spoke to me.

I tried to soothe her. "Sheeva, I'm truly sorry for what happened. No one wanted that to—"

"You're so full of shit. They put Jason in jail because they wanted to punish him because of a stupid law that says we can't feel anything between us because we aren't old enough. You put him in jail because I'm supposed to be too young to know my own mind, but guess what? I loved him. He never raped me. We were in love. I wanted sex with him. You should arrest me because I made him have sex with me.

Sheeva glowered at me, "If we were married, you wouldn't have cared, you wouldn't have charged him with anything, but because we weren't, you made it a horrible thing. Now Jason is dead. I don't want to help you; I don't want to talk to you. You killed my boyfriend."

Again I tried to reason with her, saying, "Sheeva, I can understand your anger. What happened was horrible and should never have occurred."

Then Sheeva said with a faced streaked with tears and a voice breaking from emotions, "You're so right, Ms. Special Agent, whatever your name is. It should have never happened, but it did. Do you know that Britney Spears's sister Jamie Lee got pregnant at sixteen and her boyfriend was nineteen, but nothing happened to him because she's a celebrity, but I'm not, so my boyfriend gets arrested, ass-raped, and beaten to death in one of your fucking prisons for nothing." Sheeva's bravado faltered and she succumbed to her emotions. Her emotions were real; her body shook uncontrollably with her sobs, and she pulled a pillow to her face to stifle them.

I said to her quietly, "There is nothing I can say that will make it better. A terrible mistake was made, and our entire country is suffering because of it." My heart was telling me to reach out and hold Sheeva, but the FBI agent part of me told me not to. Sheeva looked like a small child hiding behind a pillow and her anguished sobs tore away at that place in me that kept my emotions in check.

In a voice choked with emotions, Sheeva said, "I loved him. Do you under-

stand that? His death is like a huge weight dropped on me, and I can't breathe. Since Frank told me Jason was killed, my whole world has been turned upside down, Ms. Special Agent Lady. My head has been spinning, my heart pounding, and I swear I feel him around me, whispering to me." She broke down in tears again, and her voice broke as she again pushed her face into a pillow to stifle her sobs. She looked at me with all this anger and said, "Now you want to talk to me? Isn't it just a little late?"

Suddenly someone was knocking lightly on Sheeva's door, interrupting our confrontation. I heard the handle of the locked door jiggling and the unmistakable voice of a very young girl asking Sheeva, "Why are you crying? Didn't Santa bring you anything? Do you want a present?"

I saw Sheeva try to get control of herself. She bit her lip and wiped her nose with the back of her hand. From some place deep within her, she gathered the strength to answer the child. "I'm okay, sweetie, I have presents. Thank you for caring though."

Then the little girl asked, "But why are you crying?"

Sheeva didn't reply, but just sat there trying to maintain control of her emotions and her voice.

The little girl didn't go away and continued, "Are you sad?"

"Yes, I am, but I will be okay. You have a merry Christmas, and don't worry about me," Sheeva replied in a controlled voice.

"Okay, merry Christmas," the little girl cheerily responded. Then a small

handmade card appeared under the door. It showed a child's drawing of a Christmas tree with two stick figures next to it holding hands. Mother and daughter—or maybe it was Sheeva and the little girl. Scrawled across it were the words "Merry Christmas, Sheeva." I heard the little girl's footsteps fade away, and I glanced at Sheeva as she sat on her bed looking completely defeated.

I was totally choked with emotions, my voice of authority transformed into that of a grieved mother talking to a suffering daughter, "Sheeva, please listen to me. I want to make things better for you. I really do. I'm so sorry about what happened to you, to Jason, to everyone. I promise you, we are going to investigate and punish those who were responsible for what happened to Jason, but I do need your help now. Was your father responsible for these attacks on Christmas morning?"

I could hear the trepidation in Sheeva's voice as she replied, "Before I tell you anything, I want a lawyer who will help me make sure what happened to Jason will not be forgotten. So get me a lawyer."

I told her, "Sheeva, you are not charged with anything. We don't provide lawyers to people who are only witnesses. We believe this is what Jason came to tell us about on the twenty-third. Was it?"

Sheeva was still torn between anger and grief, and her eyes sparkled with tears as she glared at me and said, "I'm sure you can find me a lawyer who would want to represent me."

I realized then that I probably could find a lawyer to represent her under these very odd circumstances, so I replied in desperation, "Okay, Sheeva, I will look for a lawyer, but in the meantime, can you tell me if this was the attack that Jason was here to tell us about on the twenty-third?"

Sheeva stared at me for a long moment and in a barely audible voice finally uttered, "Yes."

I felt a great amount of anger spreading through me when her answer confirmed what I'd already suspected. I knew this horror could have been averted if common sense had been used instead of illogical policies. I smiled as best as I could under the circumstances and said, "Thank you, Sheeva. Really, thank you. Give me a minute with my associate, and then I'll be back to help you get your stuff together and get you out of here. You are not under arrest, but we feel it's best that we have you stay in a location where nothing could happen to you, someplace where you have someone guarding you."

Sheeva continued to look off into the distance and didn't respond. Her attention seemed drawn to the sprinklings of snow sticking to her window, and then she uttered, "In Chicago, Jason and I'd walk in the snow and take hundreds of pictures. They were so beautiful. He was going to be a great artist."

Chapter 56
The Attack on Indian Point Nuclear Power Plant

I was fortunate to interview Jon Van-Zile, one of the survivors of the Indian Point Nuclear Attack. The attack began at 6 a.m. Christmas morning, when a three-vehicle convoy of military vehicles displaying the insignia of the local National Guard Unit approached the main gate. It was believed that after killing the gate guards, the attackers were able to enter the plant's grounds in less than a minute. What is so shocking about the attack is its brevity and the apparent ease the attackers enjoyed as they went about destroying it. Jon's first-person account of what he experience that morning illustrates the terrible weaknesses of the plant.

> *It was early Christmas morning, about ten minutes to six, when I entered the break room. Five guys and two women were there, sipping coffee and chatting. I bought a coffee and a pastry from a vending machine and sat down at a table with another engineer I vaguely knew, and we exchanged Christmas plans. He was off for a week after his shift, heading to Colorado for a Christmas skiing vacation with his wife and son.*
>
> *Just as the six o'clock news was coming on, I excused myself and headed to the men's room. I was standing in front of the mirror and washing my hands listening to Christmas carols over the intercom when I heard a bunch of yelling and explosions. It sounded like it was coming from the break room or someplace nearby.*

I moved to the door just as a screaming woman rushed at me. Behind her, a smoking automatic weapon was aimed at her or me. I remember seeing the flashes from its muzzle. The next thing I remember was finding myself pinned down on the bathroom floor. On top of me was the body of the woman I'd seen running toward me. Some of the bullets had hit her in the face and it was now grotesquely blown apart. Pieces of bone or teeth were visible through a bloody opening where the side of her face should have been. Her hair was just a mat of blood, pieces of flesh, and I guess brain matter. She was dead and somehow or other she ended up lying on top of me. I was still dazed and not sure how hurt I was. As I absorbed what happened, I realized that the gunman might still be around to kill me next. I didn't dare move, but I did try to peer about the hallway to see if I could see anyone. My eyes darted about, but the hallway appeared empty. The scene of the shooting replayed in my mind, and I thought I remembered the gunman was wearing a uniform. Maybe it was an employee who went postal over some girlfriend or something. Suddenly I recalled the sound of the gunshots before she was shot, and fear gripped me that he might have killed others. If that was true, I had to find out what was happening and find a safe place to hide.

My arms and legs seemed okay, and I gingerly pushed her body off me while I looked all around for anyone with a gun. I heard other shots and yelling, but it was coming from a distance. I reached up to my face, and when I pulled my hands away, they were covered with blood, pieces of flesh, and slimy gray stuff. I hoped this was from the woman and that I hadn't also been shot. I listened for a couple more minutes and then attempted to get up. I realized then that my head was feeling very odd. I pushed the woman's body out of the doorway and into the hall, and then closed the bathroom door. I went to the bathroom's mirror. What I saw made me feel faint. There was a hole in my face where a bullet had ripped open my cheek, and blood was trickling down my face. Some of my teeth were missing, and part of my gum was gone. The back of my head was all matted with blood. I reached up to see if I had a bullet wound, but all I could feel was my blood-soaked hair. I didn't feel any hole, but there was a large bump on the back of my head that was bleeding. I soaked up the blood with a paper towel, but when I reached back again there was fresh blood. Then reality hit me, and I realized that I better worry more about staying alive than how hurt I was. I could still hear gunshots and large explosions and some very loud bangs. I folded up some paper towels, stuck them in my mouth, and bit down on the paper wad to stop the bleeding. While I was doing that, the plant's warning siren sounded with its wailing sound. Its loudness made my head throb even more.

I realized there was nowhere to hide in the bathroom. I reluctantly moved to the door and opened it just enough to peer out. The hallway was empty, and I thought if I could get to the break room's kitchen, it might provide me a place to hide. I needed a cabinet or closet or someplace I could hide until help came. I walked silently down the hall, leaving the body of the woman on the floor. As I reached the break room, the smell of smoke hit me. When I peeked into the break room, I was shocked to see that all the people I'd been sitting with were sprawled all over the floor, tables, and chairs with puddles of blood surrounding them. In fact, the blood was everywhere, one wall displayed large circles of splattered blood that glistened in the dim light. I stood there in utter shock viewing the tangle of bodies, the sprays of blood trickling down the white wall, and a plume of smoke spreading across the ceiling.

I tore my eyes away from the gore and saw that a couch and a couple of chairs were burning and their flames were leaping toward the ceiling. The room was filling with smoke that hovered beneath the ceiling.

My first thought was that I should try to extinguish the fires, but I quickly discovered there was no sprinkler system or even a fire extinguisher in the break room, so my focus returned to hiding from this carnage. From the gunshots and people yelling outside, I figured the gunman had left the building. I moved to a window, glanced out, and saw workers running everywhere. They were trying to escape three men on a four-wheeler who were systematically shooting holes in pipes, generators, and people. Steam poured out of punctured pipes. From one large pipe, water gushed, creating a pool of water that steamed in the cold air as it spread across the frozen ground. The lights blinked on and off as one of the men riding the four-wheeler fired what looked like a fifty-caliber rifle at one of our large backup diesel generators. The generator shuddered to a stop as smoke poured out of its cooling fins.

The siren kept up its incessant warbling, and all of a sudden I realized that this wasn't someone going postal, but an actual attack on the power plant. It was then that I realized I had to also worry about radiation exposure. My fear of being shot grew stronger with the realization that these people were here to destroy the plant and probably kill all of us. I began to wonder what would kill me first, a bullet or radiation.

The smoke had become so thick in the break room that I had to leave or be asphyxiated. Every time I coughed, bloody spittle sprayed from my mouth. In fact, breathing was almost an impossibility with the wadded paper towel in my mouth. I wanted to remove the blood-soaked paper towel, but I felt it lessened the bleeding from my torn-up mouth. Pain had set in, and it felt like how your jaw feels after you have had a wisdom tooth extracted and you forget to take your pain medicine. My swollen tongue probed the area where my teeth and gum had been pulverized. My tongue could feel the shredded pieces of flesh that was once my gum and even the sharp bone fragments that protruded out of it. I hadn't tried to speak out loud, but when I caught myself swearing out loud, I found my speech was just a weak garble.

I moved into the hallway outside the break room, which also had smoke drifting about. The air seemed a bit easier to breath and didn't burn my eyes as bad. I'd torn off a piece of my blood soaked shirt and tied it around my face in a feeble attempt to filter out some of the smoke. I had to get down on my knees to really see and find air that was breathable. As I crawled along the corridor, the smoke above me looked like an evil, undulating black cloud.

I could see the control room area and hastily crawled to it. About ten feet from it, I saw an entire section of bulletproof glass just dangling in its frame like some jeweled-encrusted fabric.

I could see flames flickering inside the control room. I crawled a few more feet and glanced through an unbroken pane of glass. Inside the large control room, bodies laid everywhere. Much of the equipment was on fire and the room was in shambles. Consoles were smashed, and bullets and shrapnel holes were everywhere.

I realized I had to get out of the building. Between the smoke and my aching jaw, it was very hard to breath. When I coughed, it felt like my head was about to explode. I worried that my coughing would cause an aneurysm.

Another problem I encountered was that my knees and the palms of my hands were bleeding from the broken glass that covered the control room's floor.

I was crawling toward the building's exit when suddenly all the lights went off. The whirl of turbines, generators, and other plant sounds went silent. The only noise I could hear were the crackling of the fires and a few explosions and shots from outside the building.

As my eyes adjusted to the darkness, I recognized a reddish glowing rectangular shape thirty feet or so in front of me. It was the building's main entrance. The fires burning outside had created a wavering glow visible in the doorway. As I crawled beneath the ever-present cloud of smoke, trying to catch my breath, the glowing rectangle became larger and more pronounced. It was straight ahead of me, but every inch was more and more painful. Every movement caused pain to shoot through my body. My knees and hands were lacerated and bleeding. Broken pieces of glass were embedded in both knees and in the palms of my hands. Crawling on them was so intensely painful that my leg muscles convulsed as I inched forward, gasping and dribbling bloody spittle. I tried calling out for help again, but the only noise I could make was a whispery, wheezing sound. My voice was gone.

Somehow I kept going, and between coughing spells and searing pain shooting through my head, I finally reached the door and thanked God it was open. I crawled over the threshold and tried to stand up, but the effort was so excruciating that I collapsed back to the floor and almost passed out.

I felt a little bit safer because I could hear the distinct sounds of police sirens and ambulances. But along with the sirens were the sounds of gunshots. The shots sounded like they were off in the distance.

I tried again to stand, and this time I staggered to my feet successfully. I took my first step into the cold Christmas morning air and steadied myself once more. I was still gasping for air as flecks of snow lit onto my face, and the cold reminded me that I was alive. The shock of all the dead people I'd seen hit me, and I was overwhelmed with emotions. Why was this happening? How did it happen? Why didn't the guards stop these murderers? My God, this is Christmas...what a horrible day for this to happen. I cried silently. I felt so bad that I'd been unable to help any of those who had been shot and died, probably not even knowing why they were being killed.

In the dim light from the glow of the fires, I looked at my hands and saw a few shards of glass protruding from my mangled skin. It was painful, but I thanked God that I was still alive. Bleeding, yet alive!

It was still dark out. It was probably 6:15 or so Christmas morning. I looked around for anyone moving. The plant was lit up from the numerous fires. I noticed that none of the yard lights were on. The electricity had been off now for about five or six minutes or maybe longer. It appeared the killers had destroyed all of the backup generators.

The thousands of gallons of diesel fuel intended for the generators had been spilled onto the ground and set on fire. The fire burned furiously with lots of black smoke.

Over all the noise of the burning, alarms going off, gunshots every few seconds, and the occasional explosion, I heard a crackling voice coming from a bullhorn saying, "Evacuate the plant, all employees are ordered to evacuate the plant immediately." This was the first voice I'd heard since this horror had started.

I listen intently to the voice and watched others moving toward it. After I staggered to the corner of the building I'd just exited, I saw a person in the dim glow of the fires. He appeared to be one of our own local National Guard members. I clearly saw the distinct unit patch on his sleeve. It was a unit I'd once belonged to. Tears of relief filled my eyes as I stared at him. He raised the bullhorn again and barked out, "All employees are ordered to immediately evacuate the plant." As two employees approached the guard, he told them to put their hands on top of their heads and join the other employees, who were patiently waiting to be evacuated.

I slowly hobbled over to a building, closer to where I could hear the employees frantically talking among themselves about the attack. One woman standing in the line was crying in relief and thanking Jesus for saving her. A soldier wearing a National Guard uniform and a face mask stood guard over them. The sight of the National Guardsmen made me feel so relieved. I actually shook with relief. Someone was actually here to save us. I tried to cry out for them to help me, but my voice just wouldn't work. Just a small hissing noise came out. Another guard walked over to the group and joined his partner. I was in great pain and feeling terribly weak. To make things worse, I discovered that I could hardly pick up my arm to even wave to the guards to get their attention.

I looked over at the employees waiting to be evacuated, trying to figure how to get their attention, when suddenly the two guards started spraying bullets all over the people standing in the line. A couple employees tried to sprint away, but were shot in the back. I watch the men and women who had been standing with their hands on their heads crumpled to the ground. Some wiggled a bit, and then one of the men in the National Guard uniforms went over and shot them again.

I was stunned at what I'd just witnessed. I felt terrified and so sick that I was sure I'd vomit and they would see me and kill me. But then something wonderful happened. The man with the bullhorn suddenly pitched forward and tumbled to the ground. He struggled to get up, but his head suddenly exploded and his body fell. I think I remembered one of the other men who shot our employees being hit in the head and collapsing, but that might just have been wishful thinking.

It was still too dark and too much was going on for me to really be sure what had happened, but like I said, I think someone shot the bastard. That's all I remembered because I apparently passed out. With my blood-matted hair, a bullet hole in my face, and hands covered in blood, I assume I looked dead enough that no one felt it necessary to shoot me again.

Then, like waking from a nightmare, I opened my eyes and found two medics in hazmat suits hovering over me. I was in an ambulance strapped to a gur-

ney speeding away from the carnage. One medic told me I was one of the lucky ones that some state police heroes discovered when they entered the plant's grounds to end the carnage.

The ordeal seemed like an eternity, but my medical records showed that I was picked up by the ambulance only thirty-seven minutes after six o'clock Christmas morning. It astounded me that, in just minutes, a small group of jihadists had destroyed Indian Point Nuclear Power Plant and caused a million or more people to lose their homes and livelihood. What had happen was very sad, and it reminded me of a phrase I'd read from a book that stated reality is the final arbiter of arguments, proving the impossible possible and often very inconvenient.

Chapter 57
The Evening News

By eight o'clock Christmas day, it was even more obvious that things were still in a tremendous turmoil that had no end in sight. All the Christmas day football games had been canceled. Thousands of movie theatres were closed across the nation. People were requested to stay home, unless they were needed for emergency assistance or security. Because airports were closed, military personnel on leave found it difficult to return to their units.

TV stations reported disturbing body counts of people who had been killed at hospitals and churches across the country. These Christmas day death counts were accompanied by horrifying scenes of burning buildings and people weeping as they watched firemen and police carry out body bags of the dead. In some scenes, people appeared to be holding candlelight vigils. The broadcasts were punctuated with sound bites from people struggling through these horrors. While a clip of a smoking hulk of a hospital wavered on the screen, a young man holding his crying wife said, "Our baby was in there when the bomb went off. We don't know if she is alive or not, or if any of the babies in the nursery survived. They won't tell us anything."

There was a flickering picture of fires burning brightly at the Indian Point Nuclear Plant, with a soot-covered police officer emotionally exclaiming, "We got officers down, but you can't get near them unless you want to die. I hope people are praying for our men, because they need a miracle."

I switched to another channel and watched a sad but captivating first-person account of a guard who escaped from the Waterford 3 Nuclear Power Plant. It gave a snapshot of the chaos that workers at the plant encountered.

Samuel Boudreaux, a resident of Killona, Louisiana, had worked at the plant as a guard for the last six years. He told his story to Diane Wolfe, a reporter on the Taft, Louisiana, Live at Five news show:

> *Well, I was just walking out to the parking lot when I heard what I thought was a car crash. I turned around and saw that a truck had smashed through our perimeter fence and had been stopped by these big concrete barricades that surround our perimeter, but suddenly a ramp dropped from the rear of the truck and four wheelers came racing out of the back, right over the top of the barricades. I think there were probably four of these four-wheelers and a couple or more men on each. It happened so fast that I can't really say for sure.*
>
> *One of them raced toward me, or at least that was what I thought, but they were really going to the parking lot. Another one raced to this big pylon out in front of our compound, and a guy hopped off the four-wheeler and slapped something on two of its legs. The guy hopped back on the four-wheeler and raced away. This all happened in less than a minute. I mean less than a minute from when the truck smashed into the fence. Apparently the packages he strapped to the pylon were bombs, because a few seconds later there were two huge explosions, and the pylon started to collapse. The wires snapped, and electricity kept*

arcing from the snapped wires even as the pylon fell to the ground.

Suddenly I found myself on the ground, and I had blood all over my hands. I realized I'd been shot. Blood was all over my shirt, and I was trying to figure out where I was hit. One of the four-wheelers raced by me and a couple more shots were fired at me, but they missed, at least I thought they had. My head was facing the parking lot, and I watched them race through the center of it spraying gas or something on the ground and cars. As they raced out, they lit it on fire. Fire raced back and forth through the parking lot as cars started to burn. It was a complete inferno. I tried to pretend I was dead as the same guys raced by me again, heading further into the plant.

I heard more shots, and I saw employees running for the gate. A few of them were being helped by others so I guess they also had been shot or hurt somehow. A whole series of explosions started then. I think they were blowing up our backup generators and storage tanks where we stored our diesel. It seemed flames and smoke were everywhere now. We had cars burning, and clouds of black smoke filled the sky from the burning diesel fuel. Fuel tanks in the parking lot were exploding, spraying flaming gas everywhere. Some of the four-wheelers were driven by people wearing hazmat suits. At first I wasn't sure if they were our guys or not, but as soon as they started shooting holes into pipes and machinery, it was obvious who they were. Employees were still running around trying to escape, and anyone who ran near these guys were just shot down. They seemed to know where everything was and just raced here and there blowing things up and shooting anyone in their way.

I tried to get up, but I could not use my left arm at all. As I struggled to get up, a friend of mine, Matt Verde, saw me. He was a guard also and he ran over to help me. He got me up, and that was when I realized I'd been shot also in the leg. I'd never felt either of the bullets hit me, that was how hyped up I was. I was bleeding profusely from the leg wound and that worried me. I definitely was wondering how much blood I could lose before I was dead.

My friend Matt...he was a damn hero because he helped me all the way to the guard shack. As we got close to it, I saw two of my best friends lying on the ground dead. I was stunned, probably in shock, and all this time more explosions rocked the plant. I could hear police sirens in the distance, and me and Matt just kept hobbling toward River Road. My heart felt like it was smashing through my chest, it was beating so hard. I expected to feel another bullet come ripping through my back any second as we hobbled along.

A police car slid to a stop in front of us, and we started toward it just as two police officers jumped out and pointed pistols at us. They told us to stop and raise our hands. I couldn't move my left arm so I just smiled at them and said we are the good guys as Matt eased me back on to the ground.

Diane Wolfe thanked Samuel Boudreaux profusely for his story and the bravery he displayed in the deadly situation. She added that fourteen people had been grabbed as hostages by the terrorists, complicating any quick rescue or takeover of the plant by the first responders to the scene. The responding police, one with only eight months on the job and the other with only a month, lacked hazmat suits so they were unable to enter the site because radiation levels were already elevated enough to trigger alarms around the plant.

Chapter 58
The Talking Heads

In between news reports of America's nuclear tragedy, the TV stations would interview various so-called experts to provide a better understanding of what was happening, how it came about, and what the future might hold for the US. One such expert was Dr. Philip Hart, a nuclear physicist from Canada.

He was interviewed by Kenna Olson at a Boston Fox affiliate's station:

> **Kenna:** *Dr. Hart, I have read so much of your work, and we are so glad that we were able to get you to appear on our show. We hope your expertise can help our viewers understand this nuclear tragedy better. The first question, I think, that's on everyone's mind is how on earth did these monstrous, well-guarded sites get overwhelmed by these terrorists?*
>
> **Dr. Hart:** *Kenna, you're so sweet! I want to tell you it's always a pleasure and an honor to be on your show. I always look forward to our exchanges, and I hope this one will be the best yet and answer the questions that are bothering your viewers about this terrible nuclear nightmare.*
>
> *How did the terrorists do it, you ask? Well, they were committed teams of well-trained commandos willing to die for their cause. We, on the other hand, had security forces staffed with underpaid, undertrained, poorly armed, and uncommitted men who really had no business protecting such highly dangerous facilities. My God, these terrorists were like military units with no rules of engagement*

fighting a rag-tag group of men burdened by bureaucratic rules and the fear of a lawsuit if they are wrong. While our guys pondered, "Oh God, should I shoot?" they were mowed down by the bad guys, who never even gave killing the guards a thought.

In battle, a split second of hesitation will get you killed. Killing someone is hard for those who have grown up respecting and fearing the law. Another major advantage these terrorist teams have is their high degree of camaraderie. These guys want to show off to each other, they don't want their comrades to see them as cowards or soft on the enemy. Running in packs seems to make men more savage and deadlier than men standing alone. A battle-hardened soldier once told me that, to him, death is preferable to being labeled a coward by his comrades.

Kenna: *Dr. Hart, are you saying they are simply more gung-ho than the plant's guards?*

Dr. Hart: *Well, partially yes, but of course it's a lot more than just that. These guys were well-trained and knew the plant layouts and what to destroy or disable to create a nuclear catastrophe. They knew where the hazmat suits were stored, and police and military reported that the terrorists donned them right after they shot their way into the plants. Wearing hazmat suits made it virtually impossible to know if an individual was a terrorist or a plant worker. Then these guys went about destroying transformers, cooling systems, generators, electrical control panels, critical pipes, and even the control rooms. They caused a "conventional" re-*

actor accident just by destroying the plant's safety systems.

Kenna: *Could you tell us where you think they found these kinds of people who were smart enough to carry out such sophisticated attacks?*

Dr. Hart: *Well, Kenna, thousands of people in this big world have the knowledge to conduct such an attack. Security at nuclear power plants has never been strong enough to withstand a determined attack. Security has sort of been a joke at these installations. I would call it more show than substance. For example, nuclear power plants conduct these mock terrorist attacks to test their ability to withstand the real thing. Now we are talking about a test that pits about five aggressors against the plant's entire security force. And what do you know? The bad guys win about half of the time. That should have been a big red flag to the NRC, but apparently it wasn't, and now we are faced with a total nuclear catastrophe.*

There is an old Hindu proverb that says, "When an elephant is in trouble even a frog will kick him." Well, right now the NRC is the big elephant, and I'm the frog wanting to kick the hell out of him. What the NRC claimed was improbable has become a nightmarish reality, with lots of people dead and dying. These nuclear disasters should never have happened. The blame lies not just with the terrorists, but with a lot of government officials and people in management who didn't do their jobs to ensure that those plants were safe.

Kenna: *So you feel this is something that the NRC should have realized and should be held accountable for?*

Dr. Hart: *My God, Kenna, if a major league football team was defeated by a five-man squad half of the time, you would fire the coach and replace the players. But that's not what the NRC does. They let these security companies repeat their failed test until they finally pass. Once the plant's guards defeat the bad guys' team, they become exempt from further force-on-force tests for three years. The mock attacks aren't even anywhere near real. The bad guys are burdened with rules of engagement. They cannot hurt anyone, damage property, must attack between 8 a.m. and 5 p.m., and cannot interfere with the plant's operation. Boy, that sure sounds like a realistic test. Oh, did I forget to mention that the nuclear power plants still failed half of these sham tests? Hell yes, these NRC people are culpable for this disaster and should pay a big price for their failure to do the job they were paid for.*

Kenna: *You sound very angry about this.*

Dr. Hart: *That's because I am. This Christmas morning attack has been anticipated and feared for years by our intelligence services. Nuclear power plants were considered a prime target by the 9/11 attackers, and plans for attacks on nuclear power facilities were found in documents left behind by Osama bin Laden as he was chased out of the Tora Bora mountains in Afghanistan. As they say, you don't need to be a nuclear phys-*

icist to figure this one out. No pun intended.

Kenna: *How much truth is in these pronouncements that these nuclear power plant disasters will exceed all other previous nuclear disasters?*

Dr. Hart: *Good question! To start with, we have to understand that an out-of-control, radiation-spewing nuclear power plant doesn't kill in the same fashion as a nuclear bomb. A nuclear bomb has a cataclysmic explosion that creates tremendous heat, tornado-force winds, and an initial blast of radiation, but after its huge mushroom cloud of radioactive debris settles, the deadly emissions quickly subside. A rampant nuclear power plant, however, contains tons and tons of radioactive material that will continue to spew radiation into the atmosphere for years if the scientific community cannot find a way to stop it.*

Kenna: *That's hard to believe that an out-of-control nuclear power plant can be more deadly than a nuclear bomb.*

Dr. Hart: *Unfortunately, that is what most of the scientific community believes we are faced with. The sites the terrorists attacked had large stockpiles of fuel rods stored in pools. In fact, these plants had stored far more rods in their pools than what they had been designed for. These terrorists targeted these pools because they knew how deadly their contents would be if they could cause the pools to ignite. They cut off water to them and used explosives to decrease the coolant and damage the rods so they heated up quicker and boiled the remaining water away. Once these fuel rods heat up or* *are on fire, they release a tremendous amount of radioactivity.*

No one knows for sure yet, but it's also believed that the terrorists used military ordinance to blow holes in the containment buildings. As I'm sure all viewers are aware, these power plants are currently impossible to enter by humans. The nuclear reactor and the pools lack any type of functional cooling systems, so they are continually spewing untold amounts of radioactivity into the atmosphere.

A sabotaged nuclear power plant is like a monstrous dirty bomb contaminating miles and miles of surrounding land and making it uninhabitable. Many more people will die from these nuclear disasters, but gratefully less than if it had been a nuclear bomb.

Kenna: *How long will it be before the people who were evacuated can come back to their homes and businesses?*

Dr. Hart: *This nuclear disaster is not like Three Mile Island. It's a far worse scenario. All three of these incidents are level seven incidents on the International Nuclear Event Scale, or INES as it's called. Unfortunately, very few of the evacuees will ever be returning to their homes. Draw a circle twenty miles out around these power plants, and it will give you a fairly good idea of what is contaminated. This contaminated area will be unusable for probably twenty or more years to come. The contamination will be so severe that even entering these zones would be virtually impossible. Millions of people will lose their homes and businesses from this catastrophic attack. This* *attack is going to cost our country trillions of dollars.*

Kenna: *Which area is doing the worse, New York, New Orleans, or San Diego?*

Dr. Hart: *Well, if you're asking which place has the biggest crisis, I guess I would have to say the Indian Point Nuclear Power Plant because it's snowing there, which prevents the radioactive steam and dust from disbursing. It simply flies up into the air and is then swept away toward Manhattan. New Orleans isn't much better, but the radioactive clouds spewing up from the crippled San Onofre power plant are at least blowing out to sea. That's something we all should be grateful for.*

Chapter 59
Sheeva's Letter to Jason

All day Christmas, Elizabeth and I stayed perched in front of the television. Like the rest of the world, we immersed ourselves in the catastrophes caused by the Christmas Special attacks. We didn't leave the house, even to set out the garbage or shovel the snow off our walk. We just couldn't pull ourselves away from the constant specials and on-site reporting of the tragic events. There were a staggering number of news outlets providing different narratives and international perspectives of what the attacks would mean to the world.

One thing that was already obvious was that these sixty or so stateless terrorists had succeeded in changing our way of life. In California, for example, their attacks had resulted in the evacuation of the entire Camp Pendleton US Marine base because of its proximity to the San Onofre Nuclear Power Plant. The marine base had fallen into what was called a "high radiation zone," which allowed only personnel performing critical tasks to remain in the area.

The nightmarish nature of a radiological attack created fear in millions of residents living near the nuclear power plants. The fear resulted in a chaotic evacuation of epic proportions, as compared to the more orderly evacuations by citizens from hurricanes or floods. Those trying to evacuate feared not only the invisible, tasteless rays that could possibly kill them, but also the authorities who might hinder their escape to safety. They even feared other evacuees, who might further contaminate them. Civility was lost in the panic to escape, cars ran out of gas, and few people were willing to help stranded families. Closed stores along the evacuation routes were broken into by people looking for bottled water and food, while others saw it as a perfect opportunity to steal anything they could grab, even deep within the evacuation zones.

The fear and chaos caused by the attacks tainted Christmas even more by causing dozens of murders by individuals who so feared radiation poison that they killed others to save themselves.

I think I kept watching the television and listening to the radio, hoping that somehow, something great would happen that would wipe out the horrors of the day, but of course that didn't happen.

Elizabeth and I had basically forgotten about what we would traditionally be doing on Christmas. Beneath our Christmas tree, piles of beautifully wrapped presents remained unopened. We felt guilty just thinking about opening one of them while so many people were fleeing their homes or worse, mourning their dead. Instead of celebrating, Elizabeth and I just stayed glued to the television until sometime around three the following morning when I finally fell asleep.

While I slept, an Air Force C-20B twelve-seater Gulfstream III was landing in Davis-Monthan Air Force Base in Tucson, Arizona, with Sheeva Hanson on board. She had been spirited away from the Beaumont homeless shelter by FBI agent Felicia Burke and two US Marshals. Her new home would be a safe house located deep within the Davis-Monthan Air Force Base.

On Sheeva's flight from Beaumont, Texas, to Arizona, she had been given no access to the news, and Special Agent Felicia Burke had chosen not to tell her about the death of Jason's brother Frank. Felicia thought Sheeva was too distraught to handle this additional piece of bad news. The following excerpts are from a letter Sheeva wrote to Jason. They tell much about her mental state the first night at her new home.

Sweetheart,

Jason, as I write this tonight, I struggle with the words to express myself to you. I just can't believe you're really gone. I hope you're somewhere still close. Someplace out there where you can see me and hear me. I don't know how all this works when someone dies; if they just disappear into nothing and leave their loved ones behind, or do they stay a while to help with the grief? Are you there to kiss away my tears? I'm so cold. Even now on this cold December day you would be all I need to warm my soul, my heart, and my body. I am sure I wouldn't even notice the cold if you were still with me. I'd just notice you.

I wish I had my mother now. I hope you meet her. I'm begging Allah to grant you entrance to paradise. All of the flight from Texas to here, I prayed for you to be welcomed by Allah. Jason, I miss you so much. I need your shoulder to lean on and for you to listen to all my stupid problems again. I know you can't really be here for me this time so don't be sad that you can't. You were so wonderful to me and I pray to Allah that he will reunite us once again.

Jason, thank you for being there when no one else was. I'm so sorry that my family caused you this terrible thing, or maybe I should see it as something good where Allah has freed you from the evil that's here on earth. Baby, I just want you to know how happy I was to have you in my life and I thank Allah for bringing us together. Thank you for the love and the joy you brought me. You've changed my life so much, and you will live with me forever in my heart.

You were the one who made my heart beat with excitement just being near you. Your handsome face still glows within my mind with those beautiful eyes and sexy smile. Do you know that my feelings for you were so strong that I didn't even have to see or hear you come into the room; I would just feel it. I felt it someplace deep within me. Your kisses made me melt, but as only Allah knew, it took but a single glance from you to make me weak in the knees. Do you know that I would often entertain myself by stealing glances at you just to take in your face? I love you so much, Jason. Every touch, every word, every glance, or smile from you captivated me. I couldn't get enough of you, Jason Wilgers.

You taught me so much...how to handle life, how to solve my problems, and to face them without any fear, but now that you're gone I'm afraid once more. I'm sorry and ashamed to tell you that, but I am.

I'm sure I will think and dream about you every day. It's odd how my days are now a living nightmare, but my sleep fills me with wonderful dreams about you and me together. Sometimes in my dreams, I see you looking at a virgin in paradise and then the dream turns into a nightmare as my jealousy flares up. I get very agitated when I think about you making love to anyone else, even a virgin in paradise. My emotions get the best of me when I think about things like that. Things I shouldn't even think about anymore.

When they first told me what had happened to you, my stomach churned like I was seasick. It's so odd that our emotions can make our entire body ache and get sick. It was like being hit with a ton of bricks, as you often would say, and then my crying wouldn't let me stop to catch my breath. It's a physical reaction as well as emotional. It rocks me inside and out, and it hurts terribly. I wonder when these feeling will go away. How much time will have to pass before the pain subsides? I can't remember ever a time when I felt as sad as I do for losing you, Jason.

I guess in some ways you don't belong to me anymore. You belong to Allah. He's the one you smile upon now. He is who your heart glows with love for and I'm okay with that. I just want you to be happy, even if that happiness isn't with me. A part of your life force will stay within my heart till the day we are once more as one. Because that's what true love really is.

No words can describe all the feelings I have swirling around in my mind and heart for you, but those three words, "Ana b'hebbak," or "I love you," I guess say it as best as humanly possible for the emotions that consumes me.

Jason, I finally feel like I can sleep for a while, but I will write to you again tomorrow my love. Remember, Ana b'hebbak.

Chapter 60
The Day After the Christmas Special

The day after Christmas, gifts still sat untouched under millions of Christmas trees. The news was reporting that the president had ordered army troops to take up positions around all nuclear power plants in anticipation of other terrorist attacks. Civilian airports were taken over by the military. All private planes were grounded. All National Guard units were mobilized, as were all university ROTC units and even those from high schools.

The morning after the attacks, the threads of disbelief were still tightly woven into the fabric of society's consciousness. It was obvious that mornings were going to be like awakening from a horrible recurring nightmare for some time to come. The type of nightmare that should disappear as soon as you sit up and turn on the lights, but this nightmare would persist in all states of consciousness. The aftermath of the Christmas Special permeated our conscious and subconscious thoughts for days. The terror was not just from what had happened, but how much more was still to come. There was no escape from the event and its aftermath; talk shows focused on its every minute detail, and friends, workers, acquaintances constantly gossiped and bickered over every nuance of the attacks. It repeated in the brain until it felt like there was no room for anything else.

People were afraid to close their eyes and sleep, and when sleep came, many were bothered by screams and scenes echoing in their minds from the images that flashed all day across the TV screen or lurked in their minds from their own dark experiences on the morning of the Christmas Special.

Now, suddenly the war on terrorism was being fought right here on American soil, right on our front porch. No further attacks happened after Christmas, but people could feel an evil presence. It was an almost palpable presence, waiting like a patient vulture until its carrion became unguarded so it could swoop back down for more.

Even on the second day after the attack, it was impossible to understand much of what the attack would mean to the safety and everyday life of America. This was not an attack for which we could seek revenge on some country and destroy our enemy. We could not even declare a war against those responsible, because this was a stateless enemy who lived in shadows and killed itself as a part of its mission to gain passage to the promised land where eighty thousand servants and seventy-two wives awaited in a dome of pearls, aquamarine, and ruby.

The day following the Christmas morning attacks, TV channels reported the aftermath without pause. CNN covered the exodus of people fleeing the New York area. I re-watched a CNN news clip dated December 26. It was a film taken from a helicopter hovering above Westchester County, with reporter Merl Whitney trying to describe the horrible scene below: "All you can see are cars bumper to bumper on the roads leading away from Westchester. It's an unbelievable sight, there are cars abandoned everywhere. Cars still operating are trying to find ways around the stalled cars. Numerous cars appear to be stuck in the snowdrifts running adjacent to these roads. Many cars have run out of gas because all gas stations are closed in this area. The long lines of cars appear to be totally stopped. To add to the horror, local officials are reporting that people have actually frozen to death in some of the stalled cars. Many sick and elderly have succumbed to the added complications of acute radiation sickness and have died in their vehicles while attempting to flee the area.

"Some experts have estimated that more than three hundred thousand people are attempting to flee Westchester County. As you can see below, helicopters are attempting to evacuate the Hudson Valley Hospital Center, which has been running on emergency power since the meltdown of the Indian Point Nuclear Power Station. They are only one of many hospitals in the area seeking assistance in evacuating their patients."

Chapter 61
Tales of the Day after the Christmas Special

It goes without saying that the Christmas Special attacks provoked a maelstrom of emotions in people across the nation. Christmas spirit and feelings of goodwill quickly morphed into fear, anger, sorrow, hopelessness, hatred, confusion, sadness, vengeance, and more. Reactions to the attacks were mixed, but for all it was a date to remember and a deed that would change America and Christmas for decades to come. It would be another infamous day where people wouldn't only remember what happened, but where they were when they first heard the horrifying news.

To give you a broader view of how America reacted, I have included numerous first-person accounts, anecdotes, and news reports that I hope will create a collage of that day of infamy. Many of the events of that day will never be known to the larger world, because the enormity of the attacks on New York, New Orleans, and San Diego became the focus of the majority of TV, radio, and newspaper reports. The attacks in towns like Bellows Falls, Vermont; Lewiston, Idaho; Springfield, Missouri; Wichita, Kansas; and many other locations were given little press, but these are the attacks that truly define the reach and scale of the Christmas Special attacks.

An excerpt from the "The Day After Edition" of the *Billings Daily Chronicle* read:

> *Yesterday, Christmas day, a terrible tragedy struck the small town of Havre in north central Mon-*

tana. Saint Joseph Hospital was bombed in what is believed to be a part of a coordinated attack launched by terrorists that targeted churches, hospitals, and nuclear power plants across the nation.

Nothing could have prepared residents of this 118-year-old town for the horror and devastation caused by this bombing. If suspicions prove true, this community of 9,621 residents is now one of the latest victims of terrorist attacks in America.

A temporary morgue has been set up to accommodate the large number of casualties that resulted from the bombing. Many families were still waiting to learn the whereabouts of their loved ones two days after this devastating attack. Sue Smart, public information officer for Havre, said that more than one hundred people are still unaccounted for. To complicate matters more, it's not clear if the twenty-six confirmed fatalities are included in the number of unaccounted. As more information is received from the coroner's office it's suspected that the death count will rise.

The Havre Coroner's Office is trying to expedite the process of identifying loved ones by bringing in forensic experts from the nearby communities of Beaver Creek and Chinook. Because of the concern for misidentification, Havre's coroner has taken extra precautions to lessen this possibility.

Spokesperson Sue Smart said, "We recognize how difficult this time is for the people of Havre and especially those who have loved ones missing since the attack, but we must take appropriate measures to assure proper identification of the deceased."

Saint Joseph Hospital was still burning Christmas evening, and the debris littered parking lot and adjacent highway offered ample evidence of the power of the initial explosion. Twenty-four miles west on US-2 in Chinook, people were reporting seeing the black smoke from the roaring blaze.

The people of the Hi-Line area, known for their compassion, have rallied around those directly affected by this unbelievable tragedy and opened their homes and wallets to help those in need. Many of those affected were invited by neighbors to join in their Christmas celebrations.

Residents had also set up a large tent outside of the coroner's office. The tent was to provide shelter for those whose infants had been patients in the bombed nursery or who had relatives in the hospital recovering from heart attacks, accidents, or other ailments, as well as the stricken relatives of staff members who are now missing.

This chilly tent has become the epicenter of Havre's tragedy. In-

side it are the heart-wrenching scenes of mothers with tear-streaked faces waiting to hear if their infants are alive or dead. Distraught wives and husbands also jammed into the tent, praying for the survival of their loved ones. One woman sat in a chair doubled over weeping and begging God to spare her eight-year-old daughter from death. The girl had been rushed to the hospital just hours before the bombing because of acute appendicitis.

When a coroner's assistant approached a man in his forties to assist in the positive identification of his wife's burnt remains, the man burst into uncontrollable sobs. This makeshift shelter of lost souls will continue to echo the moans, muffled prayers, and heart wrenching sobs of Havre's broken until the last remains of this terrible horror are identified.

Members of the community expressed outrage, shock, and dismay over this tragic event. Nancy Smith, a nurse at Saint Joseph's, was counting her blessings because she was scheduled to work Christmas morning, but because of vehicle trouble didn't arrive till after the bomb had exploded.

"If my car hadn't acted up, I could have been among the dead," Nancy said, holding back tears. "I cannot stop thinking what my children would have done or felt if I'd

been killed on Christmas morning! It's just so sad. So sad!"
Nancy's poignant remarks typify the feelings of Havre's citizens.

The front page of the *Billings Daily Chronicle* featured condolences from leaders of many countries. I include some of them:

"Our friends to the South will always stand for those that cannot stand for themselves. For that reason, they have become the target of those who oppose freedom and even life itself. We stand by you, America, and we promise that Canada will be there, by your side, as you rebuild."
—From Canada

"This heinous act is not just a problem of the United States, but a global dilemma. Israel declares this day as a day of national mourning. The whole world suffers with you."
—From Israel

The president of China sent a message to the American people offering his sincere condolences to all the victims of the attacks and their families. He pledged his country's support and stated that China stands with all Americans in shock, outrage, and concern. He also expressed his regards for the safety of all Chinese citizens visiting America.
—From China

The Russian president echoed the same. Speaking from the Kremlin, the Russian president expressed his deepest sympathy to the American people and challenged the entire international community to unite in the struggle against these barbaric acts of terrorism, which he defined as a blatant attack on the whole of mankind. He further called the incidents acts of mass insanity by individuals who have proven themselves less than human.

—From Russia

Mexico's statement read, *"You have our most profound condolences, and we stand in solidarity with the people of the United States. We reject this criminal act of terrorism. We wish to express our solidarity and our support to all the victims of these horrible acts of terrorism and to all of their family members. We reiterate our complete, emphatic rejection of all forms of terrorism."*

—From Mexico

Even the Cuban government expressed condolences, announcing, *"Our history has been long and tumultuous, but the people of Cuba stand by you in this battle against evil. We offer our medical facilities to our proud northern neighbors. This is a time to heal our wounds and unite against an evil that threatens all of civilization."*

—From Cuba

The paper contained many more expressions of condolences from our allies. These expressions demonstrated the common belief that most countries felt threatened when America was attacked by dangerous nation-less organizations. America's response could easily trigger more war and bloodshed.

Chapter 62
Church Burning

The brutal insanity of the Christmas morning attacks is no more clearly illustrated than by the sad story of a sixteen-year-old Keene, New Hampshire, girl named Rachelle. She had been walking her dog early that Christmas morning. This is Rachelle's first-person account of what happened:

> *I was walking my new dog down Maple Street early Christmas morning. I wanted to let my dog do its stuff before we got busy opening Christmas presents. It was quiet and there was still a lot of snow on the ground.*
>
> *I was close to the Calvary Church, where my older brother and my boyfriend Darnell worshipped. I wanted to see if my boyfriend and his family might be attending so I could wish them a merry Christmas. By the time I was half a block away, I knew the services had already started because I could hear the choir singing. If Darnell was there, his car wasn't so I was ready to return home. My dog Chewie was also ready. We were both freezing, and Chewie was tugging on her leash to return home.*
>
> *I turned to walk back home, and that was when I first noticed this big gray cargo truck. You know the ones with all those tires. The truck was about a block away, idling beside the road and I could see this skinny guy sitting in the cab. The guy looked like he was singing or maybe praying. His head was tipped back and his mouth was moving. Suddenly he stopped and looked out the window in my*

direction. I felt like he was looking right at me. Then the cab door flew open, and he jumped down onto the road.

He freaked me out because I thought at first he was coming after me. My dog started yelping and barking, and the man turned away from us and went to the back of the big trailer and I guess climbed up into it.

A few seconds later, I thought I could see smoke coming from the rear of the trailer. It was dark so I was not sure what was really happening. Then I saw like a glow at the rear of the trailer, and I was sure something was burning. I thought maybe I should call 911, but I was undecided. The wind blew the smell of smoke toward me so I was sure there was a fire. I started to punch in the numbers on my Droid and suddenly the skinny guy comes running up to the cab and hops back in.

He revved the engine and pulled the truck back out onto the road. By this time, smoke was really pouring out of the back of the trailer. By then I think I could also see the glow of a fire illuminating the smoke at that time. Once the truck was on the road, the guy just sat there gunning the engines. The streetlights above him were clouded by the smoke. It seemed like he revved it for a long time, and then all of a sudden the truck lurched forward and started rolling toward me. Smoke was pouring out of the trailer now. I stepped over the curb and crunched through the snow to get behind some trees. I was so scared that I was just dragging my dog over the snow by then.

The truck rumbled by me with smoke pouring out the back. The back door to the trailer was open, and I could clearly see the flames inside it. The guy was going faster and faster right toward Calvary. When the truck hit the curb in front of the church, it bounced into the air and smashed into the brick archway. The bricks went flying, but the truck kept right on moving toward the front of the church. Just then, a man opened the front doors of the church and stepped out onto the stoop. The cab of the eighteen-wheeler slammed into him and the church. The man was swept into the church as the truck punched through the door, tearing a huge hole in the front wall. The entire truck and trailer disappeared into the church. It made a horrible noise as it crashed into the building. Smoke and debris flew everywhere. I was petrified, watching it rip into the church.

I just stood there staring at this horrible scene. I could see the church lights flickering, and then they were out. Through the windows and holes in the wall you could see flames and the silhouettes of people moving. Then the snow cascaded off of the roof, making huge piles of snow on each side of the church. The piles of snow that had fallen off of the roof glowed in the flames consuming the church.

I think that was when I heard a loud noise and then the steeple tottered and collapsed onto the roof. So much was happening that I'm not sure of everything I saw, but I think a bit of the truck punched through the back of the church. What I am sure of is suddenly flames were coming from everywhere. I could hear horrible screams coming from the church, and I started to run toward it but my dog wouldn't go. Chewie was whining and barking and pulling on his leash in the opposite direction like crazy. Before I could get him to follow me, a huge explosion knocked me to the ground. It didn't hurt me, but it did blow the church apart. The concussion shook the snow from the branches of the trees around me, and I was covered in falling snow. When I looked back toward the church, the entire place was an inferno of flames and smoke. The roar of the fire was so loud now that I couldn't hear people crying. I'd never forget those screams I heard before the explosion.

I stood staring at the inferno that once was my church, trying to comprehend what had happened. I was transfixed. Realizing all the people who were probably burning alive made me feel very sick. Suddenly, I realized that my older brother Albert was probably at this service. My legs wobbled from this rush of fear and the other emotions that swept over me. I still couldn't move. My eyes were locked on the burning inferno. I fell to my knees and began praying and crying. I was still there kneeling in the snow when the fire department arrived and several firefighters ran up to the burning debris to see if there were any survivors. About the same time, a police officer headed in my direction. I think he thought I was a survivor of the bombed-out church, and I guess in some ways I am.

A report from the Keene *Chronicle* covering the church bombing stated that the explosion flung body parts of the parishioners into the evergreens surrounding the church. The Keene firefighters were called upon to assist in collecting this macabre evidence from the tree branches. The article stated that an estimated one hundred Keene citizens were killed in the explosion and fire on Maple Street. Another article on the same front page touched on the Waterford 3 Nuclear Power Plant, twenty-five miles west of New Orleans. It stated that terrorists had used M3 and M2A3 US Army shaped charges in their attack. How the terrorists obtained them was unknown, but the report emphasized that these shaped charges had the ability to smash a hole three feet to five feet deep in reinforced concrete and up to twelve inches deep in armor-plated steel.

A statement from the Keene, New Hampshire, mayor appeared under his photo. It read, "It's so important that we respect the process of notifying family members, no matter how long it takes. We must remember in these trying times that these fatalities of this horrible attack aren't just statistics or names on a list of terrorists' victims. They were fathers, mothers, brothers, sisters, neighbors, friends, and always someone's precious child. We need to make sure we do all we can to comfort and support the families whose lives are now forever changed by this callous attack on our peaceful community. We also must remember that we cannot let an attack by fanatics destroy the long-held traditions of Christmas. Let's all pray for a return to normalcy."

While researching the background of the Christmas Special, I came across this Martin Luther King Jr. quote: "The ultimate tragedy is not the oppression and cruelty by the bad people but the silence over that by the good people."

It's interesting to note that in all these previous clippings and news reports, people have been careful to avoid the use of terms such as "Islamic terrorist" or "Islamic radicals."

America's politically correct culture is constantly shrinking our vocabulary to filter out words that offend an adversary or that clearly identify an enemy. The whole process of speech policing becomes as ridiculous as the collective denial and social hypocrisy portrayed in the tale of *The Emperor's New Clothes*.

Chapter 63
Letter from Roger Wilgers to Sheeva Hasson

On the evening of December twenty-sixth, Sheeva Hasson was given a printed copy of an email that had been sent to her in care of Special Agent Felecia Burke. The letter was from Roger Wilgers. Agent Burke felt that Sheeva needed to have some contact with Jason's father to help alleviate her depression and loneliness. For the next few months, corresponding via Felicia Burke would be the only method of communication between Wilgers and Sheeva. Sheeva's letters were all read carefully to remove any clue of her new location. Her emails to Wilgers were also resent from the FBI headquarters in Washington DC to create a useless trace route for anyone intercepting the emails. A copy of Roger Wilger's first letter to Sheeva follows:

Dear Sheeva,

This is a very hard letter to write, but I felt I had to reach out to you. I never got a chance to really meet you, but of course I heard many wonderful things about you. First I just want to tell you that I have no bad feelings for you. You had no responsibility for Jason's death. It was the result of some ridiculous laws and the actions of some incompetent police that killed him. I know his death must be a horrible shock to *you after all the things you two have gone through together. I realize how much the two of you relied upon each other. You were good for Jason. He really loved you.*

I spoke to Special Agent Felicia Burke about you, and she told me how hard this has been for you. I begged her to let me talk to you, but the best she could offer was emailing letters to you through her. I hope you get this quickly because I know how badly you need someone to talk to about all that has happened. I'm so sorry that Jason is gone and that all we are left with is a terrible emptiness and thousands of memories that tear at my heart.

Sheeva, I do take some comfort in knowing that what he was trying to do when he was killed was very right and very brave. Jason chose the high ground in a very difficult moral dilemma. I'm so proud of both of you, that you saw how necessary it was to alert the world about what was about to happen.

Unfortunately, even after all you have lost and gone through, people are still going to say bad things about the two of you, so be brave. Sheeva, we will be having Jason's funeral in just a couple days, but unfortunately the US Marshals protecting you have decided that it's too risky to have you attend, and I must admit that I agree with them. I know this sounds terribly harsh, and I'm sure it makes you feel that I don't understand your grief, but it's for your own safety. The US Marshals feel there is a big possibility that people might want to do you harm if you attend the funeral. I tend to agree with them. People are crazy right now and want revenge. There have been quite a few reports of revenge killings of Muslims. Most people really don't know what you and Jason were trying to do. Until the true story gets out to the media, many will continue to believe you were part of those who attacked us.

I have another piece of bad news I need to tell you. Agent Burke won't give me your phone number, so this is the only way I can communicate with you. I hate telling you about it in a letter, but it's the only way they have left for me to communicate with you.

Sheeva, both Jason and Frank have been killed. I have lost both my sons. They are gone. I know you met Frank, Jason's brother. He was killed Christmas morning. I'm devastated by their deaths.

I will briefly tell you what happened, but Sheeva, I really hate talking about it. I had some health issues, which I think you know about. My old body, I guess, reacted to all the excitement and anger I had when Jason called me, and I started feeling dizzy. I had to go to the emergency room to see if I was okay or not. All of this made me miss my scheduled flight. It ended up where I couldn't fly into Houston until late on the twenty-fourth of December. When I arrived, Frank met me at the airport. He looked horrible and wouldn't say much. He looked like he was on the verge of crying. He told me that he had things he had to tell me, but we needed to get to some place private.

When we were both in the car, he finally told me the bad news. He told me that Jason was dead and how it happened. I just couldn't believe it. I was shocked, horrified, and angry. We both sat there stunned, and yes, I broke down and cried. Frank was beyond crying, he was crazy with anger. He loved his brother, and he could not understand how this could have happened.

Frank told me he had gone over to your trailer and found the information Jason and you left for me to take to the Culper police. He was so upset over his brother's death that he didn't take the documents to the Culper police. For whatever reason, he kept the documents to himself. Apparently, he did read Jason's translations of the documents about a possible attack at the Saint Paul Catholic Church in Beaumont. Early Christmas morning,

Frank went to that church, apparently to observe the people coming and going. From what little I have been told by police and heard on the news, he eventually saw a woman wearing a long, heavy coat and acting very suspicious. Other people on the scene also claimed she was acting very strange as she neared the church. Some of them said she looked terrified as she hurried pass them. When Frank noticed her odd behavior, he tried to approach her, but according to witnesses she resisted. She wouldn't stop. She tried to run to the entrance of the church. Before she could get there, Frank caught up with her and grabbed her. She struggled with him to break free. Witnesses claim she actually fought back and punched him a few times. Some other parishioners came over to help Frank, or maybe were just being nosey, and that was when she blew herself up. Frank and all those standing around watching her were instantly killed.

This was all going on while I was sitting in my hotel room trying to deal with Jason's death. I had the TV on with the news playing, but I never saw the news clip about the local attack. I didn't even know what had happened to Frank until I called the Beaumont police station to see if they could contact him to call me. When I told them who I was, they transferred me to his lieutenant. I immediately asked if something was wrong, and the police officer I spoke with became very evasive, but at the same time very polite. When he asked me where I was staying and told me that officers would be coming over to talk to me in person, I knew that something bad had happened. I got myself together and waited for them. Of course now you know what they came and told me.

I'm going to hire a lawyer to try to get some justice for Jason, but that will have to wait till some of this craziness settles down.

So, I'm sure you understand that I'm an emotional wreck and finding this all very hard to deal with. Somehow I will get through this and hopefully meet you. I'd like to know the lady that Jason wanted as his wife, and I'm so sorry I couldn't have been there on Thanksgiving to meet you. I know he loved you very much and said many wonderful things about you. From the pictures he had sent me, I know he saw you as the most beautiful woman in the world.

Sheeva, I'm so glad he had you in his life. I have no anger toward you so please understand that. Maybe in a month or so, I will finally be able to meet you. At least that's what Agent Burke hinted. She said, we can communicate back and forth through them until they decide how long you will be in the Witness Protection Program. I'd love to hear from you. I would love to see more pictures of you and Jason, if you still have any.

Anyway, the funeral for Frank and Jason is a couple days away. I hope you can understand why it would be difficult for you to be there under these crazy circumstances. I know this must hurt you, and I'm so sorry that it has turned out this way. I hurt terribly from all of this and really feel bad that you're not able to be at the funeral. I just can't put any more people in harm's way, in-

cluding you. This funeral has to be a time when I can lay to rest my boys without the media circus that I'm sure your appearance would bring.

I'm so sorry for all the things that are happening to you. I know you are a wonderful person, and life is so unfair sometimes. I'm going to talk to Special Agent Felicia Burke and ask that they let you and I meet, after some of this dies down, so we can visit Jason and Frank's graves together. I think it's only right that they let you say your good-byes.

Sorry to bring you such bad news. Please write back. I would really appreciate it.

With love,

Roger Wilgers

Chapter 64
Bashing the NRC

Frustration, anger, helplessness, despair, and fear replaced Christmas spirit. The media kept up its 24/7 coverage of the attacks and reported on the millions who lost their homes, belongings, and jobs. Now these evacuees joined the ranks of other unfortunates herded out of the evacuation zones into the newly created evacuation centers. Chaos, fear, and despair reigned for these families as they tried to adapt to a life with no idea of where the government would ship them next.

It was clear that few people affected had been prepared for what happened Christmas day. The attacks overwhelmed the millions affected, along with the government agencies designated to assist them. Whatever had been planned for such a situation quickly proved insufficient. The Christmas Special attacks spotlighted our government's frailty and the many shortcomings of its disaster-response plans. In emergencies where people are required to evacuate, special consideration is needed to assist the sick, elderly, poor, and disadvantaged. Unfortunately, the Christmas terrorist attacks demonstrated that our government lacked any plans for quickly responding to a dirty bomb–type contingency. To make things even worse, people forced to evacuate needed cash, but many of those who had to flee were broke because they had spent their money on celebrating Christmas or simply because it was the end of the month.

A good example of the anger that was bubbling to the surface can be seen in this transcript from the December twenty-sixth Chris Tucker's *Hot Seat* show.

Chris Tucker: *Good evening, ladies and gentleman. I'm Chris Tucker, your host for CNN's Hot Seat. Tonight I have Marty Johnson, NRC spokesperson, Mike Trahan, spokesperson for the nuclear industry, and Mary Zimmerman, author of Nuclear Power: A Disaster Waiting to Happen.*

As you all are aware, America is very angry and wants to know how and what happened that allowed terrorists to destroy three of our nuclear power plants. They want to know if the deaths and trillions of dollars in destruction caused by the Christmas Special attacks can simply be blamed on three small teams of terrorists, or does the nuclear industry, NRC, and our government share some responsibility? Mary, let's start with your perspective on this catastrophe.

Mary Zimmerman: *Wow, Chris, I'm sure you know my position on this issue, but for the sake of viewers I will say once again that the numerous security deficiencies at nuclear power plants have been known to the NRC and the nuclear industry for years. The simple fact is that existing American nuclear plants were never designed to address the issue of sabotage, and nothing has ever been done to rectify this. Back in May of twenty-ten there was an article in Nuclear Engineering International discussing this very problem. It should have been even more obvious to the NRC and security experts that what nature did to Fukushima determined terrorists could do as well. If you think about what really happened at Fukushima, it was simply that they lost power to circulate their coolant. Once that* *happened, the reactor and spent fuel pools quickly overheated, spewing radiation into the atmosphere. That's what caused the Fukushima tragedy—the inability to circulate coolant. The Christmas Special terrorists took advantage of these same vulnerabilities and simply cut the power to the sites, destroyed their backup generators and coolant pumps, shot holes in the pipes circulating coolant, and destroyed the plants' control center. They didn't need a truck bomb to do this or a 767 to crash into the plant...just basic knowledge of how the plant works and men willing to die for their cause. So as you asked, "Should the NRC and nuclear industry be held accountable for this tragedy?" Absolutely, they were terribly remiss in properly protecting the public from this type of scenario.*

Chris Tucker: *Mr. Johnson, what do you have to say about Mrs. Zimmerman's assertion?*

Marty Johnson: *First of all, what has happened to our nation is truly horrible! My heart goes out to all the people who have been displaced and lost loved ones. This Christmas day attack on our citizens sickens me to know there are people in this world capable of doing such great evil.*

In response to Ms. Zimmerman, let me say this, we are a small, understaffed, and under-budgeted government agency. We do the best we can with the resources at our disposal. Our personnel are highly motivated and caring. We did follow terrorist events and tried to harden our defenses against all potential threats. We developed a threat assessment pro-

gram that used reports from other government agencies to enhance our DBT, design basis threat. We took the latest information and created a scenario projecting the maximum threat that a nuclear plant security system would be required to protect against. After 9/11, we updated our DBT to the probability of attacks by up to eight terrorists instead of three. With the intelligence we are provided, we could have never envisioned the attack scenario that occurred at the targeted plants. It's impossible to plan for every possible contingency. If terrorists are going to attack in large numbers, like 9/11, this would constitute an enemy of the state. Therefore, the protection of nuclear power plants should be given to the Pentagon. The military would be better equipped to handle these situations.

Mike Trahan: *I concur with Marty. The FBI, CIA, and Department of Defense actively monitor terrorists and their organizations. These government agencies had far more knowledge in these matters than the nuclear industry or the NRC. But people like Mary will target the NRC and the nuclear industry because of the federal government's failure to protect us from terrorists.*

Chris Tucker: *Certainly we all recognize that low-probability events happen. In fact, they happen all the time. With highly complex technology, low-probability incidents can have disastrous results. We have so many examples of this fact, such as the space shuttle Challenger and Columbia disasters. The 9/11 terrorist attack was, unfortunately, where we discovered that heat from burning jet* *fuel can weaken a skyscraper so much that it will collapse upon itself. Certainly none of these events were envisioned. So my question is, since we know even low-probability events happen, why would anyone ever build a nuclear power plant so close to a city? Isn't that just flirting with a catastrophe? Isn't there just too much at stake, just too much that can go wrong? Marty, can you respond to this question?*

Marty Johnson: *That's a hard question to address. But one of the main reasons was back when the industry was young, companies tried to cut the cost of building nuclear power sites by building them near cities to reduce the high cost of transmission lines. The Atomic Energy Commission back in 1964 more or less agreed on an informal rule that there would be no nuclear power plant closer to a city than Indian Point was to New York. This was done after many environmental studies and input from the Atomic Energy Commission experts.*

Chris Tucker: *Mary, do you have any input?*

Mary Zimmerman: *Most certainly. These so-called experts that Marty mentioned were so intertwined with the nuclear industry that Congress abolished the agency in 1974 because of the many charges that the AEC insufficiently considered nuclear hazards such as radiation protection standards, nuclear reactor safety, power plant sighting, and environmental protection. This agency that Congress abolished was in power when the majority of our power plants were created. The AEC had a history of con-*

flicts of interest. So greed probably contributed to many of the decisions of where power plants were located. Marty didn't mention it, but the NRC replaced the AEC as the new regulatory agency.

Mike Trahan: *This is truly a sad day in American history. It's right up there with Pearl Harbor and 9/11. Were mistakes made? Yes. However, nuclear power makes up to 20 percent of our energy production. This is not something you can shut down and replace quickly. This is going to be a painful learning experience for America. However, America always rises up and shakes herself off. She will do it again, and nuclear power will be part of her future.*

Mary Zimmerman: *What a bunch of rubbish! Marty, your feel-good talk is totally out of place after this horrendous nuclear catastrophe. Sure, it's going to be a painful learning experience, and I hope that applies to you people also. It's certainly time for y'all to accept that nuclear power plants are terrorist targets. I hate to keep harping about it but drawings and documents pertaining to nuclear power plant attacks were found in caves at Tora Bora in Afghanistan. In 2002, 9/11 organizers Khalid Sheikh Mohammed and Ramzi bin al-Shibh both talked about attacking nuclear power plants. In 2003, nineteen Pakistani-born men were arrested in Canada for planning an attack on a Canadian nuclear power plant. Certainly, the NRC had access to this information. It was reported everywhere. It was on CNN, ABC, and Fox news. Yet knowing the plants were potential targets, nothing was done to address the security problems.*

The hard fact is that y'all didn't do your jobs and as a result thousands of people have died or will have long-term health problems. Then there is the evacuation fiasco. The people in the ten-mile zone were ordered to evacuate immediately, which exposed them to high levels of radiation even when it was obvious there would be total gridlock. Mass confusion and mayhem resulted due to poor planning by the NRC, and people died.

Marty Johnson: *Ms. Zimmerman, it's very easy for you to sit back and point out all this after the fact. It's no different than a Sunday night armchair quarterback saying he would have never made that bad pass or called that play. You were not in the committees, not listening to experts, not creating contingency plans or doing all of the other essential things we at the NRC are responsible for. Walk in my shoes the next time we have a nuclear emergency and you might appreciate how hard it's to make these difficult decisions.*

Mary Zimmerman: *Mr. Johnson, let's hope there is not another nuclear emergency, due to the fact the NRC has dropped the ball so many times it would take a full week to address all the incompetence and failures of the NRC. But let's spotlight one of them, the flawed distribution program for potassium iodide tablets. Why did the NRC require that potassium iodide tablets be available only for people in a ten-mile radius of a plant?*

Marty Johnson: *I'm not able to comment on this particular topic. However, I can assure the American public the NRC cares about the well-being of each* *and every American citizen and does everything possible to ensure their safety.*

Mary Zimmerman: *I think the nuclear industry has been more interested in preserving its money-makers than the people they were supposed to serve. Your industry makes billions of dollars and cuts many corners to maximize your profits. On top of that, the 2005 US energy bill provided your industry with thirteen billion dollars in subsidies. It reauthorized the Price- Anderson Act, which really is a subsidy to a failed, dangerous technology that has been uninsurable from its inception due to the tremendous inherent risk associated with nuclear power. The Price-Anderson Act denies the public any real financial protection from the gigantic healthcare costs and economic losses created by a catastrophic nuclear accident. Bend me over, nuclear industry, and stick it to me!*

Mike Trahan: *This is outrageous! To imply that the nuclear energy industry only cares about profits and not the people we serve is just not true. Your accusations serve no purpose in helping the public get this terrible attack behind them and move forward with their life.*

Marty Johnson: *Do you plan on writing a book about this, Ms. Zimmerman? How much money do you think you will make off the pain and suffering of the American people? Who is really out to make money?*

Mary Zimmerman: *Well, Mike and Marty, I actually do plan on writing a book about the failures of the NRC and the nuclear industry. I think the public needs to know why these attacks hap-*

pened so easily. For example, federal rules required that at least ten guards be on duty at all times at a nuclear power plant, which is not a lot of guards for these large installations. But the nuclear power industry felt that was just too much of a financial burden on them so they begged the NRC to help them out. The good old boys at the NRC thought, "How can we help our buddies with the nuclear power industry save their money?" And lo and behold the NRC comes up with a brilliant solution: "Let's allow our buddies to cut it back to five guards as long as they install barriers, block doors, and take other defensive measures."

Come on, how could anyone seriously believe that five guards could really protect all sides of a nuclear facility against attackers? This is really some flawed thinking. With ten guards it would be a tough job, but with only five guards you have created simply a deception of security. You just have window dressing.

I think this is where bigger is better; you know where size counts, but I know you men just won't agree on that.

Chris Tucker: *That's all the time we have tonight for CNN's Hot Seat. Thank you for being here tonight, Marty, Mike, and Mary. Goodnight America.*

Chapter 65
December Twenty-Seventh

It was two days after Christmas when the media received news from the White House that the president would soon make an important statement to the nation. The announcement didn't provide details or even hints of the topic, which led to rampant speculation. About 10:30 a.m., the question on everyone's mind was quickly answered. The president announced to a thunderous applaud that Ali Hasson had been captured and was now in US custody.

"Today, the citizens of America can rest in the knowledge that the reckoning has begun for the perpetrators of the Christmas Special attacks. This morning, the accused mastermind of the attacks was returned in shackles from London to the United States to face justice for the despicable crimes carried out on December the twenty-fifth. Hopefully, Hasson's capture and incarceration will provide some solace to the victims of the Christmas Special attacks.

The capture of Ali Hasson is a step in our journey to bring peace and closure for all who suffered from this horrible event. For many of the survivors of the attacks and for the families of the dead, Hasson's capture will do little to lessen the pain or heal the wounds, but it does help to balance the scales of justice.

Our nation can take pride that at every point from the morning of December twenty-fifth to the hour of Ali Hasson's capture, we have seen good constantly overcoming the evil that Hasson and his minions brought upon our nation. We saw this good in the rescuers who have saved and have suffered with the victims. We have witnessed it in the many communities that have honored and held close the memory of their lost loved ones. We have seen it in the dedication and resourcefulness of our FBI, police, detectives, and marshals to quickly bring those who were behind these crimes to justice.

May God, in his infinite mercy, grant peace to our nation; to all the lives that were taken by this despicable act, and to the injured that struggle to rebuild their lives."

The media went wild with the announcement, trying to break the news first or give the most accurate coverage. Investigative reporters hurriedly scanned the newswires, researched other news articles and sources to try to find all the untold details of the Ali Hasson story. The race was on as journalists worked nonstop to cover what they knew would be one of the most historic days for the United States.

The news of the capture of Ali Hasson made the front pages of all American newspapers and even non-American newspapers. TV channels from all over the world covered it live and tirelessly.

In Chicago, journalists, photographers, and TV broadcasters turned out in a great numbers in front of Ali Hasson's modest two-story home, which was cordoned off by police. Hasson's unfortunate neighbors were deluged with a barrage of inane questions. A second army of news people jammed the entrance to North Mission Hospitals on Chicago's Devon Avenue. Ali Hasson had been a surgeon at this hospital, and his lauded professional practice there established him as a prominent physician in the entire Chicago area. He had even won a place on Chicago's Consumers Best Doctors' list.

North Mission Hospital primarily served the residents of the North Side neighborhood, a ten-block stretch of mostly Pakistani and Indian businesses populated with first-generation immigrants. It was mind boggling to think that this man who served so many so well was the mastermind behind the nightmare America faced.

Comments from some of the journalists covering the story follow.

A reporter from Telemundo said, "I think for everybody who saw firsthand the death and destruction brought on by the Christmas Special attacks, that Ali's capture became a pivotal point in the story of the event. We try as journalists to be as impartial as possible, but feelings can't always be turned off. When we see the utter despair, the stricken individuals who lost their loved ones, the many lives that have been totally shattered, and those thousands of evacuees uprooted with no idea of their fate tomorrow or even weeks to come, things this terrible, events this horrible, make it hard to be subjective. It really is hard! For us, the coverage will continue, not just on the attack, but everything that the attacks affected, like the health issues with the responders, the future of the evacuees. It just goes on and on."

Klaus Zimmerman of the German TV network RTL said, "Since 6:30 p.m. Christmas day, I've been covering the Christmas Special and reporting live from all over America, so I didn't get to sleep at all. But for us reporters, it's days like today that are really historic. On top of it all, I'm here in America reporting as the US correspondent...It's events like the quick capture of someone evil like Hasson that makes me love my job of being a journalist. It's one of those events you will never forget and you will tell your children and grandchildren that you were there."

John Dickens of ABC said, "The capture of Ali Hasson just intensifies the emotions of what happened on Christmas morning. Now we have someone alive to curse and hate. At least that's what I get from the people I have interviewed today.

There are many conflicting emotions; on one hand, there is the feeling that the hunt is over for Ali Hasson, the criminal has been found, but you still have thousands who have lost their lives. How can the capture of this single individual really rectify or heal our nation? It feels like something really significant has happened to turn things around, but then you look around and you're hit with the devastation. It's hard to be happy because there is still so much death and agony we all still face.

"The coming days will bring new information about the attack and Hasson's affiliation with al-Qaeda, and maybe we will be able to see better what his capture really means to us."

Stories of the chaos, death, and destruction filled the airwaves. People were jittery, unnerved, and the capture of Hasson did little to settle frazzled nerves. Now there was just more to talk about and debate over. People were already asking why he was even captured. Why didn't they just kill him like they did with Osama bin Laden or Awlaki? Arguments abounded about the reasoning. Most pundits believed that the president felt it would have been ill advised to kill an American citizen openly in a Western country.

Chapter 66
Letter of Shame

Sheeva had grown more depressed and despondent by December twenty-seventh. She had lost her combativeness and wanted to simply stay in bed all day. She was very non-communicative. She wouldn't eat, and the US Marshals were worried about her health. They worried she would attempt suicide.

As Sheeva learned of the severity of what her father had done and heard of the thousands who had died as a result of the attacks, she mentally punished herself for the sins of her father. Her salvation became dreams. Her view of life reminded me of a quote from an Edgar Allen Poe poem, "Is all that we see or seem, but a dream within a dream?" Following is a letter Sheeva wrote as she suffered with her depression.

Good Morning Jason,

I feel so confused now. It's hard sometimes to tell when I'm dreaming and when I'm awake. I wonder if my life is like in that movie Inception. I'm feeling like when I'm awake it's almost like an intermission in a play because when I sleep you're there in all my dreams. You're everywhere. Your spirit has not left me. When I sleep, you fill my heart with love and hold me in your arms, but then when I awake you disappear. All I want to do is sleep, because I love you being there and holding me, seeing the laughter in your face and those beautiful eyes that burn into my soul. You are there when I come down from those weird dreams, where I see myself just lost, standing in thin air somewhere between heaven and earth. I can see the earth revolving slowly beneath me, but not another soul is anywhere in sight. There is just blackness and a shining earth below and twinkling stars far, far above. And there is not any sound. It's just deadly silent. Then suddenly I'm back in your arms, lying in our bed that we once shared in our place in Culper, Texas. When I'm out there in nowhere, just standing there looking around so lost, I'm so afraid. I'm afraid I won't be able to find my way back into your arms. I'm afraid I will die there and no one will ever find me. I will just disappear and float somewhere high up there between heaven and earth. I actually looked this type of dream up on the Internet and it said it might have something to do with a concerned heart or just not knowing what to do. That's one prediction they got right.

Jason, I don't know what to do, and things just keep getting worse. This morning Agent Felicia Burke visited me at the safe house, as they call this place. She came early and told me that my father had been arrested in London. She told me that I should not watch the news for the next few days because it will be full of stories about my father, and many of them will not be pleasant to watch. As usual, I didn't listen to her and the first report I saw was my father dressed in an orange jump suit in chains. Two men were holding his arms helping him to shuffle through a group of armed police, and you could hear men yelling ugly epitaphs at him. The scene was so shocking and so degrading. Why did he do what he did? I'm so ashamed that I'm his daughter. I wish I'd died with the thousands of others that he killed. And Jason, I feel like my father killed you also. He was so spiritually bankrupt.

I have lost weight because I can't eat. I just feel like staying in bed all curled up with my eyes closed. I'm so tired of all this, and I just want to sleep.

I have been trying to figure out why I should continue on. You're gone, my mother is dead, your brother is dead, my father is a mass murderer, my brother is probably looking to kill me, your father won't even let me go to your funeral, and the whole world feels like I'm the daughter of a monster. Muslims hate me because I turned on my father; Americans hate me because I didn't turn on him quick enough. I have no friends and don't even have anyone my age to talk to. I am under house arrest. If I leave my safe house, they think some Americans or angry Muslims would happily kill me.

I really wanted to be at your funeral to say good-bye to you, to kiss your lips just one more time. I imagine all your friends and the tears they will cry as they lower your body into the cold hole in mother Earth. I imagine you in your grave, but with me there too. I lay there beside you in your arms and then our spirits would speed through the heavens like shooting stars and then there would be no one out there to hurt us.

I guess what I'm experiencing is depression and it just won't go away. It seems to stalk me day and night. I want to escape from it, but I can't because it's like something very cruel living within me that wants to hurt me. I struggle with this feeling, and I come to the same conclusion over and over that there is no way out. I want to go back asleep because you roam through all my dreams and I know you will find me again and hold me.

It's so confusing because deep inside of me I have this horrible hatred for what they did to you, and when I feel that way, a dark part of me thinks America got what it deserved. Then another part of me is ashamed that those thoughts ever entered my mind. What if I'm as sick as my father and just not old enough to know it yet?

When I catch a glimpse of myself in the mirror, I see a face that reminds me that I am the daughter of Ali Hasson, the most hated person in America.

What my father has done has severed my soul. He has pierced me to the core with his murderous attacks. Before he ridiculed, abused, criticized, blamed, and neglected me, but now he has drowned me in shame and guilt.

You always tried to make me feel so special, so different in a good way, you freed me from my rigid roles, but now my father's acts have soiled me forever. I feel so flawed, inferior, unworthy, and defective because of his acts. I probably would have lost you even if you hadn't been killed because billions of people feel the child of a murderer has to be bad. When I think about what he did and all the people who have died over the last few days, I experience these uncontrollable shudders that course through my body and I weep like a small child. Inside of me, I keep hearing an internal voice that whispers to me words of disgust and condemnation for my father and those who helped him.

I dread the day when I will be faced with the jeering humiliation of people knowing I'm his daughter and the rage and cruel remarks I'm sure they will hurl at me. Can any amount of my guilt make anything better for those who lost their love ones? Jason, I'm so lonely, so alone and afraid. My memories of you have become my friends and companions. They help heal the pain I've felt since you've been gone.

According to the Quran, Allah said, "And we will surely test you with something of fear and hunger and a loss of wealth and lives and fruits..."

I guess some believers might say that my life right now is some exercise of hardship to develop my spirituality through pain and loss.

Maybe the repeating dream of standing in space is Allah's way of telling me that my life is now empty and the darkness represents the black hole of loneliness that tells me you're gone, that you no longer exist, some voracious black hole that sucks my heart from my chest and sends it flying up to you in paradise. What Allah leaves behind is simply a numb shell of a woman without a soul, a shell of a woman that will never taste love again.

I love you Jason and miss you so very much

Chapter 67
Hiring of Attorney Thomas Lawrence

Within hours of the presidential announcement of Ali Hasson's apprehension and return to US soil, the Islamic Legal Aid Guild of Chicago started looking for an appropriate attorney to represent Hasson. They wanted a firebrand of an attorney, someone who had a track record both in criminal and civil rights cases. The guild sifted through a list of attorneys that possessed the desired qualifications, competence, and experience. After considerable deliberation, the guild finally whittled their list down to five accomplished lawyers. At the top of the list was the well-known attorney Thomas Lawrence.

On the afternoon of December twenty-eighth, Thomas Lawrence received an unexpected call from his secretary, Darlene Kerns. She told him that a Chicago attorney by the name of Omar Bokhari had left several urgent messages. Darlene said she was unable to extract from Omar Bokhari the nature of the call, but she sensed desperation in the caller's voice. She told her boss that Bokhari was adamant that Lawrence return his call as soon as possible.

Lawrence made the call, and it was answered on the first ring. Omar greeted Lawrence and explained that he was with the Islamic Legal Aid Guild of Chicago and that they had a very big favor to ask. I interviewed Omar Bokhari about his recollection of that call and what led up to it. Below is a portion of that interview:

Roberto: *Why did the guild take on the task of finding an attorney to defend Ali Hasson?*

Bokhari: *I'm happy to answer that question. When the Christmas Special attacks happened, we recognized that Islam would be blamed for the actions of these insane individuals. Our faith in Allah is very devout, and it hurts us to see Islam bashed as the religion of evil. Our guild felt it was imperative, for the sake of the Islamic community, to find an attorney to act as Hasson's defense and to defend Islam against the many media assaults it would face. It was obvious that these horrible new attacks would rip open the wounds from the 9/11 attacks and burn many of the bridges we had built between our Muslim community and American Christians.*

After the 9/11 attacks, our guild received thousands of anti-Muslim cases, but things were slowly getting better, and a small reservoir of good will toward Muslims was evident in some parts of America.

Roberto: *So after the Christmas Special attacks occurred you realized that what happen would seriously affect the Muslim community?*

Bokhari: *Oh yes! We knew immediately that we needed help from someone like Thomas Lawrence. We wanted someone who was a tough negotiator and brilliant strategist. We needed someone who possessed the ability to read people and the political landscape. Lawrence was at the top of our list. When we first spoke, I told him that his reputation preceded him and impressed us all.*

We had read news articles that Lawrence was often characterized as a leach, a hypocrite, and an ambulance chaser. They were articles that said he made his living by demeaning and preying on the police and law-abiding citizens. One article about a two million dollar settlement Lawrence won from the city of Chicago was most revealing. It was over a highly publicized case of five police officers molesting two lap dancers, and it prompted comments like, "If a rabid dog ripped Lawrence's throat out, the Chicago police force would celebrate it for a week." His response to that comment was one of the things that caught our attention. He said, "I practice law to win cases, not popularity contests." I was sure a man like this could help us, Insha'Allah.

Roberto: *So when you asked Mr. Lawrence if he was available for this case, what was his response?*

Bokhari: *Well, I talked to him a little about who we were and then I asked the critical question. Before he responded with a yes or a no he told me that he was not interested in ending up like the eighty-year-old attorney Lynne Stewart, who is serving ten years in prison. I'd met Stewart when she represented Sheik Omar Abdel Rahman, and I was awed at her abilities. It was a pity that this wonderful, kind woman, who was just trying to represent her client, was sent to prison for simply doing what other lawyers do all the time. This is the problem that lawyers face when representing accused terrorists in America. They have those special administrative measures to abide by that* *complicate their work immensely and undermine their client's right to a fair trial.*

Roberto: *Will you explain what those special administrative measures are?*

Bokhari: *Well, in the case of Ali Hasson, there were many. For example the pretrial Special Administrative Measures imposed solitary confinement and twenty-four-hour electronic monitoring. They also restricted him to only talking to prison officials. That restriction meant Doctor Hasson could not participate in group prayers.*

Communication with the news media was completely forbidden. He could not even read the news unless it was at least thirty days old, and they banned him from listening or watching all news-oriented media. These draconian steps dramatically impaired Hasson's right to counsel because they affected Thomas Lawrence's ability to discuss his client's conversations with needed outside experts.

Roberto: *Are these special administrative measures applied to other accused criminals?*

Bokhari: *In theory they could be, but in practice they seem to only be used against foreign-born terrorists. For example, Terry Nichols, the Oklahoma City bomber, was not subject to them, and he was held responsible for the death of hundreds.*

Roberto: *Very interesting! After knowing all this, what did Lawrence say when you asked him to represent Hasson?*

Bokhari: *His answer eventually was yes. He said it was a cause he would be interested in pursuing. In fact, if I recall correctly, he said, "Everything I've done in my career has prepared me for a case like this. I mean, Hasson will need a lawyer that understands civil rights law, criminal law, and the ability to manage the press, engage experts, interview witnesses, and anticipate the prosecutions' moves. That's what I do."*

But he also stipulated that he must first discuss this with his wife since she would certainly suffer from the negative press this case would create. And then he asked me if I realized that he was an African American. I was taken aback at this question, but I said yes we knew that. Then he asked me if I knew that he and his wife were not of the same race? I replied, "Mr. Lawrence, we read everything we could find about you. We know you came from a humble background. We know that one of your ancestors was a slave, we know you rose from being the son of a Georgia peach farmer, and yes we know that you married a white woman when interracial relations were very controversial."

Mr. Lawrence corrected me and said, "She was not a white woman but a girl from Japan. A yellow person was even more hated back in the sixties and seventies."

I laughed a bit at his correction and said, "Mr. Lawrence, these are actually the types of reasons that make you special to us. You appear to have a unique heritage that represents the coming together of two very resilient cultures.

To us, we see that as a wonderful resource."

Anyway, Thomas Lawrence called me later that day and gave me his final answer. He said he had discussed this with his family and he had decided to take the case. We were all elated. It's obvious that lawyers like Thomas Lawrence are a necessary and critical part of America's criminal justice system. Without brave men like him, who would represent the most hated? There would be no checks and balances.

Roberto: *When you hired Thomas Lawrence to represent Hasson, were you aware of his Christian background and that he often quoted scripture in his arguments?*

Bokhari: *Of course we were aware of that, and we felt it would be an asset to have a Bible-quoting Christian representing a Muslim. Sort of a blending of two religions! We knew that he knew the Bible inside and out and that he often invokes some moral tenet or quotes some piece of scripture to make a point, and we hoped that would be of great benefit at the trial.*

As I said before, we were happy to get him as Hasson's counselor. I'm not sure at first how happy he was, because for the next few months the Hasson trial and Thomas Lawrence were all anyone talked about in the legal circles. It was a constant media frenzy and became Lawrence's full-time occupation. The press and public galvanized around the case. This was an important international case because it was the kind that dredged up all the feelings that people have about terrorism.

Chapter 68
Boom Plus 4

Four days after the Christmas Special, America was still in turmoil. More and more heartbreaking stories surfaced detailing the death and destruction from the series of attacks that Christmas day. The attacks had ushered in a new way of life in America. It was one of fear and foreboding fueled by those ominous words, "We will come again." By the fourth day, many news outlets had chosen to forbid their newsrooms from playing the terrorist's recording or even uttering those disconcerting words. The repetition of the message was considered corrosive to the psyche of the survivors of the attacks, and by December twenty-ninth all of America was in some form of survivor mode.

Beside the terrible news of the many dead, the emotional first-person accounts, the constant talking heads, and the videos of the thousands evacuated and military vehicles rumbling down main streets, people were also bombarded by a whole new crop of advertisements. There were food ads for imported food that was guaranteed free of radiation; Radiacwash™ Towelettes that helped wash away cesium, strontium, and cobalt particles; hundreds of gun ads; survivor kits of canned food and water; bulk respirator ads; radiation decontamination kits; online sources for FDA approved Iosat potassium iodide pills; and the biggest new fad gadget, the dosimeter.

The fear of radiation poisoning was rampant, and everybody in America was flocking to hardware, sporting goods stores, pharmacies, and department stores to buy their very own dosimeter. These ads and specifically the dosimeters ads were a constant reminder that life in America had changed. Now people didn't only watch reports of weather, smog, pollen counts, and mosquito activity forecasts, there were also hourly radiation reports that informed you of the various hot spots across the nation. The reports were sponsored by companies selling dashboard-mounted dosimeters, click-on dosimeters, and even dosimeter badges. People joked that the dosimeter badges were only useful in telling you if it was time to order your own casket, but regardless of the jokes, people quickly embraced these thirty-dollar radiation-warning devices. They were everywhere. They swung from car mirrors, hung from necks on lanyards, dangled from pockets, and were taped to refrigerator doors. It became a social norm for friends to check each other's badge and compare the amount of exposure they had so far received. A darker color displayed on the card indicated how bad your day was really going. This new custom was very reminiscent of how monkeys check each other for fleas. It was part of the new social mores emanating from the attacks' aftermath. In fact, "Monitor. Detect. Escape.", the motto of the RADTriage™ Radiation Detector, became as well known and a part of the new post catastrophe vernacular as Coca-Cola's memorable "Things go better with Coke" slogan. How many hundreds or thousands of lives were saved by these radiation monitors? No one will ever know.

Even I quickly succumbed to the pressure of buying a dosimeter. My choice was a dashboard-mounted version and two of the clip-on versions, one for my wife Elizabeth and one for me. These clip-on dosimeters were the type that made noise. In fact, the ones that I bought gave me the ability to set an alarm to tell me if my radiation exposure reached my own personally chosen radiation level, and it also kept track of my cumulative radiation dose. The clip-on dosimeter attached to my belt, and as soon as I turned it on, it began to click incessantly from background radiation.

One primary reason that I purchased the dosimeters was to convince my wife to allow me to leave our home and visit a place that had suffered from one of the nuclear power plant attacks. Elizabeth thought I was nuts and angrily argued with me about the logic of going on such a trip. She felt I was exposing myself to untold risk and was acting like a ghoul who wanted to see firsthand the suffering of others. The arguments finally ended with my wife totally exasperated, but accepting of the fact that a fool with a tool is still a fool.

I think Albert Camus said that, "Stupidity has a knack of getting its way." So having won, I packed a few items, grabbed my camera, my dosimeter, a couple of paper respirators, and a few bottles of water as I prepared to set off to New Orleans.

I believed all the deaths, the thousand and one problems, anxieties, terrible visions, and unending worries that had bombarded my brain over those last few days had depressed me and depleted my very being.

Do you remember the Eagles song "Take it easy" and the line, "Well I'm running down the road trying to loosen my load, got a world of trouble on my mind"? That song clearly articulated my condition and needs. It spoke of a truth, because as soon as I embarked on my trip, I experienced an incredible sense of inner peace and calmness. I hoped it would help silence the chattering in my mind, which seemed to be louder than even the chirping of my new dosimeter. I needed to gain control of my inner world again and feel comfortable within it.

Before I left, Elizabeth sensed my anguish and confusion. I know the events had affected her also, but only God knows how deeply. Her eyes clearly displayed her sadness, and even more obvious of her feeling of despair was the lack of her beautiful smile, which days before had lit up her face. She appeared deeply shaken.

Regardless of all this, I felt I had to take this reflective trip. It would be a time to regroup and understand better who I was. I did feel a tinge of guilt as I waved a farewell to Elizabeth, but I also realized that spending time by myself was often a spiritual and cathartic exercise that brought us closer together. It would be a time to shore up my inner self and our relationship.

In fact, as soon as I got out on the freeway, I could feel my mind and body settling into stillness. But that serenity was violated by the music pouring from my radio, which suddenly seemed sacrilege toward the dead. I quickly turned it off and felt the peacefulness of solitude embrace me. This was my alone time. I rolled down my window, and a blast of cool air rushed pass my face, creating a tingling sense of pleasure.

I found it unbelievably refreshing just to be bathed in quiet, to finish a thought without any interruption. So many things were bubbling away in my mind, and I needed this time of solitude to let them settle. I realized that if I didn't relax, I'd dwell on them over and over. I needed to retain control of my own thoughts—I had to focus on me. I wanted to enter back into my own being. I needed to be refreshed, revitalized, rejuvenated, and overflowing with new energy so I could be myself again.

Not till I had this time of reflection did I realize how badly the Christmas Special had affected me. I suddenly found tears trickling down my cheek while an unabated hatred for those responsible for this catastrophe overtook me. Life was in such turmoil, and I finally had a chance to grasp the magnitude of all the people who had died from this monstrous attack and all the families mourning the death of their love ones.

A vision of thousands and thousands of bodies lying in rolling fields filled my mind as I tried to imagine what this many bodies would look like. I don't know why I was thinking like that, but I do know that I wanted to process this. I wanted to feel for all those murdered in the horrible series of attacks. I thought of their heroics and their suffering. The grief and despair of those who loved them—crying wives, devastated children, broken fathers, all brought upon by thousands of senseless murders.

The thought that played over and over in my mind was that they were dead and I was alive. The weight of despair and remorse pressed down on my heart. I wept bitterly and felt a tremendous sense of guilt slice through me that came from the fact that I had no way of making things any better for those who died Christmas morning. I could pray for them and wish them and their loved ones peace of mind, but that really was nothing.

As I sped down the freeway, I found myself reflecting over the last few days and striving to understand what had happened, why, and most of all, myself. I knew I was smothered by this dark cloud of sadness, maybe even a hopelessness, which I had to rid myself of as soon as possible. In addition, I had a palpable fear that terrorists would perpetrate yet another horror. This foreboding that all was not over frightened me the most. Could they still commit something even worse, with an enormity of evil dwarfing even their past deeds?

Even as this darkness filled my mind, I could not help but notice how fine the weather was. A light sprinkle of snow had made much of the scenery look so tranquil, so beautiful and picturesque. Even the bland Texas landscape appeared magnificent and amazing. A farm, a rolling field, some turn in the road, a scent of evergreen wafting on the wind, a weathered building, or a gnarled tree would suddenly trigger a long-lost memory and remind me of a previous Christmas. Some past beautiful holiday that was filled with wonderful memories of friends, families, and celebrations. And as I wept, the soothing wind from the open window snatched the tears from my cheeks and whisked them out into the world to maybe commune with the tears of all the other grief-stricken people.

When I reflected on all the deaths of the Christmas Special attacks, I realized that I no longer saw the world as it once appeared when I was five days more naïve. America had changed. It was now a country where everyone felt frightened. They feared the unknown, and they tried to think of some reason to have faith in their failed government.

The day before Christmas, I would have never dreamt of such an attack by these depraved humans who sacrificed their lives just to bring horror and death to so many others in some insane belief that their God would rejoice in the carnage. I'm glad that most of them were killed during their attack because evil such as theirs must be extinguished if we are to save humankind.

The cry had done me good. It's strange that sometimes something as simple as crying can relax you and relieve some of the grief that grows within us.

I noticed I needed gas, and luckily enough, a few gas stations were now opened so I gassed up at the first one I encountered and used their ATM to get some more cash for my trip.

Actually, the freeways were relatively empty. Between the fact that America had just suffered through a major terrorist attack and it was still the Christmas holidays, few people were on the road. As I drove south from Paris, Texas, nothing looked out of place. Motels and restaurants were certainly open for business. A few military convoys sped down the freeway, and lots of police cars were out on patrol, but the world still looked pretty normal.

I realized that I was hungry, and a few more miles down the freeway, I pulled into a truck stop to grab a bite to eat. As soon as I entered the restaurant, the new reality reinserted itself into my universe. Tired, joyless people gawked up at the flat-screen TVs as they blared out the latest reports about the Christmas Special attacks.

Diners and employees appeared transfixed by the latest announcement that evacuees from nuclear disaster exclusion zones would be unable to return to their homes for months or perhaps even years. People shook their heads in disgust and muttered epitaphs at the conclusion of the announcement. That was when I felt my seat begin to shake, and behind my booth I heard a swift intake of breath and then the quiet sobs of someone crying.

I heard a little girl's voice saying, "Mommy, why are you crying? Don't cry, Mommy, people will see you." The crying quickly subsided, but my seat continued to vibrate. I think the girl's mother was still silently crying, and her whole body trembled from her grief. I remembered my wife's words that watching people in grief was tantamount to being a ghoul, so I slipped the waitress a note that asked her to let me pay for the woman and child's meal. I hoped that little gesture would make the emotionally crushed woman feel a little better and maybe ease my conscious.

Her terrible plight reminded me of the thousands of families who had lived within the infamous Fukushima nuclear power plant exclusion zone. They had to wait six months before they were even allowed a four-hour return visit to collect belongings and check their properties. I tried to imagine how difficult it would be to lose everything to a nuclear disaster. To suddenly be forced to leave your home with the clothes on your back and whatever else you had the foresight to grab as you departed. Leaving behind your home, belonging, collections, friends, job, community, and dreams had to be absolutely devastating. When the Fukushima refugees were finally allowed to revisit their homes, it must have been heartbreaking. And what little joy was left must have been considerably diminished as they donned government-provided protective garments and dosimeters to remind them that their community was now just one big radioactive wasteland. I wondered how soon our nuclear disaster evacuees would face a similar experience.

I had this foolhardy desire to see firsthand the results of the attack on the Waterford 3 Nuclear Power Plant, and I must admit that my trip taught me how to appreciate how helpful these dosimeters could be. This investigation was on my own. I just wanted to know how bad these attacks had hurt New Orleans and its surrounding area. At that time, I had no idea that I'd eventually be chronicling the story of the Christmas Special attacks.

Anyway, as I drove along Route 90 in Louisiana I could discern an increase in the dosimeter. When I drove through Gretna and turned at Harvey to head north to River Road, the clatter got much louder. The noise from the dosimeter ebbed and waned as I followed River Road along the shore of the Mississippi. At Bridge City, it became even louder and more frantic, but not until I entered Waggaman, Louisiana, did my dosimeter really come awake. I was surprised because there was still some activity in this community. It had a mix of people just standing around a Red Cross relief vehicle, some wearing paper respirators while others acted like nothing was amiss.

In the passenger seat of my car sat my paper respirator, and I began to contemplate putting it on. But as I continued my drive through the small community, my machismo—or more likely sheer stupidity—prevented me from donning it.

Now the dosimeter was racing as I followed River Road west, bringing me closer to the Waterford 3 Nuclear Power Plant. It's an eerie feeling knowing something deadly surrounds you, that something invisible is attacking your cells and altering your chromosomes and DNA as you speed along a highway listening to Cajun talk radio and the rattle of your dosimeter. By this time I thought of the dosimeter as my very own oracle that would warn me of evil. Of course, I still had to have the common sense to follow its warning.

When I was about thirteen or fourteen miles away from Waterford 3 Nuclear Power Plant, I was stopped by military guards manning a roadblock. There were probably eight to ten heavily armed guards outfitted in hazmat suits with respirators. My dosimeter was clattering away by this point. The sheer clamor should have made me question my soundness of mind in going any further.

However, the decision to go on or turnaround was quickly made for me by the armed guards who approached me from both sides of my car and asked me why I was there. With automatic weapons trained on me, they demanded to see my identification. I gave a guard my driver's license, and he entered it into what I think was a driver's license scanner. It actually copies your information from your driver license into a database. They also photographed me and my car before they returned my license and informed me that I was "persona non gratis." They told me to leave the area immediately in no uncertain terms.

"Get the fuck out of here, SIR!" I think were their exact words. With guns still aimed at me, I quickly turned my car around and drove away. I actually could feel my heart racing. It's a bit scary being stopped by machine-gun-toting soldiers in hazmat suits a few days after a deadly terrorist attack.

As I drove away, I wondered if I would now be on some no-fly list or Homeland Security list of terrorist suspects. I also wondered what happened to anyone with a name like Abdul, Hussein, Abbas, Saud, or Faheem who made the mistake I'd just made. As I drove back on River Road, a small convoy of military vehicles raced by me, going way over the speed limit. I thought maybe they were still using the same policies developed in Afghanistan and Iraq to lessen their exposure to deadly roadside attacks. After what had happened, anything was a possibility.

It was an odd coincidence, but just about the time I was thinking about those possible attacks, my Cajun AM talk radio reported that four Muslims exiting a mosque somewhere in America were shot by a sniper. This would ratchet up the current fear and insanity a couple more notches. I searched the dial for another report about it, but to no avail. So much was still going on I was never able to find where the incident happened or if they were killed or just wounded.

I set it back to Cajun talk radio and listened to the newest big story about the famed attorney Thomas Lawrence, who would be heading up Ali Hasson's defense team. They talked about his credentials and about the fact that many considered Lawrence a civil rights pioneer. They claimed his cases and lifestyle have both evolved around his belief in an open society and a commitment to equality under the law regardless of who you were. The talk show host said that Lawrence was one of the first African Americans to graduate from Stanford University.

As he rambled on, he received a call from an irate listener who was angry that anyone would try to help this son of a beep. "This lawyer needs to go live in Afghanistan if he likes terrorists so much." The caller wanted to know how much Lawrence was getting paid for turning against his country.

After a quick dosimeter ad and a report on the current radiation readings in Louisiana, the host came back and talked about how Lawrence worked hard at integrating his own interracial family into the fabric of a very white suburban neighborhood outside of Chicago.

While I drove along River Road paralleling the Mississippi River, I noticed all those barges laden with forty-foot shipping containers and wondered if they would now become a post-apocalyptic graveyard of abandoned ships like those that lie rusting in the once busy harbor outside of Chernobyl. I wondered what damage the attack would do to the great Mississippi River. Tons of radioactive waste had been dumped into the river as people fought to try to gain control of the Waterford 3 Nuclear Power Plant.

The Christmas Special attacks had also started to create havoc in Europe. France was under siege by protesters from Italy, Germany, Austria, Switzerland, Portugal, Ireland, and Greece. The protestors were angry that France was still embracing nuclear energy as its primary source of energy. People felt France's nuclear energy plants endangered the surrounding countries. The protest started peacefully a couple days after the Christmas Special, but quickly evolved into violence.

I turned the radio off. I needed quiet again. My head was filling with just too much crap again. I was on my way home, and I needed to take advantage of this alone time. I wanted peace and solitude to embrace me once more.

Chapter 69
Other Happenings on December Twenty-Ninth

While I visited the New Orleans area to experience firsthand the destruction caused by the attack on the Waterford 3 Nuclear Power Plant, thousands of other noteworthy events took place across the nation. In fact, the most challenging part of writing this book was trying to convey in any real sense the total chaos that reigned supreme for days after the Christmas Special attacks. It's impossible to fully describe the bleak mood of Americans in the days following the attacks.

To say the least, there was a seething anger over the failure of the government in recognizing the Islamist threat and its apparent inability to understand events like the Arab Spring, America's exit from Iraq, and the president's announcement of the military drawdown in Afghanistan. The president had painted these events in glowing colors and said they were the successful result of a winning Middle East policy and a major step to the return of peace in the global community, but by many in the world, it was seen as total failure by an impotent America. A statement delivered by a representative of the Nigeria Islamist group Boko Haram praising the success of the Christmas Special Attacks read, "We congratulate our Islamic brothers in their glorious mission against the American kuffers and pledge our support to your noble cause. Now because of the grace of Allah and the bravery and cunning of our holy warriors, the war is at the doorsteps of the Americans. God willing, the battle will be quickly won and the cesspool of non-believers will be replaced with the glory of Islam and the laws of shariah.

Soon the stolen land built by the sweat of slaves to Godless Europeans will rejoice under the blessings and glory of Allah. The conquest of America, God willing, will be just one more victory after our overwhelming triumph in Somalia, Iraq, and Afghanistan.

"America's loss in Iraq and Afghanistan was so devastating that billions of dollars of military equipment was captured by our mujahedeen as Americans fled from certain death. The bullets and bombs deserted by the defeated kuffers will soon be used to strike down those who once killed our wives and children. The many defeats of the once-great America allow even small Muslim countries like Sudan to brush aside America's demands as a dog flicks away a bothersome flea. Today our holy warriors have now chased the kuffers to their own lair and will fight the final battle with the non-believers on their own cursed soil. Allah is great."

As blustery and inaccurate as the statement sounded to Americans, it rang true to the millions of Muslims who struggled through the wars in Iraq and Afghanistan. They had witnessed the flight of the great Satan with their own eyes and the following bloodbath among those who had collaborated with the Americans.

The blame game had started, and many fingers were pointing at both the Congress and the president. Somehow or another, the many lessons of history seemed to have been again forgotten by our leaders, said journalist Paul Craig, who wrote, "It has been but a few years since the 9/11 commission came to the conclusion that America's failure in stopping those attacks was due to America being unprepared. That same report went on to say that America never grasped the magnitude of the threat that had been gathering over a considerable period of time. More so, it concluded that America's 9/11 tragedy was partially due to a failure of policy, management, capability, and above all, a failure of imagination. So did we not learn anything from that tragedy?"

He was not the only one who attacked those in power. Another historian stepped into the fray and reminded everyone that there was little difference between the attitude of the government prior to the Second World War and the attitude of America before the Christmas Special attacks. America had failed to understand or believe in the nature of the forces opposing it prior to its involvement in the Second World War. According to the book *Pearl Harbor: The Verdict of History*, an editorial in the *Milwaukee Journal* describing America's attitude to the Axis danger read:

"We were all substituting our 'beliefs' for factual information available. The Axis had shown that it was out to conquer the world. A good many people did not want to believe that, so they didn't. Axis powers had demonstrated that they would strike friend or foe without warning. That was not a comfortable thought, so discard it. The time was short—too short—but if we adopted that idea, we should have to pursue a course which would interfere with 'life as usual.' So we pushed aside the disagreeable warnings."

It looked again like America had been asleep at the wheel.

On my trip to the New Orleans area, I'd missed one very important news report from Chicago. The announcements came out on the morning of December twenty-ninth. It was about new evidence found at the Hasson home in Chicago and the resulting investigation.

The two-story Chicago home of Ali Hasson had become synonymous with the Christmas Special attacks. It became more recognizable than the massive concrete compound Osama bin Laden had called home in Abbottabad, Pakistan. The Chicago house was where the most notorious terrorist had lived and plotted his attacks on America. Its innocence and inviting demeanor belied the horror and evil that came from within its walls. On the morning of December the twenty-ninth, the house took on an even more sinister character. That morning, scrolling headlines across TV screens announced the discovery of evidence found in the Hasson house believed to be linked to two recent unsolved murders.

The actual news report read as follows:

> *Sources close to the Hasson investigation have stated that hair, blood, tissue, and other pertinent evidence were found while searching the Hasson's home as part of the terrorist investigation currently being conducted. Numerous onlookers reported seeing a number of evidence bags being taken from the Hasson's home December twenty-eighth. The Cook County Sheriff's Department said during its early morning press briefing that authorities were not prepared to say what or where the evidence was found, but they did indicate that numerous articles were found in or around the home and were submitted for forensic screening. Pending completion of follow-up lab work, no definitive statements would be made regarding the identification of the suspected victims.*
>
> *"Information regarding the evidence gathered at the Hasson's home in*

Chicago will not be available to the public nor will the contents of the search-warrant affidavit. It will remain sealed during the course of the investigation." The Cook County Sheriff's Department also stated that, "As soon as we have confirmed DNA matches, we will be able to provide additional information to the media."

Information from the unnamed source close to the investigation indicated that a primary piece of evidence was a wallet with the ID of a missing Muslim teenage girl who had been a frequent visitor of the Hasson household. In addition, blood and hair evidence was found on shoes believed to belong to Abdul Hasson. Other evidence found has been linked to the unsolved murder of a neighbor's son, Steven Grubs, who had been killed and castrated a few weeks prior. Abdul Hasson, the son of Ali Hasson, had mysteriously disappeared soon after the discovery of that murder. Neighbors and high school officials confirmed that Abdul Hasson had not been heard from since around the time of the Steven Grubs' murder. Another interesting fact is that no official missing person report had ever been made regarding Abdul's disappearance.

Neighbors told Channel 4 news that Abdul Hasson was a very quiet boy who seemed to revere his father. They said that Abdul had not assimilated to America's culture and was often seen playing Afghani music loudly and talking to his friends in his native language.

When asked if the deaths could be attributed to Ali Hasson, an informed source said, "Currently all the residents of the home are considered persons of interest, not suspects. Ali Hasson is a possibility, but it's unlikely since he was in Canada when the second murder took place. The bizarre circumstances of the murders don't appear to be something that someone as cunning and thorough as Ali Hasson would be involved in. Unless these people knew of his big plan and were killed to shut them up, there is no plausible reason for him to be involved in such bizarre murders. I guess we will find out soon once the crime labs give us their reports."

A spokesperson for the Cook County Sheriff said: *"We are very grateful for community support and understanding and sincerely hope you will indulge us a bit longer. I apologize for the ongoing disruption to the community under these trying times. We are making good progress with our investigation, but clearly there is still more work to be done. Unfortunately, the crime scene will remain closed for a few more days to complete all needed forensic examinations. Again, let me say, the Sheriff's Department is grateful for the tremendous support and understanding you have given us. We will do everything possible to keep the disruption in your community to a minimum. And remember, anyone who has any information regarding suspicious activity or individuals at the Hasson's home is asked to report it to the Cook County Incident Room. Your identity can remain anonymous."*

Prominent Chicago defense attorney Thomas Lawrence visited the Hasson home late December twenty-eighth but was refused entrance. Lawrence would only say that he was hired by someone involved in the Hasson case, but he wouldn't divulge the name.

Susan Becka, a Hasson neighbor said, "This is all overwhelming, I just keep trying to wrap my head around it. They were such quiet neighbors. It's just unbelievable that a man who spent his life saving people could be involved in these horrible terrorist attacks and now this murder of our neighbor's boy. It's really scary to think that people like them can just live anywhere, and you never know it until they go crazy and do these horrible things."

Another neighbor said, *"Yesterday I joined the crowd of looky-loos in front of Hasson's house because I was interested in knowing what all these people were expecting to discover from looking at his house. These nosey crowds are very disturbing. Sometimes they end up standing in my yard or driveway. In fact, just last night, the police arrested one drunken gawker for urinating on the side of my car.*

"Another very upsetting moment was when this woman standing in the crowd nonchalantly asked me, 'Don't you think his neighbors would have recognized what a monster he was and done something about it?' Her question probably was rhetorical, but I no longer feel safe in my home or even on our street. I keep radios and lights on all the time so it will always appear that someone is at home.

"I dread going out of my house because of all those people staring like zom-

bies at me. I wish I could afford a hotel, but then I guess I'd be afraid my home would be broken into by these looky-loos. It's so bad that my husband and I can't even sleep at night, and we both are taking antidepressants."

Chapter 70
The Better Side of Humanity

All across the United States, people were still dealing with the death and destruction attributed to the attacks or the confusion and panic that followed the Christmas Special attacks. Some of the stories showed the better side of humanity. One such story was about the Eichlers' family. The Eichlers were evacuated from the Indian Point Exclusion Zone. They had lived in Ossining, New York, eight miles from Indian Point Nuclear Power Plant. After the evacuation declaration Christmas morning, they hastily packed some clothes and toiletries and headed out into the snowy weather. They struggled for six hours in bumper-to-bumper traffic, trying to get to Interstate 684, but their progress had been halted on Saw Mill Parkway.

Thousands of cars were lined up on the parkway, all trying to get onto I-684 north, and for about thirty minutes they had not budged. The cars had sat so long that snow had built up on their roofs and windshields. To make things worse, ice kept forming on the windshields. Every few minutes, the Eichlers would turn the car heater to the defrost mode and burn a new hole through the ice on the windshield.

The situation was terrible, but their daughter Cathy was oblivious to it all and happily continued singing Christmas carols as they sat stuck in traffic. As luck would have it, they suddenly got to move about three car-lengths and came parallel to a dilapidated car idling on the side of the road. Inside was a white haired man slumped over the steering wheel, looking very much asleep. Cathy stopped singing and started to question her parents if that was Santa Claus because of his white hair and beard and the fact that his face was so cherry red. Her father, Paul Eichler, also noticed how red the man's face was and something clicked in his brain. Just as his daughter asked, "Shouldn't we see if Santa is okay?" Paul remembered a TV show that had said people with heart problems or high blood pressure could turn cherry red. Under a barrage of hounding from his daughter and his wife to go check the Santa look-alike's condition, Paul capitulated.

He hated to get out of his car and be exposed to snow laced with radiation, but his concern about the elderly man's situation soon trumped his own safety. Paul went to the car and knocked on its window, but the man didn't stir. Paul knocked much harder, and finally after no response, he opened the unlocked car door. The man continued to just sit hunched over the steering wheel, breathing loudly. Paul shook the man, and when he didn't respond, something told Paul that he had to get the man out of the car and into fresher air, even if it was polluted with radioactive waste.

After a minute or so out of the car, the man came to but was totally confused and disoriented. Paul concluded that the man, whose name was Steven Hanks, was suffering from carbon monoxide poisoning and that's what was making his skin so cherry red. In fact, if Cathy hadn't noticed the white-haired man's red face, he would have certainly been dead in a few more minutes. The carbon monoxide had already rendered him unconscious, and only Paul's act of removing him from the carbon monoxide saved him. For five more hours, the Eichlers cared for him as they inched along Saw Mill Parkway and finally reached I-684. Mr. Hanks did survive and probably will remember Cathy's caroling as the best concert he ever heard.

Indian Point Exclusion Zone
962 Square Miles
East Coast
Exclusion Zone
N
S
E
W
PUTNAM COUNTY
ORANGE COUNTY
WEST POINT
FORT MONTGOMERY
INDIAN POINT NUCLEAR POWER PLANT
SING SING PRISON
WESTCHESTER COUNTY
ROCKLAND COUNTY
Danbury
Fairfield
Passaic
Stamford
White Plains
NEW YORK CITY
Yonkers
Bergen
10MI
16KM

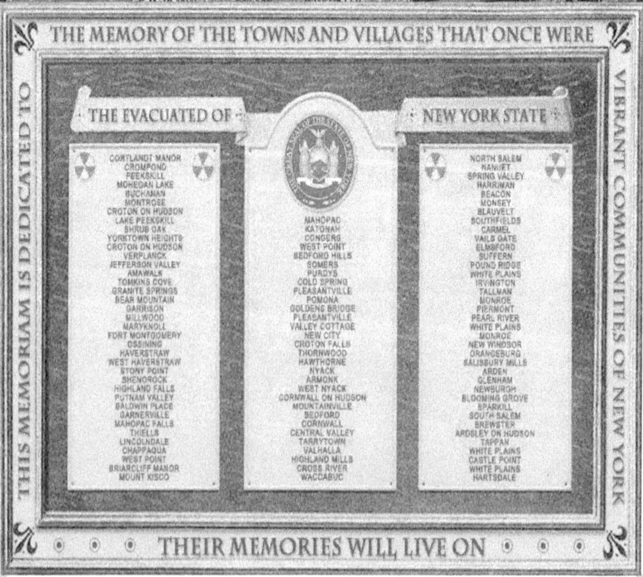

THE MEMORY OF THE TOWNS AND VILLAGES THAT ONCE WERE
THIS MEMORIAM IS DEDICATED TO
VIBRANT COMMUNITIES OF NEW YORK
THE EVACUATED OF
NEW YORK STATE
CORTLANDT MANOR
CROMPOND
PEEKSKILL
MOHEGAN LAKE
BUCHANAN
MONTROSE
CROTON ON HUDSON
LAKE PEEKSKILL
SHRUB OAK
YORKTOWN HEIGHTS
CROTON ON HUDSON
VERPLANCK
JEFFERSON VALLEY
AMAWALK
TOMKINS COVE
GRANITE SPRINGS
BEAR MOUNTAIN
GARRISON
MILLWOOD
MARYKNOLL
FORT MONTGOMERY
OSSINING
HAVERSTRAW
WEST HAVERSTRAW
STONY POINT
SHENOROCK
HIGHLAND FALLS
PUTNAM VALLEY
BALDWIN PLACE
GARNERVILLE
MAHOPAC FALLS
THIELLS
LINCOLNDALE
CHAPPAQUA
WEST POINT
BRIARCLIFF MANOR
MOUNT KISCO
MAHOPAC
KATONAH
CONGERS
WEST POINT
BEDFORD HILLS
SOMERS
PURDYS
COLD SPRING
PLEASANTVILLE
POMONA
GOLDENS BRIDGE
PLEASANTVILLE
VALLEY COTTAGE
NEW CITY
CROTON FALLS
THORNWOOD
HAWTHORNE
NYACK
ARMONK
WEST NYACK
CORNWALL ON HUDSON
MOUNTAINVILLE
BEDFORD
CORNWALL
CENTRAL VALLEY
TARRYTOWN
VALHALLA
HIGHLAND MILLS
CROSS RIVER
WACCABUC
NORTH SALEM
NANUET
SPRING VALLEY
HARRIMAN
BEACON
MONSEY
BLAUVELT
SOUTHFIELDS
CARMEL
VAILS GATE
ELMSFORD
SUFFERN
POUND RIDGE
WHITE PLAINS
IRVINGTON
TALLMAN
MONROE
PIERMONT
PEARL RIVER
WHITE PLAINS
MONROE
NEW WINDSOR
ORANGEBURG
SALISBURY MILLS
ARDEN
GLENHAM
NEWBURGH
BLOOMING GROVE
SPARKILL
SOUTH SALEM
BREWSTER
ARDSLEY ON HUDSON
TAPPAN
WHITE PLAINS
CASTLE POINT
WHITE PLAINS
HARTSDALE
THEIR MEMORIES WILL LIVE ON

Chapter 71
The Boys Return

The same morning in River View, New York, the bodies of Jason and Frank were brought home for burial. This was a tragic event for the small town, and people were astonished at the outpouring of citizens who came to meet the procession and the hearses carrying the bodies.

The sentiment of the people of River View that day is expressed vividly in the following recollections of a town trustee who witnessed the return of Jason and Frank's bodies:

> *As the mother of a soldier fighting in a war and as an elected trustee of River View, it really hits home when the children from our small community are lost to the insanity of today's pointless wars, and I'd certainly consider the Christmas Special an act of war.*
>
> *Today, I stood along the side of the road to welcome home what I considered were two fallen heroes. They were not soldiers, but they had both given their lives for the same cause our young soldiers believe they are fighting for. When I heard the story of Frank and Jason, I was astounded and proud of what these two boys from River View had done to protect others. Anyone who gives their life for you or me is a hero in my book.*
>
> *As I stood there and saw all those hundreds of lights from the cars and motorcycles in the huge procession escorting the bodies of those two boys, I said a prayer for God to protect their family and*

give them peace and comfort in this horrible time of need.

As the lights of the procession drew closer, I could feel the hot tears rolling down my cheeks I thought about all the mothers and fathers who have lost children to war. God, how do you pick yourself up and go on? As I looked around me, I felt the loving support of friends and a community that stands behind you and says, "Hey, what can I do to make your day better?"

I thought about my grandfather, who was a Black Sheep Squadron Fighter Pilot. I thought about my husband, who had been a captain and fought in Vietnam. I thought about the Purple Hearts they received for fighting and being wounded. My feelings were overwhelming. My heart was racing and my tears were rolling freely, as were many others standing near me. I was proud that so many from our town were here in support of these two heroes.

I know it bothered me terribly that these boys had lost their lives. I was proud of them, and I also felt a great deal of pride for my community of River View because hundreds of people came out to welcome these boys home as heroes, and share in the grief of their death. But why did they have to die? Why?

Before I knew it, the end of the procession went by. The taillights of the vehicles faded, and people began returning to their cars to go about their business. I wondered, with so much going on, how many would remember what they felt this tragic day? As I looked around, the flags were being packed up and chairs were being folded and put away. I noticed a friend who had her two young boys with her, and I thought, "Wow, they are the future. With all that had happened because of the Christmas Special attacks, I could only hope and pray that their future will be a brighter and better one."

Chapter 72
The Funeral

All across the nation, people mourned the dead. Town after town buried their dead, and River View, New York, was no different. Now that Jason and Frank's bodies had been returned to their place of birth, Roger Wilgers was left with the task of arranging for their funerals. The following is Mr. Wilgers narrative of those terrible memories.

> *I was devastated by the deaths of Jason and Frank. All the shit that was going on because of the Christmas Special attacks meant nothing to me. All I could think about was my sons' deaths. I was consumed by their deaths. I'd lost everyone in my life I had ever loved. I'd never got over my wife's death, and since then, my boys had become my life. They were what I thought of and planned my life around.*
>
> *Father Dolan helped me arrange the funeral for Jason and Frank. I wanted their services to be held together partly because I just couldn't figure how to divide my grief over two funerals. I had to get this behind me, or I'd be gone also.*
>
> *I found it hard to talk to anyone, and my nights were filled with my own shattering sobs that would finally drain me enough so I could get a couple hours of sleep. When Father Dolan asked me for pictures of my sons for the memorial service I just sat looking through my tears at these beautiful pictures of my two boys as they grew up and a million memories raced through my mind. I remember look-*

ing in on them as they slept, standing there staring at their beautiful faces and just feeling so proud of them. And now they are dead.

A part of me started hating Ali Hasson with a passion that I cannot describe. I saw him as the most evil thing imaginable. I wanted to kill him in some horrible way. Thoughts that I never could have imagined filled my mind of how to slowly kill him, to make him suffer for what he had done to my boys. Then I'd lift another picture, and my tears would flow again as I remembered the day the picture was taken. A picture of Jason at four years old riding his brother's tricycle, pictures of Frank wearing his cowboy outfit with a sheriff's badge dangling from his shirt. I shuffled through stacks of school pictures from elementary school, junior high, and high school that tore at my heart.

I gazed at pictures of my boys all dressed up for their proms holding their sweethearts for that year. All their dreams of what they hoped to be and what I'd hoped for them filled my mind. My breath gushed out of me like I'd been stomach-punched as I gazed down at a new picture I held in my shaking hands. It was a picture of my two boys handsomely dressed in suits standing next to me at the site of my wife's grave. The picture transfixed me. Jason was hugging my leg as he stared at his mother's casket while Frank nestled against me. My arms encircled both of them. How long I gazed at that picture, I don't know, but I finally placed it back in the box and then just sat there looking at all these memen-

toes of a life we all had once lived together. Birthdays, graduations, vacations, celebrations, bruises, first days at school, smiles, funerals, and so many more memories that lay locked within those pictures.

I finally left my stacks of memories and dropped limply onto the couch in front of the TV. Aimlessly, I flicked between stations that all seemed to emanate nothing but blurred scenes with incomprehensible gibberish. My head felt like it was being crushed as I watched those hallucinatory visions coming from the television. Through it all, I could distinguish the sound of crying and realized it was coming from me. Then another tidal wave of grief washed over me, and my whole body succumbed, folding me over like I'd been kicked in the groin. I gave into my anguish and just wept like a baby. My soul screamed out to God to give me the strength to carry on.

Father Dolan felt it would be wise to hold the services at the Cathedral of the Pines in River View. He predicted many mourners would come and only the cathedral would be large enough to hold those coming to pay their respects. He was right; the actual ceremony brought in far more people than I ever expected. A good number of police officers came to pay their last respects to Frank. Some classmates Jason went to school with in Chicago came also. The good people of River View came out en masse to pay respects to Jason and Frank. Then there were individuals who simply came because they wanted to experience the service honoring the two young men who were mentioned in the news so much. And of course, reporters from news groups across the country were also in attendance.

Father Dolan helped me with the selection of music and songs for the service. They were drawn from songs I knew were favorites of Jason and Frank. I hoped they would connect with everyone in some way. It was how Jason and Frank would have wanted it.

The music at their funeral choked me up, but I remembered every piece that was played. The songs were James Bruce's "From Grief to Glory"; "Tears in Heaven" by Eric Clapton; "Mama, I'm Coming Home" by Ozzy Osbourne;

"Fly" by Celine Dion; "Dancing With The Angels" by Monk & Neagle; "When I Get Where I'm Going" by Brad Paisley, a singer who Jason liked a lot; "Livin' Without You" by Steve Alek; and then a favorite of Frank's, "Somewhere Over The Rainbow/What A Wonderful World" by Cliff Richards; and finally their exit song was "There You'll Be" by Faith Hill.

During the service, Father Dolan offered words to soothe and comfort, words that offered support and forgiveness. In fact, he went so far as to suggest that we should all try to leave our bitter feelings behind and walk forward together. I'm not sure if there was much reality in his plea, but everyone there did pray together.

After Father Dolan was finished, I read a eulogy to my sons. I have included it in its entirety:

"In grief, I stand before you as the sole surviving member of my family. I'm awed that so many of you still had the courage and kindness to take the time to venture out to my sons' funerals even as our country struggles to move forward after a terrorist attack that shocked the entire world. It was just a few days ago my two sons were killed, but it seems an eternity to me.

"I have been to funerals and watched as a father, mother, brother, sister, or friend struggled to stay composed and express their feelings about their loved one. Now I feel the same burden standing here in front of all of you. It's so difficult, but I'm grateful to have this chance to say something about my two boys.

"It has been a couple of months since I last saw them alive. In fact, the last time I saw Jason and Frank was when Jason was hospitalized at Chicago Mercy Hospital after he sustained a brutal beating over his relationship with his girlfriend. Regardless of the terrible circumstances that brought us together then, I dearly cherish those few days of memories of the last time I spent with my sons. All of us together those few days meant a lot to each of us then, and the world to me now.

"It was my last glimpse of my sons, the last time I'd touch them and the last time the three of us would sit close together, talking and laughing. Then our time together ended, and Frank and Jason drove away to Texas. Now they lie here in caskets.

"I was blessed to have a rather simple, yet powerful and loving relationship with my boys. Jason and Frank were hard to dislike.

"They were both born right here in River View, New York.

"It's been said that you measure how a person lived by the truths they lived by, the reasons they cried, the bridges they crossed, and the way they died.

"If there is any validity in that statement, then certainly I can say that my boys lived wonderful lives.

"They knew and followed the truth that the world is a far better place to live in, if we do onto others as you would want done onto you. They both observed the truth that we have a moral code and a legal code, and that often they are terribly at odds with each other. Jason and Frank realized that the world shines brighter for those who exude optimism. My boys were certainly optimists. Their optimism shone for me in the form of encouragement—I was encouraged to fight my cancer. I was encouraged to go find a new love in my life. Just a few days ago, Jason was so optimistic about his legal issues in Culper, Texas, that he felt my help would be unnecessary.

"Both of my boys were not ashamed to cry. They cried tears of sadness when their mother died. Frank cried tears of joy when he learned that Jason was going to survive his beating. And I'm sure Jason cried tears when he realized that he might never see his love of his life again.

"Albert Camus said, 'Men must live and create. Live to the point of tears.' My boys lived his advice.

"In Jason and Frank's short lives they learned a lot, they lived many life experiences. Crossed many bridges. One such bridge was the death of their mother when they were very young and I took on the role of both mother and father.

"I did a lot of traveling with my sons and we visited places like San Francisco, New York City, and Washington DC. I remember walking with them, holding their hands, visiting New York's Times Square, the Washington Monument, Yankee Stadium, Alcatraz Island, Radio City Music Hall, and our BART ride from San Francisco to Oakland. In our travels, I tried to expose them to many different experiences and as many different aspects of life as possible to arm them spiritually and emotionally for their future years.

"One night with a full moon, the three of us walked across a covered bridge in Vermont, just like the one in The Legend of Sleepy Hollow. The boys loved to do simple things like that. A fun winter day was walking along a railway painted with snow with Jason snapping pictures of the beauty of nature and man's inventions melting together.

"And we would have movie night where Frank would eat an entire pizza before the movie was over. One time he folded up a piece of greasy pizza and stuffed the whole thing in his mouth and started choking on it. He was really choking, and Jason came to Frank's rescue with some version of the Heimlich.

According to Frank, his little brother actually saved his life that evening. I remember all these times and things as if they had just happened.

"I tried to respect and nourish all their talents and encouraged them to excel in all their endeavors. Jason had a God-given ability to create works of art. He had become enamored by steampunk art, which is simply a blending of the best of the Victorian era with the dull throwaway creations of modern time. He was a great photographer and even a better artist with oils. Frank, however, was a student of man and had the great gift of intuition. It was a gift he used wisely and is what eventually contributed to his heroic acts in Beaumont. His optimism and joy for life was transmitted whenever he smiled your way, and the girls claimed he had sparkles in his unforgettable eyes.

"Neither of my boys lived long enough to be married and have a family of their own, but Jason was in love with a young lady when he was killed.

"Frank was the oldest and became a police officer in Beaumont, Texas. I'm sure all of you have read about his heroic deeds, which saved many in Beaumont but cost him his life. I see so many police officers sitting out there in the pews and standing in the back, and I'm so grateful to all of you for your thoughtfulness in taking the time to come to his funeral. I know Frank would have been astonished and pleased that so many of his comrades in blue somehow escaped from their duties at such a trying time.

Thank all of you from the bottom of my heart for honoring my son Frank at his last farewell.

"It's a tribute to Frank's level-headedness and strength of character that, despite the most unimaginable coincidences following Jason's murder, he forged on to redeem his brother's honor and became a hero in so doing.

"The truth is that they both made extraordinary contributions to the world at their death.

"Let me tell you a little about my son Jason. He was going to school at Houston's Institute of Art. I'm sure that many of you have read or heard news stories about him. I wanted to take a few minutes this afternoon to honor him and try and set the record straight over his involvement in the Christmas Special attacks. I'm sure you know that the media prefaces my son's name with disgusting phrases like 'accused sex offender' or 'sexual predator,' but they don't really explain how trivial these assertions are, so I feel it's my duty to try and right the wrong they heap on my son's memory.

"I looked up a few quotes when I went about trying to compose this eulogy. One that I found that seemed to express the last few months of Jason's life was a quote from D.H. Lawrence. He said, 'Love is the flower of life, and blossoms unexpectedly and without law, and must be plucked where it's found, and enjoyed for the brief hour of its duration.'

"My teenage son Jason was nineteen and madly in love with his sixteen-year-old girlfriend, Sheeva. A typical teenage romance with a Romeo and Juliet

intensity to it. She loved him and in fact wanted to be here today to say her last good-byes, but because of who she is, it became impossible. For those of you who are unaware of who she is, I will tell you now.

She is the daughter of the mastermind behind the Christmas Special attacks. She is a beautiful, intelligent, loving young woman who was beaten by a tyrant of a father who condemned her for embracing American culture. She ran away from her father when she felt her life was in danger. She fled to Houston to seek refuge with my son. They had been boyfriend and girlfriend when Jason lived in Chicago, and apparently their love for each other was still burning. Jason took her in. For the next few months, they lived together as a married couple. They loved each other and took care of each other.

"A few days before Christmas, Jason discovered that documents Sheeva had taken from her father's desk contained detailed plans in Arabic of a terrorist plot on the United States. His first reaction was to report these suspicions to the authorities, but he quickly discovered that living with a girl three years and forty-seven days younger than him violated laws that could put him in prison for years. In fact, he discovered that his crime of living with his girlfriend required harsher punishment than if he had blinded someone or hacked off their legs.

"He learned that his affair with his girlfriend could lead to being a registered sex offender for the rest of his life. Even worse, since Sheeva was not seventeen, Jason would also be labeled a sexual

predator by the courts. And let me point out that if they had been married, no laws would have been violated, or if they had lived in any of thirty-one other states where the age of consent is sixteen, his love for his girlfriend wouldn't have been a crime at all. I can't really speak for all men, but I'd bet that most of us in this cathedral are guilty of the same crime my son faced that morning when he decided to go to authorities and report Ali Hasson's plot and risk being branded a sexual offender. Jason faced a terrible moral dilemma.

"He chose to go to the authorities knowing full well what problems he might face, but he could not stand by and let these attacks happen. There is no doubt that my son Jason sought to help the authorities, but his genuinely good intentions were hampered by those who should have embraced his help.

"My son tried to reason with the authorities that he should get immunity from the charges they would heap on him for living with his sixteen-year-old girlfriend, but they wouldn't give him any signed promise of exoneration. Instead, they decided to throw him in a holding cell for the night. It was in this holding cell where he was killed a few hours later because others in the cell thought he was a deviant sexual predator who crawled through windows in the dark of night raping babies in their cribs.

"Even now the media finds it still necessary to perpetuate the vilest assertions of my son as an accused sex offender. It appears to be their goal, despite his

death, to destroy even the memories of Jason.

"I'm sure both of my sons would want me today to speak out about these unjust laws. Laws that are arbitrary, irrational, unreasonable, and if really enforced, would criminalize 80 percent of our young men as sex offenders. Mahatma Gandhi said that, 'An unjust law is itself a species of violence. Arrest for its breach is more so.' Certainly that belief speaks loudly of these barbaric punishments for such a common action by teens in today's society.

"Hopefully, rational people will prevail to end these laws drafted by sleazy demagogues and religious zealots. As Elizabeth Cady Stanton said, 'To make laws that man cannot, and will not obey, serves to bring all laws into contempt.'

"I'd like to end by thanking God for the small mercies he has shown us at this dreadful time. For taking my sons in a way that showed their courage as young men and their extraordinary desire to save the lives of others even at the sacrifice of their own lives.

"Frank and Jason will always be the joys of my life. I give thanks for these two boys who were so unique, extraordinary, and irreplaceable.

"Sons, you were taken from me so young and now your souls are rising to a place I can't follow yet. You two have to take this trip without me, but at least you will have each other. Your dad has business that he must take care of to set things right before he can join you. But I will join you, and I look forward to that time when we can take those long walks

once again. It's so sad to me that only after you're gone do I realize how much of my world your love filled and how empty it is without you. Frank, Jason, I love you and always will.

Once the eulogy was finished, Father Dolan had a couple more words to offer. He said that he agreed with my view of barbaric laws that penalized our youth for perceived sins that not even the church views with such distain. God's law allows forgiveness of children who have sinned and does not curse them for the rest of their life. He reminded all that the mother of Jesus was but a teenager of thirteen or fourteen when she was chosen by God to give birth to his son.

Finally, the service was over, and a silent procession of pallbearers carried Jason and Frank's caskets to the hearses that would take them to their final resting place in the winter's frozen earth.

At the grave, I stood holding a carnation from Frank's casket. A friend approached me and placed his hand on my shoulder and offered his condolence and then said he had to get back to work. It dawned on me then that the world was continuing and people were going about their business. It was just Jason and Frank's world that had ended.

Time had also stopped for me, and I knew then that for the rest of my life these tragic moments would be frozen in time just as solidly as the frozen ground would forever embrace my sons. These two lights of my life had been extinguished by the acts of one crazed, despicable bastard, and as those thoughts crashed through my mind, my body shiv-

ered with anger and I wanted to scream my hatred to the world.

My thoughts were interrupted by Father Dolan as he approached me and told me it was time to go. I tossed the carnation into Jason's grave and felt Father Dolan grab my arm in a solid grip, moving me away from the grave. I was like a drunk wavering on rubbery legs as he led me away from the awaiting graves. They were gone.

Chapter 73
The New Year

The threat "We will come again" hung over America like a dark cloud. As the New Year approached, people feared a new series of attacks. Fear would be one of the lasting legacies of the Christmas Special attacks. After the 9/11 attacks, America had quickly lulled itself back into a sense of invincibility as people felt the worst was over. We had all this new security at airports and protection from the formidable Department of Homeland Security. We had foiled more than forty terrorist attacks since 2001, like the liquid explosives plot, the air cargo bomb plot, the Christmas tree lighting ceremony car bomb plot, the subway bombing plot, the Christmas day bomber plot, and numerous others. How could any enemy be able to mount another Pearl Harbor or 9/11 attack against an opponent as observant and prepared as America?

But unbelievably, another attack did happen, and fear rushed back into people's psyches in serious and silly ways. Fear changed the way people lived. People avoided malls and shopped online; people feared flying, taking a bus or riding the Amtrak; only cars seemed like a safe mode of travel. People were hypersensitive to anything that appeared out of place...sugar granules on a desk could cause an entire office complex to evacuate while hazmat experts investigated the spill as a possible anthrax threat.

As New Year's Eve approached, people hunkered down for the new attacks they were sure would occur. Hospitals were avoided like the plague because they were on the list of likely targets. Across the country, virtually all New Year's celebrations were canceled. The annual New York City Times Square celebration was canceled out of fear of new terrorist attacks, plus the elevated levels of radiation that had swept over New York City.

In Los Angeles, the annual New Year Hollywood galas were also canceled. America was on the alert. Thousands of troops were on standby, and National Guard units patrolled streets and stood guard over buildings. But the New Year was on its way, and nothing could stop it.

Samoa first welcomed in the New Year, and as the earth turned, the celebrations spread across the globe. New Year's reached Pakistan and Afghanistan, where people danced and celebrated the attacks on the Great Satan America. A short time later, midnight arrived in Baghdad, Iraq, and the New Year was welcomed with a monstrous celebration of fireworks that made the night appear as day. Finally, New Year's arrived in a subdued America as people huddled in their homes watching TV or listening to the radio, waiting for the first report of the new attacks. But there were no attacks; perhaps the billions spent protecting the nation that night deterred the attacks, or perhaps none had been planned in the first place. As the new year emerged, the customary euphoria of a new and better year was as scarce as truthfulness in a politician.

Since the Christmas Special attacks, the president's silence had become deafening to the American public...but on New Year's Eve, his voice was once again heard.

New Year's day was an apropos time to speak to the public, because by then many Americans had felt as if the country was simply running on automatic with no one in the cockpit. People were not only afraid of more terrorist attacks, but also the devastation to the American economy. The depth of this financial disaster would soon be evident when the stock market reopened on January second, the first time since the attacks. After the 9/11 attacks, the DOW had dropped 684 points. Analysts predicted that the Christmas Special attacks would cause even greater losses, reaching into the trillions. Thousands of jobs would be lost in Louisiana, California, and New York, devastating job losses that would have crippling effects on their economies for years.

Chapter 74
The President Speaks

The president's speech was given on the afternoon of New Year's Day. It was a somber and haggard president who looked out of the television at his American audience. The country listened to the president's words in hushed silenced, waiting for some great announcement or revelation that would free them from the shock, fear, uncertainty, and gloom that gripped them.

The president's speech did not rise up to those lofty expectations, but it did address some of the basic issues and rekindled hope for many. Excerpts from the president's New Year's address follow below:

> *Greetings,*
>
> *As this new year awakens, our nation is facing one of its gravest challenges ever. As a result of three nuclear disasters, brought on by terrorist attacks, America must now confront a crisis unprecedented in its history. On this birth of a New Year, our nation is in mourning for the many who have perished from these attacks. The true number of casualties and cost this attack has exacted on America is still being assessed. It is also too soon to tell you with any certainty what course of action America will take in response to these attacks on our nation. What we do know is that many months of work and sacrifice lie ahead—months in which both our patience and our unity will be tested. Henry Ford, one of America's greatest industrialists, said, "Coming together is a beginning. Keeping together is progress. Working together is success."*

This is a piece of wisdom that I think should be the cornerstone of our new beginning.

To win the battles before us, we must regain our national unity. We must cure this political paralysis that has crippled our government and left us hobbled. Washington needs to stop talking and start walking. It is essential that we regain the ability to govern ourselves and restore your faith in our nation's future. We cannot win this grave crisis that lies before us if we continue to allow a political malaise to erode our national confidence and rip apart the social and political fabric of America.

Containment of these nuclear catastrophes requires unity and perseverance because the solutions are long-term with no short-term panaceas. We will put all the resources our great nation has and summon all the wonders of science and engineering to return our nation to its former greatness. But we can only succeed if we tap our greatest resources America offers and that is the inexhaustible spirit of you, the American people.

We are at a turning point in our history. If we are to quickly extricate ourselves from these problems, we must close the gap of trust that exists between citizens and the government. Americans want honest answers, not easy answers, not false claims or political evasiveness. As your President, I pledge I will do my best to make these changes in our government, but I cannot do it alone. I need your help, your sacrifice, and your commitment to rebuilding our nation's spirit. Only with all of us working together can we regain the confidence and strength that has been so precariously eroded

Today, I'm asking Congress to mandate that compensation be paid to the thousands of families who were forced from their homes because of the attacks on Christmas Day. These individuals, who bore the brunt of these heinous attacks, deserve a speedy resolution to their financial burdens and our nation's assistance in rebuilding their lives.

To make absolutely certain that nothing stands in the way of achieving these goals, I will urge Congress to create a Radiation Hazard Board that will have the responsibility and authority to manage the massive undertaking of cleaning and returning the evacuated towns and cities back to their citizens.

I'm also asking for an emergency meeting of the Security Council to be convened, without delay, to take action against those responsible for these latest terrorist attacks. This resolution will call for the prompt denouncing of all terrorist attacks in the strongest possible terms.

As a necessary military precaution, security at all operational nuclear power plants has been reinforced by additional military units. I have also directed the armed forces to prepare for any eventualities that may arise as a result of these attacks.

In addition, Homeland Security has been directed to escalate and continue close surveillance of all individuals regardless of race, nationality, or religion who have displayed any reason to question their allegiance to America.

Because of the continued atmosphere of intimidation that emanates from these emboldened groups of terrorists, I am calling upon all Muslims in all nations to demand an immediate halt to the clandestine, reckless, and provocative attacks made by radical Islamists in their global jihad. The wounds and anger that perpetuate the terrorists' actions must be addressed and healed, but any continuation of such attacks will not alter our resolve and will only create greater tragedy and burden on all peace-loving Muslims.

The adherents of Islam who believe that nations and people not part of the "house of Islam" are therefore in the "house of war" portend a disastrous future for all mankind. Global peace, respect, and trust between people of all faiths are threatened by these beliefs and acts of terrorism. A chasm of perilous dimensions is growing between Muslims and non-Muslims. Those adherents of Islam who seek world domination must abandon their quest and back away from the abyss of destruction. Instead they should join with people of all religions in an effort of reconciliation and world peace.

America will not be standing alone. Other great nations, including Japan, Russia, Germany, Ukraine, and France, have offered their help in assisting us in this task of taking control of our destiny once again. They can help us with their experience and knowledge of nuclear disasters, but they cannot remedy the problem of America's lack of confidence in its leaders and government. A lack of confi-

dence that has weakened the very heart, soul, and spirit of our national will.

In closing, I pledge I will do all in my power to improve the efficiency and productiveness of your government, but I can't do it alone. For the sake of our nation, it's time for us all to join together and commit ourselves to a rebirth of the American spirit. Working together with our common faith, we will not fail.

Thank you and good night.

Chapter 75
New Year's and Angola

The biggest problem that America faced on New Year's was its fear of the future and the unknown. This folly was expressed most eloquently by the Irish political theorist and philosopher Edmund Burke, who said, "No passion so effectively robs the mind of all its powers of acting and reasoning as fear." I think the following story told by a Cajun gentleman from Mamou, Louisiana, illustrates how easy fear and a few cans of beer can be the catalyst that turns a peace-loving man into a convicted felon.

This gentleman didn't want his real name divulged for obvious reasons, but I felt his story should be a part of the Christmas Special story. It was in fact those attacks and its aftermath that created the situation that led to his imprisonment. In my interview with him, I'm just going to refer to him as Angola.

Roberto Roma: *So I understand that this is the first time you have ever been in trouble with the law. I'd appreciate it if you would tell me how you ended up here in Angola State Prison. I think what happened to you will resonate with many survivors of the Christmas Special.*

Angola: *F'sure! You want me just ta tell you da whole story?*

Roberto Roma: *Yes, please tell it in your own way, and if I have any questions, I will interrupt you to get more clarification. Like I said, I think your story is something many Americans will relate to.*

Angola: *Well, ah guess den I need ta make it real clear dat I wuz a recovering alcoholic and had been totally clean foh seventy-five months and eight days prior ta da Christmas Special. Dass da longest time I ever kept ma shit together. I'd held down a good job and wuz pretty happy wid ma life. I'd even been able ta talk ta ma ex-wife occasionally widout having any fights or arguments. She had remarried ta another coon ass, who seemed ta be a pretty nice guy.*

Roberto Roma: *I guess I'm a little late, but congratulations are certainly due for that accomplishment. So what were you doing on Christmas when the attacks happened?*

Angola: *Well, ma Christmas plans wuz ta get up and drive over ta Vidor, Texas, ta visit ma daughter and have Christmas dare, but dassn't what happened of course. When I woke up, I turned da TV on ta check da weather foh ma trip and da first ting I saw wuz a report on Waterford Tree. I couldn't believe what dey were saying bout it. It had been attacked, and a huge evacuation wuz going on all around New Orleans. I immediately switched ta udder channels ta try ta learn moh, but I swear ta Gawd every one of da channels wuz bout some udder attacks somewhar else in America. It wuz frightening dat so many attacks on us could be happening on Christmas morning.*

I got ta say raht now, I hate calling dos attacks da Christmas Special attacks cause dare wuz nuttin special bout dem. Dey should be called da Christmas shithead attack or da Christmas asshole attacks by assholes.

Roberto Roma: *You can call the attacks anything you like. I bet a lot of people agree with you about what they named those attacks.*

Angola: *Good! Like I said, when dos attacks occurred, I'd been sober foh seventy-five months and eight days. I'd been a frequent flyer wid Alcoholics Anonymous and had gotten ma life back, but all dat stuff on Christmas just wuz someting I could not cope wid and it got me drinking again.*

On Christmas, I wuz pose ta get wid ma kids and ex-wife and have Christmas at ma daughter's house, but wid all da shit dat wuz happening I wuz afraid ta being on da road. I'd tried calling ma daughter, but never could get through ta her. I wuz getting frantic and fearing someting could have happened ta her. I wuz so worried dat I started seeing all dese horrible visions of her dead burning in some church and I just broke down crying. I wuz angry and felt so helpless.

I got carried away and ma mind just started making tings worse and I thought her kids would be wid her and I just knew dat dos bastards killed dem also. Dat wuz when I opened a Christmas present I'd bought foh ma boss, which wuz a bottle of Amaretto and took a drink raht from da bottle. Dat first drink wuz like magic. Some of ma fear just flew away and suddenly I realized dat I should check her Facebook page cause she is one of dos who are always yakking on da Internet. Thank Gawd foh dat cause dare wuz six post from her saying she wuz okay, but her phone wuz always busy so she couldn't call. I wrote back ta her dat I wouldn't be able ta make it and told her I wuz okay and as far as I know ma town hadn't been hit by any of dis shit.

Roberto Roma: *Knowing she was okay must have made you feel a little better. Did it?*

Angola: *Well a bit, but I wuz just upset bout everyting. Da attacks were scaring me. It* *just seemed like no one knew what wuz really going on. I hear one story dat all of New Orleans is gone and den I hear another dat most da people can still stay dare and all dat shit just gets ta me. Anyway tings just got worse foh me between da attacks on Christmas and New Year's Eve and I found maself drinking everyday ta get rid of da jitters. I tink a drunk like me gets addicted ta da news when someting so horrible happens and dass all you tink bout. I wuz off all dat week so dass all I wuz tinking bout. Each night I hooked up wid some guys at a safe bar in Mamou. It wuz dis place called Fred's Lounge. Best damn Cajun bar anywhar. Dey had great band dare dat played good live Cajun music.*

Dis is a place whar only we coon asses go ta. I mean it wuz just people who had lived in da community foh ever and been going dare since dey were old nuff ta drink. It made you feel better just being wid a bunch of friends and neighbors who you knew were not gawd-damn terrorist wanting ta blow you up.

New Year's I sat dare da entire day talking ta friends I'd made since da day after Christmas. On New Year's day, dey are serving black-eyed peas and cabbage and it's as much as you can eat along wid Cajun sausage cornbread. Dass what we call tradition foh New Year's.

Roberto Roma: *I think that's interesting that in some of the small towns people were still celebrating New Year's in the traditional way.*

Angola: *Well, not really, cause we would usually be shooting off fireworks and some shotgun rounds, but dey had some law dat made us not do it on dat New Year's. Anyway, Ah'm sitting wid ma friend Bobby most* *da whole day and we are talking bout all dass going on. He tells me how mad he is cause his sister Cherri wuz evacuated from Reserve and also lost her job at da Saint John Airport. Now he don't know whar she is no moh. We guess she is in one of dos evacuee places da government had set up. He wuz pretty drunk and he got ta crying bout her. She had a real hard life and he loved her a lot. Her boyfriend, some low-life, just beat her up a week before and knocked out two of her teeth, Bobby told me. We drank some moh beers and I wuz eating some pork roast when Bobby brought up dat Muslims don't eat pork. He guessed you ain't going ta find no Muslim at no Cajun New Year's celebration.*

Roberto Roma: *So no one comes to this bar accept Cajun people?*

Angola: *No udders do, but I tink once one of dos Arab guys step a foot in our place, we would recknize dem real quick on New Year's. Dat made me and Bobby feel good cause we just didn't trust no one like dat who goes around blowing up people cause dey ain't a Muslim. Bobby started telling me da reason why we are in all dis trouble is cause we don't have no good leaders any moh. Dey are all chicken shit. One of his heroes wuz General Patton cause his dad served in da army wid him. Bobby said his dad would tell him all bout General Patton and dat he wuz no panty waist sissy like all da politicians and generals now.*

Bobby said his dad claimed dat General Patton told him dat when he get home he would be able ta say, "He didn't shovel no shit in Louisiana. Nope, he rode wid dat son of a gawddamned bitch named Georgie Patton!"

Bobby's dad loved General Patton and wuz proud he wuz in his army. He said George Patton swore a lot, not like dese pussy-ass generals we got now. Bobby's dad would tell us dat General Patton told his men ta rip out da living gawd-damned guts of da Krauts and use dem ta grease da treads of dere tanks if dey wanted ta win da war. Lot of times when we were talking bout problems in da Middle East at Bobby's house his dad would say do what general Patton told us ta do, "Murder dos lousy cocksuckers by da bushel-fucking-basket" and den you ain't got no moh problems.

Roberto Roma: *I have read some of the stories about General Patton. He was a real character and his men loved him, they say.*

Angola: *Well, I know Bobby's dad loved him. Anyway moh we talk bout tings, Bobby just gets moh madder bout what da Arabs did on Christmas. I tink part of it's all da whiskey he wuz drinking, but he just gets madder and madder. Finally he gets dis idea dat we need ta be like General Patton and kick some rag head ass. He wants ta go find a couple Arabs and beat da shit out of dem, but I tell him he is too drunk ta fight anyone. Den he says okay let's go ta Lake Charles and fuck up dere Gawd-damn church. I aks him what he wants ta do and he says let's find a couple pigs and put dem in dere church. I tell him he is fucking crazy, but he don't give up. He comes up wid another idea. "Okay let's get a bunch of pig knuckles and pour da shit all over dere place," He tells me. We are feeling better now and laughing our ass off. He tells me he got his ta-toe gun in his truck and we can load dat wid pig knuckles and shoot dem all over da church. I wuz pretty drunk maself and just feeling good. I didn't tink dis wuz not any big deal, cause we do a lot of crazy shit in Mamou and no one really cares dat much. We decide ta do it, and Bobby brings me over ta ma house and I* *get a bottle of whisky ta bring wid us and two six packs of beer.*

Roberto Roma: *So you were really drinking all the time, even at your home?*

Angola: *Yea, I wuz totally off da wagon. I ain't going ta deny it. So we had an hour or so ta drive so we wanted ta get going before it got too late.*

As we drove ta Lake Charles, we stopped at some convenience store and bought up most of da jars of pig knuckles and a few packages of pork sausage. We were going ta make balls of pork sausage foh da spud gun also.

We had got an address foh da Muslim church and had it plugged inta our GPS and we got dare real quick. We drove around da block a couple of times and it looked pretty quiet so we decided ta first just park da truck out front and Bobby got in da bed of da truck and got da ammo ready. We were laughing our ass off at da time. Anyway I wuz going ta be in da cab and be da lookout and he wuz going ta fire a few balls of pork sausage and pig's feet at da church.

Roberto Roma: *Did you see any lights on in the mosque?*

Angola: *No, dat wuz da funny part. It looked like nobody wuz dare, and den when Bobby shot a few times, dis guy in a robe comes running out of da place and is all yelling and mad as hell, but Bobby just shoot some moh pig's feet and sausage balls at him. I tink da guy got hit wid some of da stuff, but he keeps coming toward our truck and yelling all kinds of shit dat I can't understand. I tink he wuz talking in dat Arab talk. Just bout dat time I hear a police siren and reckon it's time ta get loss real quick. I yell at Bobby, who is still laughing like hell and doesn't hear me. I tried* *ta tell him da cops are coming but he is so wound up he don't hear me or he don't care. I gun da engine and we go flying out of dare. Bobby falls on his ass, but I can still hear him laughing. Ah'm going already like sixty miles an hour and take a turn down dis udder road and a cop car is coming down da same road raht at me. I step on da brakes, but ah'm going so fast dat ma car slides raht into da cop car and I smash ma head against da steering wheel real hard and split it open. I got blood dripping out all over me.*

Da cops are already out of dere car and are pointing guns at me. Ah'm in a terrible mess cause ah'm hurting from da accident, and I realize I need ta pee someting awful. I get out of da truck and try ta stand but Ah'm weaving all over da place. Dis cop comes towards me yelling some shit at me, but I can't hear him cause now I got like ten of dos Arabs all around me talking and yelling all kinds of shit Ah doan understand at all. Ah'm tottering and suddenly start falling toward da cop in front of me. Ta keep from falling I start staggering toward da cop and he tinks ah'm attacking him or someting and hit me in da head wid his flashlight and bust ma head wide open in da back. Now I got ma head cracked open in da front and in da back. I fall on da ground and dey all jump all over me. Ah'm trying ta do what dey tell me ta do but someone steps on ma fingers. I mean dey were squashing ma fingers like dey were a stomping out a cigarette butt. I tink it's one of dos Arabs standing on ma fingers and dey break two of ma fingers. Man, Ah'm trying ta pull ma hand back and da cop tinks ah'm fighting him so dey try ta taser me, but in da confusion da cop who has da taser presses it down on da hand of dis udder cop who wuz pushing me back down on da ground.

Roberto Roma: *You mean one cop tasered another cop?*

Angola: *Hell yes, swear ta Gawd! Wid all da shit going on around me, I could still hear him yelling at da cop wid da taser and calling him a fucking son of a bitch. I just can't hold it anymoh and piss ma pants and den dey hit me again in da head and dass all I remember until I wake up in a hospital all strapped down ta ma bed. When da cops talk ta me, dey say dey got me and Bobby on resisting arrest, attacking a cop, vandalizing a place of worship, and doing a hate crime. I thought dey would give me a fine and put me in jail a couple days, but no, dey got me dis crap lawyer and he tells me I should plead guilty ta all dis stuff cause dey are going ta go hard on people now after da attacks. So I take his advice and end up heah in Angola. I got ta do tree years heah before dey will even consider letting me out. It just ain't fair. Well, dass ma story.*

Roberto Roma: *So now in retrospect are you sorry about what you did?*

Angola: *Hell no, I ain't sorry! Ah'm sorry ah'm in prison. Shit, dese Arabs blow up our churches, and I go and just throw some pig parts on dem and dey act like I wuz da terrorist. But ah doan have a big time lawyer and a bunch of money ta protect me so ah'm in prison before dey even start trial foh dat Ali Hasson guy. He gets a big shot lawyer ta protect him and I get shit. He kills all kinds of people and blows up hospitals and churches and gets treated like royalty and I get da shits.*

Chapter 76
Final Notes on the New Year

I would be remiss if I didn't mention two very big news items that were announced on New Year's Day. The Chicago Tribune's headline blared the news that Abdul Hasson, the son of Ali Hasson, was wanted in relation to the murder of Steven Grubs and the disappearance of Hidi Najjar. Forensic evidence linked a purse found in the home of Abdul Hasson to the missing Hidi Najjar. It was believed the purse still contained some items of identification. Hidi Najjar had not been found, but sources close to the investigation indicated that a witness had been located who had information linking Abdul Hasson to her disappearance.

According to the article, police believed that Abdul Hasson had fled the country and was assumed to be in Europe or the Middle East. A taskforce had been created to find Abdul Hasson and bring him to justice. A tip from a reliable, confidential informant provided information that led authorities to believe that Hasson might be in the Waltham Forest area of London, England. This area of London had a large population of Muslims Against Crusades, or MAC, whose members would presumably assist in hiding Abdul Hasson from the authorities. Regardless of the alleged crimes of Abdul Hasson and his father Ali Hasson, many members of this predominantly Muslim community saw them as Allah's soldiers and heroes.

On some talk shows, there was even speculation that the award-winning physician Ali Hasson was innocent of the terrorist charges and that his son was the mastermind behind the Christmas Special. Others wondered why Ali Hasson was going to London when he was captured. Was he there to meet with his son? Many suspected that Abdul Hasson was very involved in the Christmas Special attacks.

For many days to follow, pictures of Abdul Hasson flashed across television screens, along with grainy surveillance videos of four other individuals who were suspected of being involved in the Christmas morning hospital bombings.

By New Year's Day, FEMA was handling the herculean task of coordinating the relocation of the thousands of people driven from their homes by the three nuclear disasters. FEMA used numerous resources to provide temporary housing for the evacuees. Military bases, state parks, thousands of FEMA trailers, private homes, and cruise ships had become a part of the solution to shelter the homeless families. Over twenty-two thousand people were being housed on cruise ships anchored in Mobile, Alabama; Los Angeles, California; and Bayonne, New Jersey. FEMA was in the process of contracting for more cruise ships because they provided a safe environment, were set up to feed and house large numbers of people, and they allowed FEMA medical staff to monitor and administer treatment for any health issues related to radiation exposure.

An additional announcement was made that free mental health services were being offered to all those affected by the nuclear disasters. Immediately, the ACLU and other legal watchdog groups warned that this type of service presented many legal problems for the evacuees. The fact that the services would be paid for by the nuclear power companies implied that the information collected in the study could be used to the detriment of the evacuees in the compensation process. Diagnosis of mental health concerns or the lack of any could be used against an evacuee's claim for compensation. Pre-existing mental health issues could be used to dismiss or mitigate the actual distress and other mental problems brought on by the loss of their homes, jobs, and communities as a result of the nuclear disaster.

Senator Katherine Laforge of Texas entered into the fray of politics surrounding the attacks with a proposal for a bill that would provide free medical care for life for those nuclear disaster evacuees aged eighteen and younger. A similar benefit in Japan was considered for the children who had been exposed to radiation from the damaged Fukushima nuclear power plant.

From the Chernobyl and Fukushima experience, it was evident that many children exposed to high levels of radiation would have continuing health issues—some that would kill them.

An email from a woman to her husband stationed in South Korea provided some sense of the urgency and chaos that existed as she and thousands more tried to evacuate from the town of Taft, Louisiana, near Waterford 3 Nuclear Power Plant.

> *Dear Russell:*
>
> *Well if you're reading this, I'm sorry, but I just could not hold on any longer. I won't be able to tell you in person how much I love you, but I did leave you a very beautiful Christmas present, your brand-new daughter Kirstin. She is a part of you and me, and she now needs all the love she can get. You need to give her the love I would have, along with all your*

own love. You're going to have your hands full. I hope you can handle it.

When they told me you were coming home from South Korea, I was so excited. It gave me strength, but all that radiation from the damn nuclear power plant was just too much for me. It's so scary that you can't see it or feel it or anything, but it's there and it creeps into your body and changes your cells just like cancer does. Honey, I made a big mistake when I pressured you into buying that cheap land near a nuclear power plant.

You loved me too much. You should have told me I was an idiot. Anyway, I hope you get compensated for all the grief and loss it has caused us.

I don't feel bad right now, so it's hard for me to believe that I'm dying, but that's what the doctor is telling me. I decided that while I was still able, I wanted to tell you what happened so you get the truth. I'm sure you know that we had to evacuate when they attacked Waterford 3. Well, I was still in bed while the fighting was going on. I was just lying there trying to think about what I'd left to do for Christmas when I thought I heard the siren going off. At first, I just dismissed it and tried to get a few more minutes of sleep. Then Brian came barging into my room and yelled, "Hey, Mom, you hear that siren?" It was probably like 5:45, and when I went to the window and looked out I saw lots of cars out on the road and a red glow in the sky over the nuclear power plant. The terrorists had set fire to cars, fuel and bunch of other stuff, and flames were shooting up in the sky. I turned on the TV, and they said there were terrorist attacks all across the country and many nuclear plants had been attacked and were spewing radiation into the atmosphere.

I'd forgot I was pregnant with all this excitement, but then I felt a sharp pain in my stomach and real quick I was reminded that Kirstin was waking up. She wasn't due till the twenty-eighth, so it would be a few more days before I got to see her. Anyway, I decided to call Mom and see what they were doing, but of course the phone lines were busy. We had electricity, and things seemed like normal so I heated up some coffee. I know, I should not be drinking any when I'm pregnant, but it's hard for me to quit.

So I sat down at the kitchen table and clicked from station to station on the news and I saw they were saying people were evacuating from Taft, La Place, Killona, Montz, Luling, and everywhere close to the plant. The reporter said people should leave immediately and try not to be exposed to the air any more than necessary. We were supposed to keep the car windows up and just circulate the air in the car and not let any from outside in. Well, the reports were scaring me. I knew we were only two miles from the plant, so I knew I needed to leave.

I grabbed a bunch of clothes and packed our Beetle and also picked out some of the Christmas presents for Brian. I just left everything else on and got out on the road as fast as I could. I had the car radio turned on and was hearing all kinds of stories about people being shot and explosions and some hospitals that were blown up. It sounded like a war was going on right here in America.

I didn't even know where I was going once I got out on the road. As we were driving down South River Road, we got stopped by a four-car pileup and had to go around that. I had to drive over the grass alongside the road, and the car was bouncing around like crazy, and this old Lincoln or something behind me was honking at me to move faster. Anyway, that was when my water broke. I couldn't believe it. I was going into contractions. I gave the guy behind me the finger, and he pushed his car right into the back of the Beetle and started pushing us along.

Brian realized something awful was going on because I was moaning and screaming, and he got up on the seat and started yelling at the guy pushing our car and he backed away. I pulled the car further into the grass and stopped and tried to catch my breath. I realized that I was going to have Kirstin right there, but the Beetle was so small and packed with so much stuff I knew I could not have her in the car. Brian kept asking me what was wrong, and I told him mommy was having a baby and I needed his help. I told him he had to try to stop someone to help me get to a hospital. He gave me a quick kiss, told me he would get help, and jumped out of the car. Next thing I see him running up and down the side of the road yelling at cars. It was awful at first because no one was paying any attention to him. They wouldn't even roll their windows down to ask him what was wrong. Then the traffic came to a halt again, and he started to bang on people's car windows to get their attention.

The bastards still wouldn't help him, but then Harry Watkins, the young guy who was the janitor at Brian's school, recognized him and came to my rescue. He had a truck full of stuff, but they had some blankets and they made like a mattress in the bed of his truck for me to lie in. His wife, Shovonya, got in the back with me and tried to comfort me. She tried to keep this handkerchief over my face, but I was screaming so much it was useless. I was gulping in that air like crazy. I think that was what got me. She had one of those masks you use when you're painting, and I think she is okay from what I have been told. Anyway she helped me a lot.

I think my screaming traumatized Brian. He said I just screamed and screamed for what seemed like forever. Harry tried to get us back into the line of cars on River Road, but it was very hard because no one would let anyone else get in front of them. Finally, he got in there, and I think Kirstin was born while we were inching through Mimosa Park. They said I passed out, and it was not until I woke up in the hospital that I knew Kirstin was okay. Next to my bed, our wonderful son Brian was sitting and waiting to say hello to me. When I came to, he came over and kissed me all over. Brian is so much like you. He is very brave and does all the good things. Anyway, I could tell he was trying not to cry.

He was shaking and didn't want me to see his face, so I tried to kiss him and that was when I felt my face feel like

I had a sunburn or something and my lips were so dry. A nurse noticed I was stirring and went and got a doctor. Doctor Arnold came to my bed and asked the nurse to take Brian outside so he could talk to me. The first thing I thought was he was going to tell me that Kirstin was dead, but of course that was not what he had to tell me. He told me I'd lost a lot of blood and unfortunately had been exposed to a very large amount of radiation. He didn't come right out and say I was going to die, but he said it was best that I try to use this time to get all my things in order just in case. He told me that Kirstin seemed fine, and she would be brought in so I could see and hold her, but Doctor Arnold warned me that I wouldn't be able to nurse her.

It broke my heart that they were saying I was so sick with radiation that my milk could harm her. I wanted to see her, so they brought her in along with Brian. Kirstin was beautiful. She was all little baby smiles and was not even crying. Brian was all smiles watching and told me that after I'd passed out he got back in the cab and held Kirstin all the way to the hospital. I could tell he really didn't know how sick I was.

As crazy as it might seem, I'm very grateful for this trial or whatever it was. Even while people were trying to kill us, I gave birth to a beautiful baby. They couldn't stop that. God is telling me something or you something. He sure gave us something beautiful. That has to mean something. Every Christmas is not just the birth of Jesus; it's also our daughter's birthday.

Wow and what about our son? What a wonderful boy. I'm so proud of him. He has a heart of gold.

We had such a beautiful home. You were so talented. It makes me sad that it's gone now. I'm sure it will be in this new exclusion zone for fifty years or more. No one has any idea when anyone could ever move back, but if we are as bad as they say, then we can use Chernobyl and Fukushima to know it will be many, many years and probably not in any of our lifetimes. I did take some beautiful pictures of the house decorated in Christmas lights before this all happened and you can see them on Facebook.

Russell, I know this has to hurt you because I know how much you loved me. As odd as it seems, that gives me some comfort to know that my life meant that much to someone. I know how sad I'd be if they told me you were dead. I want you to know that I really couldn't have asked for anyone better than you. If you feel sad, just think back to all the memories that we shared. Look at Brian and Kirstin and how beautiful they are and remember that we made them with God's help.

I know I don't need to remind you, but please be strong for them. Remind them about me and tell them how much I adored both of them, more than anything else in the world. Make sure Kirstin does not feel guilty about what happened to me and that she knows her birth was one of the best days of my life. She was certainly one of the best things that ever happened to me. Her smile and laughter rep-

resent all that's good and beautiful in a world that is so screwed up with hate.

Please tell them that Mommy is in heaven with all the angels, and I will watch over them and protect them always. I love you, Russell. But never be afraid to do what you need to do to be happy. Our children will need a new mommy, and you will need a new wife. I will be watching that you do move on in life and find another special person who will love you and care for them with love. You may think this is impossible right now, but it's not.

Sweetheart, better days are coming. I'm so happy I got to share the days I had with you. Please make sure Kirstin, Brian, and you have a wonderful life together. Give them my love often. I love you so much and hate to say good-bye, but as they say, all good thing eventually come to an end.

I love you.
Your loving wife,
Celia

Waterford 3 Exclusion Zone
Right outside New Orleans
N
W
E
S
Lake Maurepas
Lake Pontchartrain
Convent
New Orleans
Marrero
Woodmere
Jean Lafitte Preserve
Thibodaux
Timken Wildlife Management Area
Schriever
Raceland
Lake Salvador
NEW ORLEANS 5
THE MEMORY OF THE TOWNS AND VILLAGES THAT ONCE WERE
THIS MEMORIAM IS DEDICATED TO
VIBRANT COMMUNITIES OF LOUISIANA
THE EVACUATED
OF LOUISIANA
STATE OF LOUISIANA
UNION JUSTICE
CONFIDENCE
KILLONA
MONTZ
LAPLACE
NORCO
KENNER
HAHNVILLE
LULING
ST. ROSE
RIVER RIDGE
RESERVE
HARAHAN
AVONDALE
VACHARIE
LOUIS AMSTRONG INTERNATIONAL AIRPORT
NEW SARPY
GOOD HOPE
WAGGAMAN
AMA
DESTREHAN
GARRYVILLE
EDGARD
LUTCHER
GRAMERCY
ST. JOHN THE BAPTIST PARISH AIRPORT
PARADIS
BOUTTE
THEIR MEMORIES WILL LIVE ON

Chapter 77: Where in the World Is Abdul Hasson?

The search for Abdul Hasson intensified after the announcement of his suspected involvement in the death of Steven Grubs and Hidi Najjar. Interpol jumped in and issued a Red Notice on Abdul Hasson on January second. All 188 Interpol member countries were notified that Abdul was wanted for murder and possible terrorist activities. All border control agencies were also notified of Abdul Hasson's Red Notice status and were asked to help in his apprehension. As tight as the noose appeared, Abdul Hasson was not quickly apprehended. In fact, his whereabouts were unknown until months later. Initially, Abdul was tracked to London, but then his trail evaporated.

Where was Abdul Hasson during the search? For those first few months, he was given refuge in a London mosque.

To learn what I could about Abdul's escape from arrest, I talked to the Mufti Alhaj Manik Ahmed in London, who gave sanctuary to Abdul. The transcript of our conversation follows.

> **Roberto Roma:** *Thank you for taking time to talk to me about Abdul Hasson. When did you first meet him?*
>
> **Mufti:** *Well, Mr. Roma, as odd as it might appear, I'd never heard of or seen Abdul Hasson before the afternoon he sought my help. Another man who I will not name brought young Hasson to me. When I realized who he was, my first inclination was to cast him out so our*

mosque wouldn't be seen as supporting terrorism.

Roberto Roma: *You knew he was wanted for murder and terrorism?*

Mufti: *Of course. Something as big as the attack on America, I'd know. The attack on America was an attack on Islam also.*

Roberto Roma: *So why wouldn't you turn him in? It seems to me that if you had turned him in, that act would have told the world that you're against terrorism and you don't condone the actions of these radicals. Plus, there was that two million dollar reward for Abdul Hasson.*

Mufti: *Well, Mr. Romano, I must admit that I had a very strong desire to do just that and for most of the reasons you mentioned, but I also have an obligation to provide sanctuary for those who seek it here at the mosque. When a person enters the mosque, he is in a sacred place, a place where only Allah's laws are followed. He came to me for sanctuary, and I must give it to him, Allah willing, regardless of man's laws.*

Roberto Roma: *I thought you didn't give sanctuary to criminals?*

Mufti: *Mr. Hasson was not a criminal, only a man accused of a crime. He hadn't been convicted of anything. He was wanted for questioning, and this is London. We don't abide by rules made in America. It's important that your readers understand that we don't just harbor Muslims from persecution. As a Muslim and as a religious leader, it's my duty to grant asylum to anyone who seeks it. In fact, the Prophet Muhammad preached that we should grant refuge indiscrimi-*

nately, unconditionally, and humanely to all seeking it, regardless of their religion. The granting of refuge was so important to Muhammad that he started our Islamic calendar based on the first day he was given refuge in Medina.

Roberto Roma: *Well, I must admit I had no idea of how important the custom of granting asylum was to your religion. I can understand the dilemma you must have felt facing this responsibility of making the decision to turn him over to the authorities or giving him refuge.*

Mufti: *It really was not very much of a problem to make the decision. Allah had made the decision for me, and it was my duty to follow his commandments. You see, Islam, our mosque, and our religious leaders have time after time been faced with asylum seekers, and Allah willing, our response should always be the same. Remember, "No discrimination" was Muhammad's command. Mr. Roma, we are very proud of the bravery our religious leaders have demonstrated in granting sanctuary to people who might otherwise been imprisoned or even murdered by their persecutors. The imams of the Grand Mosque of Kigali and the madrassa of Nyanza Rwanda are famous for sheltering Hutus, Tutsis, and Christians during the 1994 Rwandan genocide. In fact, while this good deed was being done, over a thousand Tutsis were being slaughtered in a Catholic Church in Nyange, Rwanda, because the priest, Athanase Seromba, gave them false refuge. In fact, this man of the Christian God helped in their slaughter and now serves* *a life sentence for the crime of genocide and crimes against humanity.*

Mr. Roma, I don't say these things to imply that Catholics are evil...that's not my intentions. It's simply an observation that in all great religions we will find a few cancers growing that must be excised before they metastasize and kill the entire body.

Roberto Roma: *I agree there will always be a few rotten apples in the barrel, so it just makes me wonder even more why you wouldn't have at least cast Hasson out of your mosque and made him hide somewhere that didn't tarnish your image?*

Mufti: *My image would have been tarnished forever if I hadn't followed the custom of granting asylum. This is a custom, a good custom that goes back hundreds of years. It's even written in your Western literature as a good thing.*

For example, in that famous book Les Miserables you have Valjean, a convicted criminal, given refuge in a Catholic convent to help him escape his pursuers. People saw that as a good thing.

Roberto Roma: *You make a good point. There are not simple solutions to these questions. How long did Hasson stay with you?*

Mufti: *Abdul Hasson stayed a few months with us. I cannot give you the exact length of time, but during his stay he was isolated from all of us except those who fed him and counseled him. I know you would like me to tell you where he went, but that's information I don't have because I didn't speak to those who finally came and moved him to a new refuge.*

I'd suspect it was somewhere else in London because he had many admirers here in London.

Roberto Roma: *I understand you didn't socialize with Abdul Hasson, but did he mention anything about what he was accused of?*

Mufti: *Abdul, of course, denied he had ever killed anyone. However, he claimed he did know who did these killings, but that America wouldn't want the truth to be known. Abdul believed that your government would just want to kill him because he was the son of Ali Hasson. He was convinced that he would be killed in the same fashion that America killed Osama bin Laden and Anwar al-Awlaki. He feared that if he was taken into custody he would be killed by American thugs who would say he was reaching for a weapon, just like they did with Osama. America's justice system is not one many Muslims have much faith in any longer. When Muslims see that the president of the United States orders the killing of Muslim men at whim without trial or appeal, it paints America as a country of hypocrites.*

Roberto Roma: *You truly believe that Muslims see America as a country of hypocrites?*

Mufti: *America talks about the high ground, but it waddles in the mud of hypocrisy. History is not only taught in America, but in all countries, and many things that America preaches that other countries do are as evil as the things it does itself. America does not publicize its sins as it does the sins of others. Do you know who Posada Carriles is?*

Roberto Roma: *No, I must admit the name does not ring any bells. Who is he?*

Mufti: *Posada Carriles, or Bambi as your CIA called him, is a man much of the world thinks of as the "bin Laden of the Americas." He lives in Florida under the protection of the United States and is believed by many to be the mastermind behind the blowing up of a Cubana Airliner that killed fifty-seven people, as well as many other bombings in Cuba. Venezuela requested his extradition for seventy-three counts of murder, but your country refuses to turn him over.*

Think about how America would react if the government of Cuba or Venezuela carried out a targeted assassination of Posada Carriles in Florida. A secret operation of assassination right on American soil, as your country did in Pakistan with Osama bin Laden. What would America do if President Raul Castro announced to the world that "justice had finally been served, that commandos had put a bullet right in Posada Carriles's face" and then dumped his body in the Gulf of Mexico, which prompted Cubans and Venezuelans to dance for joy in the streets.

Do you doubt that in just a few hours there would be an emergency meeting of the UN Security Council condemning the action and authorizing the U.S. to take "all necessary measures" to protect its national security and residents, including sanctioning retaliatory attacks aimed at Cuba and Venezuela? What do you think would happen? Is this a valid question?

Roberto Roma: *You make a good point. As I said before, I know nothing about this man you claim is a terrorist, so it wouldn't be fair for me to answer your question without first researching the story behind Posada Carriles. I do promise you that I will look into this person and mention your comments about him in my book. Is there anything else you can tell me about Abdul Hasson?*

Mufti: *No, Mr. Roma, there is really nothing I can add to what we have already discussed. I must return to my duties now.*

Roberto Roma: *Well, I want to thank you for your time and your candid remarks. I hope your comments will help others understand the complexities of your obligations and the rights of seekers of sanctuary in your mosque.*

Chapter 78
Justice for Jason

On January the second, a couple hours after the opening bell of the New York Stock Exchange, the DOW Jones hemorrhaged almost seven hundred points. The bloodletting was so fierce that within three hours, the market sputtered to a stop and stayed closed till two that afternoon. Once it reopened, the losses continued unabated, and by the closing bell, America had bled away more than $1.4 trillion.

The containment of the nuclear power sites was still an ongoing battle with man making little, if any, real headway. Brave men fought these deadly radiation-spewing monsters, but all three nuclear power plants remained out of control. By now, the National Security Council was being skewered by the press as incompetent bungling bureaucrats who had proven to the world that man is still capable of life without a functioning brain. One reporter quipped that staffing the National Security Council with comatose individuals was perhaps just too an extreme application of the American Disability Act.

The National Security Advisor admitted that, in hindsight, they should have seen the nuclear power plants, especially Indian Point, as an inevitable terrorist target.

Downwind from the IPEC were high value targets, Times Square, Ellis Island, the New York Stock Exchange...virtually all of New York City. The perfect conditions for a deadly release of radiation was on a day with a strong southerly wind, which is exactly what happened on that Christmas morning. And it happened times three across the country. The radiation levels quickly reached critical points, and the governors of the three states ordered the evacuation of their most heavily irradiated areas. Millions of people fled and hunkered down wherever they found suitable lodging. Everyone hoped and prayed the worst was over, but it wasn't.

The largest single-day drop in the stock exchange's history happened January the second. By the end of that first week, however, that number had continued to drop to a loss of almost 1,100 points. The estimated loss sustained by America because of the Christmas Special attacks was put at $5.5 trillion. This price tag exceeded America's total cost of fighting the Second World War, which hovered around $5 trillion. The fact that a mere handful of determined terrorists could create such financial devastation was mind-boggling. But these numbers were easy to comprehend if you considered that these nuclear plants were located in areas that encompassed essentially 10 percent of America's population. The three targeted nuclear power plants were high-value targets because they were surrounded by airports, refineries, military bases, prisons, and thousands of other essential businesses. Their destruction would have a crippling effect on America and devastate the nation's morale for years.

The obvious indifference to the risk these nuclear plants had posed to their communities had been so pervasive among the employees and local residents that sympathy quickly began to wane for the victims.

The closing of West Point because of its proximity to Indian Point Nuclear Power Plant and the evacuation of most of Camp Pendleton because of its closeness to San Onofre was a tremendous financial loss but also a stinging symbolic loss to America's military. It seemed unfathomable that three terrorist teams of fifteen men each could create such a catastrophe...but they did. They had succeeded in making the financial losses caused by the Christmas Special attacks dwarf the 9/11 attacks by trillions of dollars.

Beside the flood of lawsuits by residents of the evacuated areas who were trying to get compensation for their lost homes and livelihood, the collapse of the stock market opened another floodgate of litigation. As stock prices plummeted, shareholders sued corporate officers and directors for negligent hiring practices, conspiracy and negligence, breach of fiduciary duty, and simple mismanagement. Many of the lawsuits had merit and proceeded, with millions of dollars eventually awarded to the plaintiffs. The Christmas Special had created a plethora of business for lawyers.

One lawsuit that took shape soon after the first of the year was Roger Wilgers versus Culper, Texas Police Department, et al. On January third, Roger Wilgers found a Texas lawyer named James Pearson who was confident he could win a wrongful death case against the Culper, Texas, police department. He felt there was a clear case of deliberate indifference demonstrated by the Culper police force and their district attorney. I talked to Roger Wilgers's attorney, James Pearson, about the lawsuit. A part of the conversation follows.

Roberto Roma: *After the death of Jason Wilgers, his father, Roger, asked you to file suit against the Culper, Texas, police force. Could you tell me a little about what the lawsuit was about?*

James Pearson: *Well, the death of*

Jason was a terrible injustice and a horrible emotional blow to his father, Roger, but making it even worse were the circumstances around his death. Jason Wilgers died because he was trying to do good. The plain and simple of it was Jason was willing to put his future at risk to stop the terrorist attacks. Jason would have been the proverbial Paul Revere of the twenty-first century—if he hadn't been muzzled by a bungling detective and a nine-to-five district attorney who was a holiday drunkard.

Remember, Jason was the first to really know that a terrorist attack was going to happen on Christmas morning. If due diligence had prevailed and they had listened to him, the entire attack on America could've probably been prevented. Unfortunately, Culper's police department appeared more interested in arresting and prosecuting Jason for ridiculous sex laws that December the twenty-third than looking into his claim.

Roberto Roma: *Could you back up a bit and elaborate why you said the district attorney was a drunkard?*

James Pearson: *Buddy Parks, the district attorney of Culper, was well known for his drinking. In fact, on the afternoon of December the twenty-third, he took off early to attend a Christmas party at the Shady Lady Gentleman's Club just off of I-10 before you enter Houston. This was a big, loud party of police officers from around the Houston area being entertained by virtually nude women from eighteen to fifty-three. Old Buddy had an eye on a certain damsel at the Shady Lady who he frequently slept with instead of* *his wife of twenty-six years. She was a petite but large-busted Brazilian lady who had worked at the Shady Lady for a year and a half and slept with Buddy so she could keep her job there. She claimed he had told her that he could send her back to Brazil if she wasn't nice to him. Anyway, when officer Krewell was interrogating Jason, he called Buddy to see what he should do with him. According to Krewell, the district attorney said something like, "Hold the little prick over for the night and I will deal with this pervert in the morning."*

Krewell claimed he told the district attorney about the terrorist threat, but Buddy claims he didn't. The call wasn't recorded so it's anyone's guess what really was said. Krewell claimed also that good old Buddy instructed him to hint to the other detainees what Jason was in there for. Krewell claimed that Buddy wanted him to get a good scare in him that night. The pole dancer corroborated the story that Buddy did get the call and after hanging up continued to have sex with her. So much for shopping for his wife!

Roberto Roma: *In retrospect, that makes a very sad, pathetic story.*

James Pearson: *And you only heard a sliver of it. So while Mr. Law and Order, Buddy Parks, was boinking Miss Brazil, Officer Krewell was bringing Jason down to the holding cells. Krewell was in a rush because he hadn't finished his Christmas shopping and wanted to complete it that night. The total lack of professionalism in dealing with this situation infuriated me. When I got four statements* *from individuals who were in the holding cell at the time Krewell pushed Jason into it, I knew I'd won the case. They all told me that as Krewell walked away from the cell, he said to the guard really loud, "Watch this guy. He likes them really young, a regular Pebbles banger."*

Roberto Roma: *What is a Pebbles banger?*

James Pearson: *Slang for a pedophile, a guy who likes little girls really young like Pebbles from the Flintstones. Officer Krewell just wanted to get some heat going on Jason, but he forgot who was in that cell. He had a couple really rough characters in there with Jason who probably were the ones who eventually did the deed, but we can't prove it.*

Anyway, Jason started getting harassed right off. No one wanted him near them. Every time he tried to find a place to stand or sit, he was told to go somewhere else in the cell. Some pushed him, some kicked him, and a few actually punched him in the face. The guard either didn't watch his monitor or thought Jason deserved what he got. Bottom line, no one interfered in Jason's beatings.

After about thirty minutes of this harassment, Jason punched back at one of these guys and landed a lucky one in the guy's face. That infuriated everyone so they grabbed Jason and dragged him over to the steel toilet that everyone shared. Someone decided that Jason was due a HIT, which is something like a Swirly shown in a lot of movies about geeks. A HIT, however, is even more degrading. It's basically forcing a person's head in the toilet water while their body is used for sex. In Jason's case, it was even more degrading and ugly. Someone removed Jason's jail-issued sandals, bunched them up, and forced them up into his anus. This act ripped open the skin around his anus, and he was bleeding heavily.

Roberto Roma: *How long was Jason in the cell before he was killed?*

James Pearson: *It was probably only forty-five minutes. It's hard to say precisely.*

Roberto Roma: *What was the cause of Jason's death?*

James Pearson: *Jason's death resulted from asphyxiation, which could have been caused by the numerous injuries he sustained or even from drowning.*

Roberto Roma: *Drowning? Could you explain that.*

James Pearson: *The autopsy revealed that Jason had water in his lungs. His inhalation of water from the toilet bowl was sufficient enough to have actually drowned him. In fact, even a small amount of water can cause drowning if the water blocks the alveoli. In Jason's case, as he struggled with his killers and tried to breathe, it resulted in him drawing in considerable amounts of water from the toilet bowl.*

Roberto Roma: *Do you agree with that or you feel that his injuries could have been what killed him?*

James Pearson: *The Culper, Texas, medical examiner believed that the actual cause of Jason's death was a crushed larynx. This certainly could have been what ended Jason's life because a* *crushed larynx would have prevented him from breathing.*

Both the Culper police and my investigation agree that during the time Jason's head was forced into the stainless steel toilet bowel, his throat was pressed down onto its steel edge. Someone held him there with their hands, feet, or by pressing a knee down on the back of his neck. Between Jason's struggle to free himself and his killers' intentions of holding him there, his larynx was crushed, making it impossible for him to breathe. In either case, Jason died because he could not breathe. He was asphyxiated.

Roberto Roma: *Did you feel you had a good case that would win?*

James Pearson: *If you want to call a sad situation like this a good or bad case, well, I guess I had a good case because of how foolish those Culper officials treated Jason.*

Yes, I did feel like I had a grand slam once I knew more about the case. A district attorney in bed with a pole dancer when he should be taking care of business and the idea of hinting to others in the cell what Jason was in for assured me of a win. At least that's how I felt. Just the fact that they decided to hold Jason in a holding cell with violent criminals was a negligent act by itself. But they went further by announcing to the perps sharing the cell that Jason was there for sex with a minor. That was just stirring the pot. They wanted something to happen. They wanted him to feel uncomfortable. This was a case of deliberate indifference.

The whole country read about the stupidity of Buddy and Krewell, and they were hated almost as much as Ali Hasson. If those two officials had handled the investigation professionally, they could have saved many lives and billions or trillions of dollars, but their insistence of shirking their duties made them culpable.

I decided to settle for $2.4 million with the city because I knew much more would break them. It wasn't enough to make anything really better. In fact, no amount of money would make things right, but it was some solace to Mr. Wilgers that the city apologized for its mistake and offered what was a considerable sum of money for a town of that size. Roger Wilgers understood and accepted the deal and that was it. I haven't talked to him since we signed all the papers and set up trust funds for the distribution of the money.

Roberto Roma: *So who actually killed Jason?*

James Pearson: *That's something we probably will never know. Surveillance videos showed only a cluster of individuals clustered around the area where the toilet was located. Jason is not visible at all in the video so it's difficult to assign blame to any specific person.*

Roberto Roma: *My God, what a horrible way to die. I've got to thank you, counselor, for all the information, and I want to tell you I'm glad you won the case.*

Chapter 79
The Big Storm

At 10 a.m., on the third of January, Thomas Lawrence's secretary Darlene Kerns handed him an envelope from the prosecution that he hoped contained some of the government's evidence against Ali Hasson.

Lawrence knew that early discovery was imperative in terrorist cases if he had any hope of winning, or at least having his client's charges reduced. In fact, the day after he accepted the case, he started an aggressive press for full and complete access to all material and witnesses that might help in building the defense. Without the prosecution's evidence and exculpatory material against Hasson, it would be virtually impossible to plan a defense strategy to use against the government's claims.

Lawrence tore open the envelope and removed its contents. He unfolded the document and saw that it was not any type of evidence, but a plea agreement that stipulated if Ali Hasson pleaded guilty to the stated charges, he would be spared the death sentence. A handwritten note clipped to the documents stated that the offer was good for only the next seventy-two hours. It also stated that the government was seriously considering labeling Ali Hasson an "enemy combatant," which would allow them to hold him for an indefinite period of time—uncharged and without access to counsel.

Lawrence knew the government's pressure was just starting. The prosecution wanted a conviction and fast. They wanted to put this case to bed and with the least amount of media coverage.

To provide a clearer picture of what the Lawrence law firm was doing January third, I've included my interview with Darlene Kerns, who was Thomas Lawrence's private secretary.

Roberto Roma: *Thank you for helping us tell Thomas Lawrence's story.*

Darlene Kerns: *I'm glad to have the chance to do whatever I can to tell his story. He was a wonderful man and a great lawyer.*

Roberto Roma: *Do you remember what was going on January the third, the day you received a plea offer from the prosecution?*

Darlene Kerns: *Oh yes! That was a terribly bad day. As Mr. Lawrence's private secretary, I helped him on many issues, not just legal matters. The first thing we looked at that morning was how much money he was down because of the stock market crash. He had lost hundreds of thousands of dollars, at least on paper. Our office mailroom was stacked high with hate mail and packages from our fans that were often full of excrement. We opened a few of the letters and then decided to have others on the staff review them because their words were so hateful and divisive. It made you feel like people were going to charge through the door any minute and hang us all for Mr. Lawrence being Ali Hasson's defense lawyer.*

Roberto Roma: *Why didn't you just throw all that mail out?*

Darlene Kerns: *We couldn't just destroy all our mail because some of it might have been from someone who could help our case. We had to hire experts in dealing with this mail issue because some* *of the boxes were rigged with springs that would fling their contents everywhere.*

In fact, we first asked a couple interns to handle the job, but they were quickly ready to quit when some of the rigged boxes splattered them with who knows what. Some of the boxes contained stink bombs, which produced a horribly nauseous odor. We were under siege by the government, the citizens, and also the weather that morning.

Roberto Roma: *How did the weather affect you?*

Darlene Kerns: *Well, on the evening of January third, Mr. Lawrence, along with some of his investigators, was supposed to fly to Toronto, Canada, to see the terrorist training camp and interview the neighbors who lived around it. Of course, it didn't happen because of the huge snowstorm that hit that day. If you remember, that storm just devastated the northeast and hit us so hard that O'Hare was shut down for over twenty-four hours. The snow was a foot deep on the runways.*

I had a sister who lived in Blackstone, Virginia, and they even received a foot of snow, which is more than they normally receive the entire winter. So because of the inability to fly out, Mr. Lawrence decided to switch gears and get a statement out to the media to try to create pressure on the government to try Ali Hasson in federal court as an American citizen.

Roberto Roma: *Why did Lawrence want to do that?*

Darlene Kerns: *Well, since we were having tremendous problems with* *discovery, Mr. Lawrence considered the note from the prosecutor's office a signal indicating that we would have to really fight for any discovery. Luckily, Thomas Lawrence had already started his own investigation into the charges against Ali Hasson. In fact, by the evening of January the second, his staff had completed interviewing over sixty potential witnesses. These were just the people who knew Ali Hasson in and around Chicago.*

Thomas thought that if the firm could get the media talking about the case and how the government was hindering it, folks would demand that the government be more transparent with the evidence and what was happening. People were angry at the government, and Mr. Lawrence hoped that the attorney general would concede to the public's desire and have this cased tried in public court just like the O. J. Simpson murder trial or the Julius and Ethel Rosenberg case. He was sure that if he could secure favorable media coverage, the government would have no alternative but to try Hasson in federal court.

Roberto Roma: *So what did Thomas Lawrence say in his statement to the press?*

Darlene Kerns: *Defending Ali Hasson had placed Mr. Lawrence in the celebrity arena, where his most mundane utterance was reported over and over and dissected by every pundit who breathed.*

The press clamored for his comments, and when he announced that he was having a press conference at our office in Chicago, all the major networks fought the snow and showed up. The con-

ference room was jammed full, and more reporters stood in the hallway. It probably wasn't just the fact that he was defending the most hated terrorist ever...excuse me, I should have said accused terrorist...the media had also become increasingly keen on terrorist cases in which no information about the evidence behind the government's assertions were provided.

Anyway, Thomas Lawrence was an excellent orator so his statement was well received. Let me read to you the statement that he made:

"I want to thank all of you for finding the time and courage to venture out into this horrible storm. I hope that what I have to tell you will make your trip worthwhile. So with no further ado, let me start with sharing with you the correspondence I received from the government earlier today.

I received a written threat that my client, an American citizen, would be declared an enemy combatant by the attorney general of the United States unless Ali Hasson immediately accepts a plea agreement admitting to all charges.

So what might you ask is the significance of all that? What does all that mean? Well, it means that the government of the United States apparently does not want its citizens to ever know what really happened and who may have been complicit in this terrible attack on America. The choices my client were given preclude the story ever being told, and the citizens of the United States deserve to know the truth behind the devastating Christmas morning attacks.

The fact is, if my client Ali Hasson is declared an enemy combatant, he will be whisked away to indefinitely rot in some secret prison, and the American public will be denied the facts. With no trial, the American public will be cheated out of knowing why the attacks happened and how.

Ladies and gentlemen of the press, the Christmas Special attacks were sophisticated attacks, using military vehicles, powerful explosives, high-powered weapons, C4, rocket-propelled grenades, shaped charges, and other military equipment. How did these terrorists acquire all of this? Why were these nuclear power plants such soft targets? Why wasn't our government ready to respond to these events more efficiently? If Ali Hasson is guilty, who did he represent? Or was this simply an attack by a nationless enemy? Who financed these attacks? If the government refuses to try Ali Hasson in public court, those questions and many others will never be answered for the public.

As heinous as the crimes my client Ali Hasson has been accused of, it's still incumbent on our government that he be afforded the same rights as any other American accused of a crime. Unfortunately, that has not been my experience so far in my attempts to defend Ali Hasson. I have been rebuffed and denied access to much of the crucial evidence that the government claims it has against my client. It is obvious the government is willfully denying my client's Fifth and Sixth Amendment rights to fair trial and due process. I cannot mount a proper defense for Ali Hasson if I'm not provided the evidence the government has against my client.

I think it's important that the citizens of America have a chance to know what contributed to these incredible attacks and learn why we were so vulnerable. It has been just a little over a decade since the 9/11 attacks shocked the world. It took years before a reluctant government finally created the 9/11 Commission to investigate the attacks. The watered-down results still painted a horrible picture of ineptitude. The report showed that our nation had been ill prepared for such an event, but at the same time we were expecting an attack.

The horror brought on by the 9/11 attacks and the embarrassment of our vulnerability afflicted our nation with a mass amnesia. America found it more comfortable to will itself to a state of forgetfulness of what had happened in 9/11 and didn't prepare for another attack. But now we are faced once more with a similar fate, where a small group of dedicated adversaries have succeeded in seriously wounding our great nation. Isn't it important this time for our citizens to know how history once again repeated itself?

I sincerely hope you will do your part in demanding that our citizens be allowed to know the truth, regardless of how uncomfortable the truth may be. Contact your congressman and senators and demand what is rightfully yours. Thank you all again."

Well, that was his prepared speech, and the reporters ate it up and went back and blasted the government with pronouncements of a cover-up and some even harped about denying citizens their Fifth and Sixth Amendment rights to fair trial and due process.

Roberto Roma: *So would you say Thomas Lawrence hit a home run with his speech?*

Darlene Kerns: *In a way, we did. The media got people talking about the need for the government to keep the public informed. Congress heard from millions of constituents, and the president and his administration were attacked for trying to erode the rights of citizens under the pretense of protecting the nation.*

There was some backlash by the nuclear energy industry and lobby. Those people just wanted Hasson to quickly go away so the story wouldn't be told. They were afraid of more political fallout. The day the story broke, more problems were reported at the Indian Point Nuclear Power Plant. Apparently, many of the pipes at the plant had eroded considerably over its almost forty years of use, and when the three-day snowstorm hit, they froze and split open, spewing thousands of gallons of highly radiated water all over the plant grounds. This, of course, froze into huge radioactive ice sheets. This was very similar to what happened at the Fukushima plant a year after its nuclear catastrophe. The split pipes made it even more complicated to find an effective way to pump coolant to the stricken plant. So those directly affected by this new complication probably would have liked to see Ali Hasson and Mr. Lawrence both lined up in front of a firing squad.

Roberto Roma: *Very interesting day. Were there any other highlights you remember from January the second?*

Darlene Kerns: *Well, yes, there was a lot more we did that day. We made up list of obvious witnesses we wanted to interview. Of course, on the list were Hasson's two children, Sheeva and Abdul, but one was under protective custody and the other was in hiding. We also wanted to talk to Mr. Wilgers, the father of Jason Wilgers. We wanted to hear everything he might know about the plans Jason supposedly found and translated.*

We also wanted to explore the theory that Abdul was the real kingpin behind the Christmas Special attacks. We wondered why he ran and why he was so hard to find. The government had been looking for him for over a week with a multimillion-dollar award, and yet not a single clue to his whereabouts had been reported. Maybe the CIA had him in custody and was unwilling to divulge the information.

With the total lack of cooperation from the government regarding discovery, we decided to mount a full-court, frontal assault on every aspect of what we knew about its case. Lawrence told his assistants they would have to fight hard to have the evidence declassified, and then we would have to thoroughly examine it for any mistakes in the propriety of the government's investigation.

Much of our attacks would be launched by using the media to stir the pot. We wanted the government to feel it necessary to tell the public the premise of its case. Making members of the admin-

istration feel the heat from its citizens and the ridicule of the media pundits often forced their hand, and that was what Thomas Lawrence was counting on.

Chapter 80
White Christmas at Sing Sing

The historic snowfall of January had tremendous repercussions on the towns within the Indian Point exclusion zone. Since the attack, most of the area had been without any electrical power. The reasons were many, but primary was the fact that the Indian Point Nuclear Power Plant was no longer producing any power. Since its demise, New York City and the surrounding area had to adjust to having 30 percent less electrical power available. To compensate, electricity was diverted from the entire exclusion zone. This included the towns of Buchanan, Jones Point, Verplanck, Montrose, Peekskill, Tomkins Cove, Annsville, Pleasantside, Crugers, Furnace Woods, West Haverstraw, Mount Ivy, New City, Hamman, Mohegan Lake, Ossining, Jefferson Valley-Yorktown, Yorktown Heights, Pomona, Shrub Oak, Wesly Hills, Highland Falls, Buckberg, Finktown, Mount Airy, Dixie, and even West Point Military Academy. During the three days of bitter cold and record-breaking snowfall, frozen water pipes in thousands of homes burst, causing tremendous water damage to these deserted homes. However, many evacuees saw this as a positive thing and hoped the damage would allow them to collect from their homeowner's policy for the water damage because nuclear incidents were an exclusion on all insurance policies.

Other major crises were developing in the exclusion zone. As a sage once said, "Left to themselves, things always go from bad to worse." That's exactly what happened at Sing Sing Prison in Ossining, New York, after the Christmas Special attacks. It was one of the many institutions in the exclusion zone that lacked any feasible plan to deal with a nuclear catastrophe. When the terrible snowstorm of January third hit, it turned a terrible situation into an intolerable dilemma for those people who had been forced to "shelter in place."

The saddest thing about what happened was much of it could have been avoided, but the belief that a nuclear catastrophe would never occur had precluded any serious planning.

There wasn't a plan to evacuate Sing Sing even in the most dire nuclear catastrophe. In fact, even as late as December 2011 at a hearing of the Nuclear Regulatory Commission, this issue was discussed and testimony was given that the proposed idea of "shelter in place" would be a very risky way to deal with the prison population of seventeen hundred prisoners.

The prisoners were housed in the huge open-air buildings with broken windows and poor ventilation systems that would expose the occupants to radiation. The additional problem of the lack of necessary food supply or bottled water to sustain those left locked up complicated manners even more. And even worse, it was noted that prison guards were not taught what to do in case of a nuclear catastrophe. Most correctional Officers didn't even know if the prison had a stockpile of potassium-iodide pills and, if so, what to do with them.

The lack of a feasible plan to evacuate prisoners angered even the commissioner of social sciences for the Westchester court, who complained the situation was insane and showed a lack of respect for the lives of the prisoners. It addition, it was noted at the December 2011 NRC meeting that the New York State emergency preparedness plan of 2009 also failed to include any plans to address the evacuation of prisoners from Sing Sing prison.

My following interview with Maxwell Ellsmore, a former inmate of Sing Sing, illustrates the consequences of this poor planning and lack of vision by the state of New York.

Roberto Roma: *Thank you for agreeing to talk to me, Mr. Ellsmore. I understand you were incarcerated at Sing Sing on December twenty-fifth, the morning the terrorists attacked Indian Point?*

Maxwell Ellsmore: *Yeah, I guess you could say so. I was doing a three-year bit for a bum fraud beef. Man, I was there when it happened, and I was there for the next twelve days while all the good people of Westchester County were cooling it in hotels, cruise ships, and with their families. By the time they let us out, we were all glowing, and that ain't no joke.*

Roberto Roma: *How did you initially find out about what happened?*

Maxwell Ellsmore: *We were eating breakfast in the mess hall and we noticed the COs whispering and acting strange. You know, like real nervous. Christmas is usually a day when the COs don't really hassle us that much, but all of a sudden they wanted us back in our cells. We weren't even through with our chow, but they were yelling for us to get up and get in formation. When we got back to B Block, we were locked down again, and that just don't happen on Christmas. We asked why, and they wouldn't tell us shit, but something was happening because you could hear sirens wailing outside. I'd never heard these si-*

rens before, and then some bro yelled it was the evacuation signal for a nuclear accident. That got everybody yelling at the CO about what was going on, but he wouldn't tell us shit. Over the PA system an announcement was made that we would be kept in lockdown while they waited for further information. Our tier CO was a new jack. He was looking real serious and worried. They kept us locked up all that morning, and when the shift change came for the guards it was obvious that many didn't show up for work. That scared us. In the afternoon, the CO on our tier told us it was a serious armed attack on the nuclear power plant and people were being evacuated. He told us we were all safe in the prison from radiation but that once they got the buses together we also would be evacuated. The sirens were still blaring somewhere in Ossining. It was a loud warbling sound you could hear above even the constant chatter in our block.

Roberto Roma: *How long were you in lockdown?*

Maxwell Ellsmore: *The first day, it was almost the whole day. I was locked up on S Gallery, which is on the Hudson River side of B Block. There were like four hundred guys in B Block. Christmas is also a big day for many to get visitors. I ain't got no one, so I wasn't thinking about it, but a lot of the guys were wondering about it. When you're in lockdown, no one gets to see nobody. We knew whatever had happened was big. And by nighttime, things just got worse. Instead of our Christmas dinner we each got a bag with a sandwich in it.*

Roberto Roma: *Were you given anti-radiation tablets, potassium iodide?*

Maxwell Ellsmore: *You got to be kidding me! We barely got food and water. Even people who had heart problems, asthma, or diabetes weren't given their meds. There was nobody on the prison staff who had any idea of what to do. They just locked us up and hoped someone would tell them what to do with all of us. The majority of the guards not on that shift just went ahead and evacuated with their families. We had a lot of guys on the gallery who had radios, and they tuned in on what was happening so we followed the news and knew we were being left behind in an evacuation zone. There was not a beep of news about prisoners being left behind. Not a very nice feeling to know that they don't give a shit about you! We weren't the only ones forgotten. Apparently they didn't have evacuation plans for the VA hospital or nursing homes either.*

Roberto Roma: *Did Sing Sing ever evacuate you guys?*

Maxwell Ellsmore: *It was two days later they got to evacuating some of our prisoners who were incapacitated or needing medical treatment. By then, we were starving. We were getting a bag with a peanut butter sandwich or a couple slices of bread with a single piece of salami hid in it. On our block, which is maximum security, the convicts were yelling and screaming and tearing the place apart. When we were not in lockdown, we could at least walk around and talk to one another, but they just kept us locked in our cells. We were going nowhere. No* *one really slept that first night. Guys were whispering to each other and listening to the radio, trying to catch the latest reports about the attacks and how bad Indian Point was.*

Roberto Roma: *So there was no rioting that first day?*

Maxwell Ellsmore: *I know there was a lot of trouble in the A Block, but not really a riot. A Block is even bigger than our housing. The morning after Christmas, there was not even a wake-up call and no count. Usually they do a head count four times a day, but all day Christmas nothing and then the next morning nothing. We didn't even have a CO come onto our gallery that morning. When we looked down to the flats we saw COs moving about wearing hazmat suits, yet we didn't even have paper respirators? We also noticed that the Metro-North Railroad had stopped running. Sing Sing straddles the railroad tracks so we always could hear it and feel it as it rumbled by, but it just stopped. On the radio, we were hearing about all this stuff about radiation poisoning and that everybody should be taking potassium iodide, but here we were, just locked up like animals in a slaughterhouse. I guess the attitude was since we were criminals, who cared if we contracted cancer and died?*

Finally at about noon, a single CO wearing a hazmat suit rolled a food cart onto our tier loaded with bags of sandwiches. He told us to get back as he tossed these bag lunches into our cells. While we were grabbing our sandwiches, he explained that we needed to start holding a wet cloth over our nose and mouth to filter out any radioactive debris floating around in the air. Two guys started demanding potassium iodide pills, and this bull just started moving away from them and holding out his mace. The two got even more boisterous with him, and he blasted them twice with pepper spray. The stuff floated over to my cell, burning my face and neck. It actually peeled the paint off the bars in my cell. I was burning and guys were getting mad as hell for being sprayed with mace.

This was when we all started thinking about what we need to do to protect ourselves. We had to do something to save ourselves. We had to fend for ourselves. We heard from the radio that only bottled water should be drunk. They said that all the reservoirs in Westchester County had too much radiation to drink the water. We had been drinking that water for two days now, and we were sure no one was going to tell us not to.

Roberto Roma: *So did you guys get bottled water?*

Maxwell Ellsmore: *We didn't get bottled water that day, and in fact we didn't even get a meal. We were just locked down in the block without food, water, or a CO on our gallery. I guess they were really short on COs. They had one on the flats, that is the ground level, and one on U and Z level, which is the top gallery, but that was all. On the morning of the twenty-eighth, they brought us pills, water, and more bag lunches. Everyone was settled down, and we hoped they would let us out of our cells so we could walk around a bit on our tier. Somebody must have been listening to our* *prayer because at about 1 p.m. an announcement came that they were going to let us out of our cells. Sure enough, they did, and just about everybody tried to find something to block their cell doors from closing again. We were not going to let them lock us up in the cells again.*

We figured they were so few COs that they couldn't force us all back into our cells. More than half of the COs had just deserted Sing Sing. We still couldn't go nowhere. There was probably another ten steel doors to go through just to get out of the block.

Roberto Roma: *Were the prison staff taking care of people with medical problems on the twenty-eighth?*

Maxwell Ellsmore: *No, and by the twenty-eighth we'd had quite a few suicides and guys dying from medical issues, I think. Around Christmas and New Years, we always have some suicides, but this year we had seventeen just in our block. COs used to get in trouble if a guy committing suicide wasn't found before he was all stiff with rigor mortis, but now they just didn't care. We had guys dead in their cells for a couple days before they got them out of the cells and off the gallery. It was really sad. When they opened the cell doors and we got to look in other cells, we found guys dead who had cut their wrists. One guy looked like he beat his head so hard against the bars that he died from the concussion. Some guys had heart attacks. It was awful just being stuck in this monster building locked up like a bunch of chickens breathing in radioactive particles and no one to help us. No one cared about our problems.*

Roberto Roma: *I know things were bad for you during those days, but tell me about what happened when it started snowing on January third?*

Maxwell Ellsmore: *That was the end of it for a lot of us. By then we had been eating next to nothing and drinking three bottles of water a day on a good day. All we ate was cold sandwiches, and people were dying. It seemed like there were a lot less guards. We didn't have our customary counts, and we hardly ever saw a CO on our gallery. Anyway, the snow started falling, making things worse. It snowed so much that power lines broke, and we were on backup generators. It was less than a day before they failed, and we were in the dark and without heat in freezing cold weather.*

They still hadn't given us any type of masks to protect us from breathing in radioactive stuff so we were all trying to hold wet rags over our face, but it was so cold the rags just froze solid. Everyone just threw them away and hoped for the best. Most of us had frozen snot caked to our upper lips, and those with mustaches found them crusted over with a thick coating of frozen snot. It was hard to talk because your face was so numb from the cold. We were never issued any gloves so you had to keep your hands in your pockets to keep them from getting frostbitten. It was seriously cold. By the second day, we didn't have much choice but to make bonfires out of the few belongings we had. We stacked stuff out on the halls farthest from our cells and huddled around the fires to keep warm. Lots of us had bought long johns in December because we knew they always kept the block cold in the winter to save money on fuel. Some guys just didn't have the money to buy them from the commissary so they were really freezing. If we found someone dead, we took their clothes and gave them to guys who didn't have enough to stay warm.

The smoke set off the fire alarms, and they just kept blaring. There was no way for us to turn them off so they just kept sounding the alarm until the battery died. Because of all the smoke, we also had to break out more windows, which let in even more cold. I think we were luckier than some because all the fires below us were heating us up a little also. Lots of guys were choking from the smoke, however, and people who had asthma were suffering something awful. We had guys who froze to death during the first night. The thirteen guys who were still locked in cells, the guys in keep-lock, all froze to death except one guy who was with the Latin Kings. Somehow he made it. I didn't know it then, but they would be carrying out another twenty-seven frozen guys from the box when it was all over. The box is where they lock you up and forget about you. You know, solitary confinement.

Roberto Roma: *Did prison staff help you at all during the snowstorm?*

Maxwell Ellsmore: *The most help we got was boxes of sandwiches and packages of bologna tossed into the block. They didn't come in. They just tossed the food through the door. They fed us like we were caged animals. The nights were the worst because it was so dark and cold. I* *had to move around all night to keep warm. You didn't dare sleep because you could freeze to death. We walked around wrapped with blankets. There was no place to go to get warm. Everyone had burned their mattresses to keep warm. We didn't have any thermometer, so I can't tell you what it really was in there, but I can tell you that by the second day the water in the toilet bowls was frozen solid. Snow was blowing in through the broken windows and piling up on the floor and not melting. Since the toilets were frozen, we started shitting and pissing in the far end of the tier where the dead keep-lock guys were. It didn't smell the place up much because it froze solid in about an hour or so. The floors were all steel and concrete and stayed so cold that a lot of us were ending up with frozen feet. Guys were staggering around because they could not feel their toes or feet. Things were bad. No food, no heat, and no news about what was going on.*

Seeing all the bodies, we were convinced we were all going to die in the next few days. Being in prison is bad, but freezing to death in prison with no food is the ultimate hell. Some guys were actually talking about if it got much worse we would have to eat some of the dead. I don't know if they were kidding or not, but when anyone died, we went through their pockets and their cells looking for any scrap of food. And we would take all their clothes, strip them, and carry their bodies down to the same place we were using as a toilet. We didn't care about radiation by then. Just staying alive was all that was important.

Roberto Roma: *Did you hear the train arrive on January the fifth?*

Maxwell Ellsmore: *The wind was still blowing pretty hard, and snow was still falling. Some guys thought they had felt something like the train rumbling by, but the rest of us just figured it was the sound of snow falling off the roof. By the third day of the snowstorm, everyone was exhausted from lack of sleep, no food, and the constant cold. Our eyes burned from the smoke from the many fires that were burning in the block.*

It was about noon when we heard commotion on the flat. We looked down and saw a hazmat-suited goon squad. Many of them had shotguns and other weapons. One of them had a bullhorn and shouted at the guys on the flats that they would be evacuated, but they first had to be manacled together. He said, "The quicker you cooperate, the quicker you will be on a warm train leaving Sing Sing and sipping a warm cup of mud. So cut the shit and let's get moving so everyone can get out today." A platoon of hazmat guys moved toward a group of half frozen cons, and thank God they didn't resist. I think I had tears freezing on my face at the sight of that weird-looking hazmat-suited goon squad putting chains on everybody. The chains weren't necessary because most of us were too weak to run, had frozen feet, and could just barely stand.

They didn't get to my gallery for two more hours, but when they did, we were all standing in line for them. We weren't going to give them any shit. Just chain us up and get us on the train. We were out of B Block in less than thirty minutes. When they marched us to the train, it was the first time I'd been out of the prison in over two years. For most, it had been many more years. When we got on the train, it was warm. In fact, it soon felt like my face and hands were burning from its warmth. They brought hot coffee in paper cups with lids and a small hole to sip from. I don't drink mud normally, but that afternoon it tasted and felt great. Along with the coffee, they brought us another sandwich of peanut butter and grape jelly and a box of raisins. Once they had finished passing out the sandwiches, they brought us paper facemasks. I guess they didn't want the outside world to know we were without any for twelve days. We had chains around our waists, we had chains hooked to our legs, we were chained to each other, and we were all chained to the seats so no one was going nowhere. We had armed guards in the front of the train car and more in the rear of the car. We sat there for another two hours while they tried to clear the rest of B Block, I guess. The windows in the train car were all covered so we really couldn't see what all was going on outside. The warmth of the train just made me want to sleep. I was having a hard time staying awake even with all the commotion. All my body wanted was sleep. I felt safe enough on the train so I could sleep without worrying about freezing to death.

Suddenly, I felt the train lurch forward we were on our way to somewhere. Away from Sing Sing, and I could feel my entire body shaking with emotion. I was alive and overcome with relief to be leav-

ing this hell-hole called Sing Sing and hopefully leaving behind the worst days of my life.

Roberto Roma: *Where did they take you?*

Maxwell Ellsmore: *Well, for me the next stop was being gated out...you know, freedom. Just about every Christmas and New Years the governor of New York pardons or commutes the sentences of some convicts. This year I was on his lifeboat list. So my prayer was answered. I was gated out.*

Chapter 81
Valentines for Sheeva

January crept by, with each day another deadly struggle with the radioactive demons spewing death into the air and waters. The fight was like the battle mortals waged against the monster laundry press in Stephen King's horror story "The Mangler." No matter what they tried to do to stop the massive laundry press, it just continued to kill and destroy. It was an unstoppable mechanical beast that appeared to have its own mind and will to be free of man's control.

Indian Point, Waterford 3, and San Onofre had become similar monsters. They had not broken free of their bonds, but they spewed deadly radiation into the surroundings and resisted all efforts to tame them. They were wild and unbelievably resilient. Man had lost control, and they were not going to give it back—at least not very easily. They were masters of their own destiny. They were possessed behemoths with the strength of giants to fight for years to maintain their freedom. Man might finally lock them in a sarcophagus, but even then, inside those walls their heart would continue beating, waiting for the concrete to crumble, the steel to rust, or an earthquake to free them so they once again could release their Furies on mankind.

The Olympian struggle between the rampant nuclear power plants and man reminded me of a passage from the book of Enoch: "And when men could no longer sustain them, the giants turned against them and devoured mankind." It was true that thousands had died and many more would before the battle was over. Every day, an army of engineers surrounded the beasts and sprayed them with chemicals and water, tinkered with machines, and argued among themselves what they could do to kill or cripple them. However, no one really knew because what had happened was an impossibility. These were events that could never have happened, so a solution wasn't part of any plan. If they could just cool these fiery monsters and keep them cool, maybe they would sleep—at least that was what they hoped.

February came, and the war continued with no real change. In Arizona, Sheeva Hasson was still struggling with her own demons and perhaps faring better than the thousands of scientists fighting their battles. Jason was still paramount in her mind, and Valentine's Day pulled at her heart worse than ever.

Sheeva had been assigned a therapist to help her recover emotionally from the trauma of Jason's death and the shame she felt for the acts perpetrated by her father and brother. She had temporarily been pulled from the abyss of sadness that had almost claimed her life. Sheeva was still obsessed with her loss, but she was also healing. Her daily letters to Jason were no longer considered a concern, because her new therapist actually felt they were therapeutic. Her Valentine's letter to him illustrated her continuing love but also showed shades of reality returning. Following is Sheeva's letter to Jason on Valentine's Day:

Happy Valentines, Jason!

Much has been happening lately. Your father wants to meet me. This really frightens me. He said he has something for me that you would really want me to have. I don't know what it is. He has been very nice to me and sent me a box of pictures and other things we had in our home in Culper. The stuff he sent me just makes me miss you even more. He has been helping me accept my situation. In his letters, he tells me it won't always feel this bad. I wonder if he really knows? He never forgot his wife.

He wants me to accept those around me who are trying to take care of me. It's so confusing because you have been gone a couple months, but often it feels like you have only been gone a moment. Maybe our souls are still locked together and that's why you feel so close.

I hope you're there. I hope you feel my kiss when I press my lips against your pictures that I cherish so much. Maybe I'm going crazy. I know they think I am. I swear I can smell your cologne sometimes floating in the breeze. I think you're out there close by, but I just can't see you. And I do look. When a breeze flutters my hair, I think it's you caressing me again.

They think I'm nuts writing to you, but it keeps me close to you. It keeps your memory fresh in my mind, and that makes me happy. But looking at all these pictures of us makes me realize how little time we had to share our lives together. I never had time to show you just how much I loved you. Now I feel that you were my savior. I'm sure I would have been killed by my father or brother if you hadn't taken me in. We shared love, and you showed me how wonderful it feels to be loved. Your love gave me strength to stand up against those who wanted to hurt me. I couldn't believe the feeling I felt in my heart for you. Every time we kissed and our lips touched, I could feel that love. Your kiss touched my soul. Each time, I felt that same magical feeling as our first kiss. When you held me close, I could feel our hearts beating together as one.

At night when I feel so alone and tears fill my eyes, I look up at the sky and see the stars dancing way up there, and I wonder if you're one of them. You were certainly my star. I always knew I could turn to you when I needed help, and at the end you showed the world how brave you were.

Your father told me to learn to smile when I look at your pictures. He said that's what you would have wanted. I'm trying. I am trying to just accept what we once had and thank Allah for that happiness he gave me those months with you.

I have framed that picture of you at my birthday party last year. It shows you with your mischievous smile. It now sits on my nightstand. Strangely, when I wake in the middle of the night, it feels like your eyes in that photo have been watching me. Are you watching me?

I hope you are. Each day I pray to Allah that you're safe. Jason, you were my soul mate, the man of my dreams. I will be with you once again, I know, and it will be forever.

Love always,
Sheeva

Chapter 82
Revisiting the Past

Eight months after the attacks, in late August, Thomas Lawrence traveled to Ding Dong, Texas, a small community a short distance south of Killeen, Texas, and the home of Fort Hood army base. He was there to visit Deek Collins, owner of the defunct Deek's Motor Pool, once one of the largest military vehicle rental companies in America. Thomas Lawrence had flown into the Killeen Fort Hood Regional Airport on one of the hottest days in August. It was 107 degrees Fahrenheit when he disembarked from the plane. Thomas Lawrence had come to Ding Dong to interview Collins regarding his knowledge of where the terrorists obtained the military vehicles they used in their attacks.

Before I provide Deek Collins's interview, it's important to summarize how America fared in the eight months after the Christmas Morning attacks.

By August, all over the country, Americans were slowly recovering from their shock and confusion. America had never been so severely wounded as on that Christmas morning. Not even Pearl Harbor or the 9/11 attacks had affected Americans as strongly as the terrorist attacks on that infamous day. The attacks were devastating enough, but a bigger element that contributed to the shock and confusion was the lack of mental preparation for such an event. There was a total disbelief that America could have been so vulnerable. The pervasive belief before the Christmas Special was that America would never suffer the agony of another 9/11 and that its nuclear power plants were impervious to terrorist attack. Then when it happened, those truths were shattered. The shock of those obvious fallacies resonated with a degree of intensity and disbelief probably equal to the confusion that engulfed the world when Galileo made his heretic pronouncement that Earth was not the center of the universe.

Americans were traumatized by the attacks and mentally affected by the haunting threat of “We will come again,” and of course the unrelenting reports of what had happened on that day of infamy.

Traumatic as the attacks were, their crippling memories quickly receded for many. I don’t think anyone can say Americans are callous or unfeeling, but we are a nation of people that quickly moves on, and fast. In the eight months after the attacks, the ability of Americans to dust themselves off and keep going exemplified one of the redeeming strengths of the nation.

It’s true that many minimized the tragedy by numbing their minds with alcohol, drugs, or incessant TV watching or sleep, but others let life push them forward. The events’ aftermath didn’t allow many much time to grieve because America needed its citizens to assist in preserving its existence. Plus, as the bills poured in and people slowly realized that most of the world was still functioning as normal, they realized they once again had to resume their place in society. People had to work, they had to stay on track and not let fear of the past cripple them.

The Christmas Special attacks caused the loss of many jobs, but it also created many new ones. Security companies could not hire applicants fast enough to fill the demand. Virtually every business, school, hospital, church, theatre, mall, nightclub, store, or any place where people might congregate had metal and bomb detectors installed and managed with armed guards who also patrolled their premises. Bulletproof vest were sold by the thousands to people who wore them in public just in case a bomb detonated nearby. Some found the added weight of the bulletproof vest a plus as a way to shed pounds. Trained bomb-sniffing dogs were sought out by those who could afford the luxury. Security cameras were everywhere, and new companies sprung up that sold monitoring services to those who could not monitor their own cameras full-time. Thousands of workers were hired to constantly monitor these feeds.

The biggest new employer, however, was a consortium of nuclear power plant owners and the federal government, which needed thousands of brave citizens to come to the aid of their country. Signs appeared all over the country soliciting recruits for these seriously high-paying jobs of assisting in the cleanup and taming of the rampant nuclear power plants. These were American workers who performed the same dangerous tasks that the liquidators at Chernobyl and the Fukushima Fifty did to contain those nuclear disasters. The pay was often over a thousand dollars a day, but the risks were even higher. In fact, many of the workers would die from radiation-related diseases or suffer debilitating health issues for the rest of their lives.

Thousands of workers were hired to help stabilize and clean up the debris from the stricken nuclear power plants. America's nuclear heroes moved thousands of tons of sand, lead, clay, and neutron-absorbing boron into the stricken plants with the help of hundreds of helicopters. They also pumped millions of gallons of water into the reactor buildings and spent fuel pools. This, of course, added the new problem of millions of gallons of highly radioactive water ending up underground or leeching back into the nearby rivers at Waterford 3 and Indian Point or into the Pacific Ocean at San Onofre.

Numerous TV specials aired reports of the deserted towns with their serene, idyllic landscapes that now encompassed over three throusand square miles of nuclear wasteland. The towns were still festooned in Christmas decorations. The reports showed miles and miles of uninhabited streets crisscrossed with garland, large wreaths, and wilted Christmas trees still towering over nativity scenes in town squares. The front lawns of many homes still displayed large Santa Clauses or snowmen, a reminder of when the catastrophe happened. Eight months after the attacks, the bloated carcasses of dead animals continued to litter the country, along with the skeletal remains of those who died months earlier.

Much of the foliage south of the Waterford 3 Nuclear Power Plant had turned a coppery red, similar to what occurred near Chernobyl after its nuclear accident. The once-picturesque Hudson River shoreline, south of the Indian Point Nuclear Power Plant, was strewn with rotting fish killed by the radioactive soup pouring from the crippled plant.

Short-term environmental concerns were ignored in favor of the bigger concern of doing whatever was necessary to contain the catastrophes as quickly as possible. Millions of residents of New York had deserted the city, leaving thousands of apartments empty and causing a terrible decline in the financial well-being of the Big Apple. New York was no longer a magnet for visitors from around the world, and with its glamour gone, it quickly spiraled into city of boarded-up buildings and crime.

For those in August still fighting to take control of the nuclear power plants, it was day after day of hell. In San Onofre, the late August days averaged around ninety-seven degrees, and working in a hazmat suit at those temperatures was exceedingly difficult. Worst yet was Waterford 3 at Killona, Louisiana, which baked in temperatures over a hundred degrees of heat, coupled with high humidity and the threat of another hurricane. If a hurricane was to hit, its rains and wind would spread radiation even further.

In Buchanan, New York, the workers at Indian Point fared no better. The temperature was near a hundred and many had problems working in such heat while wearing a hazmat suit. Accidents happened more often in August than any previous month. Numerous workers were hospitalized, seven were killed when a beam fell on them, and two more drowned in a flooded basement of radioactive water at one of the plants.

Two months after the Christmas Morning attacks, America ended its military mission in Afghanistan, bringing home all of its troops to help secure the nation. Even the small military contingent that had remained in Iraq was ordered back to the States. The end of the Afghanistan mission had happened so fast that billions of dollars of assets were left behind. Vehicles, building, food supplies, and even weapons were deserted as the troops hurriedly evacuated their positions to get back to the States.

Like water pouring in from a breeched dam, the Taliban flooded into the military bases and areas deserted by the Americans. A bloodbath among those who had assisted in

America's mission in Afghanistan followed. The killings continued for months. Mass hangings and beheadings were publicly held to remind all Afghanis who was back in charge. Afghanistan once again became a haven for the most radical form of Islam, with thousands of foreign militants flocking back to this now-fabled country that had defeated the two largest superpowers. Missionaries were rounded up and summarily hung for spreading the words of a false god. All Bibles, Torahs, translations of the Book of the Dead, and copies of Guru Granth Sahib, God Speaks, Hebrew Bibles, the Book of Enoch, and other religious books were tossed onto roaring bonfires. This was a part of a great Afghani celebration commemorating the holy uprising against Americans triggered by the burning of Qurans by barbaric US soldiers in 2012.

The vacuum created by the American's desertion of Afghanistan, according to Muslim historians, gave birth to a new Taliban. Millions of young Muslim men wanted to be a part of the victorious Taliban movement, and its ranks grew exponentially. Their holy warriors became a powerful force to reckon with. By August, the Taliban's forces had taken control of Peshawar, Pakistan, its tribal areas, and the Kyber Pass. To demonstrate their control and the impotence of the rest of the world, they destroyed Gor Khuttree, the ancient holy place of the yogis and Hindus in Peshawar. The world was so busy trying to ward off more urgent dangers that little attention or protest was given to this terrible act of destruction aimed at another historical relic of man's cultural past.

In America, people were suffering from new terrorist attacks. The many forest fires raging out of control across the country were believed to be the work of a small cell of Islamic terrorists. In all, thirteen major forest fires burned on three million acres of forest and farmland. In some areas upwind of these fires, people feared that the huge plumes of smoke billowing across the heavens were mixing with radioactive particles still floating high in the sky. Many scientists claimed it was certainly a possibility, while others scoffed at the idea.

Europe was also struggling with Islamic fanatics. France, which produced the majority of its electricity by nuclear power, found itself under tremendous pressure by radical Islamic elements to accede to their wishes. They threatened to attack France's fifty-eight nuclear power installations if their demands were not accepted. They wanted more control of their Muslim enclaves, including the adoption of shariah law in these areas and changes that would ensure that Muslims were better represented in the French government.

The threats were real, and as long as there was nuclear power, terrorists had an easy avenue to destroy large cities like Paris whenever they chose. The threats started in April and escalated over the next few months to the point that terrorists even threatened that the closing of any nuclear power plant would result in an immediate attack on the remaining plants. The terrorists' manipulation of France was similar to the control a master holds over a dog when it wears an electronic shock collar. If the dog does as he is trained, he will not be punished. However, if he makes too much noise or tries to go outside a designated area, he is immediately shocked. France was now wearing a proverbial shock collar—but a much more punishing one. Additionally the consequences of any negotiations between France and Islamic terrorists could easily harm neighboring Germany, Spain, England, Italy, or Switzerland. France was in a dire situation that was becoming more and more difficult to resolve and more and more threatening to its neighbors.

This was the August that Thomas Lawrence and the rest of America were experiencing the day Lawrence arrived at Ding Dong, Texas, to interview Deek Collins.

Deek Collins was a former CIA agent who opened his own military vehicle rental service after he retired. His business, Deek's Motor Pool, had been forced into bankruptcy as a result of the federal government's investigation into the Christmas Special attacks. The investigation resulted from the fact that three vehicles used in the attack on Waterford 3 Nuclear Power Plant had been rented from his company. Deek's Motor Pool normally only rented to major movie production companies, but occasionally it rented military vehicles to civilians for parties, parades, or other events. Deek was also an expert in explosives and military munitions and often assisted movie companies in creating realistic combat scenes.

Below is a copy of Thomas Lawrence's interview with Deek Collins.

> ***Thomas Lawrence:*** *This is quite a place you have here. It definitely reminds me of a real motor pool. Very impressive!*
>
> ***Deek Collins:*** *Well thanks, but unless I can get my business going again, what's left will soon be just piles of damn rust. Nine months ago I probably had twice as many vehicles along with some 105 howitzers and thirteen more tanks. Sadly, those tanks are all gone now.*
>
> ***Thomas Lawrence:*** *So how did you get yourself involved with the terror-*

ists who used your vehicle to attack Waterford 3?

Deek Collins: *Well, Mr. Lawrence, it was real easy. I simply rented to a customer who had rented from me four times before. Apparently, he had been working with this terrorist cell for the last few years. He would rent a jeep sometimes, or a jeep and a truck. In fact, last year, as I told government investigators, he rented a jeep and two trucks at Christmas, claiming they were for his father to use to bring Christmas gifts to the poor. He said his father was a former colonel in the army and liked to dress up in his old uniform and caravan around with a friend dressed as Santa Claus. The military vehicles were filled with presents they gave to poor kids.*

You know, you just don't suspect that a former customer is part of some major terrorist group.

Thomas Lawrence: *Had you rented to a lot of Muslims?*

Deek Collins: *In most cases, I never knew if they were Muslim, Jewish, or Christian. I mean, we don't ask, "Hey, what religion are you?" This guy Zaid Khalidi, sure his name sounded like he was a Muslim, but then it didn't make any difference. This guy was always smiling and acted like everyone else. Always asking about what movies my vehicles had been in. He would look at all those signed autographed pictures of actors I'd met on various sets and ask me questions about them. He just seemed like a regular customer.*

Thomas Lawrence: *Did you talk to him or see him after the rental?*

Deek Collins: *What kind of question is that? I'm sure you know he was found dead in a Louisiana bayou half eaten by alligators or something.*

Thomas Lawrence: *Sorry, you're right, I knew that. It's just a bad habit I have asking questions I already know the answer to. Who do you think killed him?*

Deek Collins: *Who do I think killed him? I'd guess it was whoever had him doing the rentals. They didn't want him telling who was providing the money for the rentals. They were paying in cash, in one hundred dollar bills. He was the link to those who were involved in the plot. I bet he was killed right after he delivered the vehicles to the terrorists. He seemed like a nice guy. He probably never knew what the vehicles were really for.*

Thomas Lawrence: *Looking back, do you remember renting vehicles to any other Muslims?*

Deek Collins: *Look Mr. Lawrence, a lot of Muslims are in the movie business. I mean, back in 2011 you had that big movie The Help. That was produced by Mohamed Al-Mazrouei or something like that. He is a big-time producer. He did the movies The Fair Game, The Double, and The Way Back. These were great movies. In fact, my wife loved The Help and was pissed that it didn't get any Academy Awards. This producer plays with the big boys. You think if he wanted to rent my vehicles, I'd question him? Hell, no! I'm in a business. I want to rent. I would have felt blessed if he had come to me and rented everything in the damn motor pool. And then you got that sexy actress Shohreh Aghdashloo from the House* *of Sand and Fog. Goddamn great movie! For her I'd discount everything 50 percent. Look Mr. Lawrence, it's a strange world we live in. You got bad people and good people. I think you know that, since you're working with that piece of shit Ali Hasson. I'm sorry, no offense, but I hope the government puts your client in a meat grinder and makes sausages out of him to feed to the hogs. Your boy really fucked up my life. I lost my business, business associates, and lots of friends who are afraid to have anything to do with me because they are not sure if I was involved with your boy Ali. My wife left me because she could not stand the pressure. I'm only answering your questions because I have to.*

Thomas Lawrence: *I'm sorry all this happened to you, Mr. Collins. I know you had nothing to do with those attacks, and by the time this trial is over, the rest of the world will know that also. I wish I didn't have to ask you all these questions, but that's my job. You know, we are both caught up in a bit of history. Anyway, I only have a few more things to ask. Did the government ask you how you got all these vehicles?*

Deek Collins: *Absolutely! And that's where some of my real issues are. I mean the FBI, ATF, and Homeland Security all seemed surprised that I could buy an army truck from someone on Ebay or that other businesses like mine had so many tanks available to rent to the public. The Internet has military vehicles for sale all the time. Most of the military vehicles on Ebay are in great shape, and if I rent them out a couple times, I usually can* *quickly double my money. I also advertise my vehicles on Ebay and sell the ones I feel are not going to hold up much longer. I used to have two mechanics on staff here, all the time. I needed them to make sure the vehicles always worked and looked clean. We even had all the military TMs on each vehicle, and we had friends at Fort Hood who kept us updated on anything new about any of our vehicles.*

Thomas Lawrence: *Did Zaid Khalidi ever ask you about munitions or where to buy firearms?*

Deek Collins: *Absolutely fucking not. He never asked one fucking question about guns, explosives, or anything like that. I can swear on a stack of Bibles that I never rented or sold him nothing like a weapon or explosives. Like I said before, he talked about movies and yakked about some of the actors I had pictures of hanging on my wall, and that was it. I had nothing to do with them having all those high explosives.*

Thomas Lawrence: *Where do you think they could have gotten all that stuff, like C4, shaped charges, and automatic weapons?*

Deek Collins: *For Christ's sake, the weapons and explosives those terrorists used are all pretty damn easy to buy or steal. One of our best goddamned congressmen here in Texas, Lamar Smith, brought this up a few years back. He said something like, "It's literally easier to buy a ton of explosives than it's to buy a small-caliber pistol." Now that's a pretty damn scary statement. I think he reported that tons of explosives had been stolen, and most were never recovered. Heck, we* *had C4 and TNT stolen right out of the Corpus Christi Police Department storage unit just a few years back. The thieves used a torch to break in and of course never got caught. That was their own damn police storage unit. That's pretty fucking embarrassing, wouldn't you say? Then out in New Mexico a couple years ago, some thieves got away with thousands of blasting caps, couple hundred pounds of detasheets, and a whole lot of detonation cord. Who knows? Some of those stolen detasheets might have been used for some of these attacks. That stuff is very powerful.*

A lot of thefts happen near mining or demolition sites. Lot of those thefts aren't even reported because it's too much red tape for the company that got ripped off.

So it's not very far-fetched that some militants could have been stealing this stuff or just buying it on the black market or even just smuggling it in from out of country.

They probably been gathering up their explosives and arms over a couple years. If they had different people getting the stuff and funneling it back to them, it would have been real hard to stop.

You know, Mr. Lawrence, you really can buy just about anything out there, if you just look. Hell, people have machine guns, even Browning .50 caliber machine guns. If these terrorists had a gunsmith among them, they could buy weapons that weren't suppose to function, but with a few minor changes they would be just like what the army uses. From what I read, they made their own mortars, but of course you know more about that than I would.

I do think with an operation like what those Christmas Special terrorists had going, they could have smuggled in C4 from Canada after buying it from some of our enemies like Iran, Iraq, Syria, Afghanistan, or even Saudi Arabia. But that would be hard to prove. I'm sure they could have also bought it from arms dealers right here in America for the right amount of money. But I think with all the FBI stings going on back then, it's more likely that it was obtained in some other fashion.

The rocket-propelled grenade launchers were also something that, as weird as it may sound, are quite easy to obtain in the States, but again, it's more likely that these weapons were shipped into Canada from offshore ships or hidden in one of the thousands of cargo containers unloaded on the Canadian docks every day. No one is really talking, so it's hard to prove this, but that's what I'd suspect. Then all they had to do was bring the weapons into America across the huge American-Canadian border. This is all speculation, you understand?

Thomas Lawrence: *Yes, I understand, but your knowledge or speculations have helped me understand a lot about how terrorists could have obtained all of the weapons they supposedly had.*

Deek Collins: *Well, I'm glad that I have helped you. Now if you would just rent a couple tanks for a few thousand dollars you would be helping me get out of my bankruptcy.*

Thomas Lawrence: *What if I just take you out to dinner instead?*

Deek Collins: *You sure as hell owe me after your boy screwed up my life like he did. I got to tell you, though, there ain't any great places to dine here in Ding Dong, Texas, but we do have a Texas Roadhouse up in Killeen, if you like Steaks.*

Chapter 83
Sheeva meets Jason's Dad

At the end of August, the marshals guarding Sheeva in protective custody received permission to escort her to Jason's grave. This was an important event for Sheeva because not only would she finally get to say her last words to Jason, she would also meet Jason's father, Roger Wilgers. He had been corresponding with Sheeva since the murder of his two boys. Through these letters, the two of them had found solace in each other's words.

They would first meet at the Lucky Greens Hotel, right off the freeway into River View, New York. This location was also very close to the cemetery where Jason and Frank were buried. This would give Roger and Sheeva some time to get acquainted, before they would face the emotional task of visiting the graves.

This meeting was also a prelude to their probable meeting at the commencement of Ali Hasson's trial in December.

Over the previous eight months, Sheeva had regained much of her sanity and miraculously appeared to be a much more stable person.

Below is Roger Wilgers account of meeting Sheeva:

> *The day before I was to meet Sheeva, I went out to the cemetery to check the gravesites and put more flowers on them. It was a good thing I did because someone had defaced Jason's headstone by drawing a big red heart with lipstick on it. In the middle of the heart, the person had written their ini-*

tials. I had no idea of who it could have been, but I knew it had to be removed before Sheeva arrived. I used some Windex that I had in my car and ended up using my shirt as a rag to scrub the headstone clean.

That night I couldn't fall asleep. I tossed and turned all night, thinking about my meeting with Sheeva. I should have taken a sleeping pill, but by the time I realized I could not sleep it was already about 4 a.m. and I had to be up at least by seven so I just got up and went surfing on my computer.

It was one of those beautiful August mornings ushered in by a sunrise that promised to brighten anyone's day regardless of what they faced. It was beautiful with a glowing red hue that spread across the skyline. That old saying, "Red sky in morning, traveler take warning," popped into my head as I read a story about the Detroit freeway shotgun killer, who had just taken three more lives. Really scary stuff going on in the world.

I left my house about seven-thirty and got into some light traffic with people going to work. My mind raced with all kinds of scenarios of what I'd say and what she might say. I was totally consumed mentally with my meeting with Sheeva

I arrived at the hotel about an hour earlier than our planned meeting. I knew it was odd that a guy my age would be so nervous about meeting a sixteen-year-old girl that my son had dated, but I was. Part of it was probably the fact that I knew the meeting would dredge up a lot of ghosts from the past. Would I be able to keep control of my emotions? That was my big concern.

Even after eight months, my boys were still very much on my mind; really, I don't believe a father can ever forget his days with his sons. I think back sometimes with a guilty longing for those rose-tinted days of their childhoods when they would hug me and tell me how much they loved me. I'd begun watching reruns of The Wonder Years, which reminded me so much of how things once were. It was one of those shows that would bring tears to my eyes as it portrayed events that were so similar to experiences I once shared with my boys.

Sitting in front of the hotel, I tried to convince myself that I was strong enough to console Sheeva and even tell her that Jason was in a better place, that he was in heaven flitting around with the angels, but somehow that vision seemed very hollow. I sat there a few minutes longer, staring at the hotel's entrance and finally decided to go in and have a late breakfast while I waited for our official meeting.

One of my biggest questions was who Sheeva really was. Would I like her, or would I wonder why my son had taken up with her? I really hoped she would prove to be someone I would have really approved of so I wouldn't feel angry that he was dead because he fell in love with the wrong person. It was a selfish thought, but it did linger in my mind.

I wondered what she would be feeling and thinking while she waited to meet me. She probably also was worrying about proving to me she was someone I'd like. I knew she must have a ton of guilt that she was living with.

She had to feel bad about what her father had done and that Jason and Frank died as a result of it.

I understood from the marshals that this was going to be Sheeva's first real outing since she had been placed under protective custody. I was sure she would want to get a feel for what awaited her out there in the world. Maybe she would want to get a glimpse of her future, maybe she would want reassurance that she could be a part of the bigger world again or maybe she would want to know that someone again cared for her.

While I moved my food around on my plate, the memories rushed back. What struck me most was not how much I remembered, but how much I'd forgotten during the last eight months. Those memories were racing back into my consciousness as I sat there, but it was unsettling to realize how many memories of the biggest moments of my life had faded. I wondered how long it would take to forget more about my life with my boys than I remembered. I also realized then that those days with my sons were now only mine and mine alone, and once my mind erased them from my memory, those days would be essentially gone forever. That was the kind of dumb thinking I tortured myself with as I toyed with my food.

The time finally arrived when I was supposed to meet Sheeva. The meeting room, 523, was on the fifth floor about ten rooms from the elevator. I walked up to the door, hesitated a second, and knocked on it. It opened and two marshals stood facing me. They smiled and asked my name and wanted to see my ID. I thought this was sort of stupid, but I guess you could not be too careful under these circumstances. Anyway, they accepted that I was who I claimed to be and let me in.

The room was a spacious hotel room, but there was no Sheeva in it. I asked the marshal, who had introduced himself as Tom Russell, where she was and he said, "Before you meet her we need to make sure you understand that she is still highly emotional and if a situation arises where she gets to distraught we will have to terminate the meeting. If that should happen, you must not interfere, and if you do, we will use whatever force necessary to protect her."

He continued, "Sheeva is very excited about meeting you, and we hope this meeting will help her mental health, but we don't know for sure. We can't promise you anything. Hopefully, we all can go out to your son's grave, which is something she has been demanding for months, but that's still a bit iffy. Basically, it all depends on the next ten to fifteen minutes. Are you ready to meet her?"

I told him yes and he smiled and said, "Okay." He pointed me to a door on the east side of the room and walked with me to it. Russell opened the door and waved me in.

I stood there speechless for a moment facing this dark-eyed, raven-haired beauty in the middle of the room. She smiled at me, and I finally said in a quivering voice, not taking my eyes off her face, "Hello, Sheeva. I'm Jason's dad, Roger Wilgers." As that spewed out of my mouth, I thought how stupid I must sound. She moved a little closer to me, looked up at me, and said, "Mister Wilgers, I'm so sorry for your loss. I really don't know what to say, except that from Allah we were created and to him we shall return. I know that Jason is now in paradise. I hope you can forgive me for anything you feel I did to bring on the death of your sons. I realize that if I hadn't run away to Jason, he would probably still be alive now."

Her voice broke, and tears started streaming down her face. She reached up and dabbed a tissue against her eyes and kept saying she was sorry. Her reference to Allah made my blood boil, but I maintained my composure. It struck me as highly inappropriate, since my son Frank was killed by a woman screeching "Allahu Akbar!" as she detonated her bomb.

Regardless, I suddenly found myself hugging Sheeva and telling her it was okay as my own eyes filled with tears. I think we stood there for a full minute or so before I finally let her loose and suggested that we sit down and talk a bit. The marshals offered us some drinks and tried to stay out of our way, but they were always just a few feet away.

I was astonished at how much I liked this girl. She was smart, beautiful, and I could see why my son had been so infatuated with her. She must have trusted me because she started telling me all kinds of things about Jason and her. She told me how sorry she was for all that had happened and how ashamed she was to have Ali Hasson as her father, but it was nothing she could change. She told me how she hoped I'd like her and be someone she could talk to as a friend. She told me about her life of exile with the marshals. We exchanged stories about Jason and shed more tears, but somehow among all the sadness our stories evoked, I started to feel better. Our talks and tears were a catharsis for both of us.

Two hours zoomed by, and finally it was time to visit Jason's grave. I was surprised, but Sheeva had brought with her a couple of Jason's presents from the Christmas they had missed because of the attack. She wanted to bring them to his grave and leave them there. She told me she had never been to a funeral or to a grave. Visiting Jason's resting place was a major emotional event for Sheeva, not just because of her fear of how she would feel standing in front of his grave, but also because Islam has very confusing conventions regarding a woman visiting a grave site. Sheeva told me that many Muslims say that Allah forbids women from visiting graves and curses those who do. The conversation irritated me, but I realized she was a prisoner of her religion and feared the wrath of her God if she defied him.

The time had come to go out to the gravesite. Sheeva and I were led to an awaiting sedan, which was part of a three-car caravan. As soon as we entered the car, the marshals whisked us away.

The trip to the cemetery was short, probably less than ten minutes. On the way, we talked a bit more, and she asked if my cancer was still in remission. I was happy to report that it was. Maybe God wanted a couple souls from my family and decided once he had Jason's and Frank's he needed me to clean up all the mess left behind. I asked her if she was still going to school, and to my amazement she replied that she was being tutored every day at the place where they held her.

When we got to the cemetery, they drove just about all the way to my family plot. I could see as we approached that Jason's and Frank's graves were virtually covered with flowers.

The vehicles stopped, but before the marshals would let us out of the sedan, they had an agent and a bomb-sniffing dog approach the gravesites. The dog sniffed around the flowers and barked a little, but the only thing he seemed to find was a good spot to pee. Finally, the marshal with the dog waved at us to come on, so we exited the vehicle and walked over to Jason's grave.

As soon as Sheeva was close enough to read the inscription on the headstone, she broke out in sobs, which brought tears to my eyes. She stood in front of the grave repeating things that I really didn't understand accept for an occasional "Allah" and how sorry she was. She placed two unopened presents on Jason's headstone and said something like, "O Allah, forgive and have mercy upon Jason, excuse him and pardon him, and make honorable his reception. Expand his entry, and cleanse him with water, snow, and ice, and purify him of sin as a white robe is purified of filth. Exchange his home for a better home and his family for a better family. Admit him into the garden, protect him from the punishment of the grave and the torment of the fire."

She stood there silent after her prayer just staring at the headstone. The guards or marshals were milling around and looking inpatient. Finally, Marshal Tom Russell told me we had to wrap it up and leave. He gave me five more minutes so I moved over to Frank's headstone and said a couple of prayers.

Sheeva came over also and seemed to be praying, but not as she had done at Jason's grave.

Finally, it was time to walk back to the sedan and get out of Dodge. On the way back to the car, Sheeva looked at me and said, "This is a present for you." She kissed it and then reached out to hand me a leather-bound book inscribed in gold. It was a Quran.

She smiled as she held it out for me, but I began to boil inside. I wanted nothing to do with this object that had espoused all this hate that led to the deaths of my sons. I think I jerked away from it like it was something on fire. Sheeva's smile faded and turned to a perplexed look. I told her that I was sorry, but I didn't want a copy of the Quran.

I knew I'd hurt her feelings, but it was not something I could pretend to accept. I tried to comfort her and said something like, "Sheeva, please don't be offended, because I like you and hope we can stay friends, but the stuff your religion preaches killed my sons. I hope you can understand how I feel about that. I just don't want to hear anything about Islam. Let's just share the things that we really have in common, like our love for Jason and Frank. I really do like you, and I can see why my son loved you, because you're a very nice and beautiful young woman."

Sheeva didn't reply, but gingerly replaced the Quran back in her purse. We got into the back seat of the sedan, and there was complete silence between us. Our driver started the car, and we drove out of the cemetery in utter silence. Marshal Russell, who was sitting in the front passenger seat, broke the quiet and said that if we didn't mind he was going to turn on the radio and listen to some music. He did, and the car was filled with some country music by someone I had never heard before.

As the music played, Sheeva finally broke her silence and said in a quiet voice, "I do think I understand how you feel, Mr. Wilgers. I probably have similar feelings toward my father. It was his hate that really was responsible for all these deaths along with those who believe that killing non-believers is right. I do understand."

I reached over and touched her hand and said, "It's okay, Sheeva," and I felt her tremble with emotions as she tried to stifle her sobs. I told her again that I hoped we would stay friends because I knew Jason would have wanted that.

I had something for Sheeva, which I had held back until I knew more about her. It was something I felt Jason would want me to give her. From the $2.4 million settlement I received from the Culper, Texas, lawsuit, I decided to give fifty thousand of it to Sheeva to help her with college or to start a new life when they released her from protective custody. She had no one in her life, and I really had no one else in my life to help, so why not?

I pulled an envelope from my pocket and passed it over to her and said, "This is something I think Jason would want you to have." She looked at me inquisitively as she took it from me. I told her to open it.

She tore open the envelope and read the note I'd written to her. It read:

> *Dear Sheeva,*
>
> *I realize we don't really know much about each other, but before Jason's tragic death he had told me many wonderful things about you and the love he felt for you. I know in the last few months you have agonized over what happened to him, but it was not your fault. I want you to know that I realize that and*

that I'm proud of my son helping you when you needed his help.

"You're a young woman who has many years ahead of you, and you need to live those years to their fullest. I know with all that happened between you and Jason that his memory will be with you forever, but you must move on and start a new life. Jason would have wanted it that way, and we can't let what happened to him now destroy you. I have a little present for you that I hope will help you build a better future. It's something that Jason would have wanted you to have.

I have opened a fifty thousand dollar trust fund for you. I hope it can help you go to college or get into business or whatever you decide to do in the future. It's not much, but hopefully it will be a little nest egg that can make some difference in your life. There is no one else in my life that's more deserving. You gave love to my son and made his last months the best time of his life. Thank you for being that person. — Love, Roger."

Chapter 84
Protest and Death in Washington DC

Another December arrived. It seemed impossible that almost a year had passed since the Christmas Special attacks, but the days had flown by, and the anniversary of that horrible day was just a few weeks off. A lot of thoughts and memories were going to return to millions of Americans who suffered through that infamous dark day. This was one of those events people remembered where and what they were doing when it happened. Many would re-experience many of the same emotions they felt that day. They would again feel the fear, anger, confusion, sadness, and shock, and some would even experience the fatigue and headaches they had endured during the catastrophe.

Many Americans were still trying to digest that this event really did happen as reported. It was another one of those events that fell into the list of impossibilities that couldn't have happened yet did. It ranked up there with events like the collapse of the Twin Towers, the sinking of the *Titanic*, the attack on Pearl Harbor, the nuclear catastrophes at Chernobyl and Fukushima, or the impossibility of firing three shots accurately with a bolt action rifle in seven seconds that killed President Kennedy.

The government had scheduled Ali Hasson's trial for December with the hope it would quickly conclude, and people would take solace in the fact that some form of justice had been served. For most, it was a foregone conclusion that Ali Hasson would be found guilty; the only question was how quickly they would execute him. Americans could enjoy the upcoming Christmas with a sense of relief that this monster would be sitting on death row. Or at least this is what the government hoped.

The new trial of the century was on the court dockets scheduled to start on December third in a highly guarded courtroom at the Chicago Federal Building.

The streets around the courthouse were lined with an army of armed men in blue. Large concrete barriers were place in strategic places around the courthouse to prevent truck bombs from coming near the building. Positioned behind the barricades were actual Abrams M1 tanks with their turrets sinisterly pointing down the high-rise-lined streets. Surveillance cameras protruded from building walls, roofs, and poles like the wavering legs of centipedes. Every bit of life within their view was recorded and monitored by technicians seven hundred miles away in Washington DC.

Ali Hasson's trial even called upon man's best friend to help with security. Bomb-sniffing dogs tethered to armed men in blue patrolled the courthouse grounds. Additional security precautions were taken within the courthouse, including more metal and bomb detectors. Most of the new equipment was set up in the courthouse lobby to accommodate the anticipated deluge of citizens trying to witness the trial.

Up on the sixth floor of the courthouse, a large pool of prospective jurors were being interviewed and questioned by the lawyers from the prosecutor and Thomas Lawrence's defense teams. Next to Lawrence sat the monster of the decade quietly staring blankly at Judge Garth. Garth was a seasoned, no-nonsense judge who had served on the bench for over fourteen years.

Sitting among the crowd in Judge Garth's courtroom were numerous plain-clothes detectives and agents with visible ear pieces, their eyes constantly scanning faces, gestures, and movements among the occupants. Garth had also taken extra security measures to protect the identity of the prospective jurors. Each one was given a number and referred to only by that number. Instructions were given to all individuals in the jury pool to not divulge their real name or any personal information to other jurors. Anyone discovered doing so would be held in contempt of court, fined, or given a week in jail. Judge Garth wanted his juror's real identities kept secret from the media, or at least that was what he had hoped these measures would accomplish.

This was part of the prelude to the most anticipated trial of the century. It would be a case where its details and meaning were regurgitated continuously over all the news networks and print media. Headlines in major papers heralded the upcoming trial as stories reexamined every tidbit of evidence known to the public to the point of *ad nauseam.*

In Washington DC, another story was brewing, but it was far down on the list of national news priorities. In fact, many Americans felt reticent to even discuss or read about the year-old misfortunes of the hundreds of thousands of evacuees converging in the nation's capital.

The refugees from the nuclear catastrophe demonstrating in Washington DC viewed Ali Hasson's trial as a point of closure that could further obfuscate their demands for justice from the government and the nuclear industry. It had become relatively evident that their dilemma no longer stirred the nation's sympathy as it did when they were the symbol of a wounded America. The refugees and their problems were fading shadows of a time of darkness that most Americans wanted to forget. So while the preparations of Ali Hasson's trial continued, America's displaced masses desperately tried to get their share of the media and government's attention.

The majority of those evacuees still had received very little, if any, compensation for their losses. The funding set aside for compensation was totally inadequate to help the large number of families, businesses, and municipalities devastated by the nuclear catastrophes. Battles in Congress had raged since April, trying to find what they considered an equitable formula to determine a fair dollar amount to award those who were evacuated.

Much of the hardship, altered life situations, and lost fortunes that evacuees endured were hard to fathom unless you had walked in their shoes. I was fortunate to have received a letter containing a very illuminating account of life after evacuation by a man named Jacob Morrison. He and his family, I think, represented the typical evacuee and his story reflected much of the hopes, problems, tears, and transitions they experienced.

Mr. Roma,

My name is Jacob Morrison, and I'd like to thank you for seeking out real accounts of life for the evacuees after the Christmas Special attacks. I think my family's ordeal following our forced evacuation from Buchanan, New York, is typical of the various problems evacuees were forced to endure. It's certainly a story that has many lessons for those who have never been uprooted from their homes and lives.

Our home was located four miles from the Indian Point Energy Center, so when the evacuation was called we were one of the first families forced to leave. We had to evacuate so quickly that we were

only able to take the clothes on our backs plus a few personal effects and heirlooms. When you're under that type of pressure, you really don't think that clear.

I was so busy trying to assure my twelve-year-old son, Miles, and my wife, Nora, that things would be okay that I failed to think about what I really needed to take. Worst yet, it hadn't occurred to me that we were leaving forever. That was a grave mistake.

To further complicate our situation, my wife, Nora, and I were owners of a small corner grocery store in the heart of what is now the exclusion zone. We also had to abandon our store, leaving behind all of our merchandise and equipment. Thousands of dollars of meat and crates of fruits and vegetables were left rotting in freezers with no power. It's terribly sad to see your dreams erased, but even worse when you realize you should have been more circumspect of living in the shadows of a nuclear reactor.

Without our livelihood, we had little left once the area was declared off-limits. Our lives, like so many others, were changed permanently.

I remember Miles asking me as we threw our belongings into a couple suit-cases, "Where are we going, Dad?"

I couldn't answer him because I realized I didn't know. It made me feel very powerless because I really didn't have any real plans for this evacuation. We had never given any real thought to what we would do if a nuclear catastrophe occurred. The one thing I did know was that I wanted to evacuate using our brand-new Ford Focus. It was Nora's early Christmas present.

My wife Nora was in a bit of a daze as she tried to collect her wits and belongings so we could leave before the roads were packed with other evacuees. Looking back at that Christmas morning, it was very odd. Christmas music was playing in our house while outside the early hour quiet was filled with the shrill sound of Indian Point's warning sirens. It seemed to get louder and louder, its sheer intensity making you want to leave. Lights began popping on along our street as other residents took notice of the commotion.

For years, we had enjoyed our life in Buchanan, New York, but as we drove away and watched our neighbors frantically running in and out of their homes with loads of stuff in their arms, we realized we had just become refugees. And as I listen to the radio about the attacks, another realization grew that I'd never be living in Buchanan again. I was driving to safety, but it didn't prevent the terrible anxiety and sadness that overtook me. Where was I going and what was I going to do?

How quickly things can change. I went to sleep looking forward to a beautiful Christmas morning, but woke up to a nightmare. Those last hours replayed in my head as we joined the caravan of cars fleeing Buchanan. I'd been asleep when the attacks started, but the sirens woke me. Nora was already up starting to prepare the turkey for Christmas dinner. I went out in the kitchen to join my wife and get a cup of coffee. I asked her what was going on, and she said probably another test or the siren going off accidently. That had happened a few times before. We turned on the TV and checked out the news, and of course that was when we discovered this was a real nuclear event.

The news was very sketchy, but it was clear that attacks were occurring across America. The frantic news reports, coupled with text messages from my concerned mother in North Carolina and Nora's sister in Michigan, helped us to put the pieces together quickly. We learned that a team of terrorists had successfully breached the security at Indian Point Nuclear Power Plant and had killed numerous employees while destroying the plant's cooling systems, control room, and backup power sources. The terrorists were still in control of the plant.

The report claimed that the National Guard had been called up and would be helping with the evacuation process. I did my best to maintain my composure, but when I glanced over at my wife, there was no doubt what was on Nora's mind. She had been a die-hard activist against nuclear energy since we married sixteen years ago, and since the disaster in Fukushima City, Japan, she had become even more adamant that nuclear power was a terribly risky way to produce electrical energy. If anyone here fully understood what our evacuation from Buchanan meant, it was Nora.

I couldn't help but wonder how many years it would take before Christmas morning was once again a joyous occasion instead of a lingering memory of a horrendous terrorist attack.

The coming months were incredibly trying for all of us who had been evacuated from the exclusion zone surrounding Indian Point. The magnitude of the attacks displaced millions of Americans.

Our new home was a FEMA trailer in a large encampment outside Andrews Air Force Base. At first, our situation generated a great deal of largesse from society, but soon it dwindled to a point that we all knew we were yesterday's cause. We had just become another relic adrift in an ocean of the catastrophe's debris.

The government did provide medical assistance. In fact, medical tests were conducted on a regular basis, likely in an attempt to gather information regarding the lasting effects of radiation exposure.

In May, the president finally visited our trailer park, and despite our plight, his encouraging words buoyed our spirits and renewed our hope. Just about everyone got to shake the president's hand and pose for a picture with the president. We were told that everything possible was being done to help us return to the lives we had left behind, all we needed was patience. The president said that we were in the hearts and minds of our country's leaders every day. We believed this—for at least a while.

It took three more months before everyone began admitting aloud that we weren't going to be setting foot ever again in our homes. Our entire town had been emptied and deemed "off limits" to everyone; for all practical purposes it was like Pompeii, a lifeless place lost forever. However, we would later learn that looters had cleaned out just about anything of value throughout the evacuated areas.

My mind wandered to our valuables...Nora's jewelry and my grandfather's priceless coin collection. There simply wasn't enough time to scour the attic for our family heirlooms prior to our evacuation, and now it appeared they were gone.

We were given huge stacks of government claim forms that were supposed to provide us with an easy way to get compensated for all that we lost. However, the ungodly amounts of information requested made it appear that the government was purposely trying to prevent us from getting any compensation. We had to list all that we had lost, describe the items, and indicate when and where they were bought. If it was an heirloom or a collectible, where did we get it appraised and did we ever list it on floaters on our homeowner's insurance? They asked for receipts or records of checks from our checking account to prove we had bought the item. They even requested that we contact our credit card companies to get records from them. Many of the financial services charged us fees for the information the government required, but claims were still rejected because of some technicality or a lack of supporting documentation.

The government wanted to just pay a lump sum unrelated to what we really owned. All while this was going on, credit card, mortgage holders, and finance companies continued to hound us for our monthly payments. Most evacuees had zero income, and soon credit cards were canceled, cell phone services were turned off, and people found they had no way to live other than accepting the low-ball settlement offers from the government. People became so depressed that suicide was a frequent event in our trailer camps. Life just seemed to get worse and worse.

Nora, Miles, and I spent nights reading books that were donated by thoughtful families across the country. I did my best to remember that my family was relying on me for support and an upbeat attitude, so I was careful to bury my negative thoughts and anger over the "government assistance" that was always just out of reach.

As things got worse and the government help dwindled and slowed even more, people and their families began to leave "New Buchanan," as the camp had been nicknamed. It was impossible to get a job in an area where thousands of evacuees lived. Employers and employees didn't like the idea of these people, who could have grievous health problems, becoming part of their work force. Jobs were scarce before the Christmas Special, but now it was worse—unless you wanted to work at containing one of the nuclear power plants that were spewing radiation everywhere.

I realized that we honestly had no place to go, as my mother had passed away two months after the Christmas Special attacks. I wasn't even able to attend her funeral, as I received the news a week after her death. I wept quietly in the tiny kitchen of our trailer as Nora and Miles sat silently with their arms around me. I was beginning to question myself as to how long I could keep this up...

In October, Congress passed the Catastrophe Recovery Act, which was designed to quell much of the national dissent regarding the lack of assistance that many who were affected or displaced through the attacks were receiving. However, the bill included more red tape than had been included in New Orleans during the Hurricane Katrina catastrophe. The requirement that we provide "reasonable evidence" of the items we had been lost made the bill very unfair to most of us. There was virtually no way to receive any level of "fair" value. Further, lost wages were excluded in the newly refined compensation package, so we were essentially given no chance of full recovery. Basically, we were being given the news that our lives had been "reset," and we were going to be on our own from here on out. By this time we felt the public and the government had slowly ostracized us and characterized us as a million begging losers.

The watered down Catastrophe Recovery Act stimulated many of us to become active in the protests that were raging in Washington demanding more comprehensive compensation for all of us who were forced to evacuate. Nora, an activist at heart, felt we should step up and add our voices to the struggle. So all of a sudden, I found myself living in a small encampment of protestors on K Street in Washington DC. Being at this K Street encampment quickly made us realize that we were obviously not alone in our belief that America's "recovery plan" had excluded the refugees from the exclusion zones.

It was incredibly ironic that we would begin our weeks-long protest in the shadow of the White House as fat cat K Street lobbyists financed by the nuclear industry belittled our plight to congress, the media, and to the president's people.

The lobbyists claimed that evacuees were trying to profit from an emotionally packed situation and ripping off the nation's taxpayers. The lobbyists portrayed us as greedy opportunists who knew there were major risks involved in living near nuclear power plants, yet chose to ignore those risks. They compared us to smokers who are constantly warned that they could get lung cancer, cardiovascular diseases, emphysema, and a sundry of other deadly diseases, but still expected society to foot their healthcare costs when the inevitable happens. Basically, the lobbyists claimed that if we were good Americans, we would accept the stipend offered in the Catastrophe Recovery Act and move on and let the government focus on keeping the entire nation safe and prosperous.

An older gentleman, a former University of San Diego professor who had been displaced from the exclusion zone around San Onofre, took a leadership role to help unite our voices to combat the lobbyists' portrayal of us. His name was Anderson, but everyone just called him Doc. I don't know why, but that was his nickname.

"Jake," he would tell me, "if we want to be heard amidst such chaos, we must maintain two things: organization and dignity."

Those words became our mantra. Despite the irritation that so many of us justifiably felt toward our government and society in general, Doc never let any of us speak of violence. He believed that it would undermine the entire purpose of the protests. I couldn't agree more, and his demeanor definitely calmed all of our nerves.

I cannot say how many of us were camping there at McPherson Square. If I had to guess, I'd estimate our numbers were in the thousands. Nora, Miles, and I had a small, four-person tent the three of us called home, and we spent our days holding crudely made signs demanding to know where the "recovery" funds went. Working in shifts, we marched on the U.S.

Treasury building and held candlelight vigils just outside of the White House's North Lawn. The first few weeks were everything that a peaceful protest should be. However, when the government announced that the trial for Ali Hasson, the mastermind of the Christmas Special attacks, was about to begin, things really began to take a turn for the worse.

On December 4, a female police officer was attacked a few blocks from where our protests were being held. She was badly beaten, and the media theorized that someone from our encampment was responsible. Things were never the same from the moment that poor officer was beaten.

Public pressure began to mount, and many of our protests were met with opposition. Media outlets were flooded with editorials claiming that we had gone beyond asking for compensation and that compensation wasn't necessary for those who chose to live so close to nuclear power plants. Our plight was beginning to create such a divide in the American people that we knew it wouldn't be long before we were forcibly removed from McPherson Square. What they didn't realize or care about, however, was that most of us had lost everything.

We did our best to not let the opposition get to us, though. The first Christmas since the attacks was near, and our encampment was alive with the singing of Christmas carols and even a small Christmas tree. We protested by day and shared stories of holidays past through the night. In a strange way, we were able to find a great deal of comfort through this camaraderie. For the first time in nearly a year, there were smiles on our faces. I remember being amazed at our resiliency.

The morning of December 9 started as any other day. We woke up, enjoyed a communal breakfast, and were briefed by Doc regarding our protest plans for the afternoon and evening. Progress was being made, and we were beginning to believe that we were gaining ground on the psyche of other Americans and the US government.

Our plan was to again march outside of the North Lawn security gate. This was something we had done several times in the past, but when we arrived, we were met by the opposing protestors. We had grown somewhat used to their presence and did our best to simply ignore them. Could they not see that we had no place to go?

Our group and their group stood opposite each other on the street. We endured shouts of "Rebuild your own life!" and "Everybody's hurting, deal with it!" But we held our ground. I kept Nora and Miles close to me, as there was no telling how this situation might turn, when suddenly a young woman, just yards from us, collapsed. Her head was bleeding, and a shattered glass bottle lay next to her on the ground. Before I could even process the situation, someone from our side of the street tossed a full water bottle at the opposing protestors in retaliation.

The scene that erupted resembled a medieval battle, as the street was suddenly flooded with protestors kicking, hitting, swearing, and punching each other. Miles's first instinct was to rush the street and join the fray, but luckily, I was able to snag him, grab Nora, and pull them away from the skirmish.

We retreated to McPherson Square, and within minutes, we were joined by others from our group with torn clothes, bloodied noses, and swollen faces. They mentioned that the DC police department quickly arrived in full riot gear and began making arrests. I was sure that because of this event, combined with the recent attack on the police officer, our stay in

McPherson Square wouldn't last much longer.

As the nation was chatting around water coolers about the Hasson trial and debating whether or not a death sentence was a one-way ticket to martyrdom, we were fighting a battle few understood, but many would undoubtedly read about in history books for years to come.

Around 4:30 p.m., we were gearing up for another march on the North Gate when we were met by members of the police force's riot control team and an infantry unit from the National Guard.

A bullhorn siren was followed by a concise message: "You are ordered to disperse immediately. Vacate the premises."

They marched into McPherson Square—a wall of military might complete with horses mounted with baton-swinging riders. They were all dressed in malignant black uniforms with blue helmets. Their horses were outfitted with wrap-around visors that covered their eyes. The wall of horses made an impenetrable wall that slowly moved toward us. Their hot breath in the chilly December air made clouds of condensation, virtually blurring their riders from view. Immediately, protestors began to scatter, although a few attempted to stand their ground. Nora and I immediately grabbed what supplies we could carry and frantically scanned the scene for Miles...but he was nowhere to be found. Then things got worse as gunshots rang out.

Cries and screams could be heard across the square, and our search for Miles became more intense. I cursed myself for taking my eyes off of him for a single moment. I heard Doc calling for medical assistance amidst the chaos, and within moments, we were hit with a rush of running protestors. How could it have ever come to this? Americans firing on Americans?

A second round of gunfire cut through the air, and I discovered that I'd been struck in the lower leg with a rubber bullet fired by the police. A rubber bullet hurts like hell

Nora was near hysterics, but she managed to help me retreat from the square. Miles was still unaccounted for, but we clung to the belief that he would emerge unscathed from this melee. What a helpless feeling—knowing your child is in danger with no way to assist him.

We fell back to L Street to search the crowd for our son. I was hobbling from the pain in my swollen leg muscle where the rubber bullet had hit, but the adrenaline rush of what was happening and finding Miles conveniently dulled it.

Ambulances were onsite within seconds, almost as if they had been on stand-by before the forces moved into the square. Nora was a frantic mess, sobbing and asking anyone who would listen about Miles. Finally we found him, but the news wasn't good.

Apparently, he and some other protestors had attempted to head off the marching police as they entered McPherson Square. Feeling threatened, the officers fired. Miles took a rubber bullet to the left eye. Its impact destroyed his eye completely and knocked him unconsious. Two retreating protestors carried him with them to L Street.

I stared in disbelief at my son's destroyed eye as Nora collapsed on the sidewalk just inches from him. Everything transpired so quickly, yet that moment felt like an eternity. The rubber bullet I'd taken to the leg was little more than a flesh wound, but the one that destroyed his eye created a hole inside of me that would fester for the rest of my life.

Nora, Miles and I left Washington DC, never to return. Eventually, we accepted a small compensation for our financial losses, but never received not even an apology from the government for Miles' loss of an eye. It seems that he would become just another forgotten casualty of the Christmas Special attacks.

While we have attempted to rebuild some semblance of a life together, there is no doubt our days at McPherson Square will haunt us forever. I still cannot make sense of how and why Miles was blinded. Nora rarely speaks of it, but when she does, I can see anger, sadness, and fire in her eyes.

The Christmas Special attacks were horrible, but their aftermath should never have resulted in the blinding of my son by a mob of calloused Americans who saw our existence and financial predicament as an inconvenient truth that no one wanted to deal with.

Chapter 85
Opening Statement for the Defense

The Ali Hasson trial finally commenced on December the sixteenth. Judge Harold Garth presided over the proceedings. The Chicago courtroom was packed, and after the judge gave his customary instructions to the participants he requested the prosecutor, Daniel Compton, to state the people's case against Ali Hasson. Compton's opening statement riveted the jury, but failed to introduce any information that was not already known to the world.

The jury appeared engrossed. They all listened intently. Compton's presentation was powerful and expertly delivered, complete with a few jokes to lighten the palpable tension that filled the courtroom.

He said, "You heard what Judge Garth stated, that you must base your decisions on the testimony and proof presented during the trial, but I've got to tell you that sometimes that is a difficult task. One very experienced defense attorney recounted to me what happened when he was instructing his client about how to testify in his own defense. He told him that you are required to swear to tell the truth and nothing but the truth. He asked his client if he understood that and his client, looking glum, replied, 'Yeah, I do.' When the lawyer asked his client if he understood what would happen if he lied on the stand. His client looked at him with a smile on his face and said. 'Heck yes, I imagine that our side would win.'"

On December seventeenth, Thomas Lawrence delivered his opening statement. His presentation was also expertly delivered and gave a peek at how complicated and contentious the trial would become. The transcript of his statement follows:

OPENING DEFENSE STATEMENT in the Ali Hasson Trial

May it please the court, my name is Thomas Lawrence, and I represent the accused Mr. Ali Hasson.

My client and I have waited a long time for this moment to discuss with you, the ladies and gentlemen of this jury, the questionable evidence that the government claims will prove my client guilty of some very serious charges.

The outcome of this case is a life-and-death issue to Mr. Ali Hasson.

You will be presented with evidence in many forms that will establish not only a reasonable doubt but show that my client is in fact innocent of the crime that Mr. Compton has outlined to you. I will begin where counsel for the prosecution began. As he said, it was Christmas morning. Inside the Indian Point Energy Center located in Buchanan, New York, business was being conducted as usual. Electricity was being produced to power the millions of Christmas lights that adorned the millions of Christmas trees in the New York area. It was 6 a.m. Eastern Standard Time. It was still dark outside, and a small flurry of snow was falling. To those at the plant, it was just another morning of doing the same old thing they had been doing day after day. The guards at the gate were probably counting down the hours till their shift ended and they could go home to their families and enjoy Christmas like most Americans would be doing that morning.

Out of the early morning gloom, the guards spotted a military convoy coming up the road toward them. We can only speculate what happened after that, but we do know that all of the gate guards except one were found dead due to being shot or having their throats slit.

What we don't have to speculate about is the whereabouts of my client, Ali Hasson. He was ten thousand feet up in the sky over the Atlantic Ocean on his way to London, England. Ali Hasson was not anywhere near the Indian Point Nuclear Power Plant. He was, in fact, taking his customary Christmas trip to England, a custom Mr. Hasson had practiced for the last three years.

Seconds after 6 a.m., a group of heavily armed terrorists swarmed into the Indian Point Nuclear Power Plant. Just south of the plant on the Hudson River, two more terrorists in a small boat were busy directing remote-controlled speedboats laden with high explosives into the plant's water input pipes. The end result was the destruction of the water intake pipes, which moved 2.5 billion gallons of water daily through the plant's cooling system.

For approximately the next forty minutes, these terrorists went about destroying Indian Point Nuclear Power Plant's infrastructure and systematically killing any employee who stood in their way. The carnage on that Christmas morning quickly filled the airwaves, and for the first time in hundreds of years

Christmas was postponed or, for many, canceled.

For most Americans, the Christmas Special attacks have become a nightmarish event by which we now measure time. It's one of those dark spots in man's history that will be written about and discussed for many years to come, just as Pearl Harbor and 9/11 are remembered.

The severity and devastation from the attack was so great that it was evident that the nuclear power plant owners had never seriously considered or prepared for anything of this magnitude.

That Christmas morning, the plant was guarded and controlled by some of the plant's most inexperienced employees. The warning sirens were not sounded until nine minutes after the attack started. The confusion and impotence of the government's response to the power plant invasion demonstrated that no contingency plan or armed response had ever seriously been devised or practiced to counter a serious ground attack against a nuclear power plant.

During the attack, the Buchanan, New York, fire department was one of the few agencies that responded in a professional manner, within minutes of the attack. They quickly realized the severity of the situation and began pumping water over the walls into the compound to try and extinguish some of the fires. They moved from a two-alarm fire to a six-alarm fire within the thirty minutes they dared remain at the plant. A small contingent of poorly armed Buchanan police officers lacking adequate radiation protection sat outside the gates of the compound trying to use a bullhorn to talk the terrorists out of the plant. The police threatened to storm the compound with deadly force, but because the terrorists were on a suicide mission, the threats fell on deaf ears. A small contingent of the National Guard was assembled Christmas morning and dispatched thirty-five minutes after the attack started. But by then, the radiation around the plant was so great that all civilian and government employees were ordered to evacuate the area.

Ali Hasson is not a war criminal. The only evidence the government has connecting Ali Hasson to this terrible crime are some statements extracted from unknown prisoners, probably after being interrogated, abused, tortured, and deprived of sleep. Ali Hasson, who is a citizen of the United States, was never read his Miranda rights or provided a lawyer to protect his rights when he was first arrested.

Ladies and gentlemen of the jury, everyone in America was affected by these attacks in some way, and you have been given the difficult task to determine whether the allegations made by the government against my client, Ali Hasson, are true beyond a reasonable doubt; that is to say, whether he is guilty of these crimes beyond any reasonable doubt in your mind.

Mr. Compton has outlined to you the government's case, the evidence, or at least some of it, which he hopes to present and prove. I will be disputing much of what he will present and introduce extensive evidence to the contrary, including witness testimony, photographs, tran-

scripts of conversations, videotapes, and other physical evidence. In reviewing the evidence in this case and in the proof that will come, you must use the wisdom of Solomon to decide what is really relevant and true.

The question that you will be deciding is, did the federal government get the right man? If you have any reasonable doubt in your mind, you are obligated to acquit Mr. Ali Hasson of these charges.

Many of the witnesses that Mr. Compton claims he will produce have never been questioned by the defense. So in many cases, we will be interrogating these witnesses for the first time right in front of you, the jury. I will be asking them about conversations they had with the prosecution months ago that we were never made aware of.

The government wants to win this case. They want to have my client, Ali Hasson, held responsible for what happened that Christmas morning. They want you to rush to judgment just as they did.

But I believe Ali Hasson is innocent of the government's charges, and I think you will find that the evidence will tell a different story than the one Mr. Compton alluded to yesterday in his opening.

So let me first begin with telling you about Ali Hasson. He was born in Afghanistan, the son of Hussein Hasson, and it's believed his mother was Hussein's fourth wife, Meena. Ali Hasson was the only male child of Hussein and his five wives. When Ali was seventeen years old, his father was killed by an exploding land mine. Gulbuddin Hekmatyar, a noto-

rious warlord who was friends with Hussein Hasson, took Ali in. He recognized Ali's intelligence and helped him get his education.

Ali went to college for the next nine years in various Western countries and excelled in his studies. He honored Gulbuddin Hekmatyar's belief in him by becoming a physician. He returned to Afghanistan and practiced medicine in Kandahar, providing care to members of Gulbuddin Hekmatyar's mujahedeen group.

A couple years later, Ali married and had two children, his son Abdul and a daughter named Sheeva. Ali Hasson witnessed the occupation of his country by the Russians, the Taliban, and then the Americans. After his village was freed from the control of the Taliban, Ali Hasson provided American troops important information about Taliban-aligned militias near his area. His heroic help undoubtedly saved the lives of many American troops, but in so doing he greatly endangered himself and his family.

Ali Hasson dreamed of coming to America, and because of his aid offered to our country, the State Department decided for humanitarian reasons to grant Ali Hasson political asylum and moved him and his two children to America.

That is how Ali Hasson and his family ended up in Chicago. His successes continued, and within a short time he had established himself as a very talented surgeon saving many more American lives.

During his many years as a practicing physician, he won numerous awards for his expertise and was sought out by patients because of his reputation and expertise.

That was then. Now Ali Hasson is despised and depicted as a monster, a man with no conscious or soul.

But that portrayal of Ali Hasson is the furthest from the truth.

Now let's talk some more about the weak evidence that the government bases their case against Ali Hasson. Before we get to that, I want to say a few words about evidence types. You will learn that there are two kinds of evidence, direct evidence and circumstantial evidence. Direct evidence is the testimony of someone who had firsthand experience in seeing, hearing, or feeling something they are testifying about. For instance, if the government produces a witness who testified that they saw Ali Hasson at Indian Point Nuclear Power Plant on the morning of December 25, that would be direct evidence. We don't have such evidence, however.

They do have circumstantial evidence, and that is a much different type of evidence. It's distinguished from direct evidence by the fact that it requires us to assume or infer from a chain of situations or coincidences that something did or did not happen. This is the type of evidence that the government will use in their case against Ali Hasson.

The entire case is based on circumstantial evidence consisting of hearsay and suppositions. It has been said there is no class of evidence known to be more dangerous, manipulative, or misleading as circumstantial evidence. So please use the utmost caution when con-

sidering this type of evidence in judging the guilt of my client.

The government will claim that the fact that Ali Hasson visited the farm used by these terrorists means he must be one of them, but his visits were simply to provide free medical aid to American Muslims who were attending Islamic studies there. Yes, it was in the spirit of his religious beliefs that Ali Hasson provided medical assistance to members of what we now label as terrorists, but did Ali Hasson know their plans? The answer is no. Doctor Hasson was simply doing the calling of his religion and what is required of him from his Hippocratic Oath as a doctor. Remember, not even the neighbors surrounding the farm had any idea of what was really going on there.

The prosecution claims that some notes and money found in Ali Hasson's desk by his daughter were proof that he was involved in this terrible terrorist attack. But the original notes have never been found. We have only the word of his estranged daughter and an English translation of the notes, which were originally said to have been written in Arabic. This translation of the Arabic notes was done by Sheeva Hasson's boyfriend, Jason Wilgers. We must point out that Jason Wilgers was just learning Arabic and was using these notes and attack plans as bartering chips to exonerate himself from statutory rape charges, harboring a runaway, exposing himself to a minor, and numerous other criminal charges. Unfortunately, Jason Wilgers was killed in jail while being held to face the charges. The original notes, along with a few thousand dollars that were supposed to be in the trunk of Jason Wilgers's car, were never found. The prosecution contends that Wilgers's car, which was parked a few blocks from the Culper jail, was broken into as it sat on the street, and the money, original pictures, and notes were stolen. So did these notes and pictures really ever exist?

Christmas is not a holiday Ali Hasson celebrates, but the night before those horrible attacks he did, as he had made it his custom, to deliver gifts to the children spending their holiday in his hospital. He also gave presents to the children of his colleagues. Do these sound like the actions of a terrorist intent on destroying America?

The prosecution portrays Ali Hasson's normal habit of visiting London at Christmas as evidence that he was fleeing the United States after he had put into effect this chain of attacks across America. This, ladies and gentlemen of the jury, is the kind of very weak circumstantial evidence I spoke to you about earlier.

When we are talking about circumstantial evidence, we are talking about a chain of coincidences or actions that all together could reasonably support the belief that something is probably true. However, all the links of an evidence chain must be proved beyond a reasonable doubt or the entire chain of evidence must be discarded. That is the law, and that's the law you have sworn to apply to the evidence.

Finally, ladies and gentlemen of the jury, you will see there is no real evidence that links Ali Hasson to these crimes. Plus you will see that there was absolutely no motive for the commission of this crime by him. There is not a scrap of evidence in this case proving any criminal intent by Ali Hasson regarding the Christmas Special attacks. If the evidence does not prove the government's case beyond a reasonable doubt you must acquit Ali Hasson.

However, if the weak circumstantial evidence presented by the prosecution still leads you to believe that Ali Hasson could be complicit in these attacks, please weight his culpability against his strict religious culture.

If I can have a few more minutes of your time we need to talk about culpability, laws and how religion may play a part in this case.

Let me first indulge you with a little American history of our own sins..

In the 1700s, laws existed to regulate the ownership of slaves. One law proclaimed that if a slave tried to run away or refused any task requested by the master, the master had the right to beat the slave till he learned to obey. In fact, in the state of Virginia, the law read, "If any slave resists his master and while the master is correcting such slave and shall happen to kill him, the master shall be free of all punishment...as if such accident never happened." So that was the law of the land a few hundred years ago regarding the institution of slavery in America.

During that period of our history, we rationalized reasons to place others in bondage and made laws to enforce those policies of enslavement. Now as you and I well know, once a law is in the books, people no longer question its logic, but see it as a just and right thing to do.

How many times have you heard someone say, "It's the law," as if that makes following it moral and just.

Our country has had many laws that in retrospect we now find reprehensible. A few of them were the Fugitive Slave Act, where citizens were required to turn in runaway slaves; laws preventing women a vote; and America's eugenics laws of the early twentieth century where sterilization was forced on people deemed unfit to reproduce because they were said to be mentally or morally deficient. As bizarre as these laws sound to us now, our ancestors blindly obeyed them, and very few questioned their fairness. For the sake of Ali Hasson's defense, it's important that you remember and recognize how blindly as citizens we follow our manmade rules, regardless of their logic, fairness, or how barbaric we see them now.

Another fact I need to establish before we start putting this all together is the federal court's recognition of the existence of God as evidenced by its practice of swearing in its officials and having them state the words, "So help me God."

The federal government additionally affirms its belief in God's existence by its declaration of "In God we trust" on its currency. Every session of Congress begins with a prayer by a government-paid preacher. This is an established practice that has existed for over two hundred years. There are many other actions the federal government performs that attest to its acceptance of the existence of God. Even in our pledge of allegiance we state "One country under God."

Our government's actions provide ample evidence that it believes in a supreme being, and so does my client Ali Hasson. He has believed in this supreme being for as long as he can remember. When God called upon him to do something, he would do it. He would do it because, in his belief, it was his duty as a servant of the great creator of the world, his God.

His God created a path for him, saving him from death during twenty years of war in Afghanistan. He was chosen to survive because God had plans for him. God provided him with an education and made him a doctor. God provided him with a way to move from his war-torn nation to America. Once in America, he realized it was his duty to his God to convert as many non-believers to Islam as possible. This was his new calling.

Ali Hasson was a pious man who fervently believed in the words of the Quran. These are the words and wishes of God. The Quran is not a catalog where you can pick and choose what you will believe and what you will follow. To be a Muslim, you must believe in and follow all the instructions of the Quran.

A little over a year prior to the Christmas Special attacks, Ali Hasson made his pilgrimage to Mecca. This is a religious duty that each Muslim is required to carry out at least once in their lifetime. Each year, over two million Muslims participate in this pilgrimage. It's an outpouring of humanity from all nations of the world that come together to praise and pledge their obedience to Allah. The enormity of this pilgrimage changes many of those who participate. It's overwhelming in its magnitude and the brotherhood they feel in Mecca.

The Hajj pilgrims visit the site where Abraham was told by the angel Gabriel that God wanted him to sacrifice his son Ishmael to prove his love and obedience to him.

Millions of Muslims visit the three places where Abraham was tempted by the devil to disobey Allah and not sacrifice his son Ishmael. Those temptaions were rejected and Abraham continued to the place in Mina, where he was to kill Ishmael. Just as Abraham prepared to do Allah's wishes, Allah mercifully interceded and provided a sheep to be slaughtered as the sacrifice to him.

Now, during the Hajj pilgrimage, Muslims commemorate Abraham's willingness to sacrifice his son by the slaughter of over seven hundred thousand sheep, camels, and other animals. These celebrations, rituals, and the sheer enormity of the event changed Ali Hasson, just as they have to so many others who have participated in the Hajj pilgrimage.

Ali Hasson had considered himself a servant to Allah since the day he was born. His father and mother had been devout believers who taught Ali the importance and the need to submit to Allah.

Ali Hasson was surrounded by devout Muslims, and like most impressionable children he absorbed their culture like a sponge. Just like other children, he readily accepted what he heard, was told, or saw as truth, especially when it came from his parents or other powerful adults.

These are the formative years when blind beliefs root and become the foundation of what is right or wrong and what is good or evil. So for Ali Hasson, his servitude was not a result of manmade laws, but by the laws he was taught that came from his maker Allah. This is not a strangely held notion by some radical Islamist extremist, but by the mainstream of all practicing Muslims. This belief is ingrained into each Muslim child from the day they first have the ability to comprehend words. They accept Islam and the Quran as the true word of a God, their Allah.

If Ali Hasson, as a servant of Allah, is ordered by God to use violent jihad to spread the spirit of Islam; should he not answer to that authority? Does man's law trump the laws of Ali's religion, or is the law of Allah higher than the laws of man?

And what if you have been so indoctrinated with a philosophy that instills a fear of eternal hell's fire for refusing God's calling, in fact providing no option but to obey? These are some of the disturbing questions you will have to consider as you ponder this case.

If we are to believe in the words of our Pledge of Allegiance, then we also accept that our God's law trumps man's law because it states, "One country under God." We pledge that we accept that we are under God's rule.

Let me bring you back to my relatives, who were brought up as slaves and lived as slaves for many generations.

When they were given freedom, they shunned it. They feared it because they had been taught that they bore the "sin of Ham" or "the curse of Canaan."

They were born to be slaves, and as they had been taught from 1 Timothy 6:1-5 of the Bible, "All who are under the yoke as slaves are to regard their own masters as worthy of all honor so that the name of God and our doctrine will not be spoken against. Those who have believers as their masters must not be disrespectful to them because they are brethren, but must serve them all the more, because those who partake of the benefit are believers and beloved."

So to throw off this heavy yoke of slavery, one had to cast away what the church had taught them, what their experiences had taught them, and what the beatings and preaching of their masters had ingrained in them.

Since God never speaks directly to his minions, followers must depend on the insight and directives given by holy men who are God's envoys here on earth. This is where a great deal of trouble lies, because how can one know if the directions given by God's envoys are his will or only that of the mortal giving them?

So what does this all have to do with my client? Well, Ali Hasson has been under the yoke of slavery since he was a small child. It's a part of his persona and as real to him as his beating heart. He fears hell's fire for disobeying God's wishes just as my ancestors feared their damnation by their earthly master and the God who made them slaves.

So if you conclude that Ali Hasson shares culpability in any of the horrendous crimes he is charged with, you must also consider these extenuating circumstances I have just discussed regarding culpability.

You have a difficult job ahead of you in bringing justice to this case. God bless you and thank you for your consideration.

Chapter 86
The Trial Continues

The morning sunshine of December 18 was a welcome sight after a night of arctic air that dropped Chicago's wind chill readings to twelve degrees below zero. The National Weather Service issued a wind chill advisory and urged those out and about to dress warmly and, if necessary, take refuge in any of the numerous warming centers throughout Chicago.

In short, Chicago was freezing cold on December 18, but Thomas Lawrence probably found the chilly air invigorating. This was a day after he had delivered his poignant opening defense statement for the trial of the twenty-first century. Lawrence knew he was considered by many Americans as the new Benedict Arnold for defending Ali Hasson, and he had come to accept this caricature. Regardless of how people felt about him, they listened to what he said. In fact, his opening defense statement was the lead story that morning, and many readers prayed to their God that jurors would dismiss its every word. They wanted Lawrence to lose. They wanted Ali Hasson declared guilty. For most of the public, the case was already settled. As one commentator said, "The quicker the case concludes, the sooner we can celebrate Ali Hasson's execution." This was an opinion that was shared by many, and unfortunately, the commentator who made this brash statement was a former superior court judge for Cook County.

A significant part of the Muslim population of America didn't believe Hasson was the ghoul the government claimed he was. Many outspoken Muslims expressed their doubt of his guilt and even prayed for his acquittal. A substantial sum of money had been raised to help in Hasson's defense and this provided a distinct financial advantage that previous terrorist trials had lacked.

Lawrence's wife, Barbara, said he left their home unafraid that morning and very upbeat. She said he had told her that he had prepared for this case his entire life. He claimed he was even ready for the tsunami of reporters and cameramen who would converge on the courthouse.

Lawrence knew the trial would consist of many thorny jurisprudential issues, and this morning the real trial would begin as the prosecution marched out its first witnesses.

From his courtroom notes, it was evident that he worried most about the judge following the law and not showing a bias for the prosecution. The Ali Hasson case was the biggest news story since the terrible attacks on the previous Christmas morning, making it obvious that millions of people would watch it.

There is a tremendous pressure to render a guilty verdict when a courtroom is surrounded by a lynch mob whose chants and cries of revenge add an extra chill to the air. A large contingent of federal marshals and Chicago's finest escorted Thomas Lawrence through the roiling crowd, but they could not prevent the glistening globs of spit that started to spot his camel hair coat. One observer said the mood of the people was so intense that when Lawrence appeared, it was very likely he would have been beaten to death if he had not been so well protected. "People wanted to cut out his heart and slice up his liver," the man elaborated.

The first witness to be called to the stand was Dr. Badawi, who had met Ali Hasson at the Water Tower Place mall a few months before the attacks. When the prosecutor asked Badawi if he felt Ali Hasson could have orchestrated these attacks he answered "Yes" before Lawrence could object to the question. The answer infuriated Hasson, who stood up and chastised Badawi, calling him numerous curse words in Pashtun and finally being restrained by marshals, who forced Hasson back into his chair. Ali continued to yell at Badawi and at the court that all would soon suffer the wrath of Allah. The judge admonished Ali Hasson and Lawrence and threatened Hasson that if he could not control himself, he would be removed from the courtroom.

The prosecution's examination of Dr. Badawi continued, and Ali Hasson sat calmly glaring at Badawi as he explained how he came to know the accused. When Badawi testified that he had opened the sealed envelope he had given to Ali Hasson, an angry Hasson once again interrupted the proceedings.

Upon hearing that the parcel was opened and resealed by Dr. Badawi, Hasson began to yell, "Badawi, you're a traitor to our people. You're scum. America sleeps once again. Pearl Harbor, 9/11, the Christmas Special. You're all pompous fools. Those who hate you will devour you." As the outbursts continued, court officers struggled with Ali Hasson, ending with Hasson and the officers on the floor. Hasson ended up being dragged, still yelling, out of the packed courtroom by two court officers. What happened after his removal is recounted by Julia Maxwell in her first-person account of the resumption of the trial.

My sister and I had been awarded two of the reserved seats for victims of the

Christmas Special attacks. My sister's husband had been killed in the bombing of his church on Christmas morning. Luckily, my sister, Jacqueline, and her son had not accompanied him to service that morning.

My sister had told me that her husband, Mark, wanted to take his seventy-two-year-old mother to Mass that morning. As soon as it was over, he had planned to bring her back to their home to celebrate Christmas with the family. Instead, they both perished that morning.

This was our second day at the trial, and the morning session had just started when Ali Hasson became very belligerent over the testimony of a witness. He was told by the judge to control himself or he would be removed from the courtroom, but he continued to rant at the witness. I hated that man more than I'd hated anyone in my life. He looked so smug sitting in the front of the courtroom dressed in some expensive suit and looking annoyed at even being there. Just the way he looked infuriated me. He was the man who had killed my brother-in-law, ripping apart my sister's life and leaving her alone to raise her two-year-old son.

His last outburst of swears and threats at the witness brought Judge Garth down on him. He told the guards to remove Ali Hasson from the courtroom. Ali Hasson actually fought the guards as they dragged him out of the courtroom still yelling. I was glad to get that smug-faced bastard back in his cell where he belonged. All I could think was, "Thank God we don't have to look at his fucking face anymore." If I could have been the person executing him, I fervently believe I would have enjoyed it

After Hasson was removed from the courtroom a quiet hush replaced the previous commotion. During the lull, I grasped my sister's hand to calm her and gave her a smile of reassurance. Jacqueline's composure, however, didn't change, and you could see the strain the last year had put on her. Jacqueline's face was no longer girlish. Her eyes no longer smiled when you looked at her. Now all I saw were worry lines, dark circles, and graying hair that she no longer cared to color. It just didn't matter to her anymore.

As soon as the judge called the court back to session, the prosecutor continued questioning the witness. I turned away from Jacqueline, but continued to hold her hand and gave it a gentle squeeze. That was the last thing I remembered before everything went black. Whatever happened knocked me out because the next thing I remember is waking up to darkness.

I was so stunned that I couldn't comprehend anything. All I could see was swirling dust or smoke perforated with pencil-thin beams of light slicing through the blackness. It didn't make any sense to me. Why was everything so dark and what were those little beams of light? Why was I so cold?

I felt panic and tried to figure out what happened. The courtroom came back into my memories, but at first I still could not figure out why I was in all this blackness. The noises around me seemed muffled and distant. I tried to move and realized that my legs would not respond.

I wondered if I was in a coffin and dead. Really, the thought entered my mind and lingered there as I looked around my dark prison.

As my eyes search the darkness, I realized I could vaguely see hunks of concrete and broken pieces of chairs, and an idea started to form in my mind as to where I was. I knew something horrible had happened, and suddenly I knew I'd been in the courtroom and it must have blown up.

I thought my legs were missing, but I was able to reach down and touch them. I couldn't move them at all. A huge weight was bearing down on them. Suddenly, I remembered Jacqueline and called out to her, but there was no answer. As the ringing in my ears subsided, I thought I could hear screaming and moaning around me.

Then I heard a very faint, raspy voice. It said one word, "Julia?" The voice said it a few times. I knew it had to be Jacqueline. I summoned all my courage and managed to pull myself together enough to reply.

"Jacqueline, is that you?"

"Yes. I'm pinned under something, and I can't see out of my left eye. The weight of whatever is on top of me is making it difficult to breathe. Where are you?"

That was a hard question for me to answer because I hadn't yet oriented myself to where I was. I was just beginning to realize I was trapped under a pile of debris, but I didn't know much more than that. I didn't know how badly I was hurt or how far away Jacqueline was.

I called to Jacqueline, "I'm close to you, under some debris. I'm trying to pull myself free. How are you?"

While I waited for her reply, my senses were slowly returning, and I felt something dripping on my face. At first I thought it was water, maybe from the sprinkler system, but then the mist cleared just enough for me to see an arm, a grotesquely fat, severed arm dangling between two slabs of concrete directly above me. Blood dripped off of the end of a bone that protruded from the severed arm. I moved my head to the side and realized that my hair was soaked in blood, maybe from the severed arm or maybe from my own body.

I lifted up my head to see if I could view my legs and the rest of my body, and I saw a large mound of something lying across my stomach. I could see that I was in a very narrow opening between some slabs of concrete and smashed chairs. I reached out to touch the mound, and to my shock I realized it was the body of a large man. I tried to push him off, but moving his bulk was like trying to pick up a water mattress. There was virtually no leverage for me to pull or push him off of me, and I wasn't even sure where I could move him to. I also realized that when I'd reached down to touch my legs earlier, I had probably touched this body instead. My legs were probably numb from the bulk of his body pushing down on them. There was probably very little blood flow to them.

I could hear Jacqueline's raspy breaths, but she still didn't reply. I knew I had to free myself. I again grabbed the dead guy who was slick with blood, and pulled with all my might on his intact arm. I felt him move a centimeter or so. Blood still dripped on my face or made little splashing sounds as it fell into the pool of blood surrounding me. After an eternity of pulling, I could tell I'd shifted his bulk. I was trying to move him so he would be next to me instead of on me.

I continued to pull on the dead guy for what seemed like hours, but I finally managed to slide him off of me and on to the floor. The beams of light were much fainter now. By this time, the smoke and dust had dissipated, and I realized that the little bit of light I had seen had been coming through chinks in the rubble over me. The beams were fainter now because the sun was low on the horizon. I had no idea how much daylight was left, and all I could think about was if I would die here

I thought I heard noises like a dog barking and hoped it was a rescue team so I tried to yell, but my throat was so dry from all the dust and no water that I could hardly utter a sound.

While I'd been pushing the corpse off of me, I'd been constantly calling for my sister, but she wasn't responding. I did hear her raspy breathing occasionally…at least I thought it was her.

There were lots of strange sounds as things moved and wind blew through the rubble and people cried out for help. I could hear sobbing, yelling, praying, people talking to someone, and constant pleas for help. So there was no way to be sure if the breathing sounds close to me were from my sister or someone else.

Through the dimmed light I strained to see if I could figure out what was on my legs. It looked like wood from a courtroom bench wedged in with a large piece of concrete. I'd thought all the weight on my legs was from the dead guy, but now I could see I was still trapped from my thighs down. I couldn't feel my legs, and I didn't know if that was due to the weight of the debris or if I was paralyzed.

I lost it for a little while. I started to cry, and give up hope. I knew the sun would be down soon, and a December night in Chicago is no place to spend outside, exposed to the elements. I closed my eyes and just waited to either bleed to death or freeze to death. I knew I was done.

I don't know how long I just lay there waiting for death to take me, but when I finally opened my eyes again, it was pitch black. Something else had changed. I could now hear voices all around me. I quickly realized these voices were the rescue workers desperately working their way through the rubble and the corpses. I tried to call out to them, but my voice was so soft that I knew they couldn't hear me over the noise of their equipment. I heard their dogs barking, and it sounded close. I squeeze a few more sounds out and hoped the dogs would hear me, but time passed and suddenly I realized they were gone.

I thought again about giving up, but the image of Jacqueline's three-year-old son, Andrew, flashed vividly in my mind. Little Andrew was safe at the Comfort Inn with our parents, who were prob-

ably going crazy with the little knowledge of what had happened.

I must have passed out again because suddenly it was déjà vu and I didn't know where I was.

Why couldn't I move my legs and why couldn't I see anything? Then it all came flooding back, and I wanted to cry.

I found some strength again and began to try and move the debris still on top of my legs. Nothing moved, not even an inch. I kept trying until I could barely breathe and my arms were too tired to try anymore. I racked my brain for more ideas. How was I going to extricate myself? How was I going to find Jacqueline?

I started to squirm in hopes of pulling my legs out from under the debris. Suddenly I felt I had moved out of the debris a little. It wasn't far, but it gave me new hope. I continued squirming, and every once in a while I'd feel my body move another inch or so. It was extremely slow, but eventually most of my body was free from the wood and concrete. I was beginning to think I would live and that I'd find Jacqueline and everything would be great.

As I tried to pull my feet from under the debris, a big piece of concrete shifted and scraped across my left ankle. I screamed as I felt it peel the skin away. It burned and throbbed, but at least I knew my legs weren't paralyzed. I didn't know how badly hurt my legs were, but I did know those types of injuries heal.

That piece of concrete falling on my ankle gave me a new sense of purpose. It's amazing how something negative can give us that last piece of motivation we need.

I took one more deep breath, and with all my strength, I pulled my legs out from the final pieces of debris. I was free.

I tried to get on my knees, but I couldn't get any further than rolling over onto my stomach, and even that was immensely painful. When I tried to rise up onto my knees, the pain was excruciating, and I screamed such a horrible noise that I was surprised I had it in me to still make such a noise. My throat felt like it was burning with acid. It was raw and probably bleeding. I realized as I prostrated myself that crawling was not an option.

It was so dark, but I felt I had to try and find a way out from this tomb of concrete, wood, and corpses. I began to drag myself in the direction I thought I'd heard Jacqueline's voice, but I had little faith that I'd find her.

I slowly inched my way across the floor, trying to push debris out of my path whenever possible or wiggling myself around it like a snake. I'd crawled only a few feet before I was blocked by a body. I tried to wiggle the person to see if they were alive, but I quickly realized they were very much dead. A large hunk of the woman's head was missing, and she was surrounded by a sticky pool of coagulated blood. I blocked out all of that and tried to find a way around her. I still had hopes of finding Jacqueline. I called her name over and over, but no reply. As I pushed my body over the corpse of the dead woman, a beam of light cut through the darkness, and I heard a cry from someone above me saying, "I've found a live one. She's over here. Bring the paramedics."

My heart skipped a beat. Maybe that was Jacqueline and she was alive. I started to cry for joy. My hope for my sister was short-lived because suddenly a light was shining in my face and someone was saying, "Stay calm, we are here to help you."

Then I felt something warm fall over me, and I realized the rescuer was covering me with a blanket. I was the one they had found alive.

"My sister is buried here also," I croaked. "Please find her, she is right around here." I kept pleading as the paramedics swarmed around me.

They carried me out of the rubble and loaded me into an ambulance. I was told later that I became hysterical and they had to sedate me just to take me to the hospital, where they operated to repair my injured left leg and stop some internal bleeding.

I don't know how much time passed before I woke up and asked for Jacqueline. No one was able to tell me at first. It wasn't until hours later that I learned that they found Jacqueline sometime the next afternoon. Her injuries were extensive: two broken legs, a broken pelvis, and a bad gash on the left side of her head that had bled slowly throughout the entire ordeal. I immediately asked when I'd be able to see her. I could tell by the look in the doctor's eyes that he didn't want to answer that question.

"Where's Jacqueline?" I screamed.

They told me later that they had sedated me during my outburst, but I don't remember that. I just remember the anguish and intense anger that consumed me at that moment.

Now, seven months later, I can look back at that day without crying, without feeling extreme anger or guilt. It's not easy, but I can do it. Jacqueline is dead, and I can't change that.

I now know that I was right that Andrew needed a mom. I just didn't realize that mom would be me. I now know just how wonderful and amazing it is to have a son. He's almost four years old, and although he's been through so much, he's just a happy, loving child.

I watch him play sometimes, when he doesn't know I'm watching, and I can see Jacqueline in him, mostly in his smile. I can see her carefree nature and easy laugh. I can see her tenderness and also her sometimes simmering temper, but most of all I can see her love of other people in Andrew.

My body is mostly healed. I can now walk with only a slight limp. Life is far from perfect, but at least Andrew and I have each other, and I know that bastard Ali Hasson was crushed to dust by his own actions. That fact actually gives me a little relief from everything else. He is dead and can never harm anyone again. That is certainly something to celebrate.

Chapter 87
Thomas's Last Words

Thomas's body was hemmed in between chunks of concrete and debris from the collapsed courthouse. He had little hope of escape, but he continued his recording regardless. This is the transcription from the final minutes of that recording:

> *Barbara, I know I have been rambling, but I want to tell you once more how wonderful you are. I want you to know that I'm truly sorry for the pain my dream-chasing has caused you. This last dream case turned into a nightmare that has brought pain and destruction into many lives, including yours. For that I'm truly sorry. Ali Hasson and those bastards like him are a plague on all humanity, and I'm ashamed that I tried to play the justice game with him.*
>
> *You have been my life force ever since we were dating back at Howard. It has been your support and love that has been my driving force. Without you, I would have accomplished very little. Even now, it's the love I feel from you that blocks out the pain of this moment. My vision of your smile erases the darkness around me and gives me these precious moments to still be with you. So many memories of wonderful times shared with you and Scott have flooded my mind, reminding me of the beautiful life we lived. I hope you two will cherish those same memories and lock them in your hearts.*

Thomas's voice broke here, and he paused, but his unsteady breathing continued. In the background, the noises of the building in its death throes were still discernible from the recording. You could hear sounds that were probably slabs of marble or concrete still settling.

Suddenly Thomas's voice returned:

> *Please don't let those memories fade. Keep them strong. With those memories, I will always be with you and Scott.*
>
> *Being close to you, Barbara, has always allowed me to leave my fears behind and become happy in the world that existed just between you and I. I can remember many a night where I felt myself floating away from one of my dark days into your inviting arms.*
>
> *Barbara, I want you to know that I don't fear death. I loved life—I've had you, a beautiful wife, a great son, and a perfect home. I don't want to leave you, but reality is often cruel and doesn't give us what we want. My choice would be to stay with you, to love you and protect you, but I guess you could say I'm being liberated from this existence and will move on to what follows.*

Again Thomas stopped talking, and the groans of the building filled the silence. I could also hear the blaring of sirens mixed with Thomas's labored breathing. After about a minute of this background noise, he spoke once more.

> *Barbara, don't let what has happen steal your hope and spirit from you or Scott. Especially Scott!*
>
> *Make sure Scott listens to this recording. At least the part that's for him. Scott, I'm sorry I was not there with your mother to see your school play this afternoon. I should have gone, because I didn't*

have the best of days here at the courthouse. I'm sure you did well, and I'm also sure I would have loved watching you. Anyway, I wanted to leave you this message and tell you how proud I am of you and that I love you. Putting it bluntly, son, your dad has got himself into a mess that he is not going to get out of, but I have a couple moments to say a few words to you.

Thomas's voice broke again, and you could hear him trying to regain his composure. He momentarily composed himself and said,

"I'm so sorry, Scott, this is not how a dad should act. I hope you will understand."

More silence followed, with a few audible sobs, and then Thomas continued with his message to Scott:

You and mom are going to have some bad times, but with spirit and hope you can move on to great things, and that's what I want for you. Life is so unpredictable and rough. It's full of games and tortures, and worst of all, it can change within seconds. That's what it did with me.

Scott, you need to be optimistic about life and use your tremendous spirit to deal with any pain or loss you might feel from all of this. Your mom loves you, and that should be comforting to you. And I know you might not really have thought of me as loving you, but I do. I have been so proud of you, worried about you, wanted you to have everything a young man could ever have. I wanted you to have all the advantages. I may not have got all of them for you, but you were blessed with the greatest advantage, and that was love from your family and so many others.

I need you to be brave, for yourself and for your mother. This is going to be your biggest challenge. Being brave when things seem so wrong is hard, I know because I have been there. It's hard for me to ask you to do what might first appear impossible, but the impossible becomes possible when you have the courage to maintain your hope and spirit.

I always wanted things to be exciting and beautiful for you; I wanted to be a dad you would be proud of.

Scott, I hope you will remember the times we were together. The times we watched movies together, told jokes, or just shared a smile between us. The memories might be painful at first, but eventually I hope you will just know I'm still with you, even if only in spirit.

People believe all sorts of things about what happens when a loved one dies. Well, the one thing I believe…is that in remembering that person and thinking about them, we often discover more about our selves.

When my dad died, it was a sad and difficult time for me. But as with all sorrows, eventually time erases them. Even though he left me twenty years ago, I still think of him daily. I wish he would have been with me longer, but a part of him has always remained with me and also with you, Scott. When you have children, a part of your grandfather will be with them also.

A person really never dies. My dad still has a presence in my memories, in my heart, and his memories are woven into so many things that I see and touch.

So Scott, I want you to do your best and help your mother through this. I hope you will study hard in your coming years so you will have the knowledge on which to build your future. I won't be around to give you my advice, but your mom is wise, and I hope you will possess the wisdom to recognize that. I have a feeling that a huge number of people are going to admire you, and I want you to know that I'm one of them.

I do have one last piece of advice for you: live your life with honor, don't be afraid to dream, and march to your own drum.

I have a request for both of you; it might sound stupid, but I want you to celebrate Christmas. I mean celebrate it like before the attack. Evil wins if everyone lives in fear of celebrating Christmas.

I know what is happening now and what happened the day of the Christmas Special has made Christmas a day of darkness for millions, but December twenty-fifth is Christmas. It should remind everyone that we are all part of one big family and celebrate the day as recognition of the spirit of good in all mankind. The next Christmas might be hard, but you can do it.

All of a sudden, the staccato sound of a machine gun or perhaps a jackhammer filled the recording, blocking out any other sounds. This went on for quite some time. It was intermittent and sounded as if the sounds came from different directions and distances. In between the chatter of this loud noise, you could hear a coughing or heavy breathing and a couple curses coming from Thomas.

Finally, the clamor subsided and once more you could hear Thomas uttering a few words:

> *"Barbara, I hate to say good-bye, my sweet angel, but it's time for me to rest. I'm running out of power and I need to rest."*

A series of coughs interrupted Thomas's words. It was a serious coughing bout, but then it subsided.

A few seconds later, Thomas, in a thin voice, uttered his final words,

"I love you guys."

Chapter 88
What Did Ezekiel See?

The day after the Chicago Federal Court was bombed, the president of the United States gave a short address to the nation. In it, he reiterated what previous presidents have said after prior Islamic militant attacks.

"On this occasion we must reaffirm that the United States is not—and never will be—at war with Islam. It's imperative that this is understood, that our war is not against Islam, but with those individuals who are mass murderers and have indiscriminately slaughtered anyone who stood in their way, including Muslims. Ali Hasson's demise should be welcomed news to all who believe in peace and human dignity."

The president's statement shared the front page of most papers with the story of how five Chicago police officers happened to book the same Hajj tour to Mecca as Ali Hasson a year prior to the Christmas Special. The Hajj is an important religious duty to all Muslims so it was not odd that they all went on the same tour. What was startling was that two of the five police officers were the suicide bombers who blew up the federal courtroom where Ali Hasson's trial was taking place. It was theorized that both police officers wore explosive vests that were detonated simultaneously from a remote location.

Some people theorized that the police officers must have been forced into this mission or were unaware that their bulletproof vests were packed full of explosives. However, most Americans believed they were willing participants and did this as their jihad duty to punish the kuffers and kill the crusaders who were defiling Islam with man's corrupt laws.

The courtroom destruction gave cause for celebration to millions of Muslims in Pakistan, Afghanistan, Iraq, Iran, and Saudi Arabia. People celebrated in the streets and burned American flags and statues of the American president. Huge posters of the faces of the two Chicago police officers who were responsible for the blast appeared everywhere, and they became instant heroes to the masses.

The government concluded that the bombing was a plan to free Ali Hasson that went awry. They theorized that Ali Hasson was supposed to have been further away from the blast when the bombs detonated. Instead, Ali Hasson was caught in the avalanche of falling concrete and crushed in the rubble. The falling concrete severed a gas pipe, and a fire quickly ensued that burned Hasson beyond recognition. His remains were identified by his glasses, shoes, and one of his fingers. The finger had apparently been severed by a chunk of falling concrete and crushed, but it was protected from the fire. The crushed, roasted finger was checked against Hasson's DNA and came back as a match. The glasses, which had been issued by the prison's optometrist, matched Hasson's prescription. The bodies of the two guards who had been escorting him were also found next to Ali Hasson's remains.

Most of America was happy Ali Hasson was dead, but at the same time saddened that his death had resulted in so many innocent people dying. As many pundits proclaimed, it was time to put this all behind us and move forward. As they said, "What is done is done; nothing can change it, but we can change the future, and that is what we need to focus on."

But as most major events in America go, there is always someone with another story, like the Kennedy conspiracy theories and the 9/11 conspiracy theorists who believe the government was complicit in the attack. Ali Hasson's death had its conspiracy theories also. My interview with a Chicago street preacher who called himself Ezekiel raises a few questions about the government's explanation of Ali's death. Although his version of what he saw is totally discounted by the government investigation as the ramblings of a confused drunkard, it does make you wonder. The interview follows:

Roberto Roma: *Ezekiel, I'm glad to finally meet you. You have become quite a legend since the courthouse incident, but I guess you know that.*

Ezekiel: *It's my mother's fault, I wasn't like this till I was born. I hear you're big-time writer. I don't do no writing, but I do a lot of reading, mostly Bible stuff. You know my name is a biblical name?*

Roberto Roma: *I thought it sounded like one.*

Ezekiel: *My namesake, Ezekiel, was commissioned by God before Jesus even walked the earth. God called Ezekiel the Son of Man in the old book, you know. Ezekiel was really important to God. My father was a preacher, and he told me that Ezekiel was really as important to God as Jesus was, 'cept when they killed him and Jesus became more famous. God gave Ezekiel a tough job just like the one he gave Jesus. He was sent to people who were not so keen to obey God's voice, and you know I'm still trying to do that since I bear his name. That's why I'm here to help you.*

Roberto Roma: *I can use all the help I can get. Tell me, where were you the day they blew up to courthouse?*

Ezekiel: *It makes me shiver just thinking about that day. I remember it well. I'd been holed up in the rear of an old van because it was one of those winter days so cold that if a dog pissed on a fire hydrant, he'd be stuck there till spring. I'd found this van in the long-term parking lot that had been left unlocked, so I felt I could chance sleeping there for a few days. I figured that the owner would be gone a spell since they were in the long-term parking.*

Roberto Roma: *I think you could say you were at the right place at the right time for this event. So what happened?*

Ezekiel: *I ain't sure you could say all that. I got a bullet shot straight through my shoulder and another that put a hole right in my liquor flask that was right over my heart. That bullet went right through by coat, two sweaters, and hit that flask dead center in my shirt pocket. The bullet punched through one side of the flask and pushed out the other side like a tit. Knocked the shit out of me. It broke two of my ribs. The good thing is, it got me closer to God again. Since then, I bought me a new flask and keep red wine in it all the time now. I think when they saw the red wine stain on my jacket, those guys thought I was dead. For now on it's gonna be Boone's Farm Tickle Pink as my favorite wine for salvation.*

Roberto Roma: *It's a miracle you're alive.*

Ezekiel: *That's an absolute fact.*

Roberto Roma: *So I guess you're a church-going man.*

Ezekiel: *I don't need to go to no church to be a God-fearing man no more than a man standing in a barn makes him a farm animal. I been doing a lot of my own preaching. I'm sort of what Ezekiel of the Old Testament was. I try to bring God to the people by just seeking out those who need it the most. I live with them. I even have to sin sometimes to bring people closer to God. I was trespassing the day I witnessed what others say is a bunch of bullshit, but it ain't. You know what the FBI, Homeland Security said about me?*

Roberto Roma: *Yes, they said your story was not believable.*

Ezekiel: *No, what they said was that I was a delusional drunkard who couldn't tell a pile of dog shit from a bowl of pudding. I might be slightly burned out, but my brains are still smoking big time.*

Roberto Roma: *Well, I'm not like them. I'd love to hear what you witnessed.*

Ezekiel: *I told you where I was, in the back of the van. Well, I was about to step outside to take a piss just as I saw this police car come screeching into the parking lot. It stops just a few feet from my van, and then these two cops jump out...or at least that's what they looked like. They are all glancing around like crazy, and then they open the back door of the squad car and pull out a man dressed in a real nice suit, but all messed up and crumpled. His left hand's got like a towel wrapped around it and looked all bloody. I squinted to get a better view of* *the guy, and then my eyes bugged out like a stepped-on toady frog as I realized this was the guy who was the big terrorist, Ali Hasson. I can still see that face in my head. He looked like he was in a daze, like the pictures of Jesus after he was put on the cross. The guy couldn't stand up. They were just pulling him along. Suddenly I realized they were coming right to the van I was in, so I grabbed my pack, threw open the door, and ran as fast as I could, but one of them pulled a pistol and shot at me. It missed, and I just kept running and got another few feet when he shot at me again and that bullet hit me in my shoulder and spun me around. I fell up against a truck, and as I was falling the second bullet hit me. I guess they saw the spray of wine blowing out my coat and thought he had hit me in the heart. Anyway, I think it knocked me out as I hit the asphalt. Next thing I know, the van is backing up fast, and then it just speeds away. I can't sit up my chest hurts so bad. I was sure I'd been shot in the heart or I was having a heart attack.*

Roberto Roma: *It sounds like you were in one terrible situation.*

Ezekiel: *I think you could definitely say I was and it would be no lie. I was there on the ground in snow, and it was as cold as a whore's heart. My whole body was shaking worse than a dog shitting razor blades. I reached up to my coat where all that red was and it was slicker than greased goose shit. I knew I was going to die. I was trying to think of all the bad things I had done and ask God for forgiveness, but I realized he was going to have to let me live a bit longer if he was* *going to listen to all the shit I had on my sin list. Suddenly, I saw a person coming toward me. He was glancing around all nervous also, and I am thinking, "Oh shit, he is coming to finish me off." I put my hands up like I'm praying and he shouts to me, "Hey, you alive?" I yelled back and it hurt like hell, "Well, I'm right now, but I been shot in the heart." The guy says, "Oh shit, I better call you an ambulance." He pulls out a phone and diddles around with it, but he ain't moving much faster than a bug on fly paper. I'm getting a little worried, so I yell at him, "Hey, bring the phone over here and I will call them." This guy, bless his heart, was as dumb as a barrel of spit and half as useful. He walks over to me and hands me his phone and I dial 911. He just stands there and he ain't got nothing to say, but he says it anyways. I realized God had him there like a messenger or something for me so I could call 911 and be able to go about and do my work for God.*

The ambulance came with its alarm blaring in just a few minutes. The noise hurt my head. The first paramedics who showed up were big ums. One was this woman I swear was so ugly she would have to hang a steak around her neck just to get a dog to like her. The oth er was just a bit old and had more chins than a Chinese phone book, but the two seemed to know what they were doing, and when they opened my jacket they both sniggered and told me I was going to be okay. They lifted the flask from my pocket and wine dripped from it. The ugly one said, "Mister, you're lucky. You probably got some bruised ribs, but you're go-

ing to live." She looked at my shoulder and told me it would probably take a couple stitches but it would be fine. The ugly one kept chatting with me and asking what happened, and I told her and she comes back and looks at me funny and says, "The news said Ali Hasson was killed at the courthouse." I told her that what I said I saw was what I saw. He was wobbly but alive, and they were all talking that gobbledygook Arab talk. I knew it was him. Hell, I'd seen his face on TV about hundred times a day for the last year.

Roberto Roma: *His face was certainly one that most Americans would recognize. It was strange that you felt you had seen him but others claimed you had to have been mistaken.*

Ezekiel: *It got even worse when I got to the hospital. By the time the ambulance arrived at the hospital, a couple of feds were waiting for me. Before I even got to see a doctor, they were asking me all kinds of questions, and I told them the same story I told the medics, but they wanted to know how much I'd been drinking that morning and if I did drugs. They wanted to know why the people who shot me couldn't have been some guys who had maybe robbed some drug dealers and were dressed as cops with a stolen cop car. They wanted to know how good my vision was. They asked me if I remembered what color Hasson's suit was and if he was wearing a tie. It happened so fast that all I remembered was he was wearing a dark suit. Maybe it was blue or brown or gray, hell, I don't really recollect. I know the guy who* *looked like Ali Hasson had something like a towel wrapped around his hand and it was all wet and bloody looking.*

I think they didn't believe me. They joked around with me and gave me their card and told me to call them if I remembered anything else and that was it. I never heard from them again. The Chicago police did a little investigating too, but a couple days later, once I started checking with them about who shot me, they tell me the feds are covering the case.

I could not believe they didn't have anything in the papers about what I saw, so I contact a reporter at the Chicago Tribune and told him my story. They run it, but it reads like a joke. Enough people read it, however, and realized that what I saw made sense. They never found Ali Hasson's body in the courthouse rubble, but they did conveniently find one finger from his left hand that they claim was proof he was dead and burned up or blown apart or something. So I get to thinking, maybe it's like what happened to Osama bin Laden. You know they say they killed him and dumped his body in the ocean, but then those Stratfor emails leaks from this government guy named Burton claiming that Bin Laden's body was on a CIA plane heading to Dover Air Base. Makes me really wonder if he was even killed or just drugged up and is now in one of those high-security prisons and being made to eat ham sandwiches every day. So the more I think about what I saw, I realize the government is trying to paint me like I'm some sort of drunken moron. I get to thinking, what if they were really police who grabbed Ali Hasson?

Hell, they might be taking him away to join Osama bin Laden down in Guantanamo. Or maybe it was not real cops, but terrorists dressed up like cops who were freeing Ali Hasson. It might even have been real cops who were Muslims and who were part of a plan to free Hasson. A lot of Muslims liked him and wanted him freed. The bottom line is we ain't seen no dead body, and I'm sure I saw him with those guys. So what's going on? Is he dead or not?

Roberto Roma: *From all the people I have talked to, I can assure you that your claim definitely has people questioning what the government has been telling them. Do you have anything else that will shed more light on what happened?*

Ezekiel: *I have been doing a lot of deep, critical thinking since that day. I been thinking about spiritual truths and literal truths. I know God is looking out for me. He wants me to finish my mission. He saved me that day so I could continue on. He has helped me many a day. I can remember times when I was so hungry that my belly button hung out my asshole, but all of a sudden I'd get food. So I don't worry about food, money, or any worldly things, because all I need is to believe and he will take care of me. God wants me to help others to see the differences between the literal and spiritual.*

The Bible warns, "Be not a minister of the letter for the letter kills, but the Spirit gives life." That's from Corinthians. In straight talk, what that all means is that the Bible, the written word of God, should not be taken literally, and if it is, people are going to wind up dead. That's what has been happening because you got a bunch of people doing the literal instead of the spiritual. We all got to move on and follow the spiritual part of the Bible. Following the literal part causes war.

The Bible is a book of light and can only be understood by those with spiritual sight. I have spiritual eyes, and it's clear to me that most of the stories in the Bible can never really be understood by common folks, 'cause they don't have the ability to comprehend the spiritual side of the stories. Most people have a sick soul or are vain or are just plain dumb. So today, that's what I'm trying to do, help people on their spiritual path of understanding, so they can see the Bible the way it was intended. That's why I'm not dead. It's because God had this mission for me and needed me here on earth to help him with his nation of panicked sheep.

Roberto Roma: *Well, from what I can see, the world is much better off because of that miracle of you being saved.*

Part Three
A New Beginning

AKRANES
Iceland
Cgmj/DHearne
The Christmas Special 2013

Chapter 89
Sheeva's New Diary

After the bombing of the federal courthouse in Chicago, a great deal of chaos happened between Muslims and non-Muslims in America. As much as the president had promoted the importance of unity between all people, America was torn apart religiously. Non-Muslims distrusted and feared Muslims, and most Muslims felt the same towards the non-believers.

The distrust and fear manifested in many ways. For example, many non-Muslims feared using doctors who they thought were Muslims; they boycotted Muslim-owned businesses; and they stayed away from areas where Muslims lived. The darker side of the fear resulted in mosques being firebombed. In retribution, cathedrals and churches were desecrated and set on fire. Both Muslims and non-Muslims were beaten by hateful mobs, and many more Americans died as a result of the Christmas Special attacks and the hate that it fostered. Finally, eighteen months later, sanity appeared to return.

All during this time of unrest, Sheeva Hasson was living under the Witness Protection Program in Arizona. She had regained much of her sanity from the emotional trauma inflicted by the death of her boyfriend and knowing that her father was responsible for the death of thousands in the name of Allah. She had not lost her faith during this trial, and even when her father was killed she accepted what ensued as Allah's will and his way of punishing her father for the horror he had inflicted on so many lives.

Her brother, Abdul, was still a wanted man, and many believed he had been given refuge in Saudi Arabia. Very few clues had surfaced in regards to his whereabouts. It was common speculation that Abdul had been the mastermind behind the Chicago courthouse bombing and the attempted freeing of his father, but there was no real proof to support those assumptions.

Sheeva's life was threatened by the million-dollar fatwa that had been offered to any jihadist as a bounty for killing her for her betrayal of her father and Islam and as punishment for her whorish actions of sleeping with a kuffer. Because of these threats, the Witness Protection Program decided it was time to move Sheeva to a more secure and permanent location. The United States decided to move her to a country with a very small Muslim population. Her identity would also be changed, and she would have a totally new history and name.

On her departure to her new destination, Jason's father, Roger Wilgers, bought Sheeva a beautiful diary to record the start of her new life. The following excerpts are taken from her first entries as she talked about the new Sheeva.

> *Dear Diary! You mean a lot to me because my would-have-been father-in-law, Roger Wilgers, bought you for me at the Tucson International Airport just before we started our journey to Iceland. I love your cool cover in its steampunk style of brass cogs, gears, and the emotion indicator. How many diaries have an emotion gauge? Today, it read*

that I'd be 68 percent happy. Anyway, I want you to know that I'm going to share with you everything about the new me in Iceland. What I mean by the new me is that I'm no longer Sheeva. According to my passport and other papers, my new secret identity is Sonya Walsh...yup, Sonya Walsh. I looked the name up and it's Russian and means "wisdom." The story goes that I'm moving to Iceland to start my life over after my husband Chris Walsh was killed in Afghanistan. I have a whole lot of new stuff to remember. Maybe writing it down will make it easier to keep it fresh in my mind.

Jason's father, Roger, has become like a real father to me. Once, it was hard to have him around because he reminded me so much of Jason, and that made me sad. After my father's court tragedy, we just sort of ended up communicating more and more, and finally it was like Roger was the person who was always looking out for me.

The marshals didn't like me communicating with Roger and con-

stantly told me I was breeching my security, but he was the only person I could talk to who understood what I'd gone through.

It was hard for the marshals to stop our communication. Every time they monitored my email and deleted emails I was expecting, I'd call Roger from my cell phone or a payphone or even from one of the marshal's phones and ask Roger if he had written. Quite a few times we had it out with the marshals that they should let me at least talk to this one person. I think they finally just gave up trying to stop me from contacting him. It's not like the terrorists have an intelligence department or organization that can monitor email correspondence and phone calls, so why the big problem?

When the Witness Protection Program informed me they had found a permanent home for me in Iceland and I told Roger, he was very upset. He agreed that the new location would be a far safer place than where I was, but he wasn't happy that the great distance would end our frequent visits. A day later, he shocked me when he told me he was selling his house and moving to Iceland also. That was when I realized how much I meant to Jason's dad and how much he meant to me. I think he sees me as his connection to Jason. Maybe I remind him of his son in a good way. It makes me happy to have someone close by who I love and trust.

At first, the federal marshals were furious that I'd told Roger about the move, but after a couple days my sin was forgotten. A week later, when Roger's plan was discovered, the federal marshals were dumbfounded that he was also planning to move to Akranes, Iceland. They were so upset with Roger that they threatened to arrest him for interfering in my relocation. They said he was interfering with a federal witness. Finally, Roger hired a lawyer, and two days later the federal marshals accepted the fact that he could really go and live anywhere he wanted.

Roger had already visited Iceland and told me he had found a house very close to where he suspected I'd be living. I asked him how he found that out and he said my new home was in a small community where nothing was really secret. He said it was a place where if someone was told a secret they would swear another best friend or spouse to secrecy and in turn that person would do the same till finally the whole town knew the secret. He told me I'd love the place.

So finally, on a 109-degree, sunny July morning in Tucson, Arizona, we started our journey to Akranes, Iceland.

After about eleven hours of flying and layover time, we landed at the Keflavík International Airport some thirty miles south east of Reykjavík, Iceland. It was about 1 a.m. when we landed so I really couldn't see much of anything, but to my amazement I was told that sunrise was only two hours away. Carol Williams, the federal marshal escorting us, said that in Iceland during July, the sun rises about 3:30 a.m. and sets around 11:30 p.m. While I was thinking about this big change in my days, Roger and I were also being processed through customs.

Marshal Williams chatted with the customs agent in Icelandic during the entire procedure. I think they knew each other quite well; a lot of smiles and laughs were exchanged between them. Roger noticed it also and looked at me with his "what-is-going-on?" grin, but the flirting probably helped us get through the process quicker. The customs guy stamped our passport and in broken English said, "Here you are, Sonya." We were then directed into a corridor that led to the main terminal.

We didn't even have to retrieve our luggage, Carole had arranged for another marshal to pick our bags up and deliver them to our new home. Marshal William's job was to get us to our new residence as fast and as safely as possible.

As we walked through the terminal toward the airport parking,

I saw a beautiful stained glass mural hanging from the ceiling. It was huge, with a couple of strange faces and weird things that looked like flying machines with wings. It had a distinct steampunk look to it, which of course triggered memories of Jason and his love for steampunk art. I stood there looking at it, but only for seconds because Marshal Williams said we had to hurry. One other thing in the terminal that really caught my eye was a spa that used naturally heated geothermal sea-water. I thought that was neat, but Marshal Williams said that most houses in Iceland use geothermal heating to keep them warm.

We were passing several shops when Marshal Williams suddenly decided we did have time to order coffee and pastries. She stopped at a place called the 10-11 store, very similar to a 7-11 back in America. They had a coffee bar, and Carole treated us to coffee and pastries to take with us on our drive into Reykjavík. I was too hungry to wait for the drive and started nib-

bling on a pastry as we continued to the parking area.

As soon as we stepped outside, the cold hit me and I shivered. It was probably forty degrees with lots of moisture in the air. It felt colder than it probably was. I quickly learned that fifty-five in July was considered a hot summer day.

In the parking area, Marshal Williams pointed out a new Toyota Yaris Terra and told me it was my new car. She was in such a rush that I didn't even have time to look it over. She handed me a new driver's license with the name Sonya Walsh on it and told me to stick it in my purse. I was actually excited about driving in my new country, but she wouldn't let me. She said it was important that we get to Reykjavik quickly because we had to catch a ride to Akranes on a ferry that was really a training ship for sailors.

Riding on a ferry was not what I'd expected. I thought we would be driving through the Hvalfjarðargöng tunnel and I had been looking forward to the experi-

ence. Marshal Williams, however, killed that plan. Carole said she hated going through a three-mile, poorly lit, and badly ventilated tunnel in an area that sometimes has hundreds of small earthquakes in a single day. If a big earthquake happened while you were in the tunnel, what would you do? She had a point; the tunnel was not only about three miles long, it was also under water. It would be very scary being in there even during a small quake.

By the time we got to the port in Reykjavik, the east was glowing red as the sun rose over the horizon. The sunrise was so beautiful. It made me think of Jason and how he would have loved to photograph all of this beauty. I think Roger was also thinking about Jason or Frank because he looked withdrawn and had become non-talkative. Maybe he had hoped that Iceland would be so exciting that he wouldn't think of his son's death.

We arrived at the port just as the ferry was preparing to depart.

Marshal Williams's timing had been perfect...two more minutes and the ferry would have left without us. The ramp was still down, so she drove my Yaris up onto the ferry, and we were now on our last leg of our journey.

The ship's foghorn sounded, and I felt us slowly edging away from the dock. We got out of the car just as a man rushed over to greet Marshal Williams. He first spoke in Icelandic to Williams, but then switched to English as he welcomed Roger and me with a big smile and handshakes. His name was Ragnar something. I couldn't pronounce his last name. He ushered us over to the railing and gestured to the city of Reykjavik that we were slowly moving away from. He told us in heavily accented English that Reykjavik was Iceland's capital and his home. A third of Iceland's population lived there, about 120,000 people he claimed. I couldn't help but think that back in Tucson, we had half a million people living there, more than Iceland's entire population.

For my first morning in Iceland, the sunrise was spectacular. The clouds and haze cloaked the sun, making it look like a huge orange ball of fire. It laced the sky with a mixture of pinks, reds, oranges, purples, and blues. Ragnar told me that, at some times of the year, a sunrise or sunset can be three hours long. It was a beautiful way to first see Iceland.

As Reykjavik faded from view, we moved to the bow to catch our first glimpses of Akranes. The first thing I noticed were rays of sun lighting up a huge mountain that jutted up behind the town of Akranes. Big clouds hovered above it painted by the rising sun. Ragnar said the mountain was called Akrafjall and it was about six hundred meters high. He told me I'd have to climb it and see the beautiful view from the top.

As we got closer to the Akranes harbor, I spotted a lighthouse and noticed the many colorful boats bobbing about in the water. A lot of the boats had their hulls painted ca-

nary yellow, bright blue, or even a rose color. In the background, you could also see colorful roofs of buildings. Ragnar told me I'd love Akranes and that this was the town where the best football team in Iceland came from.

Just a few minutes before we were to dock, Marshal Williams took me aside and asked me if I was alright and felt comfortable with my new place. I told her that it was too soon to really know, but I was excited about being in this new place. She reminded me that Iceland had only a few hundred Muslims and very few in Akranes so I should not be noticed by someone wanting to cause me harm.

A few Palestinian families had been resettled in Iceland by the United Nations High Commissioner for Refugees, but they were struggling to survive after losing everything and living in squalid, harsh desert tent camps on the Syria/Iraq border. These weren't people to fear, but she warned me for the hundredth time to tell no one my real name or story.

I thought it was sort of ironic hiding from the very people who should make me feel the safest, but remembering the million-dollar fatwa placed on my head always clarified the why.

Chapter 90
A Spy with No Eyes

The million-dollar fatwa on Sheeva Hasson attracted many wannabe jihadists. The killing of Sheeva was an obligation that many in the Muslim community felt was necessary because she had brought such dishonor upon Ali Hasson's family name. Her sins were not only that she defied her father and slept with a kuffer, but also that she had become a traitor to the Muslim community and was assisting the government of the Great Satan. Many devout Muslims prayed for Sheeva's death with the same zeal that farmers pray for water during a drought.

The claim that Allah had already started to punish Sheeva was preached in fiery sermons by numerous mullahs. They claimed that Allah had ripped her soul from her fouled body and sent her blasphemous kuffer boyfriend to the ever-burning fires of hell. They declared, "She was just a walking, soulless shell of a human who was hated by Allah as much as Jews and pigs."

The need to consummate the fatwa against Sheeva led to a strange group of bedfellows who united and formed an organization to find and assassinate Sheeva Hasson. The group called themselves the Avengers. This group of improbable partners consisted of former intelligence officers from Iraq, Saudi Arabia, and Iran; they represented Sunni, Wahhabi, and Shiite Islamic ideologies. They had agreed to work together to end this affront to Islam by expediting Sheeva's trip to the fires of damnation.

Although the Avengers were a clandestine organization, their activities were quickly recognized by American intelligence.

A little more than a month prior to Sheeva's relocation, the National Security Agency reported that it had been hacked and some of its databases had been accessed. The few clues left behind suggested that the objective of the attack was probably to find information about the whereabouts of Sheeva Hasson. New security measures were taken at NSA, and additional guards were assigned to protect Sheeva. It was believed there was a possibility that the hack might have been successful in extracting information that might endanger Sheeva's life.

A week after the NSA hacking, newspapers reported three loud explosions on the tarmac at the Davis-Monthan Air Force Base in Tucson, Arizona. The base, which was Sheeva's temporary home, claimed the explosions were some small ordinance that was accidently ignited while rearming a plane. A follow-up article stated that a thorough investigation was in progress to prevent any similar incident from occurring. The report stipulated that no one was hurt and only minor damaged was sustained.

The same week, two Langley, Virginia, CIA agents came up missing. Their whereabouts remained unknown for about two weeks, until on a hot June afternoon, a resident of Reston, Virginia, encountered a macabre scene.

The woman who reported the incident desired to remain anonymous. However, I can say that she was the mother of a boy who had just finished softball practice and they were both on their way back home when it happened. They were driving down a rural road leading to their home when they came upon the nightmarish vision of bloody person standing in the middle of the road. The mother stopped her car in front of this strange apparition as it started to plod toward her car. She stared at it in shock, numb by the grotesqueness of what she was seeing when suddenly she heard her son calmly say, "Mom, that's a lady who is hurt." The lone figure on the road was indeed a woman. Her partially nude body glistened with smeared blood. A red-stained, metallic garment covered her crotch and posterior. Her head was shrouded with blood-soaked hair that stuck to her grotesquely mutilated face, and her arms swung aimlessly back and forth as she tottered about like in a daze. Small plastic bags were taped to her wrists, hiding her hands. The mother got out of her car and went to the bloodied woman and frantically started to ask her questions, but the only replies were indiscernible grunts. The woman shied away from the mother and fell to the asphalt. The boy, who had stepped out of their car, handed his mother her cell phone and told her to call 911, which she did. She told the emergency operator of the strange encounter and was told to cover the victim up and wait for the police and ambulance to arrive. The mother told the operator that the woman was badly injured and perhaps dying from loss of blood. The 911 operator continued to attempt to calm the mother and told her to see if the victim needed anything, like water or clothes.

A police car with two officers came screeching down the road. Its wailing siren erased the afternoon quiet. Barks from dogs and the constant groans from the woman added to the cacophony of sounds.

The first responders were two Fairfax, Virginia, police officers. When they looked at the victim, they were also shocked and bewildered at her various injuries. Her face looked as if it had been burned. Much of its skin was missing. Parts of her nose and ears were totally burnt away. Her eyes looked glazed over and unseeing. The eyes moved within seeping red slits that were devoid of skin. When the police tried to give her water, they discovered that most of her tongue was missing. The woman had been the victim of a monstrous attack in which the perpetrator had tortured and mutilated her face and body.

The answer to the questions of why and who tortured her was revealed after she arrived at the Fairfax Hospital. The metallic panties turned out to be layers of duct tape. As it was removed from her body, a small flash drive secured within a plastic bag was discovered pushed up into her vagina. Obviously, the purpose of the duct tape was to ensure the discovery of the flash drive and not to provide the woman some measure of modesty.

The removal of the garbage bags from her wrists revealed that her hands had been amputated and barbarically cauterized to stem the bleeding.

The woman's life was saved, but the injuries and trauma she experienced at the hands of her torturers would cripple her physically and mentally forever.

The flash drive contained a warning message and a video that recorded the torture of the woman and a man who had been kidnapped along with her. I was able to find a copy of the video, which was distributed on the Internet and is still featured on many jihadist sites.

The footage of the torture was nauseating. It was proof again that the fiery words of scary books written centuries ago still possessed the power to cause a madness in man that led them to kill one another.

I will not describe the entire video, but only what is necessary to help you understand its viciousness and the message behind it. In fact, the video was so grisly, so evil, that I wondered as I watched it how insane these men were who carried out the horrible acts.

The video opened with just these words displaying on the screen, *"Tabari VIII:122/Ishaq:515.*

It was then followed by this verse: *"The Prophet gave orders concerning Kinanah to Zubayr, saying, 'Torture him until you root out and extract what he has.' So Zubayr kindled a fire on Kinanah's chest, twirling it with his firestick until Kinanah was near death.*

Then the Messenger gave him to Maslamah, who beheaded him."

This message lingered on the screen for nearly a minute until an unknown voice finally said, "This message is for all kuffers who are plotting against Allah and Islam. We are watching you at all times and will punish all who stand in the way of the word of Allah the Most Beneficent, the Most Merciful."

The message disappeared from the screen and was replaced with an image of two naked people standing with their hands chained above them to hooks in the ceiling. The room was nondescript, with bright lights casting eerie shadows over the shackled individuals against a backdrop consisting of a hanging dark blanket or darkened piece of canvas. The shackled individuals were the two CIA agents who earlier had been kidnapped by unknown Islamic terrorists. One of them was the mutilated woman who had been found half dead on the road. The other was a man who worked with her.

The two CIA agents said nothing as the interrogator asked where the apostate Sheeva Hasson was hidden. The interrogator stated that the laws of America had interfered in Allah's shariah laws and it was their obligation to correct this. The voice proclaimed that the male agent would be put to death for America's attacks on Islam, but the woman might be spared. Her survival depended on how quickly and truthfully they answered the questions put to them.

The interrogator's voice said, "Death can be quick and merciful, or it can be a lingering preview of what hell will be like in your next life. Let me remind you that hell is the punishment that Allah has prepared for you, the unbelievers. The torture and horror in it cannot be imagined by mortals, but I intend to give you a glimpse of what you may soon be enduring. We want answers. Where is Sheeva Hasson hidden?"

No one answered the interrogator and then suddenly a hand was seen coming into view from the right side of the scene. The hand was gloved in rubber and held a plastic sprayer. A mist of some liquid was sprayed over the man's genitals. At first he stood there shaking and then suddenly let out a piercing yell. The liquid was sulfuric acid, and it immediately started to burn away his skin and the tissue beneath. His body shook, and his legs flailed frantically, but to no avail as the acid continued to burn away the tissue.

The woman yelled out at her tormentors, "Please stop it, don't hurt him!"

Her pleas were met with a pompous religious harangue, "Whore, it is said that if an unbeliever calls out for help in hell, he will be helped with water like molten copper which will scald his face. I will abide by these words and do as you requested."

The rubber-gloved hand appeared again in the scene. This time it pointed the spray bottle at the man's face. The CIA agent tried to turn away from the spray, but it still hit the side of his face. The acid glistened on his ear, hair, and even a part of his arm as it burned deep into his exposed flesh. He jerked his head about, trying to relieve the pain, and clumps of hair slid off his scalp displaying raw, weeping pink flesh.

On the screen, superimposed over the writhing, tortured man, was the following message: “Quran Surah 69:The Reality. Those who don’t believe in Allah will be chained up and cast into hell-fire where they will eat filth.”

I will not provide any further details of the torture other to say that before the video ended, both of the woman’s hands were sliced off with a hacksaw while being simultaneously cauterized with a red-hot sword blade. To end the torture, the woman finally told the interrogators that Sheeva was being held somewhere within an air force base in Arizona. The faceless interrogators and torturers decided they had the truth and that it was time to kill the male CIA agent. The scene changed, and the CIA agent was shown tied to a chair. As he sat naked and in terrible agony from the acid and beatings, a large hook tethered to the ceiling was push deep into the agent’s chin. The hook forced his head to tip upward. Suddenly a sword flashed through the air, and the agent’s severed head swung back and forth as the female agent screamed in terror. A new message appeared over the shot of the headless CIA agent reading, “Quran 5:33: The punishment for those who wage war against Allah and His Prophet and perpetrate mischief in the land is to murder them, to hang them, to mutilate them, or banish them. Such is their disgrace. They will not escape the fire, suffering constantly.”

The video provided evidence to back up the rumors that the three loud explosions on the tarmac at the Davis-Monthan Air Force Base in Tucson, Arizona, were from mortar rounds. Officials continued to deny that an attack had occurred, but fewer and fewer people found the government's explanation credible.

The end of the video displayed another ominous verse from the Quran: "Quran 21:44: Do they not see us advancing, gradually reducing the land (in their control), curtailing its borders on all sides? It is they who will be overcome."

Chapter 91
Sheeva's First day in Akranes

The events in Virginia and the attack on the tarmac at the Davis-Monthan Air Force Base in Tucson, Arizona, were kept from Sheeva and Roger Wilgers. A more thorough investigation of the explosions at Davis-Monthan suggested that the mortar rounds had been fired from a moving truck. This complicated the task of discovering who was behind the attack. A surveillance video near an industrial park supplied proof that such a vehicle existed and at least one shot was recorded on the tape, but the film was too grainy to provide the face of the driver or a license plate.

Sheeva was not told of the incident, but it was responsible for her quick departure from the States. I have included further excerpts from Sheeva's diary as she settled into her new life in Iceland.

Marshal Williams had told me that I'd love Akranes, Iceland, and it was the perfect place to start over. Pulling into the Akranes fishing port and looking around, I wasn't sure if I'd agree with her. I stood near the railing of the ferry as we approached the dock. The ocean spray and wind blew in my face. The spray made my face feel so cold that it was awkward to move my mouth even to talk. Lots of men were busy getting gear on their boats. Fishing was a big part of the town of Akranes. This town of six thousand was about the size of Culper, Texas, where Jason and I once lived together...what beautiful memories. In the distance, I could see colorful houses. Many of the ones that were visible were painted in pale colors with bright roofs; it varied, but I could see blues and reds popping in the sunlight.

I felt a hand on my shoulder and turned to see Roger looking down on me. He looked sad. Roger told me it was time to get back in the Yaris because we were about to dock.

As we got into the car, Ragnar came over to say good-bye. After telling me how much he enjoyed talking to me, he said in a very serious manner that the women in Akranes were not going to like me. That gave me a sinking feeling, and I timidly asked him why. He replied with a little wink, "Because you're going to be the prettiest woman in Akranes," and then he started laughing.

We rolled off the ferry and turned toward the street. A street named Faxabryggia bordered the port. There was a car waiting for us with two well-dressed men sitting in it drinking coffee. Marshal William said they were the guys who would escort us to our new homes.

I watched my new town pass by; just about every sign and advertisement was in Icelandic. I certainly had some learning to do. There were a few funny looking letters I couldn't even figure out. All the road signs were in kilometers. I'd forgotten that I'd have to use the metric system in Iceland. I saw the temperature earlier, and it had displayed twenty degrees. I was trying to sort out what that exactly meant. I should have figured this stuff out before I left, but I didn't.

Akranes was a small fishing town with lots of charm. As we rode to our new destination, I studied the people we passed, eager to see what was normal here. As far as I could tell, the fashion was much the same here as it was in the States. It was bad enough to be almost alone in a new country, let alone worrying about if my clothes fit in or not. Something else that struck me as we drove through the town was the sheer amount of color...so different from back home. Everything was bright; the ocean, the houses, even the sun seemed brighter.

We drove down a quiet street lined with a few bungalow-style houses, where children were playing in the street with their parents watching them from their stoops. The name of my new street was Vesturgata. I think I can already pronounce it, which is great because I find Icelandic very difficult so far.

My new house was pale, grayish green with a grey roof and a bright blue door. Roger had been correct about where I was going to be living because the house he had bought was just two houses down on the opposite side of the street, with a blue roof.

Williams handed me my keys, and I was led into my house. The two men who escorted us were never introduced to me, but they did accompany Roger to his house and helped us carry in our luggage.

I was thankful I had my own place and even more grateful that Roger was living so near.

The Witness Protection Program had set up a bank account in my new name and given me money to live on, a new credit card, and cell phone. A lot of worries off my back! And Roger's money from the lawsuit would take care of him for a long, long time.

After being shown around my new place, Marshal Williams suggested that I relax, get some rest, and she would look in on me later. It sounded like a great idea because I was exhausted. The bed was inviting, and I was dying to try it out.

Williams and her two associates left, and even though I was exhausted, I decided to visit Roger. His house was very nice, but you could not tell it from the way he looked. He was just roaming around the rooms looking distressed. I suggested that he take a nap and we get back together later to explore the town for a good place to eat. Unexpectedly, he smiled, gave me a hug, and said that was the best idea he had heard in the last twenty-four hours. He gave me one of his house keys and told me to just come over when I was ready. I returned to my new house, set my cell phone alarm for noon Iceland time, and hopped into my inviting bed.

At twelve noon, the incessant phone alarm woke me, and I got up feeling a lot better. I showered and put on some clothes I hoped would be appropriate for my first visit with locals.

I went over to Roger's house, but he was still sound asleep. He looked peaceful, and his snoring told me he needed more rest. I decided to let him sleep and left him a note telling him where I was going.

I was hungry so I decided to find a place to eat. I drove around my new neighborhood to get a feel of where I was. A couple blocks from my house I spotted a restaurant. It was on a street named Kirkjubraut and its sign, reading "Café 15," was one of the first signs I could understand. I pulled up in front and went in. It was a quaint little place, at least that was my impression. They served alcohol, coffee, and a small assortment of local dishes. I stumbled a little bit with communicating with them, but I managed to order some lamb kabobs and a braised whitefish over rice, both of which were very good.

Most people in Iceland could speak English to some degree, but it would be nice to talk and understand their language. Learning Icelandic was going to take me a bit of time, considering just how different it was from what I was used to. The owners of the café were kind enough to give me a little bit of information in English about places to visit, stores, churches, and of course, their football team.

I realized that I better remember the name of their football team, which was Íþróttabandalag Akraness, a name I couldn't pronounce, but its short name was IA, which I could handle. In Akranes, not knowing the stats of the IA and its players would make me an outcast for sure. I was also glad to discover that there was a local museum and a library just a few streets over.

After lunch, I headed back home. My street was quiet when I returned. A stiff ocean wind was blowing, making it feel much cooler, definitely far colder than what I was used to for July in Tucson. I decided that tomorrow I'd buy better clothes to wear for this kind of weather. I checked on Roger again, and he was still sleeping so I left him alone. I decided more rest was also what I needed and I got back into bed and turned on the TV to see what was happening in the world. I found the Icelandic version of CNN, but I could easily tell what was going on from the pictures. A video showing a protest in Washington DC was still big news. It looked like it was another million-man march demanding that the president step down. Police were all over the place and were caught on camera clubbing people, much like what the world had seen when Egypt and Syria had their uprisings. I watched a bit of it and listened to a commentator explaining his view of the significance of the march. They were claiming it was caused by the pent-up frustration of the American people over the government's glacial response to the Christmas Special attacks. With the constant news coverage of the attacks, I wondered how soon it would be before someone recognized who I really was.

Chapter 92
Day Two in Iceland

While Sheeva adjusted to her new home in Iceland, Marshal Williams stayed busy coordinating twenty-four-hour surveillance schedule of Sheeva's activities with the Akranes' police. The events at Langley, Virginia, the mortar rounds in Arizona, and the increase in chatter on the jihadist networks heightened the need for increased security. There wasn't any real evidence that Sheeva's move to Iceland was known to the large number of jihadists who wanted the glory of killing her, but Williams felt it prudent to assume it might have been leaked. Unknown to Sheeva, she would now be tailed at all times by either a marshal or an Akranes police officer.

Plainclothes police would also patrol her street constantly. This was a job that the small police force relished because they hadn't had anything this exciting for years, and to make it even more palatable the US government supplemented their monthly pay with 200,000 Icelandic kronos, about another fifteen hundred dollars.

The surveillance was not easy because Sheeva visited many locations in her exploration of Akranes. From the following diary pages, it appears that she naturally adapted to her new home in Iceland, although she had some difficulties in the pronunciation of Icelandic words.

Day two of Sheeva's diary in Iceland:

This is my second day in my new home. This morning, I got up around seven o'clock and remem-

bered that the sun had been up already for three hours at least. Weird! I opened my bedroom window and sat in front of it drinking my morning coffee and looking out onto the quiet street. There was a nice breeze blowing through my window, and I could even smell the ocean. I even thought I could hear the roar of the ocean, but maybe it was just sounds in my head. Then suddenly my coffee started sloshing around and spilling onto the table. I was not sure what was happening as the whole house seemed to be shaking.

Then as suddenly as it started, it stopped. I thought I'd experienced some sort of hallucination, but I noticed the lights were swinging back and forth and realized it had been an earthquake. I remembered that Iceland experienced earthquakes often. I guess this was just a normal one because no one was running around on the street, and I never heard any sirens.

I calmed down from the excitement of my first earthquake and my mind flashed that this house was the first place I'd lived in for the last two years that was really mine. That was a very overwhelming realization because the last place I considered home was my place in Culper, Tex-as, with Jason. Just that thought brought tears to my eyes. I promised myself that I'd start making my new house into a real home. If I was going to live here, my house had to really feel more like it was mine. I needed to decorate the place and do some shopping for food and other stuff.

I started unpacking some of the things I'd shipped here. I got my clothes unpacked and filled the dresser with them. I realized I'd brought a lot of clothes I'd never wear here. I unpacked a few photos and set them against the wall. I found one from my first date with Jason. I don't think I'm quite ready to put up that photo yet. I ended up crying for a good half hour after I found it, remembering all the great times we had. I never knew that thinking of all of the good times could hurt so much. I wish I could get it behind me because I hate feeling sad every time I see his face or remember him. I guess part of it is I feel so responsible for his death. If I hadn't fallen in love with him, he would still be alive.

I did hang two of his framed steampunk paintings on the wall, and that took courage because they reminded me of him every time I walked by them. I loved things steampunk too, so it was also a part of me. I'm still wearing the steampunk ring he gave me on my sixteenth birthday. It's what I fiddle with when I'm really nervous.

I spotted one of my neighbors this morning while he was heading out to work. I introduced myself, but he didn't have time to really talk to me. His name is a problem for me because I just can't pronounce it. He did invite Roger and me to a traditional Icelandic dinner for tomorrow night with his family. It will be very nice to have a family dinner again and get to know my neighbor. I hope Roger will also want to go.

I found myself excited to explore Akranes today. I wanted to go over to Roger's house and get him going, but I first had to get my makeup on and pick out something to wear. I stopped in my kitchen and took a couple bites from last night's café leftovers. Tasted great last night, but it really wasn't what I wanted to eat for breakfast; I needed to get Roger going because I wanted to visit some café and have a real Icelandic breakfast.

I went over to Roger's house, and he was still in a sour mood. He said he didn't sleep well and was still exhausted. I know he has been having bad nightmares lately, and of course that's understandable. I do hope that he is going to be all right in time. I know he misses Jason and Frank a lot.

We finally went shopping, but it didn't seem to help Roger's mood. I'm really concerned for him. He seems to really miss Jason, Frank, and the States. I have noticed that his irritation gets worse when a shopkeeper talks to us in Icelandic instead of English.

The grocery store we found was on Gardagrund, which is only a couple blocks away. I think it's close enough to walk to. I shopped there, but found it hard to read the labels. I made due and purchased enough food to get through a week easily.

While shopping, I picked up an Icelandic cookbook in English. It has many Icelandic recipes that I want to try. There were a few odd dishes in it that I'm sure I will never try, but most of the food looks pretty easy to make and appetizing. I learned from the butcher that most meats are locally farmed. They had a lot of lamb in their display. The fish also comes from the locals. I just hope I don't get tired of lamb or fish anytime soon. I also found a book on the Icelandic language so I could get started trying to understand the locals a bit better. Wow, there is so much for me to do, I can't figure out where to start, but life is really exciting here in Iceland.

After we got home, I offered to cook but Roger wasn't hungry and seemed only to want to be left alone.

I noticed that today seems to be lasting a lot longer than yesterday. Last night, I went to bed early so I never noticed. It's now eleven at night, and I can still see the sunlight. I guess I will get use to it eventually. I'm looking forward to the three-hour sunsets...wow!

I decided to set up my computer. It was still the crazy one that Jason had altered with its case of brass, leather, and wood. I was afraid the Internet wouldn't work well here, but I was way wrong. Internet in Iceland is faster than it was back in the States.

I yearn to have friends and realized I'd have to get involved as Sonya, even with the groups that I previously was with. I had really got attached to members on the thesteampunkempire.com blogs and chat room.

In Arizona, I spent half my day chatting with my steampunk friends as I hid in my safe house. I missed them and tried to decide if it was safe to keep contact with them or not. I vacillated back and forth about setting up a new account using my new name or just using my previous screen name. The username I previously used was not my real name, and its listing only showed the city and state where I lived. I decided to just update my previous profile with my new city and country and keep all my steampunk friends. I know this would piss off Marshal Williams, but she really wouldn't have to ever know. These cyber friends had been there for me all during my difficulties, and I just loved them.

Chapter 93
Interview with an Akranes Police Officer

The graphic torture video released by the clandestine American jihadists caused a greater focus on Sheeva. The anti-terrorist intelligence community also noticed elevated jihadist chatter on the Internet, prompting them to raise the national alert status. This response was appropriate because, an ocean away, Sheeva's brother Abdul Hasson seethed in anger at the attention focused on his sister and vowed to find and finally kill her. His family's honor drove him toward this goal, not the reward that was offered in the fatwa sentencing her to death.

How the plot unfolded is detailed in statements given by an American jihadist named Jose Oktar. His account of the search for Sheeva and the speed with which her assassins descended on her was startling.

Jose Oktar was a convert to Islam who had attended high school with Abdul in Chicago. The two knew each other, but were not close friends. Jose idolized the older Abdul, but Abdul rejected this new convert's friendship.

The aftermath of the Christmas Special changed things, however, and Abdul realized the benefit of having more people in his corner.

A few months after the infamous Christmas attacks, a stranger approached Jose Oktar just as he was getting into his car after a day of work at Fenton's Flower Shop.

The stranger was a tall elderly man who greeted Jose with the familiar Muslim greeting, "As-salaamu alaykum." The man didn't introduce himself, but described himself as a devout Muslim. He told Jose that a very important individual wanted to talk to him. The nameless man provided Jose a throwaway cell phone and told him that later that day he would receive a very important call. The man warned him that this phone was to be guarded at all times and not to be used by anyone else. He also warned Jose that talking to anyone else about this encounter would be very unhealthy. Jose was in shock, but very intrigued that he had been apparently picked for some clandestine event. He asked the man what this was all about, but was told simply to be patient and that the call would answer all his concerns. The man blessed Jose and then left him standing by his car greatly confused, but excited.

About two hours later, Jose received a call and to his amazement discovered he was actually talking to Abdul Hasson. Pleasantries were quickly exchanged, and Abdul explained the true purpose of his call. He asked Jose to become a part of the jihad against America he and his father Ali Hasson had launched with the devastating Christmas Special attacks.

As Abdul suspected, Jose was thrilled and honored to be considered by the son of Ali Hasson as someone who could help the jihadist cause. He quickly accepted Abdul's request and said he was ready to do whatever was needed to support the jihad against America. Jose felt proud as he placed this special phone back into his pocket. He was one of the chosen.

A few days after the call, money was clandestinely delivered to Jose. The funds were to be used by Jose in his search for Sheeva. Months went by with minimal progress in the search, but then a few months after the courthouse bombing, Jose's luck changed. In his inquiries about Sheeva and Jason, the mention of their involvement in the steampunk culture came up several times. At first it meant nothing to Jose, but after further consideration he realized this was an avenue he had to investigate. He submersed himself into its culture and visited every steampunk site he could find, combing through the member's profiles and their posted photos. After three weeks of scrutinizing these profiles, he suddenly found himself staring at a photograph of a girl living in Iceland who looked very much like Sheeva. As he studied her profile and browsed through the numerous photographs she had uploaded to the site, he recognized Chicago landmarks in the background of some of them. There was a series of pictures of a big steampunk convention that had been held in Chicago a few years prior. The details had a familiarly to them that he felt matched Sheeva's life. One other thing he read from her profile was that her boyfriend had been brutally killed just before Christmas. Many of her postings talked about her fear of the future.

Looking back over her postings, he noticed that a few days after the Davis-Monthan Air Force Base attack she had posted a comment that she had moved to Iceland. She went on to say that she hoped people would now leave her alone so she could live in peace.

Jose immediately recognized the significance of his discovery and reported his suspicions to Abdul Hasson.

Abdul was thrilled with Jose's discovery and told him to immediately pack and get ready to go to Iceland. Later the same day, a cleric from a Chicago mosque brought Jose an airline ticket and money to help facilitate his trip.

A day later, Jose Oktar was looking out the fifth-story window of the Centerhotel Arnarhvollin Reykjavik, Iceland. What happened after Jose arrived in Iceland is detailed in my interview with Inspector Gunnar Steinsson of the National Police of Iceland.

Roberto Roma: *Thank you for meeting with me, Inspector Steinsson.*

Inspector: *It's a pleasure helping you in your desire to tell the world what happened here.*

Roberto Roma: *When was the first time you knew anything about this situation?*

Inspector: *When Marshal Williams told us about this American named Sonya Walsh and that they expected an attack on her by some love-crazed stalker. That was a couple days after she had arrived in Akranes. At first we were all doubtful that anyone would try stalking someone in Akranes, a fishing village of about six thousand people. Our town is virtually free of crime. We occasionally have some lout in a fistfight or an occasional stabbing, but murder is rare...very rare.*

Roberto Roma: *What evidence or information did they provide you with?*

Inspector: *When Marshal Williams came to us with your government's suspicions about the safety of this young lady, Sonya Walsh, they totally opened the file on her for us. At least that was what we believed they had done. They told us the safety of Sonya was important to the US government and that was why the marshals service had moved her here.*

They then shared with our office that the suspect had displayed a great deal of interest in some online steampunk group Sonya Walsh was involved in. Marshal Williams relayed to us how Jose had deceitfully befriended her friends to gain her trust, and then requested Sonya as a friend on this particular steampunk site. Unfortunately, Sonya fell for the ruse and even started having short conversations with Jose through the site's chat feature. Then things started to move very fast.

Roberto Roma: *What happened that made things move faster?*

Inspector: *Agents in Chicago notified us that Jose had airline tickets to Iceland and that we needed to have things in place to track him the second his plane touched down in Reykjavik, Iceland. We immediately assigned police officers to numerous tasks. We planted plainclothes officers in the terminal who would be waiting for his arrival and inconspicuously tail Jose anywhere he went. Cameras were set up to video his arrival. We wanted fresh pictures of him to distribute to our National Police force. We wanted to capture this guy in the act of breaking the law, but not just for something trivial. We wanted to let him have the ability to move around freely and feel safe enough to attempt to do whatever he was coming to Iceland for. We felt certain that once Jose landed in Iceland, he would be trapped with no way out. Iceland is a very hard place to escape from unless you have a boat and the knowledge of how to sail it.*

Roberto Roma: *So you felt very confident about your operation?*

Inspector: *Well, we felt confident about the Reykjavik part of the operation, but Akranes was a different story. This is a town of about six thousand people and* *some guy walking or riding around the neighborhood where Sonya lived was going to be noticed. People were going to introduce themselves to him, so we had to ask for some major community help on this operation. We went house to house on the streets around where Sonya lived and asked people not to talk to strangers. We told them we believed one or more outsiders might be involved in some criminal activities on their street.*

We explained to them that we wanted our suspects to feel unthreatened, but actually that the National Police of Iceland would be in position all over the street. They would be dressed in plainclothes, sitting on stoops playing cards, driving by in cars, and even stationed in various homes. We stressed to the residents the importance of staying inside and letting the police do their work. We worried a lot about people doing something that would alert Jose or whoever else might try to harm Sonya.

Roberto Roma: *That's astounding that you can count on your citizens to help in your police effort. That's not something that would happen in America. You would probably end up having national news crews swarming the place, a bunch of ambulance chasers there to sue the police for endangering the citizens, and other lawyers there to sue the police for entrapment of the suspect.*

Inspector: *Well, in Iceland villages like Akranes the whole community is like one big family. These people have lived together forever. Everyone knows everyone else. They love their community and want to protect it, even the newcomers* *like Sonya. Things did get worse, however, when we discovered that Abdul Hasson was also coming to Iceland and that Sonya was really Sheeva Hasson. This pissed off a lot of officers on the police force. We felt we had been duped into putting our citizens into a dangerous situation.*

Roberto Roma: *How did you discover that Abdul Hasson was coming to Iceland also?*

Inspector: *We monitored all of Jose's correspondence. On the first day he was here, he emailed someone from the hotel, telling them he had arrived in Iceland. He also confided that he had chatted further with Sheeva and discovered that she lived in a small town named Akranes. About thirty minutes later, the recipient of Jose's email responded back. The email had been to Abdul Hasson, and Jose's news prompted Abdul into immediate action. He told Jose to try to get more information about the town Sheeva lived in and to talk more to her online. He had written down a list of questions for Jose to ask, like could she see the ocean from her house, is she near any good restaurants, is she near any coffee shops? Apparently, Abdul was trying to figure out what part of the town she lived in.*

We were not sure when he was arriving, but he did indicate he was arriving on a ferry in Seyðisfjörður, which told us he was probably coming from Denmark. The fact that we would now have at least two people to shadow would further complicate the operation. We assigned more police to the ferry terminal and hoped we would have more info before he arrived.

We also realized that Seyðisfjörður was an eight-hour drive from Reykjavik, so we would have time if needed to alter our operation when Abdul got to Iceland.

Roberto Roma: *And all this time you didn't inform Sheeva that her brother was on his way to Iceland?*

Inspector: *No, we didn't tell her. She was safe. We had about seventy-five police assigned to this operation. That's a lot for a country with a police force of about a thousand. We also had officers from the US Marshal services involved in the operation. If we thought it was getting to risky, we would either move Sheeva or pick up Jose and Abdul before they could hurt anyone.*

Roberto Roma: *Why didn't you just pick them up before they did anything that might harm someone?*

Inspector: *We wanted to see if there was a chance of more of these individuals in Iceland. This was not just an operation to protect Sheeva, but also a chance to root out any violent jihadist cell that might be operating in Iceland. We took the events very serious. After the Christmas Special, we realized that jihadist attacks can happen anywhere. Normally we don't even carry guns, but all officers on this operation were issued a sidearm.*

Roberto Roma: *Why would Abdul take a ferry instead of a plane to Iceland? If he had flown, he could have landed right in Reykjavik.*

Inspector: *When we first discovered he was coming by ferry, we surmised he figured boarding security would be more relaxed on the ferry. You can en-*

ter our country from Denmark, England, Canada, US, and many other countries with just a passport and a valid ticket. Visas are not required if you're staying less than ninety days, so people often take advantage of that and come here on a whim. We discovered later that he used the ferry because he also brought a cheap used car in which he had hidden guns and bullets in its frame. Guns are very hard to buy in Iceland.

Roberto Roma: *So all during this time, Sheeva was just living her life like nothing was going on? Didn't you worry that a neighbor would say something to her?*

Inspector: *It would have been very unlikely that anyone within the village would say anything to her about what was going on, and they didn't. She just kept on trying to get her new life going.*

Chapter 94
Breakfast in Iceland

As Inspector Gunnar Steinsson indicated, Sheeva was totally oblivious to the events unraveling around her. She was still excited about where she was and that it seemed like her life had changed for the better and she was finally safe in this strange land where July is more like fall. Iceland was inviting to her, and she was enjoying this new life. It made her think a lot about Afghanistan, maybe because of the high mountains and snow.

This optimism is reflected in her diary:

Diary,

Today, I started my morning with a very common Icelandic breakfast. They call it porridge, but to me it's just oatmeal with slivered almonds on top. I made it following a recipe from the cookbook I bought the other day. I also fried an egg in butter and sliced some of the fresh market-bread to go with it. I can tell you that after trying the bread, I know I want to learn how to make it. By the time I finished eating and cleaning up, it was close to 8:30. The longer days were definitely catching up to me, because I felt like it was so much later than it really was!

I decided I'd take some of the porridge to Roger, with some fresh bread in hopes that he would eat something. I think he is having a harder time adjusting than me, and I can't help but be worried about him. I hoped he wasn't regretting his decision to come with me. I fixed him a bowl and went over to his house, hoping I wasn't going to wake him up. I didn't have to...he was already up. He gave me a smile when I showed him the food I brought. I was really happy that he ate it, and he said I did a good job sweetening it up just right. I told him how much I liked the bread and that I'd sworn to learn to bake it myself. He laughed! It was good-natured, though, and it made me feel good that he liked it.

I asked him if he wanted to go shopping with me, because I still needed to get some things to make my new house feel like home. He said he would rather not. He did agree to go to our neighbors' house for dinner, which I was really looking forward to.

I walked toward downtown, not really sure where I should even begin to look for stuff for my house. I got very lucky when I turned onto Faxabraut and found a very small antique shop. One of the windows was boarded up, but the "Open" sign out front was in Icelandic and English for which I was grateful. The steps into the store were rickety, and I thought the porch just might cave in. However, when I got inside, I was amazed! The whole place smelled...I don't even know how to describe it. It smelled like history, sawdust, and fabric all mulled together. It was musty, but in a good way! There were picture frames lining practically every inch of the wall: big ones with gold trim and bulky reddish wooden ones, and scattered between them were smaller ones ranging from metal to gold and silver. There was an old spinning wheel in one corner that was really neat, and the lady behind the counter told me in very broken English they pulled sheep's wool through it to make everything from shirts to blankets.

I browsed for a while, deciding on a few items. An old pocket watch that was bulky and tarnished and a music box that was made of heavy brass definitely attracted my attention. I couldn't help but think that Jason would be proud of me for attempting to make my own steampunk decorations. I also picked out an old brass lamp with a heavy shade that was made of beaded crystal; I wanted to sit it near the window because I imagined the crystal would catch the sunlight and sparkle beautifully. I picked out two picture frames; one of them was made of silver with a swirling design that went all around it, and the other I think was actually made of brass. I knew it would be a while before I put pictures in them, but I wanted to have them anyway. I found a tablecloth that was just the perfect size for the little kitchen table I had; it was lacy and off-white, almost like a doily, and I felt it would match the pale walls of my house. I picked up a few other little trinkets, gratefully paid for them, and took my spoils back home.

After I put everything up, I took a shower and spent some time on my makeup before dinner, wanting to make a good impression on the neighbors. Surprisingly, Roger met me at the door, looking sharp and ready to go! We walked next door and knocked.

We were greeted by Vigdís Steinsson, who was smiling and very friendly! She seemed so happy to welcome us into her home and told us over and over how glad she was that we had moved into the neighborhood. Her English was broken but still easy to understand.

She gave us a tour of her house, which was modestly decorated. Pictures of their family lined the walls; they had two small children, who she mentioned were eight and six. You could tell the house was lived in by a family, and I loved it.

We sat down to eat, and Gunnar Steinsson did his best to make conversation with Roger. I think he was trying to get Roger to open up and talk about himself. The first course was a traditional fish soup, which was made with cod and garlic...and even brown sugar! It was called *fiskisúpa*. I didn't think I'd like it, because it had a very sour smell, but I was pleasantly surprised that it tasted much better than it smelled. The sugar balanced out the fishiness that I was afraid of. The soup was served with something she called *tvíbökur*, which translated into twice-baked buns. Vigdís kindly explained to me that the bread was baked twice because it would last longer, and traditionally it was kept for weeks at a time. It complimented the slightly sweet soup, and its crunchiness made it even more appealing.

When they brought out the main course, I thought my eyes were going to pop out of my head. It was a stuffed leg of lamb. Once my piece was cut, I could see it was stuffed with prunes and sliced apples. I couldn't believe how good it was. Roger liked it too; he finished before me. I think Gunnar had won him over because they seemed to chat for most of the dinner. As for his wife, she offered to show me a few recipes, and I can't wait to take her up on her offer. She was so nice, and I'm really glad to have what I hope to be my first Icelandic friend.

By the time they brought out dessert, I was filled. Dessert was called hrísgrjónagrautur, which was just a really long name for rice pudding. I was glad; rice pudding was something I'd really liked. After many thanks I told them I'd love to have them over to my house soon for dinner.

Chapter 95
Meeting Aisha

The last available picture of Abdul was taken when he lived in Chicago. Interpol did not have a recent photo of him, and they realized he could have changed his appearance. They had created police sketches of various disguises he might have used. Fortunately, a photo surfaced that had been taken just three days prior.

Abdul had been living in a flat in Waltham Forrest for some weeks prior to the discovery of the photo. The photo came to the attention of the police because of a strange event in which Abdul was recently involved in. A statement from a well known street pimp named Marcus Nottage to the London police provides the details of how the pictures came about.

> *My name is Marcus Nottage, and I'm making this statement of my own free will.*
>
> *Well, first thing I want to make real clear is that I don't get no money from this girl we will be talking about. I ain't no ponce. I'm just a friend who helps her sometimes. Anyway, her name is Aisha and she is real fit, big knockers you know, the bee's knees. She is out on Brick Lane in Tower Hamlet when this bloody trick just walks up to her and out of the blue asks her if she does doggy. She thinks the bloke is a real wanker. He acts like a nonce, but she is usually okay with weird. So real cute she goes, "Bow wow, bow wow. Is that the kind of doggy you want?"*
>
> *He says to her, "That ain't what I mean, and you know it. Do you do doggy*

and how much?" She should have known he was a little wonky right then, but Aisha is easy peasy, and she is up for it.

She chats a bit more, and since she knows he is on the pull, she says something like, "Maybe fifty quid might make me like doggy, can you relate to that?" He holds out his hand with fifty quid in it. Aisha ain't stupid. She takes it and tells him to follow her to our place. So when they arrive, he wants to know her name and he wants her to strip for him while he sits on the bed with all his clothes still on.

She does this real sexy strip and goes over to him and rubs one of the bugger's hands over her knockers. He starts fondling her tits and asks if her name really is Aisha. She tells him it is and then he wants to know if she is a Muslim. She tells him we don't talk bloody religion when you're playing with my knockers. He pulls his hands away and asks again if she is Muslim. The bloke is really a knob head. Aisha tells him, "Yes I bloody well am, is that a problem for you?"

He tells her no and then starts taking off his britches. I know all this because I am in Aisha's closet watching through this one-way mirror hanging on the door. She likes me around to protect her in case a bloke gets crazy. She meets a lot of freaks, you know, down on Brick Lane. Anyway the bloke takes his clothes off and tells her to get down on her hands and knees so he can do her doggy. He doesn't want to kiss her or play with her knockers any more or anything. He kneels behind her, but he don't seem to be able to get it up. He rubs her arse a few times and then sort of stoops over her a bit and caresses her cheeks and neck and then ask her if she knew who Aisha really was. He picks up one of her stockings off of the bed and starts rubbing it along her back. Still nothing is happening to him, his tallywhacker is as limp as a noodle. I'm beginning to feel real dodgy about this bugger.

Suddenly he grabs her hair and pulls back her head. Lot of buggers do that, so I don't think much about it. He says to Aisha, "So you're a Muslim whore?" Aisha says, "Oh, you like dirty talk. Yes, I'm a dirty little Muslim whore who wants your big knob up my quim." She wiggles her arse around and reaches between her legs to put his knob in her, but he is still all soft. She says, "Let me suck you and make you hard so we can rumpy pumpy." He doesn't answer her. Instead, he pulls her head back by her hair and with his other hand punches her in the face really hard.

I didn't even see it coming. I was totally gobsmacked, but only for a moment. I grab for my baseball bat that I keep in the closet, and while I'm getting that he wraps the stocking around her neck and puts his knee into her back and starts trying to choke her. Now this bugger's knob is all hard and he is yelling at her that she is a whore who has defiled the name of the Mother of the Believers. I bust out of the closet ready to give him a good tonking, and before he can even let go of the stocking, I whack him a good one across the back. He falls over and starts cursing me, and I whack him again and tell him to get the bloody fuck out.

He starts to come at me and I step aside and whack him again right in the stomach. That knocks the fight out of him. He falls arse-over-tit to the floor panting and holding his stomach, and I grab his clothes and throw them out the front door. He hasn't still recovered his breath, and when he looks up at me, I poke him hard in the stomach with the end of the bat.

This time he honks all over the place and is panting like a dog. I grab him by an ear and start pulling his naked arse right to the front door and shove him right out on the sidewalk. He is out there all starkers, and people on the sidewalk are looking at this bald-headed bugger sprawl out like he is some green alien from Mars. I tell him don't ever come back or I will smash your head in the next time. He is still groveling on his belly.

I slam and lock the door, and then Aisha and I watch him from the window as he crawls over to his clothes all strewn over the sidewalk and hurriedly puts them on. He seems like he wants to get off the street real quick. He doesn't bang on our door or yell any threats or anything. He just gets his clothes on real fast and legs it away like nothing ever happened. At first I think that's probably the way anybody would be if they were tossed out on a busy sidewalk all naked, but then Aisha says to me, "You know, other girls around here have been killed by being choked to death by someone off their nut. The police have a poster up about it."

She tells me there is a five hundred quid reward for information leading to the arrest of this bugger. All of a sudden, I'm back in the closet checking the video camera we have hooked up to film the freaks who want a souvenir of their time with Aisha to wank off to. I just happened to have had a video camera on during all of that session. We had pictures of his face, his arse, his knob, and everything else. I think the best one is the look on his face when I bust out of the closet with a bat in my hand. He didn't know what to do. He just froze there, holding the nylon stocking around Aisha's throat with his little tallywacker sticking out in front of him. It's funny looking back at the video...even Aisha laughs at it when we played it back as I gave him a good tonking. He was bloody stupid not to think that someone as pretty and ace as Aisha wouldn't have someone wicked like me watching her back. What a bloody arse.

Chapter 96
Day Four in Iceland

By Sheeva's fourth day in Akranes, her brother Abdul and his car were floating toward Iceland. A flurry of letters to the American State Department were also zooming across the Atlantic to Washington questioning why the Justice Department had failed to identify Jose as a terrorist when they first sought the help of the National Police of Iceland.

Inspector Gunnar Steinsson had taken a close look at the woman the terrorist purportedly wanted to kill. The previous night, he and his wife had borrowed a house close to Sheeva's home and broken bread with her. Gunnar liked her and could not understand why these Islamist wanted to kill her so badly. Meeting her just made him more resolute in protecting her from them.

By the evening of Sheeva's fourth day in Iceland, her brother was also in Iceland, speeding west along Route 92 on his way to Reykjavik. Officers now had numerous pictures of Abdul from the police in Tower Hamlet, England. With the new images of Abdul, it would be easier to track him. The embarrassing pictures were e-mailed to all departments involved in the investigation. Now the National Police of Iceland could keep a more educated eye on him every mile of the eight-hour journey. During this same period, Sheeva was enjoying more and more of her new home in Iceland. Excerpts from her diary follow.

When I woke up this morning, the brightness of the sun didn't bother me as much. Back in Texas, when I would get up, the sun would still have that morning glow to it, kind of reddish-orange, and the sun still sat low in the sky. Here, when I get out of bed the sun has already been up for hours and hours, and it has an almost-midday look to it!

The first few days, I had a hard time sleeping in because of it. But today, I woke up fresh and managed to sleep in until 8 a.m.

I decided that instead of making my own breakfast, I'd go into town and get something. I thought about going over to Roger's and asking if he wanted to go, but I wanted to get some alone time. I dressed quickly, pulling on a lightweight sweater and a pair of blue skinny jeans. I decided to go back to Café 15, the place we ate when we first came into town. There was a small crowd there, all sipping out of coffee mugs and nibbling on various breads and pastries. You could smell the coffee, one of my favorite smells by far, mixed with the scent of fresh baked goods.

They had a clear glass display on the counter with all of the breads and baked goods nestled in it for everyone to see. I stood in front of it for a few moments, trying to decide what I wanted. It came down between what looked like a cream puff and a cream horn. I didn't indulge much, but I was trying to embrace everything Icelandic, and that included the food.

I settled on the cream puff, which turned out to be something called a vatnsdeigsbollur, which was what the man behind the counter called a carnival bun.

I was surprised when the man who was running the cash register came to my table to talk with me. His English was very good, and he said he could tell I wasn't from here and wanted to see how I liked my stay. When I told him I'd moved here and wasn't just visiting, he actually took a seat! We talked for a little while; he told me his name was Geir Oddsson and that he had lived here all his life. I was afraid to tell him where I came from, because I didn't want to make the marshal angry with me for giving up too much in-

formation. I told him I was from the Southwest and that I'd loved it. I also told him about how I was still trying to learn my way around the town, and he offered to take me around one day. I thought, is this a date? My first thought was that I wasn't sure if I was ready for anything like that; my mind automatically went to Jason. There was a pang in my heart that I was afraid would never go away. But then I thought about my new start here, and Roger's new start, and how Jason had only ever wanted me to be happy.

"Yes" came out of my mouth. I couldn't believe I'd said it out loud. He smiled and said, "Great, maybe I can show you around this weekend." He seemed like a very nice guy, and it would be nice to see the city with someone who had lived here his whole life. I was ready to make friends. I had my friends online, and they would always be part of my old life, but I was wanting to get into my new life.

I spent the rest of the day buried in my recipe book, making a few different dishes. I told Roger to come over around six so he could sample my dishes, and he seemed more than happy to. I was hoping he was also getting more used to his new life.

I made a few things. I wanted to definitely try some fish, because that was in abundance here and always fresh. I tried my hand at making curried haddock as a main course. It turned out pretty good, a little spicier than I wanted but it was a learning process. I made a few side dishes and burnt one. Roger smelled the mistake as soon as he walked into the house, and I was glad to see a smile cross his face even if it was because of my cooking disaster.

Over dinner, I told him about the guy I met at the Café, and how he was going to take me around town this weekend. I thought for a minute to ask Roger to go with me, so he could see the town too, but at the last minute I decided against it. I don't want him to be uncomfortable. I hoped he would start to make friends also. I could see how bad he *missed Jason, and that was surely why he was having trouble adjusting. I wondered what he thought about when he was alone.*

As we sat out on the porch, with the sun still high in the sky, I told him how I was feeling. How I felt like I wasn't being smothered anymore, that I felt free and relaxed. Like I could finally be myself after everything that had happened. He said he was glad, that this was what life is all about. We had coffee on the porch, and after our chat we just sat in each other's company for a while. I told him that after I got back from my tour of the city, we should do something, and he suggested visiting the beach. I'd been so busy seeing and learning about the town that I hadn't had a chance to go to the beach!

Chapter 97
Day Five in Iceland

On the fifth day of Sheeva's life in Iceland, her past was quickly catching up with her. Her brother Abdul had arrived in Reykjavik and met with Jose. They met in Jose's room and discussed what was to happen. Abdul wanted Jose to use his car and drive to Akranes. He wanted him to ask around if anyone knew where the new American girl lived. Abdul was sure that the people of such a small town would know where she lived. He wanted Jose to pose as a friend of Sheeva's who had come all the way from America to visit her, but had lost her contact information.

Abdul was correct in his assumption, and a few hours later Jose was asking a young man in a coffee shop Sonya had mentioned in her online chats with him. The man knew who Jose was talking about and gave him the name of the street where Sonya lived. He didn't know which house, but told Jose to just ask anyone on Vesturgata and they should be able to point out the right house.

When Jose got to Vesturgata, he spotted a man gardening and asked him if he knew where Sonya lived. The gardener just happened to be a plainclothes police officer assigned to this operation. The gardener made small talk with Jose and then said the young lady Jose was looking for lived just two houses down on the opposite side of the street, but that she wasn't home now. He told Jose that Sonya goes out a lot in the day, but he thought she would be getting back soon. Jose thanked him and decided to drive back to Reykjavik and report his discovery to Abdul. While all this was going on, Sheeva was still oblivious to the danger and enjoying life in Iceland. In fact, she was experiencing her first date since the death of Jason. Below are her records of that day.

Diary—Day 5

I woke up and felt excited for the day. The feeling was good, and I felt refreshed as I hopped into the shower to get ready for my day. I didn't bother spending much time on breakfast. I had a bowl of hot instant cereal that reminded me of the Malt-o-Meal that I used to have back in the States. Not the best breakfast, but I really didn't feel like going to a lot of trouble.

Once I was dressed, I had about an hour to waste before meeting Geir. So I sat down at my computer and plugged in the program I bought to learn Icelandic. I was just going to get a book, but I thought that this way would be better, so I could hear the words instead of just seeing them. I put my headphones on and started the first lesson. It would show me the word on the computer screen, and then say it through the headphones and tell the meaning of the word. I had to go over a few words more than once, but I think it's a nice way to learn the language. The thought of becoming fluent made me excited, and I hoped one day to carry on a full conversation without anyone's help.

After I was finished with my lesson, I grabbed a jacket and headed out the door to meet Geir. I was actually so excited that I didn't even stop in at Roger's place as I usually did when I left my home. Geir was waiting for me at Café 15, and he offered to buy me a coffee before we left. It did smell good, but I told him no thanks. He asked me if I'd done any sightseeing of any kind, and I told him I'd walked around town a little. He mentioned one of the museums, and it was one I'd wanted to visit. The place was called the Gardar Folk Museum, and it was just on the outside of town. We took his car.

The first thing I noticed when we arrived at the museum was the lack of armed guards and metal detectors. We drove right into the parking lot without being checked first by security. I was so accustomed to going through security all the time back in the States that this seemed actually odd to me. What did catch my eye when we pulled up, however, was a giant, ancient fishing ship from 1885. When we walked up to it, Geir told me it was called the Sigurfari and it was over a hundred years old. It was multicolored too, which fit the area so well.

The museum wasn't set up like a traditional one, with one big building. It was made up of several buildings, each holding a different sort of display. Most of them focused on life and customs from many years ago, like farming. The newest part of the museum focused on a more modern Iceland. It had displays for sports and information on the tunnel I hoped to drive through soon. It was called the Hvalfjordur or Bay Tunnel.

We spent more than three hours there, and before long it was time to go. I would have liked to visit more places with him, but I'd told Roger we'd go to the beach, and I thought he really needed to get out.

Geir was nice and offered to take me out again soon, and again I told him yes. He dropped me off at my home and I was really glad I met him. He was only a year older than me which scared me because he was young and handsome. I wasn't sure if I was ready to be involved with some guy yet, but I'd definitely like to call him my friend.

Since Roger and I were going to the beach, and I hadn't eaten anything, I decided to throw together a picnic, just tossing in some leftovers from my cooking adventures. He knocked on my door while I was trying to find something to put the food into.

He helped me gather up some blankets, and we put the food in the old backpack I'd used the day I ran away. That day felt so long ago, and again this relief washed over me that I was finally free. My brother could not threaten me here. His threat that, 'I would get mine,' which I'd feared for so long, now seemed oddly foolish.

I could sense Roger was waiting to ask me about my day with Geir by the way he kept glancing at me, but I didn't say anything.

We walked down a street toward what the locals called Long Beach. I couldn't imagine swimming in weather like this, it was way too cold! But it would be nice to sit and talk to Roger about what I'd seen today and how nice Geir was.

The beach was quiet; only a few families dotted the shoreline as we approached. There were dark rocks bordering the sand, which was a very deep charcoal color. I remember seeing it when we came in, but it was much prettier once we were able to actually walk in the sand. I took my shoes and socks off, so I could feel the cool sand between my toes. It actually felt really good on my feet.

We spread a blanket out, and while I dug out the food for us, Roger finally asked about my day. I told him about the museum and how I wanted to go there with him sometime. As we nibbled on some day-old bread I told him how Geir offered to show me around again, and how I accepted. I was worried that this would upset him, but he seemed glad for me. He said it was good for me to make friends my age again.

I asked him what he had planned for next week, and he told me he was actually considering looking for a job. I asked him why, because I knew he still had most of the settlement from his lawsuit against Culper, Texas. He told me he thought it would be good for him to get out and do something with his time. He thought it would be a good way for him to feel like part of the community, and I agreed with him. It actually made me want to do the same, and I knew right away where I'd want to start, Café 15. I was sure I could do something there, and with Geir working there, I would feel comfortable. I bet I could cook or at least wash dishes. And eventually I could be the cashier, once I got a better handle of the language. I asked him if he knew where he wanted to work, and he said not yet, but that a *neighbor had offered to help him find a job.*

We sat quietly for a little while, watching the tiny waves crash against the sand. I never realized how much I liked the smell of the ocean. I knew that if I ever moved again, it would have to be near the water. The salty, refreshing scent filled my nose, and every time I took a deep breath, it reminded me of what a new life I had.

Roger seemed happier, which made me happier. I hopped up and curiously stuck my toe in the water, and yeah, I wouldn't swim here. It would have to be a lot warmer.

We stayed for about two hours before we decided it was time to get back. I wanted to do another lesson with my Icelandic course.

Chapter 98
Jose and Abdul take a trip

Once again, forces were converging to change Sheeva's life. I visited Iceland's Litla-Hraun prison and recorded Jose's story of what happened on Sheeva's sixth day in Iceland.

Abdul had e-mailed me that he would arrive in the morning around seven. Meeting this famous jihadist, who was not only the son of Ali Hasson but a famous man on his own accord, would be one of the biggest highlights of my life. I anxiously waited for his arrival and was so relieved when I finally heard his soft knock on my door.

I glanced out of the peephole and saw a powerfully built young man with a shaved head standing in front of my door, eyeing my peephole. His stare bore right into my eye as I peered out at him. I knew it was Abdul when he silently mouthed, "Salem alaykum." I unlatched the door, beckoned him in, and greeted him with my own hearty, "Salam alaykum."

He didn't reply, instead he looked sternly at me and said, "Jose we do not say Muslim greetings in public. This is a country of non-believers, and we don't want to stand out. Don't give yourself away. Use words like hello, but not Muslim greetings. And don't pray in public."

Then his look of seriousness disappeared, and a big smile spread across his face as he said, "Jose, you have done what thousands of others have failed to do. You found my sister. You made me very proud. You are soon going to be a rich man because you're doing Allah's work. And this work has a large bounty that will be all yours. All yours, my brother Jose."

He then asked me to tell him all I knew about his sister, Sheeva, and so I did. We sat at a small table in the room, and I told him everything I'd discovered about his sister. As I talked, he would interrupt with a curse or say things like, "That fucking whore" or "Filthy slut," or "Sheeva the family's curse."

I was with Abdul for less than twenty-four hours, but during that period he repeatedly told me how much he hated Sheeva. It was almost like a madness. I could understand why he felt hurt by what his sister had done, but he was obsessed with his hate. I think he was also jealous of her popularity. Abdul wanted to be seen as an equal to his father, but he wasn't thinking big like he had.

Abdul was very religious and prayed often. He had developed a large zabiba, a prayer bump, on his forehead from the many times his forehead brushed across his prayer mat. The bump looked even more pronounced because his head was totally shaven. I considered myself a devout Muslim, but in my haste in packing for my trip to Iceland, I'd forgotten to pack my prayer mat. When I told Abdul, he let out an incredulous gasp. Then for the next few moments, Abdul's eyes displayed real anger toward me. He then reminded me, "We are not on vacation, we are on a jihad mission."

A minute or so later, he acted like nothing had happened and challenged me to try and trip him up on his knowledge of the Quran.

Abdul offered his Quran to me and told me he wanted to show me his knowledge of the truth. He told me he could recite any verse of the Quran. He asked me to pick one for him to recite. I did, and regardless of which verse I asked, he was able to recite it word for word. He said he had memorized the entire Quran by the age of fifteen and was the youngest Hafiz in his mosque in Chicago. He said his father was so proud of his accomplishment that he tried to enter Abdul into a Hafiz contest in Saudi Arabia, where Abdul could compete against others reciting the Quran. However, the State Department didn't grant him a visa quick enough, so he missed the contest. Abdul said his father was furious about this because he wanted Abdul to be recognized for this great accomplishment.

For probably twenty or thirty minutes, I kept asking him different verses and Abdul would recite them verbatim without a single mistake. His recital actually soothed my nerves. I'd been thinking about what we would soon be doing, and I worried about being caught and put in prison. Abdul's recitals also kept him from talking about how much he wanted to kill his sister.

From the things he talked about, it seemed like he enjoyed killing. Yes, I knew I'd signed up to help assassinate his sister, but once I met Abdul in the flesh, my feeling for why she had to be killed began to bother me.

As Abdul talked about what he had done and what his father had done, I recalled his aloofness back in high school. He and his close friends always excluded me from their group. I remembered as he expressed his hate for his sister how he used to harass me about my name. He would tell me I needed a real Muslim name not some foolish Christian name like Jose.

It was never very long before he would return to talking about Sheeva. He told me that he hoped Sheeva had dreamed about this day of her death every night since she ran away. Abdul said he hoped she felt panic every time she saw the news about the fatwa on her life. He told me there was no escape for her. She was one of the walking dead, waiting in line with other apostates and kuffers for their turn to die and face hell's fires. He joked that it was funny she should be in such a cool place right before she would be smelling the sulfur of hell and feeling her flesh sizzle.

Abdul wanted me to drive to Akranes and ask around to find out where Sheeva lived. He was tired and wanted to get some sleep, so I left and within a few hours I was able to find people who knew about this new American woman who had moved to Akranes. I claimed she was a friend, but that I'd lost her address. Once I had the information, I drove back to our hotel to tell Abdul the good news.

He wanted to lose no time, so he decided we would go to her house and kill her early the following morning. I tried to sleep a little, but the lack of darkness in Iceland in July and my worries about what we were about to do prevented it. Then, at about three in the morning, Ab-

dul told me smiling, "It's time to go hunting, Jose, we have a whore to kill."

To get to where she lived, we had to drive through this very long tunnel called the Hvalfjörður Tunnel. As we drove through it, Abdul told me that a few days after the Christmas Special, he had a dream in which the Prophet Muhammad appeared.

I wanted to ask him how he knew it was the Prophet Muhammad, and maybe he sensed my skepticism, because all of a sudden he said, "I knew it was Muhammad because he matched the description of what he is supposed to look like."

Abdul went on to say, "In my dream, Muhammad appeared in an explosion of light that showed him smiling, revealing this slight gap in his bright white teeth and black curly hair that fell to his shoulder. It was all shiny and shimmering. Above his thick beard, his face had a redness to it. Also the visitor in my dream had extremely broad eyes with very black pupils. The eyebrows were thin, but the eyelashes were thick and as black as his hair. His shoulders were broad, and he stood upright and had a commanding presence. I know it was Muhammad because Satan cannot impersonate him. When I awoke from the dream, I was sitting up, sweating, and had kicked the covers off my bed, probably from the fear of seeing Muhammad, peace be with him. I tried to remember what he might have said to me, but then I realized that anyone who is visited by Muhammad in a dream is a blessed soul and will not enter into hell. I felt a huge relief as I thought about how blessed I was. I realized that the path I'd chosen was the right one. I was special to Muhammad because I was ridding his beautiful earth of non-believers."

I wanted to ask Abdul about who he might have already killed, but I thought that such a question would probably anger him. I sat in silence as we continued through the tunnel. Abdul kept mumbling verses from the Quran as he drummed on the steering wheel. The constant hum of the tires and his incessant finger tapping made Abdul's verse recitals sound very eerie.

Suddenly Abdul stopped his recital and said, "Do you know where I was the day of the Christmas Special?" He didn't wait for me to answer before he blurted out, "I was in Saudi Arabia." He laughed a little and then continued, "I watched it all from a house of a close friend of my father's. They were Saudi diplomats who smuggled me out on a diplomatic flight. My father had made provisions for me to leave five days before the attack. He didn't tell me why, but told me to watch the news on December the twenty-fifth.

"That day, a group of us sat around watching a football game between Nigeria and South Africa, and then suddenly it was interrupted with the news that America had just suffered a series of devastating attacks. They said attacks happened across the country, the worst being three attacks on nuclear power plants that had released great quantities of radiation over three metropolitan areas. The damage was severe. A cheer of 'Allāhu Akbar' went up in the house, and

then for the next three days, most of Saudi Arabia celebrated my father's success. People from this village loved my father."

The tunnel's exit came into view, and we left its darkness. The twilight was replaced with brilliant rays of the sun. The snow on the mountains shimmered in the early morning sun. Its brightness and beauty for some reason made me feel sick with dread of what we were about to do. Abdul remarked as he took in the sight that it was a good day to kill a kuffer and then laughed.

As he got control of himself, he returned to talking about his sister and how much he wanted to watch her die.

Abdul said, "I guess I must do only what Allah wills, but I wish I could see her face as she realizes she is about to finally get what is coming to her. She has defied Allah too long, and her time to burn in hell is now. I want her to feel the panic as she tries to suck in her last few breaths of air while she struggles to stay alive. I would love to see her gasping for a few more moments of life as I step on her throat. I would like her heart to beat so fast with fear that it bursts. I hope she has dreamed of this day often and knows there isn't any escape from Allah's wrath. I have thought about this a lot and decided if I shoot her, I will try and shoot her in the right lung. I want it to be a sucking chest wound so she will feel the blood filling her lung, making her suck in little gasps of air to buy a moment more of life. They say a sucking chest wound feels like liquid fire, which is perfect before this whore of a sister takes her one-way journey to hell. Today is a beautiful day for us, Jose, and a day of doom for my sister." Abdul was quiet for a few minutes, and then he said, "This will be the last day she'll be spreading her legs and the day my father will smile on me for bringing honor back to our family. Are you excited, Jose?"

His question took me off guard, and I stammered trying to think what to say. I told him I was more nervous than excited, and he said, "You will be nervous this time, that's normal, but you will soon get use to it as you understand that what you're doing is Allah's will."

We stopped at a coffee shop close to where Sheeva lived and bought a couple pastries and some coffee. I tried to eat one but couldn't. I really wanted to tell him that I'd changed my mind, but I felt he would kill me also. He was very powerful physically, and he had a rifle. After listening to him, I didn't think he would leave me alive if I chickened out. I also felt that he might kill me anyway and try to make it look like I was the one who killed Sheeva. I no longer trusted him, but I could see no way to get out of my situation. I was mad at myself for getting into this mess.

Once he got his pastries, he drove toward Sheeva's street and nibbled on a cream puff as he drove by her house. We drove up and down the street a couple times looking around her neighborhood to see if there were any police cars or anything suspicious looking. We didn't see anything, and Abdul said, "This is it," and laughed.

We pulled up across from Sheeva's house, and Abdul rolled his window down and stared out at it. He was still eating the pastry and some cream hung from his mouth. He was wiping it away when the shadow of a woman became visible behind the curtain of a window in Sheeva's house. Abdul yelled, "It's Sheeva, Allahu akbar!" At the same time, I saw police in black uniforms aiming rifles out of windows of the house we were parked next to. I ducked down and shouted to Abdul that police were all around us. Abdul didn't hear or seem to care because he quickly reached behind the front seat for his loaded rifle. He quickly hoisted it to his shoulder and pointed it at the shape of the woman behind the curtain.

Then everything happened at once. About a thousand birds flew from their roosts in the trees nearby and fluttered over our car. I could hear the loud barking of dogs, and the barking seemed to be getting closer to the car, but I didn't dare raise my head. Abdul fired at Sheeva and I remember him yelling, "I hit her, she is down. Allāhu akbar." Then a small earthquake hit, and the car bounced about as the windshield shattered from bullets fired at Abdul and me. I was yelling at Abdul to get going and drive away as his face caved in from a bullet and he fell forward onto the steering wheel. More bullets ripped into the top of his shaven head, blowing a stream of blood out of the bottom of his skull. The spray of blood and stuff painted his seat red. More bullets slammed into the car making these horrible thunking noises and suddenly my airbag exploded and smashed me back into the seat. That was it for me. I was shot multiple times, but I don't remember being hit. Maybe the impact of the airbag or one of the bullets knocked me out but Allah's mercy let me live. I was told by a nurse that I was unconscious for two days. When I came to and realized what had happened it all felt like some impossible dream or more like a nightmare, but unfortunately I knew it was not; it was something very real and very horrible.

Chapter 99
Flying Bullets

After Jose returned to his hotel in Reykjavik, he went up to his room and relayed to Abdul what he had discovered. While this was going on, Abdul's car was covertly checked by the Reykjavík Metropolitan Police and members of the Icelandic Coast Guard for explosives. None were found, nor any residue of explosives. While they had access to the car, they installed a small transmitter under the back bumper. A decision had been made that if explosives were found, the arrest of Jose and Abdul would proceed immediately to prevent any chance of a catastrophe.

While the Reykjavík Metropolitan Police searched the car, officers of the National Police force monitored the discussions between Jose and Abdul. Abdul kept referring to a document that he was showing to Jose, but the writing was so small that it could not be read using the surveillance cameras. What was understood was that they were going to drive back to Akranes at about three in the morning to be at Sheeva's house to join her for breakfast. At least those were Abdul's words to Jose. For another thirty minutes, the two of them were heard praying and chanting and singing some Islamic verses.

On the sixth day of Sheeva's life in Iceland, things were about to once again radically change. The full story of what occurred on that morning is detailed in a story by Helga Bjarnason of the Reykjavik Monitor.

> *A gunfight broke out in the early morning hours on the quiet street of Vesturgata in Akranes, Iceland. According to a senior police officer, a contingent of local and National Police of Iceland cordoned*

off the entire neighborhood after creditable intelligence indicated an imminent attack by armed Islamic terrorists on a resident of Vesturgata Street.

The resident was Sheeva Hasson, the daughter of Ali Hasson, the mastermind behind the devastating Christmas Special attacks that occurred in America a few years back. Sheeva Hasson had just relocated to Akranes six days prior to the attack. She had been living quietly on Vesturgata Street under the alias of Sonya Walsh.

The attack was carried out by her fugitive brother, Abdul Hasson, and by an American jihadist named Jose Oktar. Abdul Hasson was already wanted for two murders in Chicago, Illinois.

The purported reason for the attack was an honor killing. Americans have witnessed many of these types of tragedies. One of the earliest in 1989 was a sixteen-year-old Palestinian girl who was held down by her mother while the father stabbed her to dead. It was believed she was murdered because she had taken a part-time job and dated an African American.

In the case of Sheeva Hasson, the grievances stem from her dressing in western-style clothes, dating an American who claimed to be an atheist, and her willingness to testify against her father regarding his involvement with terrorist plots. The grievances were considered so heinous that a fatwa was issued by a prominent Afghanistan cleric, who called for the death of Sheeva to return honor to the Hasson family. Consequently, this fatwa became Abdul's constant reminder that he was called upon to remove the stain on his family's honor. It became his duty to perform this honor killing, because it's usually done by members of the aggrieved family.

A spokesperson from the Icelandic National Police stated that early in the morning, undercover agents followed Abdul and Jose from the moment they left their hotel, Centerhotel Arnarhvoll in Reykjavik. The two suspects proceeded to the Hvalfjörður Tunnel and drove west. Another surveillance team spotted their vehicle as it exited the west end of the tunnel and continued along Route 1. The Icelandic National Police shadowed them to the village of Akranes.

When the suspects arrived in Akranes, they stopped at the Olis gas station and bought gas and then went to Skutan Coffee Shop and bought two cups of coffee and some pastries. The suspects then drove to Vesturgata Street and were observed driving up and down the street five times before parking on the side of the street directly across from Sheeva Hasson's house.

At all times the suspects were under police surveillance. After the car was parked, the two alleged terrorists sat drinking coffee and eating pastries for a few minutes. Then Abdul Hasson rolled down his window and started to scrutinize Sheeva's house.

Officers of the Icelandic National Police waited for the order to converge on the car and arrest the two suspected terrorists. While Abdul observed the house, Jose Oktar pulled a black ski mask down over his head. The police observing the suspects also noticed that Oktar placed a silver pistol on the dashboard as he positioned the mask over his head.

The sight of the pistol was enough to warrant giving the order to arrest the two. As the command was relayed, however, the outline of a woman passed in front of Sheeva's kitchen window. Suddenly, police saw Abdul reach behind the front seat of his car, grab a rifle, and press it to his shoulder.

National Police Inspector Gunnar Steinsson immediately gave the order to fire on the armed suspect. Before the snipers could fire their shots, however, Akranes was hit with a stiff jolt from another earthquake. Gunfire erupted, but not before Abdul was able to fire his rifle.

Sheeva Hasson's kitchen window exploded from the bullet's impact and the silhouette of the woman behind it quickly collapsed out of view.

A barrage of bullets continued, riddling the car. Eleven bullets struck Abdul, killing him. Jose Oktar was also struck, but only wounded. He received bullet wounds in his legs, left arm, and right shoulder. He is expected to survive and will be prosecuted in the Icelandic courts for his crimes.

An ambulance and a coroner's van were soon parked outside Sheeva Hasson's house. After about thirty minutes, her door was opened by a contingent of police officers, and a gurney with a closed body bag was maneuvered down her porch steps to the waiting coroner's van.

Police held back another American, who had ran over to the house after the gun battle. The man, who lived in the ad-

jacent home, was highly emotional and sobbing over the demise of who we believe was Ali Hasson's daughter. Neighbors said the man was Roger Wilgers, a single man who had moved into a modest house across the street from Sheeva Hasson the same day she moved into the community. It has been reported that Roger Wilgers is the father of the accused pedophile that Sheeva Hasson lived with after she ran away from her father in Chicago, Illinois.

The peaceful people of Akranes were grief stricken and outraged over the killings for such senseless reasons. A young man who had just met Sheeva Hasson was quoted as saying that she was one of the sweetest women he had ever known. He was so emotionally devastated that he was unable to express himself further. His mother stated that he had gone on a date with her the day prior to the deadly attack.

An anonymous spokesperson for the Icelandic National Police stated that an investigation is underway to determine why the two suspected terrorists were not arrested before the tragedy happened. Many people are wondering why the carnage happened and who was making the decisions that resulted in deaths.

Roger Wilgers was quoted as saying, "It's a tragedy that this barbaric tradition of honor killings still exists in the twenty-first century. Barbaric traditions and a culture of hate are what destroyed Sheeva Hasson."

Chapter 100
The Final Chapter

Four months ago, I finished my book chronicling the events behind the Christmas Special attacks, but I purposely waited till this Christmas morning to write this final chapter. I felt it would be powerfully symbolic to finish the manuscript on the anniversary of those attacks.

My wife Elizabeth and I chose to celebrate this Christmas in Mesa, Colorado, in a rustic cabin overlooking a snow-covered ravine. This was the town I grew up in, and the Christmases I had there are still treasured memories of my childhood. A number of my high school classmates still lived in Mesa, and I looked forward to visiting them this Christmas day.

This morning, as I came down the stairs, the music of José Feliciano played on a Christmas radio station. It brought back fond holiday memories of my daughter when she was four, running around singing "fleas naughty dog," which always earned her great praise from my wife and me. A couple years later, when she discovered the song's real words were "Feliz Navidad," she pouted for half a day before she forgave us.

I looked out the living room window and saw that the sky was grey with snow-laden clouds. Old timers say a grey clouded sky means snow flurries are on the way. A snowstorm on this Christmas day would actually be welcomed. Already, little eddies of snow swirled around the window ledge, and out in my yard, trees drooped their branches from the weight of their white blankets. Across the road, smoke curled up from my neighbor's chimney and lights twinkled in their windows.

A wood fire crackled in our fireplace and its smoky aroma mixed with other exotic Christmas scents. And all around our house the glitter and sparkle of decorations greeted the eye.

Christmas for us had always been a great day of celebration, where we would spend time with family and friends, exchanging gifts with loved ones and gluttonously stuffing ourselves. I'd hoped this Christmas would be a day of magic, and remarkably I could already feel the pull of that strange and beautiful force that accompanies Christmas. The magic of these holidays has always been hard to explain, but to me, Christmas should be a day of calm, peace, and happiness punctuated by a lot of joy, laughter, and song. This holiday, I hoped, would be one where its spirit would infect us all with generosity and charitable warmth and subdue those memories of that infamous Christmas morning.

I hoped today would let me feel the emotions and observe how the world is recuperating from the attacks that still seemed so fresh in my mind. I wanted to hear the sound of Christmas carols and take in all the visual beauty of the celebration. I wanted to be assailed once more by the potpourri of scents from evergreen trees, pumpkin pies, gingerbread cookies, and turkeys roasting.

This Christmas morning, I wanted to go to a church and hear a Christmas sermon, find someone in need and give them food and money, visit friends and relatives, and see how the wounds we endured have scabbed over during the last few years.

Elizabeth and I exchanged gifts, but I found myself still feeling a nervous tension that diminished the thrill which normally accompanies this custom. Part of it might have been the fact that I was trying to be overly observant of all the emotions shared on this Christmas. It was almost like I was watching a play of Christmas instead of really experiencing it. After our gift exchange, Elizabeth and I went to Saint Joseph's church to attend Christmas Mass. On the way there, we watched in fascination the brightening band of grey glowing on the horizon. The sun was rising, and the edges of the fat grey clouds shimmered like silver. Streaks of sun sliced through the gloom as the morning grew brighter by degrees. Finally, a red glow arched above the Grand Mesa. It was the beginning of a beautiful Christmas day.

There were not that many members of the congregation attending the morning service. The poor turnout was probably a result of realizing that even God no longer protects these sacred walls from the insanity of man's evil. I know I'd yet to get over my dismal resignation that metal detectors and explosives sensors were now the norm before entering churches, hospitals, theatres, or malls. Security measures involving armed guards somehow dampen the aura of Christmas.

At church, before the Christmas sermon, it was plain to see that, while some of my family and friends had recovered from the tragedy, others still struggled.

In talking to them, it seemed as if Ali Hasson was not only still alive, but actively plotting an even larger attack. They were still held captive by the mentality of conflict and fear, and without a surviving enemy, they invented enemies from shadows. It seemed like a sad misuse of their energy and intellect.

Since these attacks were not simply assaults against our nation, but also a desecration of the Christmas celebration, people saw the Christmas Special attacks as far more sinister than any prior aggression against America. For many, it was an attack on Christianity, and for others it was an attempt to blot out a day that celebrated the beauty, benevolence, and good will of all mankind.

Father Cowen was one of the fortunate priests who survived a terrorist bombing during the Christmas Special attacks. The Salem, Oregon, newspaper reported that the attack happened like a Stephen King horror novel. An older woman dressed in a long black coat entered Salem's Church of Redemption and seated herself in a pew near the front. Just as Father Cowen began his Christmas morning sermon, she suddenly jumped up, yelling, "Allahu Akbar!" and detonated herself. A piece of shrapnel struck Father Cowen in the left eye, destroying it. Now an unblinking glass eye stares from its socket as Father Cowen's right eye darts about the faithful as he preaches. I wondered if it's unremitting fear that provokes its constant motion. If it's, it's understandable because he was the sole survivor of that attack.

One truth I took with me from his sermon was this: "There is no better time than Christmas for all of humanity to come together. Christians understand the unique beauty of what that day represents in Scripture." But Father Cowen added, "Christmas has been a celebrated time of the year even before Christ. From today onward, we must respect and show tolerance to all people, from all walks of life, not just to those we are a part of. Remember, our differences are meager compared to our shared humanity."

Talking to my friends and family after the sermon, it seemed plausible that, besides those who couldn't get past their fear of new attacks, there was a seed of change. We stepped out into the cold street and saw strings of lights on lampposts, wreaths hanging on doors, and nativity scenes wherever people could find places to put them. Christmas, I thought, is truly universal. A lump rose in my throat. The Christmas holidays and a well-delivered sermon were having a profound effect.

Much has happened in the years since the Christmas Special attacks—some would say justice was served to Ali Hasson by the annihilation of his family. To many, that was the end of the story...but it's not. Now we are faced with a past that demands consequences.

We have to weigh our options and decide what course to take. And in our consideration, we must remember that every action we take will have consequences.

That's life's conundrum. Do we break the cycle of consequences, or do we transcend the event and look weak to our enemy and cowardly to those who want us to avenge the death of the fallen? Does humanity have the grace to free itself from the influence of its past? I remembered how Scrooge broke with his past in the Christmas Carol. Could a nation do the same? Can we toss away the yoke of political correctness and live in a reality that accepts that good and evil exist? Can we accept the dismal realization that evil cannot be destroyed simply by redefining it or closing our eyes to it?

I hoped for some special phone calls from some of the people I met during the years I researched and wrote about the Christmas Special attacks. Just as I was accepting that none would come, my cell phone rang. The spirit of Christmas had come through, and I smiled broadly as I recognized the number and answered the call. I cheerfully offered, "Merry Christmas."

The caller replied in her slightly accented English, "Merry Christmas to you, Mr. Roma."

I asked her if Santa had visited her way up there in Iceland.

She giggled and said, "He certainly did, Mr. Roma. I'm just so glad I am here to celebrate another Christmas and to live in peace with Erik. Thank you again for your wedding presents; we use them everyday."

Her call was an affirmation that good sometimes wins over evil. That call was one of my most memorable Christmas gifts.

I want to end by saying I hope that the Spirit of Christmas will always be with you, bringing you, your family, and your loved ones the gifts of Health, Happiness, Prosperity, Peace, Friendship, Love, and Brotherhood.

About The Author

David Hearne is the author of two previous books, including "Hulagu's Web – The Presidential Pursuit of Senator Katherine Laforge and the definitive guide of programming concepts called "Enable Command Performance". He has also written numerous articles on technology and interviewed its luminaries like Ted Wait the founder of Gateway 2000 Computers, Heidi Roizen the founder of T/Maker and a Vice President of Apple Computer.

David was a former military officer who served in Vietnam during the Tet offensive and has two sons who have served in Iraq and Afghanistan.

He now lives in Southeast Texas with his wife, daughter, numerous cats and a cat like dog at their Book Nook Inn Bed & Breakfast.

www.ingramcontent.com/pod-product-compliance
Lightning Source LLC
Chambersburg PA
CBHW051926020726
47501CB00001B/6

* 9 7 8 0 9 7 5 5 9 7 6 1 3 *